The Power to Deny

A Woman of the Revolution Novel

Wendy Long Stanley

Elizabeth Græme

Chapter 1

I should have written something of the life I have lived. To simply die without a meaningful good-bye seems a poor ending for one who spent fifty years with a quill pen in hand. They are all dead now, of course, including General Washington himself.

Ah, but I have no idea about my husband, do I?

And my first love is not dead, no matter how many times I wished it upon him. It has been decades since I held his letter in my hands, already limp from the fingers of Mrs. Abercrombie and my mother and who knows how many others. Even in old age, I am no wiser in the way of men. I should have prayed for wealth; that would have guaranteed my independence—the only thing I ever truly wanted.

It's a cruel world for women, it seems to me, as I lie here dying in a cold room in someone else's house.

Memories come gurgling back like slow-boiling water. Mother's gentle face bent over my first serious attempt at verse, exclaiming with praise, smelling of lily of the valley, her fingers stained red from jarring beets. Father lifting me from the carriage for Thomas's burial, my brother's strapping body too young and strong to be lifeless in a coffin. Jigs and minuets; clinking crystal glasses and barking laughter; the painful angel notes of Franklin's armonica making me cry all over again. Hayden and Pope. King George's stern shoes. Westminster Abbey. Thin lines of blood splayed across Graeme Park following the trail of dead foxes. Gunshots. *We hold these truths to be self-evident.*

William Franklin's face appears before me. I blink in surprise. After all this time! I shake my head to dissolve his handsome young features. I might have gone to him, I suppose. Perhaps I should have. The same way I should have gone to my husband.

I know what they'll say. *She was not an obedient wife.* Worse, I provided my husband with no sons. What if *I* had been born a male, without the prison of hearth or womb to hamper me?

Ah, well. I have my writing. My poems and books. Children of a sort. Perhaps I might have liked critical acclaim, like that writer Mary Wollstonecraft in England. I don't agree with everything she writes, but at least she gets people talking.

I'm tired.

When I wake again it is midafternoon, my chamber steeped with winter sunlight gray as dirty water. For a moment, I think I'm at Graeme Park, but of course I am not.

A servant is fussing over me. She reaches under the covers to remove the iron bedwarmer, now cold.

"What year is it?" I ask. My mind is heavy; my sleep was thick with ghosts.

"Eighteen hundred and one," she answers. "February."

John Adams is our president, then, and has been the last few years. Or is it that ginger-haired Jefferson? He's too shifty for my liking. I miss Washington. He was a better leader, much less fiery and prone to invective than that bloated Mr. Adams who succeeded him. Poor President Washington, dying like that from a simple ague. What a terrible loss his death was for us and all the country. They mourned in droves, lining the streets by the thousands, keening like animals. A pitiable noise. I'll never forget it.

"Did you know His Excellency?" I ask the girl, who is leaning into the hearth with the bedwarmer. "President Washington?"

She shakes her head, settles the iron to warm, and crosses back to straighten my bedding. "No, ma'am."

"I hope, in the end, he could forgive me," I say.

The girl's eyes finally meet mine. I can see her weighing my lucidity.

"I wouldn't trouble yourself," she says. "About what's already gone." She reaches up to feel my brow with dry fingers. What is her name? I must know her.

I feel sorry for Martha Washington. After the way her husband cheated death so many times, she must have believed him immortal. He got shot at repeatedly and escaped unscathed for years. I'm glad he died at Mount Vernon. He loved it there, with his Martha. Mr. Washington was a fine man, the finest, despite what he thought of me.

How did we manage to get through it, our war? Our revolution was such a tremendous gamble.

"I was loyal!" I exclaim, grasping the girl's wrist. "I was. A true patriot! You must believe me! I always believed in the cause. You'll tell them, won't you?"

The girl's brow creases with worry. "That's all sorted now, most like."

How different my life would have been had I made another choice. Any other choice than him.

"We were crawling in the dark," I say, releasing her arm and trying to sit up. "That's the problem, you see. It only makes sense when it's *over*. That's what people won't understand." The generations to follow will never know how it was for us, will never know that our freedom hung as precariously as a twig on a funeral pyre. The quest for our liberty was a mess for years. Necessary, oh yes, but the cost, dear God, the cost. Tears prick my rheumy eyes.

"I'll just go and fetch Dr. Rush," the girl mumbles, retreating.

Last week I wrote to Mrs. Washington and asked that she remove my name from Washington's papers, should I be in them. I suspect I am, as he was so meticulous with his diaries, and I was forced to cross the war line more than once. I still do not like to remember it. I am not guilty of what they think!

If we had not won our revolutionary war, besides the hard boot of the Crown kicking us open, my husband would have stayed.

I will leave it to the historians to fill their books with stories, real and imagined. I suspect many more words will be written on our war, and it is my prayer that I appear in none of them.

What I leave behind are my words. That is what I would like the world to have of me.

I want to be remembered. So few women are.

Chapter 2

Philadelphia
January 1, 1756

"Miss Betsy, look!"

The two boys ran toward me, the taller with newspaper in hand, faces bright with the thrill of death. They were two of the Logan children who lived next door. We were staying at our home in Philadelphia for the winter. Pennsylvania winters were far too blustery and freezing cold to endure at our estate in the Horsham countryside. Father always had to have the finest houses, and although he rented this one, it was as opulent a mansion as all the others we'd lived in since I was small.

"Money for the heads of Indians," the boys yelled.

I paused, my hand on the gate.

"Show me, then."

The broadsheet was shoved at me. There it was on the second page of today's paper, *The Pennsylvania Gazette,* January 1, 1756. "Seven hundred dollars' reward," I read the headline aloud. "For the person who can bring to the city the heads of Shingas and Captain Jacobs, chiefs of the Delaware Indian nation."

"Or three hundred and fifty for one!" Eli said. His cheeks were bright red in the cold. He was twelve, small for a boy.

"They're really bad, those Indian chiefs," his little brother added. "They've been killing the settlers out west over nothing. Governor Morris doesn't even want the Indian chiefs alive no more!"

Out west. On the frontier, where William was. My breath caught.

"So I see," I said. My eyes scanned the page. The chiefs were charged with *alienating the affections of the Indians from His Majesty and the people of this province.* Shingas and Captain Jacobs were attacking up and down the western settlements, killing and kidnapping people, and burning property to the ground.

"You should tell your gent," Eli said, referring to William. "So he can try and get the money. Seeing as he fought in King George's War and all. He must be good with killing."

I looked at the boys. The French and Indian war could not mean much to them at their ages.

"Thank you, Eli," I said with a forced smile. "I will when he returns. You see, William is already at the frontier. He left two weeks ago."

"Do you think if they caught the savages they'd stick their heads up on stakes outside the State House?" Young Arthur's eyes bulged at the thought of it. "I'd sure like to see Shingas the Terrible up there!"

"I'm not sure what they'll do," I said mildly. "Remember your Christian faith, boys. There are many good Indians, too. You had best be getting along, and I am off to see a friend."

"But these are the bad Indians," Arthur protested, and wiped at his leaking nose.

"So is he out there killing the French then?" asked Eli. "Your gentleman."

"He's building forts to protect people. He's trying to help the settlers stay safe," I said. "William is my friend, not my betrothed."

I wasn't in a hurry to marry. I knew a husband and babies would erase my time as surely as autumn frost spreads its greedy fingers across the lawn.

"Well, he should kill the French too," Eli said matter-of-factly as my coach pulled up and I climbed in. "Father says they're nothing but trouble."

"She sure is pretty," Arthur said to his brother as the door closed behind me.

Sleep escaped me that night.

My bed curtains were not drawn, and I watched the moon in the night sky through the window, a whisper of a crescent, barely visible through the swell in the glass. All I could think about was Indians murdering unsuspecting settlers.

I turned in bed and felt sweat on my nape and down my back. The moisture clung to my shift and wadded it up uncomfortably against me. It was very late, but tonight Philadelphia was unusually quiet. I could hear no sounds of wheels and hooves on cobblestone, no voices drifting from the taverns, no dock workers calling to each other on their walk home. Even the street cats were not fighting.

I felt a sharp pain in my head. When I was younger, I used to think my headaches would be the end of me. The pain was a fiery stabbing that lingered for days. I would have to lie in darkness with a towel over my eyes. What is it that Alexander Pope said in *Epistle to a Lady*, "Die of nothing but a rage to live"? I didn't believe I had experienced a rage to live yet, and that, perhaps, was what I would remedy. I had not yet turned nineteen, so time, with good fortune, was on my side. I rose up and reached for the pitcher on my table, the one with red and blue birds on it from the potter in Derby. I fumbled to find the handle in the darkness. Mother had it shipped here from England with some other pieces, I recalled. I poured water into my glass and drank thirstily.

Was William safe? Folks there said the backbone of Pennsylvania was ragged with cruelty, the killing like never before. Blood ran thick day and night. Men and women were choked with fear even in broad daylight when the sun was high and golden.

Our governor Robert Morris at first tried to ignore the problem, then announced that our colony was overrun with Indians who delighted in shedding blood. He ordered a party to head west and solve the problem. William couldn't wait to go. They were going to build stockades and prevent settlers from being killed, or at the least stop them from abandoning their homesteads in terror.

Morris put William's father, Mr. Franklin Senior, in charge of the mission. Can you imagine! Mr. Franklin! Although I was fond of him, Mr. Franklin was a man of fifty with limited military experience. What was Morris thinking? Franklin was good at many things, but hardly the sort of person you'd put on a horse and thrust into the mountains in the winter. He hid the fact that he had a gimpy foot and troubles with gout. When the air was cold Franklin senior wheezed like a bellow.

Still, off they went. William and his father and a hundred cavalrymen headed out on horseback a few weeks before Christmas.

I heard the quick patter of feet and could barely see who had entered my room when Liza threw back the blankets and banged my head with her elbow.

"Oof," I said.

She laughed and snuggled into my back. "Sorry, sneak attack."

"Put the duvet back. And do *not* put your cold feet on me!"

"I will," she said, and put her feet on my calves, "and I have. I couldn't sleep."

Liza was like another sister to me. She was orphaned as a girl overseas, but she has lived with us since she was twelve after my sister Ann's husband rescued her and brought her back to Pennsylvania. Liza was seventeen now, and my dearest confidante.

"What time is it? You could have woken me up," I complained.

"Toss," Liza whispered dismissively. She squirmed in place. "You need to tighten this bed. It's loose and lumpy."

"You have your own bed," I said drily. "Go there."

She reached out a hand to my back. "Why are you sticky? It's not hot. Are you ill?"

I swatted her hand. "No. Leave me be. I'm fine. It's late. And be *quiet*!"

Liza sat up. "You're pining for him, aren't you? You poor dear. Are you very worried?"

"Ssh, you'll wake Mother and Father," I said over my shoulder. "I'm fine. Really. Liza, either go to sleep or go back to your own bed. Or I'll throw water on you. I warn you, the pitcher's still half full."

"Oh fine." She laid down again and laid her head on my back.

The small weight of her calmed me. Eventually her breath evened out and she was asleep.

I looked at the wall, tried to sleep, and thought of William again. Even without the threat of Indian attacks, the driving snow and cold temperatures alone would be daunting, although I was more worried about violence.

The French possessed most of Canada and had pushed south into the Ohio Valley too aggressively for our King George II, who thought the land belonged to us. The French formed alliances with the Delaware and Shawnee Indians and were using them to gain a stronghold. If they could slip through the mountains at the Lehigh Gap and attack us from the west, they would.

I sighed. If only the French had stayed in Canada, where they belonged. They could have the north and we would stay here. The Indians could keep their land and everybody would stop fighting. Problem solved.

I wondered what William was doing. The truth was that William Franklin had a secret little spot in my heart that was growing too quickly. He actually *was* my man, but I did not wish to tell those Logan boys. What started as a flirtation over our lottery tickets five years ago became a serious courtship, although I still felt shy about admitting that to my mother and father, or anyone really.

After another restless hour made worse by the fact that I could no longer toss and turn due to Liza's deadweight, the water went right through me. Liza was between me and my chamberpot, and the wall was on the other side of the bedstead. I wriggled downward until my feet emerged at the end of the bed, followed by my body and head. I felt like a groundhog.

I padded around to my tinderbox and flint on the night table, feeling them from memory. With a hiss, the candle on my table surged to life. I relieved myself and placed the chamberpot back under the bed at the foot, carefully out of the way. One time I kicked it by mistake in the middle of the night and the pottery broke. Unpleasant, to say the least.

Back in bed, I stared at the wall and begged for sleep. Finally, I drifted off. I saw William in a crowded tavern, his tall frame large in the room, one boot raised on a stool. He spread his hands wide as he delivered a joke and acknowledged the roar of laughter. There was a clank of tin cups. "Good one, Will!" A man's laughter was punctuated by snorts.

The party faded to a field at Graeme Park, my summer home. William and I were in repose in the grass, surrounded by clover. He reached a hand out to flick a ladybug from my hair, pausing to stroke my cheek. He smelled like horse and tobacco and yeast from the bread we had just eaten. I could feel the warmth of the sun on my face, and the strength of his long fingers gentle on my face. Comforted, I sunk deeper into sleep until my mind offered up the next image. A sinewy brown man, sleek with sweat and grease, grabbed William from behind, wrenching his head back and, in the flash of a muscular arm and glint of metal, slashed at William's scalp. The Indian raised his prize in triumph. A lump of blood and hair swung like a dead squirrel from his hand as he grinned down at me, then whooped, racing away, and William pitched forward heavily on me.

I cried out, sleep gone, and bit my lip to quell the sound. No one must hear. Mother already thought I was overwrought. If she knew I was having nightmares, she would send me away to our friends in New Jersey, and then I'd be away for weeks and not here when William came home.

Liza rolled over, snoring a little.

Chapter 3

Philadelphia
February 7, 1756

I sat in the parlor with the newspaper, reading an article on how to get the French out of America. There were fourteen detailed points on what would succeed in evicting the French once and for all. Little Aurelius was in my lap, asleep and drooling. I also had a stack of books and the new edition of *Poor Richard's Almanack* at the ready to ward off boredom.

"Point fourteen. The five nations," I read theatrically into the empty parlor, "and our other friendly Indians, will keep the French Indians in eternal subjection."

I glanced up at the mantle clock, then continued reading. I tried for a courtly voice. "As we are MASTERS of the sea, a few ships of WAR, sent to the coast every YEAR, would FOREVER prevent the return of the FRENCH into the country. Da dum. What do you think, Aurelius?"

The dog didn't stir.

The reward notice for the Delaware Indian chiefs' heads had moved from the second page to the first, up to the top left under the name of the newspaper, and had been there every week for a month. Clearly, no Indian chief heads had been offered up. Shingas and Captain Jacobs remained on the loose.

The house was far too quiet. Mama had gone out and the servants were busy elsewhere. I missed the times when my brothers and sisters were around, when a ruckus was always taking place. Liza had gone to Princeton for a few weeks to see extended Stedman family. I put down my paper and looked around me.

I was restless. The damnation of winter. I looked down at my slippered feet, and wiggled my toes in a beam of sunshine. I wished I could have gone on the expedition. Instead, I sat here like a plum on a cake.

This house was too big for us, but Father liked his creature comforts. And status. We had more rooms than we needed, all beautifully appointed. Plasterwork decorated the high ceilings and cornices with elegantly placed leaves and flowers, carefully sculpted by the best craftsmen. Marble graced the fireplaces of the dancing and gathering rooms here on the first floor; expensive tiles decorated the upstairs fireplaces. Every wall featured a fine painting or an antique map, or several. In the corner cupboard was Mama's favorite silverplate.

Another month had passed and there was still no word of William's party. How much longer until he came home? At least I knew he wasn't dead, because Mr. Franklin had sent word to his wife that they were making good progress. Deborah said he thanked her for the roast beef she sent, which had managed to reach them. I hoped gout wasn't flaring up in those old feet of his.

I looked at the paper. Different colonies are governed differently in America, depending on how they were established. Here in Pennsylvania one family, the Penns, held power. We're known as a proprietary colony, and that is part of the problem. King Charles gave a great amount of land to William Penn seventy-five years ago, to pay off his father's debt. When William Penn died he divided up his land and wealth between three of his sons: John, Thomas, and Richard. Even though we had an elected Assembly, whatever governor was in place just listened to what the Penn men told him and not the wishes of the people. What governor wouldn't want to keep his job and enjoy being in the Penns' good graces? Even my father has benefitted from their choice appointments.

When I was younger, I didn't understand that our elected Assembly was filled with Quakers who despised violence and wouldn't take up arms, even for defense, even when they were under attack. Father said this left us with no standard for organized defense. The Penn brothers hadn't been very focused on Pennsylvania's struggles, until now, when so many were dying from Indian attacks. I guess it was no wonder that some of the Indians aligned with the French in the face of all that apathy: peace-loving Quakers in the government, rich Penn brothers not that concerned about protection or fairness. Not to mention that the Penns were often in London and not even here.

I tossed the newspaper down and reached for another.

The front door opened and closed. Oh, good. Mama was home. I heard her speaking to the housemaid and then light steps coming toward the parlor.

When she entered, I pushed Aurelius off me to get up and kiss her cheek. She smelled of cold, that satisfying scent of fresh air and icy skin.

"You weren't long," I said. "Did you find what you were looking for?"

Mama pulled a new hat from a package and held it out to me. "I was so tired of my head being cold all the time so I went to the milliner. This ghastly weather! I shall be warm now."

Her hat was rabbit fur, soft and luxurious. I admired its craftsmanship.

"Father came home while you were gone," I said. "He said to tell you he is tending to patients. I told him you were at the shops."

Aurelius, named after the Roman emperor Marcus Aurelius, leaped into my lap again when I sat back down. There was not, humorously enough, an imperial bone in him. He was scruffy, ugly, small, and nervous. I stroked one of his ears absently.

"How is he? He was in such a rush when he left."

"Weary," I said. "Yet unbending. You know he won't rest, not when so many are ill. He's in fair enough spirits, I suppose. He ate and bolted out again."

"He must be used to it by now," my mother sighed, "after all those years as port physician. He's no stranger to long days, although it must be more of a strain now that he's older." They said my father's professional rigor prevented outbreaks of disease from spreading through Philadelphia under his tenure, no small feat when so many ships piled high with immigrants streamed toward the docks.

"He's in good humor, you said?" Mama fretted.

"He is. Although he could not pass through the house without telling me what to do, as usual. He ordered me to write poems. I am to avoid the news and stop reading the papers." I laughed. That would make me too much like other girls.

"You are so bright you frighten him," my mother said. "Your sisters were easier, somehow." I've always known Ann was his favorite, although he loved us equally and none of us suffered from lack of attention.

"That's not what frightens him," I said cheekily. Mother gave me one of her looks, so I swallowed the rest of my retort.

"I expect it will be easier for him when you marry," she said thoughtfully. "You won't have so much time then to get yourself so wound up. You have far too many opinions and knowledge of affairs of the world for one so young. Have you been writing?"

Marriage, marriage, marriage, I thought peevishly. I've never been fond of the thought of it for myself, which I dared not voice. Every woman must marry, but I still found the idea overwhelming and slightly distasteful. Marriage meant managing a house and having no time for writing.

"Yes, I've been writing poetry."

"And reading your Bible, too, I trust."

I was writing a great amount lately, my pen driven by the empty hours of winter. I had composed verse since I was old enough to recognize the letters on my hornbook. Earlier today I reworked some poetry until my concentration disappeared and I realized I was stewing about William again.

Mother rubbed her hands together to warm them and reached for the brass bell to ring for tea. I reached for a quilt and smoothed it over my lap, tucking it around Aurelius's wiry neck to cocoon the both of us.

Mama had birthed ten children, but several died in infancy or childhood, and only I remained at home. My two living sisters, Jane and Ann, were ten and eleven years older than myself. They were married and had homes of their own. Jane even had a little girl, Anny, who was named after our mother and sister. When my sister Ann was a girl, she was more of what my father thought girls should be, less talkative and more focused on needlework and domestic arts and happy to be doing so. My sister Jane was between us, a combination of both of us, happier to listen than to talk. Their oldest child, my brother Thomas, was in his twenties when he died, unmarried, of yellow fever. I missed Tom, he laughed a lot and always had time to play. I never knew my other brother, William, who died before I was born when he was only ten. The other children died as babies or young children. I sometimes wondered if my Father was disappointed that none of his sons remained. It did not matter if you were a gentleman physician or a warehouse worker, your babies died all the same, if God willed it to be so.

"Tell me, how is William?" Mama asked.

I looked up from picking at loose threads on the quilt on my knees. "I haven't seen him yet. Father told me there is talk in the coffeehouse that they're on their way back. I know he'll come by or send word as soon as he arrives."

"I have been meaning to speak with you, Elizabeth," she said as the maid appeared with tea and biscuits. We waited in silence as she set up the porcelain service and departed. "You are very young and your father and I are concerned that your feelings for William may be ill-advised."

In this town, it was hard not to see that William and I were growing closer. We had the same circle of friends, although it would be difficult not to in a place where everyone knew everyone. You couldn't walk a block in Philadelphia without running into ten people who all knew each other somehow. And had been at your table or hearth.

"Well, I have no plans," I said uneasily. I took the cup she handed me. "He is dear to me, though."

Mother nodded, her mind working as her small fingers cradled the warmth of her cup. Had Father asked her to speak to me? Perhaps they were hoping William would not survive the expedition and that would bring a natural end to my "ill-advised" feelings. My thoughts instantly made me feel ashamed.

"William is . . . opinionated," Mother said slowly. Her words reflected the cleanness of her mind, like the planks of a cooper's barrel pulled tight in perfect symmetry. "And political to a dangerous end. His writings do not sit well with us. You know your father's colleagues and professional associates support the Penns. We must put our faith in them too, to lead us into the future."

I did know. And I knew they didn't like William's father, and I knew why. Five years ago Mr. Franklin senior was elected to the Pennsylvania Assembly after being the clerk there for many years. After he left the post, William took over as clerk. Franklin Senior had been outspoken about the problem of having a Pennsylvania governor that was always handpicked and jumped to the Penns' orders like a trained monkey. William and his father were dangerously stirring up stagnant waters that had been murky too long. I couldn't help but wonder if William's illegitimacy was a problem for my parents, even though Franklin embraced him as his son and Deborah had raised him as her own. People can have strong opinions about the improper shadows of the past and hold them close, even if they do not voice them.

"Franklin should stick with his science experiments," my father had muttered more than once. Mr. Franklin had retired from his printing and leased out his shop to a partner in order to pursue his interests in science and philosophy.

My mother cleared her throat. "We don't believe William is right for you."

I fought the urge to giggle. I wasn't even keen on marriage. Why must fondness for someone always come with expectation?

"William is studying the law, not going into politics," I said. "If anything, he's guilty of simply defending attacks made on his father. Father and son are very close. Wouldn't you want me to defend you from an unprovoked attack? I wouldn't let anyone speak badly of you, Mama, especially if it was untrue."

She said nothing.

"William only wants what is best for Pennsylvania," I added defensively. "He wants what we all want: safety, peace. Prosperity."

I heard horses pass in the street, followed by mad barking. It sounded like the Nesbitts' new dog, a stray they took in and called Spotted Dick, like the pudding. It was a ridiculous dog, gangly and oddly sized, a short body on long legs. Big head. The dog was so absurdly pleased with its new station in life that I had taken it a bone from the kitchen just to watch him run in happy circles.

"I'm fond of William," Mother conceded. "I am. Your father, however, is not. This makes it difficult."

She looked at me knowingly. William upset them when he published a pamphlet last fall with his old tutor, and now our friend, Joseph Galloway, called *Tit for Tat*. The brochure implied the Penns were guilty of treason for not paying taxes and supporting a proposed militia bill to keep Pennsylvania safe. Colonists who liked their bodies to stay in one piece, the brochure argued, needed to be defended from Indians.

Father was embarrassed, for even though William did not put his name on the piece, everyone knew who had written it—the man courting his only daughter still at home, and only unmarried child.

"We fear for you, Elizabeth," my mother continued. "William is a young man of ambition. You are too young to understand this now, but what you want in a husband, especially after many years of marriage, is stability. A man not too lofty in his reach. Nor too outspoken."

"He's been a good friend to me, Mama. And more than that, I admire him." *Although he's more than a friend now,* I added silently. I did not want her to know William had become a determined suitor lately.

"Yes, you two have been friends for many years," my mother agreed. "Yet you are turning nineteen this month. He is seven years older, a grown man. He will need a wife soon, and his affections for you are growing." She said this with warning in her voice. Alarm poked me. I did not know how she knew, but she did. Had someone seen us in our stolen moments?

Her message was clear: William was unwanted. I should be rid of him, for there was no shortage of well-to-do suitors in this town and all the other towns nearby. I must choose another, a husband that was better suited to the Graeme alliances. Or at least a man that did not openly contradict my father's beliefs and political loyalties. My father had served as president of the St. Andrew's Society since its inception in Philadelphia, which meant his social calendar was long, and his list of influencers wide. He had also worn many hats in addition to physician: naval officer, justice of the peace, farmer, and town leader.

Why must I listen? I stifled the urge to throw my teacup. I wanted to watch it smash into the wall. My sisters took husbands as if it required no thought, as if no *choice* was needed at all. Hummingbirds to sugar water, or rainwater falling down a spout. What called my heart was books and reading and all the words that came to me and asked to be written. I was lifted by great writing: Spenser, Swift, Locke, Johnson. Alas, this wasn't the work for a woman beyond dinner conversation or a turn around the park. As women, we made our homes and had our babies, and if we had both, we were blessed. Purpose and security were not to be sniffed at, all you had to do was ask the women who didn't have them. There were dozens living a miserable existence by the docks.

Mother took my silence as agreement. She finished her tea, rose, and leaned over to caress my cheek. "I am glad you understand, my dear. I am off to the church. Did I tell you Ann is coming by? You two can visit without me until I return."

"Surely there is no service at this hour?"

Mother shook her head, moving to the door. "Not a service. Great need. Refugees are streaming into town from Carlisle and York. So many families have fled their homes and have nothing other than the clothing they wear. They require food, clean garments, bandages. We'll provide what we can. I have old blankets still in good repair to take and a pot of stew from Gretchen." Gretchen, our cook, was as constant over the years as our tall clock at Graeme Park, chiming our days into seasons.

I was struck by how many displaced people were surging into town, how rapidly Philadelphia was becoming part of a bigger conflict. The frontier war was moving closer toward us as markedly as our creek in Horsham always swelled in a rainstorm.

"Surely the Indians will not attempt to attack Philadelphia," I mused, trying to imagine it. "Or the French troops?"

My mind discarded the thought. An attack in the middle of town was unlikely. The Indians would not stray from the way they excelled in war, attacking from trees and the protection of bushes and rocks. That was how they killed General Braddock and his men last summer at Fort Duquesne. Besides, invaders were easy targets in our wide streets. What would William Penn have thought of us now, his great experiment of religious freedom and orderly streets filled with refugees of war.

Our house in Horsham would be a more likely choice for an attacker, for it could provide food and shelter. Graeme Park was close enough to Philadelphia—not quite twenty miles—to ambush the main roads into the city from the surrounding woods. Father purchased Graeme Park when I was a baby. It had first belonged to my mother's step-father, Governor Keith.

Mother raised an eyebrow at me. Uneasiness was etched across her face.

"The Quakers have done the most so far," she said as if I had not asked about Indians attacking Philadelphia, her hand on the doorknob, "and they are strained to the limit. The rest of us must do more. Christ Church has pledged to assist, and the Presbyterians and Methodists. We'll send someone to speak to the Catholics." There were close to thirty churches and Quaker meetinghouses in town. We needed to summon resources.

"I'll help too. I'll do whatever is needed. I know Liza will too when she gets back."

Mother nodded. "Yes, but in the meantime, I think you should consider a visit to the Campbells. You haven't been yourself. You're worrying too much about William and the war and atrocities not meant for a young girl's mind. It will send you into one of your three-week headaches. A rest would do you good. Why don't you take the trip to Burlington? The Campbells would be pleased to receive you. At least think about it."

I wasn't about to leave for New Jersey now, when William was due home. I opened my mouth to protest when she slipped out as gracefully as she came in, her skirts a gentle rustle of movement. Mother was a slim reed of a woman, delicate as spun sugar.

In my mind, I surveyed Graeme Park. We had a fine stone mansion house on more than eight hundred acres. We used to have seventeen hundred but Father sold some to invest in his land. There were dozens of cows, hogs, sheep, chickens. We had plentiful vegetables and herbs in the kitchen gardens, fruit in a large orchard, grains in the fields. There was clean water in the creek and wells, and unlimited timber from thick forests that surrounded the cleared land. We had servants in outbuildings, and stables for the horses. It would be a bounty for any army. My thoughts would prove to be prescient, but I did not know it then.

I had sympathy for the native people, or at least the friendly ones. When I was growing up, I would often see Indians in Philadelphia for meetings and trade, especially in the fall, looking dignified and strong, intelligent, their brown bodies sculpted with muscle and ornate with wampum beads and paint. I purchased a beautiful basket once from a raven-haired woman, a vessel finely and intricately woven. How peculiar it must have been for the Indians all those years ago when great foreign boats sailed up to their shores, spitting out light-skinned men in odd clothing who spread European diseases like a summer wildfire.

Mother stuck her head back around the door. "I can hear you thinking from out here. Listen to your father and stop reading those papers. Focus on something else, your music or your languages. Which reminds me, have you done your tatting lately? Honestly, Elizabeth, I don't know whether it's because you are the youngest or we were too lenient with you, but you're so different than the others! I can't help it, you worry me."

I rolled my eyes but she was gone.

Our king was convinced we could share America if he could squash the French and keep the settlers and Indians separated. The Indians, wise from years of broken promises, believed their survival depended on aligning with the winning side, but who was winning?

I bent over my loom weaving as I listened to my father mull over matters of state with my mother. Tatting was too intricate for my mood, I would have wrecked the lace. It was much easier to bang my shuttle back and forth.

"If the Penns gift money to the colony for defense, an amount significantly *more* than their tax payment would be, England would have no excuse for Parliament to object! An offering, if you will." My father was excited. He saw a way to diffuse the tension without making the Penns seem weak, or obligating them to pay taxes on a regular basis going forward. "I think I've come up with a solution!"

My mother nodded. "Seems a reasonable option. They certainly need to act in some manner."

"I'll recommend it for their consideration at the earliest possible opportunity," my father said, pleased.

I felt a familiar tightness grip my chest, the restriction of not being encouraged to share my thoughts. The Penns were like family to us, and were no strangers to our parlor and wine, but I felt they should pay taxes like all the land-owners, not give gifts at a whim. Hadn't the past year proven that we needed to fund defensive measures?

Last November, a Moravian mission only seventy-five miles from here had been attacked, completely unprovoked. A dozen Shawnee Indians shot into the house, killing several men. A few women raced for the stairs and were yanked back by their feet, then abused and murdered. Before they left, the Indians then burned all the buildings, the grain, hay, horses, and forty head of cattle. Why would they destroy valuable food and livestock?

I wanted to say something to my father, but I held my tongue. I knew from experience the comments of girls on the decisions of men were not welcome. I learned that when I was very young, although I was no longer the impressionable girl I once had been. William taught me different ways of thinking. Our government wanted us to think that the Indians were savages, and perhaps they were, but William said Indian land and their way of life was disappearing as settlers pushed further westward from the coast. "Indian land is being taken like the stroke of a paintbrush over canvas," William said. "We don't honor our agreements. They are hungry and dispossessed."

I thrust my shuttle again at the memory and took a breath.

"Father, did you see they're tallying the dead from Indian attacks now?" I asked conversationally, my eyes on my work. "They're even counting the number of buildings that have been burned or destroyed."

The lists of those killed and missing were long and growing longer. I had seen it earlier in the paper. James Armstrong, Richard Cabit, Michel Paxton, John Stevenson, John Murray—scalped and killed. Henry McIllroy's son and two daughters—captured and missing. Esther Clair— scalped but still living. *Still living while scalped?* George Eberhart—tomahawked. Frederick Rifledork and wife— missing. The names went on and on.

Father looked at Mother. He had been in Pennsylvania since 1717 and was every inch the new world gentleman, but part of him would always be a Scot, with strong and fiery opinions, particularly on government and justice. He had certainly held official positions in those areas in the colony. Father was a kind and amiable man, soft spoken and gentle, until a matter concerned him and he dug in his heels. At that point, he could be as intractable as the most stubborn mule. The look he gave me made it clear he did not want me to speak on the current depredations.

"You are a young girl," he said, puzzled. He would rather I discussed Plato and the events of ancient Greece. I enjoyed those too.

"No need to concern yourself, my dear." Mother smiled at him. "Elizabeth has plenty to occupy her, for we are in the middle of the winter social season. There certainly hasn't been any shortage of dances and charity work. She is merely showing us her Christian heart and concern for all."

Why shouldn't I discuss the news? I ached to see William and hear of his party's progress. Had the forts been built? Was everyone returning in good health? I missed my handsome young Franklin. How wonderful it would be to be with someone who would speak to me of matters other than needlework and French verbs.

Chapter 4

Philadelphia
February 12, 1756

"You have a new gown," my friend Rebecca squealed when she plonked down next to me in the coach. She grabbed at the fabric under my cloak. "The color! What a handsome green. You never said you were having a new gown made."

All four of us girls collected, the coach swayed as we turned the corner onto Front Street and the wheels slid over cobblestones slick with new snow. The town's roads are always mired in winter, an ongoing source of concern and complaint. Still, snowy streets are better than the brown muck of spring.

The jerky movement made Rebecca fall into my side. She leaned into my shoulder as she fingered my skirt.

I swatted her hand away. "Be a lady!"

Cornelia and Hannah laughed. We were a giddy group tonight, for these dances were one of the only reprieves that saw us through the dark, merciless winter months. Our fathers paid for membership to the social assembly, so each year we had season's tickets to dances held every Thursday night from January through May. And of course we also attended privately held balls.

Father was actually one of the original subscribers eight years ago when the social assembly began. I had been so envious as a girl, watching Ann and Jane prance out every week night in their finery when I was too young. The dances had changed over the past few years, growing larger. We now had eighty dancers at every dance, easily, which made for a wonderful night out. Hannah's father was one of this year's directors. A successful merchant, he had been helpful in outfitting the dances, giving us an increased supply of rum and limes.

"You want to impress William Franklin," Cornelia said. "Admit it. Your handsome hero is back from battling Indians at the frontier. You plan to command his attention in your new silk so he only has eyes for you."

I snorted, rather indelicately.

"He is already impressed, you nitwit," Hannah corrected Cornelia. "Everyone knows that. She doesn't need to try."

"I'm not sure if he'll be here," I said. "I don't know if they're even back from the frontier."

"Such a dreary week this has been," Rebecca sighed. "Honestly, I hate the cold and dark, I do, I do, I do. As soon as they play a Virginia reel or a jig, I'm going to leap onto the dance floor! It's so tiresome just sitting, sitting, sitting all the time! And if Mother gives me one more sampler to work on, I'll scream."

Rebecca and I had been friends since we were young girls. Her family, the Moores, owned Moore Hall in Chester County. As long as I'd known her, Rebecca had dreamed of saying yes to the right husband. I doubted we would be friends if we met now, but when you are young, you form attachments that last even when you grow in different ways.

"I may not dance tonight," I said. "I twisted my foot this afternoon falling over Aurelius. It was the stupidest thing. I didn't realize he was there. I may play cards or dice tonight and sit out the dancing."

The inside of the carriage looked like a haberdasher's store as yards of ribbon and lace spilled away from our bodies into the small space. Our friend Charlotte should have been with us, but her family buried three of her siblings yesterday, the three youngest boys who were barely more than babies. They died from smallpox. They had inoculated the older children but thought the little ones too small to withstand the danger of the vaccination.

"Are those new boots as well, Betsy?" Cornelia eyed my lambskin button-ups peeking out from beneath my skirt. I had my velvet dancing slippers in my bag, along with my ticket, a hair comb, and a lozenge. "Very pretty."

I nodded. "The mice feasted on my other pair at the bottom of the wardrobe. Our cats are lazy and fat. I swear Gretchen feeds them, but she will not admit to it."

Hannah tutted. "Hard to be a good mouser when your belly is full. They probably just wave a paw sleepily in the mouse's direction." She raised her hand in imitation and we laughed.

The carriage jolted on. Moon gleamed on the snow, lightening the darkness. I looked out the window and saw a member of the night watch shouting over to a figure slumped against the brick wall of the customs house. The whale oil lamps, new last year, threw yellow shadows into the inky black and highlighted the form of a man. "*No place for ruffians*," the watchman called. "*Move on*." The man straightened and trudged away, shoulders slumped. It was unclear to me if the errant gentleman was lowborn or if he had consumed too much drink at a tavern over the course of the day. Winter rendered all of us low eventually.

"I keep thinking of Susannah," Cornelia said. "I wonder how the crossing went. I keep hoping for a letter, but nothing has come. I bet she is swimming in lovely new things!"

"As long as she is not swimming in the Atlantic," Hannah muttered wryly.

Our friend Susannah had left for Britain in October with her new husband, who owned an import business in Bristol that promised them wealth and a good life. Many local men drooped in disappointment last summer when Susannah's choice of husband did not swing to their favor, as Susannah sparkled like the largest diamond ear bobs and anyone who met her was drawn into her sphere of light. Her parents celebrated the marriage, despite losing her to England. Susannah was the oldest, and they had eight more at home.

"The post takes a long time," Rebecca said. "I remember it was a good three months to hear from my cousins when they went to Liverpool. I'm sure we'll hear from her soon, once she gets settled."

"I heard the postal route is clogged on the roads near the water, especially in New Jersey and New York," Hannah added. "Depending on the port the letters arrived at, the roads might not passable. We may not get a letter until the spring." She sighed. "I do miss her terribly. Susannah was such fun."

"Is," Cornelia corrected. "Susannah *is* such fun. She isn't dead."

"What if we never see her again?" Rebecca asked. "Would you take a husband from abroad? I can't imagine being tossed about on the sea all those weeks in a dodgy wooden ship! One good storm and I would die of fright. I had an awful time on Father's skiff in the lake, never mind the sea."

"You get sick just looking at the Schuylkill!" Cornelia teased. "And that's only a river."

"I would go in a heartbeat." Hannah touched her heart dramatically. "After all, consider what she had to look forward to on the other side! A husband, a family of her own, a whole new world. Not to mention the money."

"I'd like to see Balgowan in Perthshire one day," I said. "That's where my father is from in Scotland. It's the ancestral Graeme family seat. And I would like to go to Mother's home in St. Albans in England. I've heard about the gardens there; they sound lovely. England must have an elegance that we can only imagine, compared to our scrubby forests and fields. So much history there, don't you think, all those centuries of civilization piled one on top of the other."

"But the crossing!" Cornelia said. "Bad weather would be the *least* of it. Father says the sea is crawling with Spanish and Portuguese that would put a cannon ball in the side of a British ship without a moment's pause."

"I would worry about being sick just from being on the water," Rebecca added. "I can't imagine losing my stomach for days and being trapped on the ship. No escape other than by leaping overboard!"

"Then you should keep your eyes on the Nesbitt brothers here at home," Hannah told Cornelia with a wink. "More to your taste, are they not?"

Cornelia made no secret of her desire for a farming life, for she was fretful by nature and found comfort in tranquility, or at least the idea of it. In truth, her family owned a popular glazier on Spruce Street, and it amused us that she felt she was called to rural life. With the exception of visits to our country homes in the summertime, her feet had not touched many fields, and any farm animals worth their salt would run from her.

"Our Betsy already has her husband waiting in the wings right here in Philadelphia," Cornelia said, fluttering her eyes at me flirtatiously. "When he gets home."

I stuck my tongue out at her.

"Where is Liza tonight?" Hannah asked me. "Still in Princeton?"

"Yes, still visiting family. She'll be back in a fortnight." I missed her, she was the only person close to my age at home. One couldn't count the servants.

"So who do you think will be here tonight?" Rebecca asked. "The Smolen brothers? It's a shame the youngest one is so short."

I felt a familiar boredom overcome me and gazed out the window as the girls guessed their dancing partners. They had such an ongoing fascination with young men.

As we turned onto Water Street, I watched a cart pulled by work horses headed to the docks, loaded high with logs. They were on their way to a shipbuilder. Philadelphia's seaport was the largest in the colonies now. The small town of my childhood was burgeoning with growth everywhere I looked. Cornerstones had been laid for a permanent hospital at the intersection of Eighth and Pine, due to open at the end of the year, and the College of Philadelphia opened last year at the corner of Fourth and Arch. There were more carriages and wagons rattling through town each year, new merchants and tradesmen, new houses rising out of dust every week, the streets littered with construction materials. The sound of hammering never stopped. Germans filled the city by the thousands, as well as Irish, Finns, and Scots. Last week a new cobbler, a goldsmith, and a cabinetmaker all opened their doors in a section of Second Street not far from our home. There must be over a hundred taverns and alehouses now, many doubling as an inn or boardinghouse. To get to the countryside proper, one had to walk farther than a mile, as far west as Eighth Street and just as far north, although we had some nice gardens and parks in the center of town, all part of William Penn's plan.

William Penn intended his city to stretch from river to river, from the Schuylkill on the west to the Delaware on the east. Instead, our town was lopsided, tilting heavily to the right with most of the growth clustered on the Delaware River. Ships of all sizes entered our docks year-round: sloops, brigs, schooners, even the odd man-o-war. Our warehouses received goods from all over the world: silver from Mauritius, spices from India, sugar and molasses from the West Indies. From the Continent we imported tools, leather goods, books, and weapons. Our departing ships were brimming with our wheat and flour and Indian corn. We also exported beer, glass goods, rope, bricks, even dairy cattle. Mother said Philadelphia was a bounteous place to be—if God had not called you to poverty. Or, as our rector at Christ Church liked to add, if you did not impoverish yourself drinking away your wages and your senses.

"We're here!" Rebecca announced, prodding me from my reverie. Hannah clapped her hands.

The Freemasons Lodge was the new site for the dancing assemblies. When my sisters were my age, the dances were held at Hamilton's Warehouse on the wharf. Ann used to complain of the stink of the water. This new location appealed more to Philadelphia's rising upper classes, although where we danced mattered not to me so long as the music and company was good.

Our footman opened the door and held up a hand as we held our skirts and climbed down. I was the last out. I was about to follow Rebecca and Cornelia and Hannah inside when there was a light tug on my elbow. I turned to see William grinning, his tall figure silhouetted by the lamp behind him. I gasped. He was back! He motioned a finger to his lips.

We stifled laughter as the door closed behind my friends, who didn't notice I had fallen off. William clasped my hand and pulled me in a half run to the lane next to the lodge. I ignored the mild pain in my ankle. Even in half-darkness, he was an impressive sight. Dark-haired and tall, his greatcoat framed his broad shoulders like a well-fitted suit of armor.

In the shadows and privacy of the side of the building, we stopped and turned toward each other.

"You have returned," I said stupidly. Was it possible to stop breathing from happiness?

"Miss Graeme." William leaned toward me, pushing me into the brick wall behind me. Laughter floated through the night as carriages pulled up and departed. We heard others arriving on foot and horseback, the night air filled with voices as they called out to friends. "I have missed you," he said softly.

"Why, Mr. Franklin," I retorted, delighted, "I am pleased to see you but very displeased all at the same time."

William frowned. "Whatever for?"

"Not only did you not write to me, you didn't come see me upon your return," I said, my voice teasing. I couldn't stop smiling. We swayed toward each other, William's head inches from mine. I smelled the sweetness of a cigar and behind it the stench of urine from the ground around us that the snow could not mask.

"You are not correct, Miss Graeme," he said. His lips brushed mine. "You see, I did call on you but alas, I was forsaken. That led me no choice but to capture you here in this alley."

"You did?" I pulled back. My voice changed from teasing to serious. My evening bag dug into my wrist and dangled awkwardly. "You came by the house? When?"

William dropped a butterfly kiss on each of my eyebrows. "I called on Saturday, and yesterday again. How could you think I would not come? I was tossed out by that ill-tempered bull of a manservant your father employs. What's his name, Alf? Alb? The first time they said you were indisposed, and the next, not at home. That man should be set to work clubbing thieves in the market. It would be a better use of his considerable skills. He's rather brutish."

I laughed. "I swear I did not know. No one said a word." I was sure it was not an accident, either.

"Always my tormentor," William sighed.

"No. Your very great admirer."

We straightened, became serious. Our eyes searched each other's in the dim light.

William squeezed my arms. "Betsy, I thought of you a thousand times while I was away, more, even. Lord knows I had plenty of time; the going was hellishly slow, and you were a welcome distraction while we fought snow up to our thighs going through the mountains. I hope you don't think I prefer the company of dozens of rank-smelling men over you."

The mention of thighs stirred something within me, and I felt my cheeks go warm. I raised my gloved fingers of the hand without my evening bag to his cheek. "You have no idea how glad I am you are back, William. I'm so very glad. I missed you greatly."

William took my hand and moved it to his lips. "Betsy, we must talk." His eyes seared into mine.

"Yes, we do," I agreed, "But not here. We can't be alone here. We need to go in." I motioned toward the street. "The girls will be looking for me." I shifted sideways along the wall, away from him.

William stood for a moment without moving. I moved forward and pressed my lips to his. He sighed and reached for my hand. We slipped out of the alley and around to the front of the hall, two shadows sliding out from darkness.

"Will!" a man called through the crisp air. It was our friend Francis Hopkinson with a group of others. It was hard to tell who they were from where we stood, half way to the steps.

"Well done," Francis shouted. William nodded and raised a hand in appreciation. As they approached I could see that two of them were Francis's classmates from the college, Jacob Duché and John Morgan. They would be the first class to graduate from the new college this spring.

"How did it go?" Hopkinson asked.

I listened to William provide a brief answer, careful to avoid self-praise. Talk had spread quickly of the expedition's victory in the Lehigh corridor. Their work was an achievement. In six weeks, they had sealed a three hundred-mile expanse from Reading through Bethlehem, built three stockades, buried the dead, and restored a tentative peace. Some folk believed that their work halted the drums of war, at least temporarily.

"We heard you and your father rode back into Philadelphia at night to avoid a fuss," someone said.

"We did what we needed to do," William said easily. "Folks get excited." They hadn't wanted people to come out in droves, cheering, lauding them as heroes.

I grabbed a handful of snow. When Francis and his friends turned to go inside and William followed, I dropped the snow down the back of William's neck.

He roared and shook it off. "I see what our life is to be like when we are married!"

"Why should I marry you?" I teased. "An itinerant soldier? What will you do now that you are back from the wilderness? Surely going back to clerking for the government would seem rather dull after you've been dodging Indians in no-man's land. Maybe you *should* reconsider going into your father's printing shop."

I was jesting of course. William did not have the temperament for trade, could not be penned into small spaces. He belonged in the outdoors, or at least in bigger places. When he was only fifteen he had tried to escape to sea. Mr. Franklin had calmly boarded the ship William was on, still moored on the Delaware, and gently brought him back home. That was the beginning of William's military career; his Father knew he could not hold him back and channeled his son's energy into military service. William headed out shortly after that, galloping into King George's War in Albany. Military service suited him, he blossomed and settled in to himself. After he returned, we became friends, and then more than friends.

"Miss Graeme, are my affections misplaced?" I heard the tension in his voice. I had gone too far.

"Oh, William darling. I was joking." In my anxiousness, I forgot about the people walking by us into the hall. I did not care.

William held my hands. "We should have a life together, Betsy. Wouldn't you like that? We already have had, haven't we, for years. Let's make it real."

I heard my mother's voice, imploring me to be cautious. I felt the weight of my father's disapproval, stung by his child choosing a man he did not like, a man that did not share his beliefs. William embarrassed him.

I embraced William quickly. My heart reacted to his warmth, the solidness of him. I pressed him close to me for a brief moment, then took his arm and propelled him inside.

The brightness and noise was a blinding contrast to the cold winter's night. The strains of Handel's *Water Music* surged around us, the musicians warming up, as we handed our outer garments to waiting staff.

The clock inched toward twelve, the evening drawing to a close. The rules were clear: assembly dances must end at midnight, no exceptions.

My throat was sore from talking. I had moved between gaming tables, the hours slipping by in a happy haze. Bach's Minuet in G Major floated in from the dancing room next door as the current game of dice finished, and I excused myself. I had drunk enough Madeira that I no longer felt my sore ankle.

I found my friends on the dance floor. Rebecca and Cornelia and Hannah were twirling elegantly through a minuet. I stood next to a tall column, heavily decorated with scrollwork, and watched.

"Ah, my good fortune. A beautiful woman all alone," William's low voice intoned just behind my ear. He was so close I could feel the warmth of his breath and the smell of whisky.

I laughed. *"If music be the food of love, play on."*

"My lady quotes Shakespeare."

"She does. Orsino in *Twelfth Night*."

"One can only hope. I dream that my lady has an appetite for love, the love of her doting Franklin."

I laughed. "Ugh. Such simpering humor shall make me queasy."

He stood close behind me, a hand either side of my waist. I could feel my stays under his fingers, the boning suddenly tight and itching where it had never bothered me before. William bent to brush his head against mine, his temple above my ear.

"Come away with me, my lady," he said in a low voice.

Longing pulled at me. I closed my eyes, imagined it. "Where would we go?"

"Boston? New York? Before your parents' object, we can be husband and wife. Be with me," William murmured. "They would come around to the idea. Your mother likes me. I'll finish my studies and find work as a barrister. That's a fine profession for a daughter's husband. How could your father object to you marrying a man of the law?"

"I doubt *your* father would appreciate that," I said smartly. "The presence of a woman getting in your way. Besides, I'm not sure Mr. Franklin would have me for your bride. He has plans for his son."

The heat of William's hands still on my waist seeped through my body. I twisted my head to look up at him. His expression was sincere.

"Your father relies on you," I said. It was true. After William's military service, in addition to having William replace him as clerk in the Assembly, Mr. Franklin gave him a position in Philadelphia's postal service, as well as steered him into law. They did several projects together for the town, as well as embarked on scientific exploration, which included Mr. Franklin's electrical experiments. William was enthusiastic counsel and partner for all of his father's ideas. Even in the Lehigh Valley last month, reports said it was William who organized badly needed supplies for the army, mustered new recruits at each outpost, and used his military experience to drill them at his father's command. The two Franklin men were inseparable.

William merely shook his head and swayed with me to the music, the merest hint of movement. I felt like the flame of a candle, shimmering with heat. No one seemed to see us; the room was filled with bodies and noise. The late hour of the night, and the wine, made me too bold. I placed my hands over his on my waist and leaned back into him.

"Do you know, Betsy," he said above my ear, "there were times when I thought death was not far away. Not just because of the cold or the men falling ill around me. We knew the Indians were watching us while we worked, we could feel them. Only the sheer number of men in our party prevented us from being attacked. Yet all through the long days it was not an ambush on my mind, or my own death. It was you."

I felt it too. I felt our bond even when we weren't together. We were connected to each other the same way the moon pulled on the tide.

"I thought of you too," I said softly. "I could sense you."

Perhaps if my parents approved, it would have been easier to know what to do. I felt like Mr. Franklin and his rod, chasing flashes of light in the sky. Philadelphia was roiling with uncertainty these days, and I was pushed up against my parents and the war developing in the west. It was a difficult time to think of eloping.

"Your parents have known me since I was a boy," William said.

It would have been hard not to. Benjamin Franklin had been responsible for our first public library, our fire service, the new college, the hospital, even the paving and cleaning of streets and sidewalks. My father said they were a fine family, there was nothing undesirable about a man that served his community so generously.

I knew what was unspoken, though. My father may have respected Ben Franklin, but he disliked him. They were as cautious around each other as a rabbit and coyote. My father was conservative and traditional, more farmer and physick than politician. Mr. Franklin's opposition to the Penns jarred my father, agitated his sense of order. And, of course, Father's friendship with the Penns, particularly Thomas Penn, with whom he was close, kept my own ears full of the misery Ben Franklin was causing them. My father would drag me back by the hair if I tried to leave, albeit very gently, although the thought of leaving with William tempted me. William liked it when I worked on my writing, and he never tried to speak to me as if I was merely a girl.

"Come away with me," William said again.

"Do you mean what you're saying?" I asked. I did not see this coming. "Have you thought about this?" I enjoyed flirting with William, I liked our banter and teasing and the pure giddy fun of his company. He had become serious without warning this year, and I was unprepared for his sudden deepening of intention.

"Marry me, Betsy," William said, and neatly turned me to face him. "You are my best friend, my whole heart. My feelings for you—" he stopped and looked around when he realized we were not in a private moment.

My eyes met his. If I refused him, I might lose him. I could not bear that. I did not want to do or say an offense that would send him away.

Mother's warning rang in my ears. *We don't believe William is right for you.* I wanted to say yes because I didn't want him to go to someone else. I liked being with William, but I wasn't ready to marry. It felt an awful burden, not being able to keep affection without the chains of matrimony.

I thought of the day last spring I found a runaway wife hiding in our back yard. *They do what they like, don't they,* she said brokenly, nursing a bruised cheek and oozing yellow cut above her eye. I gave her food and coin to help her on her way and kept her secret. Husbands often froze their credit accounts on escaped wives so women had no access to resources beyond what they could take.

William wasn't like that, though. William was a good man.

Why was I thinking of that now? What was wrong with me?

William watched me squirm and gave a slight shake of his head, resigned. He took my hand and pulled us toward the dance floor as the minuet came to an end and a violin released a long, slow, sonorous note. This must be the last dance.

"You will be the death of me, my muse," he said. He gave me a grin that made his eyes gleam, rakish and sensual. "It appears I must wait, so wait I will."

Suddenly I didn't want to tell him about my bad ankle.

Chapter 5

To Horsham
April 17, 1756

This week Governor Morris issued a startling proclamation: murder the Indians. His orders said to kill any Delaware over the age of twelve. In his instructions, he outlined how much money would be awarded for each body. A male was worth twice as much as a female, upon proof of death. There were also monetary rewards for the return of our citizens that had been captured by the Indians. Morris explained that the friendly Delaware who were sympathetic to peace were exempt from his order.

I was distressed. The murderous order made no sense to me. From a distance or in a hurry, from the other end of a musket or a sword, how could anyone know a warring Indian from a friendly Indian? How could more killing lead to less violence overall?

There had been more brutality in the west. Each day brought new violence, confusion, and another influx of refugees into Philadelphia from the frontier. The Quakers were disgusted by Morris's killing order. They held a majority in the government but started quitting in droves while taverns bulged with men hunkered down to form attack plans on the Indians.

My mother wasted no time. "We're going to Graeme Park," she ordered. "Immediately."

She would not even allow Liza and I to stay an extra day to go to the dance, although in truth we were already scheduled to go home for the fox hunt on Saturday.

I heard her whispering with Father before we left. "Have you forgotten the Mohawks who came to the dancing assembly last year? It was also April, as I recall. It was the talk of town."

"That was different, Ann. They were *guests*. Delaware warriors are not suddenly going to walk in the streets with tomahawks and arrows. Philadelphia is the last place they would come. The streets are too wide and populated."

"You can't *know* that, Thomas."

And so we left, racing north on York Road toward our summer home. My mother tried to get my sisters to come too, but they refused.

"They are married women," my father groaned when my mother complained to him.

"We will come for the hunt," they placated her. "Don't worry, Mama. We'll be fine."

"They'll be with us soon," Liza soothed my mother. She always did that, calmed tempers and eased the worries of those around her. If she had been born a boy she would have made a good physick.

We jolted Graeme Park by the abruptness of our arrival; even the birds scattered in surprise. The servants rushed about shaking off winter. Linens were washed, salad herbs and vegetables planted, shutters thrown open, the kitchen house scrubbed clean in preparation for the months of hectic occupancy to come.

My step-grandfather, Sir William Keith, had this house built in 1722 when he was Pennsylvania's lieutenant governor. He called his property Fountain Low because of the springs that ran through it. While governor, he was well-liked by the people but not by the proprietors, for he could never manage to tow the party line to the degree required. Instead, he arranged peace conferences with Indians and tried to listen to the concerns of the people. I wondered if he was turning in his grave at the state of Pennsylvania now, with Indians on the war path (those he worked so hard to befriend) and the French poised to attack us.

"Do you miss him, Mama?" I asked my mother as we unpacked the good china.

"I thought the world of him," she answered thoughtfully. "He was my sun after my own father died. He had such a big heart, despite his weaknesses."

"Tell us about him," I said, mostly to ease the pinch in her forehead and get her mind off of murdering Indians, although I had heard the stories of my step-grandfather many times before.

"Yes, do," Liza chimed in.

"My stepfather went back to England to escape his substantial debts about ten years before you were born," she began, opening a box of Meissen porcelain. "You know he died in debtors' prison, that's no secret. He struggled in so many ways, in business and politically. Some would say he failed. There's even talk that he intended this house to be a brewery or a malt house and abandoned the plan, but I don't know how true that is. He did, however, love this land and the people in it. He cared very deeply. It cost him a great deal to leave my mother here; he thought he was coming back to her."

My mother was kind, but I heard what people said. In reality, my grandfather Keith was wily, unconscionably so. William's father told me that, thirty years ago, my step-grandfather promised to help him set up his own printing business and finance it, then left him high and dry. As an eighteen-year-old, Mr. Franklin was on the boat to London, as per their agreement, before he realized that it was all a ruse. There would be no money and no assistance when he arrived in London as a youth. He had been deceived. Franklin was forced to make his own way without resources. Unfortunately, my grandfather made many empty promises to many people. I guess he paid for them in the end. He went from being lieutenant governor in a mansion house to dying as a pauper behind prison walls in the Old Bailey.

"What a shame," Liza said, pulling the paper off a vase featuring a Chinaman in his garden, etched in silver gilt.

"Perhaps Grandfather Keith would be heartened by what Papa Graeme is doing with his property now."

I liked the way Liza called my father Papa Graeme. Obviously, they weren't related by blood, but he cared for her as deeply as he cared for all his children.

"Careful, Liza," my mother said when Liza placed the vase down a tad too roughly. "That's precious." I've heard traders call porcelain white gold.

Grandfather Keith was always scheming to make money, I thought. Fortunately, Grandfather Keith's underhandedness had not reached us. As Graeme girls, my sisters and I had been taught to be exemplary, beginning with character. *Always make good on your word. Be godly: have integrity, humility, compassion, and respect.* After our morality, the list of lessons and requirements for our education and refinement through the years was endless. We were given Bible study; a deep immersion in academia; education in languages written and spoken, including Latin, Greek, French, and Italian; we were required to be proficient in dancing and singing and reading music; even learning an instrument or three. Equally important were a thorough knowledge of hostess duties and how to manage a household. We were to be calm, graceful, and always in control of our emotions, even if someone was rolling around on the floor in front of us with both legs shot off.

Luckily, my mother educated her daughters the same way she taught my older brothers before they died, so I fared better than most of my sex, who were relegated to the domestic. The book learning was the easy part. It was everything else that troubled me. I felt like the future stretched before me like a maze with no exit. I needed to prepare to lead a house one day, a thought which made me weary. I was not fond of housekeeping at all. It put me in the foulest temper.

But here I was, unwrapping dishes.

After we finished unpacking the dry goods, I locked myself in my chamber for two days, writing. My windows had already been cleaned when we'd barely been home a day, I noticed. I always loved my windows. My chamber had a set of double windows, tall and wide, on two walls, the beauty of nature only a glance away. I sat at my desk writing, trying to leave the world behind, surrounded by books written by my favorite authors.

I was deep in concentration on Saturday morning copying verse into my commonplace book when I looked up with a start. Liza was in my chamber casually waving a pistol.

"Put that down! What on earth are you doing?" I yelped.

Liza stopped by a window and took aim at a sycamore tree. "In case any warring Indians come. We should be prepared."

I stared at her as if she had swallowed an entire bottle of opium syrup.

"It said in the paper—"

"I know what it said," I snapped. "How could you bring that into my room?"

Liza shrugged. "We are not in town now, are we, dear heart? In the country, we may need to protect ourselves. It would not be unreasonable to—"

"Get out, Liza. Now! Take that with you. Have you lost your senses?"

That was one of Father's pistols, I was sure. I recognized the engraved handle. "And put it back wherever you found it. I won't say a word."

"I am a good shot, you know," she threw over her shoulder as she departed. "You may be glad of it one day when I save us both."

"I'm a good shot too," I called after her. "I just do not shoot *people*."

"Can we go and shoot fox with the men? It would be good practice."

"Bah!" I got up to close the door firmly after her. "No. Not unless you can disguise yourself as a boy."

"It's not wrong to be prepared!" she called through the door.

I sat down again and tried to retrieve my train of thought, but it was gone. I looked at the books on my table, my authors. Silent friends. Edward Young I could open my heart to. His poem on death, *Night Thoughts*, is relatable to everyone who has someone close to them die. Where is tomorrow, he asked sorrowfully. In another world, was his answer, for his wife had died. Nicholas Rowe flattered my imagination and took evening walks with me while I mulled over his plays as I walked. And who doesn't love his version of *Pharsalia*? Joseph Addison suited me in any humor, he was so witty and insightful. His *Cato, A Tragedy* is one of my favorites. Alexander Pope I was a little afraid of because he knew the human heart so well and always made me examine my own. William Harvey I revered, for he had such goodness in his soul and could say the same thing in so many ways and still be ideal.

If I had to choose between reading and writing, I did not believe I could. Writing poetry elevated the soul. Women were educated by poetry, for a good verse helped us reach toward each other, even if we were far away from each other in distance. When we copied poems down and shared them, the words opened our minds and connected us until we could see each other in person again.

I wrote my first poems at twelve, although I shuddered now to read those. My poetry was much better now. My Latin tutor encouraged me to publish, like some ladies who write in Europe do, but I would never do that. That was vanity, and untoward. My poetry was for myself and for sharing with friends. That was why we wrote to each other using pen names, so we could be free.

I looked up. The view outside my windows was beautiful. The color of the greenery in April was sweet and dense and vivid. This was the color of crowns of laurel, of grass smelling of new life, of stories of fairies in the forest.

I dipped my quill in my ink pot and began to write:

In Nature's grace we bend

"Betsy, come," Liza called from the top of the stairs. "The Moores have arrived. I just saw their carriage."

Ah, the fox hunt.

I shelved my pen and stretched my stiff fingers as I stood. I glanced at myself in the looking glass. My hair was tame today, dark and shiny, holding up in its tortoiseshell combs. I wouldn't call myself beautiful, but I liked my hair and eyes. I was not blessed with the strong chins and broad cheeks of the girls in Da Vinci's paintings; my chin was narrow, but my eyes had been called luminous. And William said I had lustrous hair.

I gathered my shawl around my shoulders. There was a chill in the air. There had not been many warm days yet this spring.

"You'll be staying, I do hope, Williamina," Mother said to Mrs. Moore, handing their cloaks to a maid. The hallway smelled like wet sheep.

"Believe it or not, the weather was pleasant when we left Chester," Mrs. Moore said, with a nod at their wet cloaks. "Not raining at all. Yes, we'll stay two weeks, if that's agreeable."

"Oh, I'm so glad!" Liza breathed. "Rebecca, it has been weeks and weeks since I saw you. We must catch up."

"We must," Rebecca agreed. They danced away from the older women. "Betsy, come," they called from the landing.

Mother and Mrs. Moore disappeared into the parlor.

"Richard Nesbitt and his father have arrived," Clara, my maid, said to me. She was breathless from running up and down the stairs where there was a window with the best vantage point of the front driveway. "And the Lukens brothers."

"Is Reverend Smith here?" Rebecca asked.

"I have not seen him," Clara said.

"He is coming, though?" Rebecca persisted.

I nodded. I thought so.

Reverend Smith ran the College of Philadelphia and was a Church of England clergyman. He had been handpicked by Ben Franklin and the board to run the new school based on an essay he wrote while he was still in Scotland. So far he seemed unaware of the admiration of my friend.

"That's all right, Clara, we don't need to know every arrival," I called after her. There were far too many people coming to make individual announcements, besides the obvious fact that many of them had been friends and neighbors for years. No need to be too formal.

"Yes, we do," Rebecca called over me. "Of course we do! Thank you, Clara."

"We'll see everyone at dinner," Liza pointed out.

Rebecca shrugged. "*Hours* from now."

"I do so appreciate a gathering," Liza said happily. I wondered if the pistol had made it back to Father's office.

There were many parties scheduled despite the troubles we faced. We had already received invitations to the Nesbitts' for a spinning party and to the Dreshers' for a spring fête, to the Stocktons' for the wedding of Prudence to John, and to the Campbells' and Powells' and Shippens' for balls. The summer invitations had only just begun; there would be more weddings, and the Carters usually hosted a spinning bee. The Andersons always insisted on a garden party when their roses were in full bloom.

I myself preferred smaller gatherings where the conversation had more substance and was more interesting. There was only so much talk I could listen to about hat feathers and new dressmakers and who made the best indigo. Luckily, we lived in a town full of learned people, and there were always interesting folks coming and going from the continent. Even the ships from Canada and the Carolinas brought a steady stream of people eager to reach booming Philadelphia with its new industries and growing marketplace.

"Don't pick a tanner," Liza advised Ada McKean over a game of whist. Ada had confessed she was ready to court. "No one wants to be with a man who smells of dead animals."

"A man of the church," Rebecca added piously, "would be a good choice. He would have a good heart and honor."

"Well, not all of them," Edna Steuben said. "I heard about a minister in Lancaster who was behaving in a very ungodly manner with a few of the women in his congregation."

"Now, Rebecca, which man of the church would you be referring to?" Ada teased. "Anyone in particular?"

We were playing cards at a table at the end of the parlor while Mother and the older ladies were clustered around the fire talking. Mrs. Nesbitt and Mrs. Lukens had arrived. Their young grandchildren were playing jacks on the floor at the other end of the room, mostly girls and a few little boys who weren't old enough to go on the hunt with the older boys and men.

The conversation around the card table had gone from the dressmaker on Market Street offering new Indian voiles, to what the summer concerts would be, to admiration for the work of the upholsterer White & Lawrence after they redid the chairs in Edna's aunt's house. I kept a watchful eye on Aurelius, who had sniffed the children with interest, then flopped down near the brass music stand and fluttered an eye each time a tray went by. His nose wrinkled at sweetmeats and fig tarts, but he knew better than to beg. I was not as confident how the jacks would fare after he'd woken up from his nap and was looking for a good chew.

"Are you still sweet on Reverend Smith?" Edna asked conspiratorially.

Rebecca blushed. "Ssh," she murmured, looking in her mother's direction, but the older women were absorbed among themselves.

"If he isn't interested, there are new doctors in town," Ada offered with a wink. "Young and fresh from training in Paris and Edinburgh. Betsy, go, your turn."

"It's a man's heart that matters," Edna said. "Doesn't matter if he smells like tannin or spends his days making rope or laying bricks or melting metal at the forge."

"I agree that a good spouse has to be more than his livelihood," I said. "Nights by the fire can be long. We need someone to talk to." I never had any trouble finding something to discuss with William. Besides being worldly, his mind was like a lighthouse beckoning to me; he was widely read and could speak on any subject.

"Someone to talk to, Betsy? Conversation?" Edna said scornfully as she laid a card. "How boring."

"You sound like an old lady," Liza laughed. "None of us are twenty yet."

"Oh, Betsy," Ada said. "You, the last of the pretty and witty single Graeme girls, dazzling to a hundred men. The newcomers are barely off the boats and they're smitten before their feet touch land. None of your suitors will be lacking in any regard."

"There actually *is* a lineup," Rebecca said. "The problem is William Franklin's massive shoulders blocking the way."

The girls laughed too hard, and the ladies looked up. I shrugged my shoulders and studied my cards.

I had always been slightly out of tune with the rest of the world, like a violin with a string that refused to true up. If I were Rebecca, I would have planned the biggest society wedding in Philadelphia and sweet-talked my parents into a lavish wedding dinner after a ceremony at Christ Church. But I was not Rebecca. Instead, I quietly nursed my feelings and hid my thoughts from my family. I envied Rebecca, for if you were forthright and honest, you didn't need to remember what you had said or not said, and never be in a position to tally your omissions and half-truths.

"You could have a prince," Edna said to me. "You are the most delightful creature. We all adore you."

"Oh, be quiet. Stop," I said, embarrassed. I laid a card and sipped my punch. "You know what I meant. I did not say I want to be boring or have a dullard husband. I meant—"

"Yes, yes, we know. That you love your books and fancy ideas," Liza interrupted and blew a kiss across the table at me. "And that you will have no time for marriage, not ever, because you're far too busy writing loads of very important words in at least six languages."

"Well, there won't be time for writing when you and Will are married with a babe on the way and one just walking. You can save the goose its quill," Ada said matter-of-factly.

I shuddered and hoped no one saw.

"Well, *I* want dancing and music and parties and fairs and balls!" Edna said. "I want fancy carriages and expensive travel and exotic foods and all the gowns I can think of to ask for. I win, ladies!" Edna threw her last card down and stood up to curtsy.

Rebecca cheered and bowed to Edna. "You are the queen."

My maid appeared. Clara held out a bowl. "Candied almonds?"

We lounged and ate and wondered aloud how the men were faring on the hunt.

"Read one of your poems to us, Betsy," Ada said. "You said you have new ones."

"Oh yes, do," Edna said. "I love it when you read. Your voice is lovely to hear."

"I should object on principle," I said. "Such awful friends, mocking me like that."

Liza waved a dismissive hand. "Oh, please. We tease out of deepest respect."

We moved from the table to the stuffed chairs. I retrieved my commonplace book and stepped over Aurelius, whose little body was emitting loud snores and the occasional waft of noxious gas.

"My, he's a smelly one," Edna said. She made a face and waved the air with a sparrow-like hand. "For such a small mutt."

"He always stinks," Liza agreed. "But he's lovable. Betsy, we should give him a bath."

Aurelius responded with another offering of gas to greet the arrival of my sisters. Ann looked healthy, her cheeks pink and round, but Jane looked wan, I thought.

After my sisters made their greetings, they draped themselves on the loveseat near me. Our childhood evenings had been spent in front of the fire as Mother read aloud a drama and we hung on to every word.

"I miss this," Ann said with a sigh, tucking her skirt around her.

I began to read my poem.

"When one fond object occupies the mind . . ."

The light was thin, the sun low and pale as suet when we heard the men and boys coming down the road, a few dozen strong, voices raised in song.

"They're back," Mother announced.

We crowded around the windows to watch. The hounds trotted ahead of the horses, followed by the men with their kill, which was several foxes, some rabbits, two opossums, and a wild turkey. Three wild turkeys.

"I wonder if James caught anything," Jane said, looking for her husband.

"And Charles," Ann added, peering over Jane's shoulder. "They had a good year last year."

"Oh," Rebecca sighed at the lumps of fur going by, paws and tails dangling lifelessly. "Shame. That their lives should end like that."

"They are little more than vermin," Jane objected. She wiped the water drops off the window with her fingers. "They are a nuisance, killing and spreading disease. There will always be more; we'll never get rid of enough of them. That's why the government pays two shillings a piece for them to be killed." Apparently, the government wanted foxes and Indians both to be dead, I thought.

"Still," Rebecca said. "All God's creatures."

Ann shook her head. "You would never make a farm wife."

"There is naught wrong with a tender heart," Mother said from the other window.

"She was always sensitive," Mrs. Moore commented. "Different from my other children."

"Excuse me." Jane shoved Ann out of the way and made quickly for the door, a hand over her mouth.

"What is it?" Mother asked, hurrying after her.

Before she could answer, Jane vomited on the floor in the hall. She moaned, straightened, and ran upstairs.

Mother had the ghost of a smile.

"I suspect I may have another grandchild coming," she said quietly. "I have wondered."

She rang the bell on the side table. "Come quickly," she called to the servants. "Clean it before the men come in. Ann, go to your sister."

The men joined us, creating a commotion in every direction. Soon noise and laughter floated up from every room on the first floor. Bodies were everywhere, in the new dining room that used to be our kitchen before Father had the summer kitchen built, in the parlor, the hallways, even Father's office. Children under twelve were ordered upstairs for their meal and games in the nursery, including, to their disgust, the young boys who had been allowed on the hunt with their fathers.

Mother had hired extra servants for the day. Dish after dish came in from the kitchen house. Trays of cheese, bread, and grapes were passed around and bowls of oranges and dates. Then the main courses appeared: turtle, pheasant, trout, and beef. We could not eat it all. For sweets, we had brandy cake and pastries. The food and wine flowed steadily, hour after hour.

It was much later, long past sunset, when the feasting stopped. Father finished his supper and held up a hand to the men around him at the dining table. "Friends, stay and drink. Celebrate with us."

A cheer went up. "A bloody good hunt every year, Thomas," yelled Richard Powell. "To the Graemes!"

"Fetch my fiddle," Father said. Someone had a harmonica and blew out a few squeaky notes. Another man pulled out a flute.

Wall sconces were lit and glowed brightly throughout the house. We pushed the furniture in the parlor back toward the walls, then rolled up the Turkey rugs and tucked them behind the chairs. I noticed Mother had her porcelain busts of the great poets moved; one had gotten broken at the last party. Someone very drunk had used it for target practice with a spirit glass. The expensive French platters from Limoges had disappeared too.

Time shifted, receded. We spun and shrieked with laughter through jig and reel after jig and reel. It was the early hours of the morning when the dancing finally petered out. We sat down, breathless, our faces shining and our hair flying out. Friends blurry with drink and fatigue slid home without ceremony, music and laughter too loud for proper good-byes. Some left their children sleeping in the nursery and said they'd return for them on the morrow.

I took out my violin and played a Scottish folk song. I sang some silly made-up words about the hunt, and when I repeated the verse, everyone joined in, shouting the refrain. At one point, my mother sat balanced on my father's leg, her wineglass held up to avoid spilling as Father thumped her hip boisterously, beating time to the music. We laughed and sang for what must have been hours as the floors vibrated underneath us.

The morning sun shivered the black sky to dark gray as the door closed on the last guest. My sister Ann and her husband had left early, along with James and pale-faced Jane and their little baby girl, back to their homes in the city. Mother and Father finally retired, as did Mrs. Moore to the guest chamber.

Rebecca and Liza and I headed to the stairs, clutching each other about the waist as we hummed, "Yo Gentle Gales."

"Look," I said. I paused on the landing between the first and second flights and gazed outside the window at the sky. "The sun."

"This isn't the first time we've stayed up all night and watched the sun rise," Rebecca giggled. "We know how to end a party."

We climbed again and reached the second floor. I extracted myself from their arms and paused outside my chamber door. "Good night, then, dear ones. Sleep well."

"ImgladImwithyou," Rebecca said to Liza. She shook her head and clucked to release her tongue. "I'm glad I am staying in your bed, Liza Lou. You can protect me."

"Protect you from whom?" I asked, amused. "Ghosts?"

"From being kidnapped by Indians from my bed."

"Charming," I said. "I was enjoying being happy and carefree."

"Not to worry, sweet Rebecca," Liza said to her. "I know where there's a gun, and I can use it. I have been *practicing*." Liza eyed me knowingly.

"You have both drunk too much punch," I said. "You are talking nonsense."

"And wine too," Liza added proudly. "Although it doesn't taste the best with rum punch."

"I would take my own life," Rebecca continued. "I would *kill* myself, I tell you. I'm not letting an Indian touch me. I won't be like those women in the papers, slave to a savage."

"No one is coming for you, Rebecca," I said with a sigh.

"No, and not Reverend Smith either," Rebecca said theatrically. Liza and I laughed.

Liza hauled Rebecca up the next flight of stairs to their room on the third floor.

Later that afternoon, William galloped up to the house on his horse. What was he doing here?

"Go talk to him outside," my mother said, frowning.

I grabbed my shawl and ran out to meet him.

William was barely off his horse before he issued a warning. "Betsy, stay as long as you can at Graeme Park." His face was dark and anxious.

We took his horse to the stable and then walked to the creek.

"Tell me."

"Last week more than five hundred men from three of the back counties mounted up and headed this way. They are demanding a law to get armed troops."

William was as taut as a loaded bow, his usual relaxed and laconic demeanor nowhere in sight. I noticed he arrived with a musket at the ready and a knife sheathed in his boot.

"This is not news. I've heard this before."

"Betsy, this is different. These men are making their way to Philadelphia right now, armed and angry. They're bloodthirsty. *Five hundred men*, Betsy. Not five or ten, or even fifty! Morris received word and sent the attorney general and his men to meet them. They're trying to head them off at Lancaster."

If Governor Morris had sent the attorney general to head them off, he saw the men as a real threat. If he wanted them as far away as possible from Philadelphia, they were dangerous. I listened closely.

"These men, the insurgents, claim we failed them," William continued, his voice low and urgent. "They are crazed with rage. Word is that Indians either killed their wives or took them."

I thought of our festivities last night and over the previous weeks. How sobering to think we had been dancing while blood was shed. Maybe Rebecca was not being so dramatic after all.

"Violence in town, then. This is what you fear?" I asked.

"These are men at the breaking point. They'll burn Philadelphia down if they have to, to get what they want. I predict they're going to go on a rampage. They want armed troops defending the settlements on the frontier. To them, nothing else is acceptable. They know Pennsylvania doesn't have an organized defense plan. They'll kill people in town to make their point, in the streets or in church, anywhere, in retaliation for what's been done to them. Innocent people will die."

I thought of the graceful arc of Philadelphia's cupolas against the river, the spires of Christ Church and the State House, the elegant mansions and houses lining Society Hill, the merchants and their lucrative store windows, the new docks being built. William's description of the incoming raiders rampaging through my prosperous hometown didn't seem to fit.

"What can we do?"

"I don't know. Nothing has changed. You know there's no money to pay for troops. Not without taxation," William said. "The Quakers will not agree to it, and others will not pay tax for defense unless the Penns do. Even if we achieved a miracle and raised the money, we would still need to assemble and train men that are only farmers. We are unprepared and ill-equipped."

Before I could tell William of my father's idea that the Penns gift an amount for defense of the colony, William grabbed my arm. "Promise me you will stay here, Betsy. Please. Do not come into town. It isn't safe. I'm worried about you."

"I promise." I smiled to try and lighten his fear. "William, listen to me. We won't go into town while there's a chance of unrest. Father will make sure of that. We will gladly heed your advice."

I went on to tell him of Father's idea of the monetary gift from the Penns in lieu of a tax payment. I had heard that Thomas Penn was receptive to his suggestion and the money was being prepared.

William's face slowly cleared, his jaw unclenching.

We sat down on a log and watched as sunlight dappled the water with silver light. This was the place where I wrote when the weather was fair. I liked to watch the water birds come and go, crying their lonely calls. Last summer I shared the property's streams and rivers with herons, beavers, an egret, a snapping turtle, and a host of frogs and toads.

William stroked my palm absently.

"You missed a good hunt yesterday," I said against the sound of the gentle ripple of water stirred by a family of ducks. "I was hoping you would come, but I understood why you chose not to."

He nodded. "It's better that I stay back. Let your father not have to lay eyes on me for a time."

William slid down off the log onto the ground so that his back was leaning against it. I joined him, feeling the rough bark catch at the back of my short gown. He closed his eyes and arched his back over the log, stretching. He had ridden hard to get here quickly. My heart constricted. He was always thinking of me.

For a man, William had a beauty that was saved from being effeminate by his height and broad shoulders. His face was pretty, with his long nose and his features spaced just right in his face. Sometimes he wore a wig, but he needn't;

he had a thick head of hair, which he sometimes tied back with a ribbon in a queue. William had a certain slender leonine air that his father did not possess, an easy grace, a natural aristocratic manner. I fought the urge to touch the dark curls where they brushed against his ears.

William's birth mother must have been beautiful, I guessed. Mr. Franklin would never tell anyone who she was. Mr. Franklin took up with his common-law wife, Deborah, when William was an infant, and Deborah took in William as her own child. Sometimes Deborah was harsh with William, but I could not blame her. She had to endure her own son, Franky, dying at the tender age of four from the pox while her husband's son, thrown forth into the world from an unknown, and most likely lowborn woman, lived to ride into Indian territory for the king, wearing the scarlet of the grenadiers and shoulders squared with pride.

"Such scrutiny," he said, one eye opening a crack. "I feel like one of your songbirds or butterflies, about to be captured for posterity in a line of poetry. Write me up nicely."

"You need a haircut," I retorted. "Still, I cannot help but admire such a handsome man, now can I?"

William sat up and drew me to him. I settled my head into his chest.

"My dark-eyed poet with the beautiful hair," he murmured. "Whatever is to come, I feel better facing it with you by my side." I closed my eyes and rubbed my nose on his waistcoat like a kitten.

He reached for my chin, raising my face to his, and kissed me.

"Betsy, Betsy, Betsy. I could say your name a thousand times. I would like to know you as a husband knows a wife. You drive me mad. I long to marry you."

The soft coo of a mourning dove slid through the trees at the same time as a little fish broke the surface of the water with a gurgle.

"I have decided I will marry you, William Franklin," I said softly. The words dazzled me, winter sun on snow. "I find I cannot be without you."

William was grinning. I had surprised him. I surprised myself.

I put a hand on his chest. "But it's my turn to ask you for something. Promise me, William, that you'll put our union ahead of your politicking. Stop writing articles and brochures that upset my parents. The Penns are dear to my family, and criticizing them, whether they deserve it or not, will not give us any hope for an easy time of marriage."

"I cannot marry your parents, Betsy," William said and pressed his lips on mine again, so lightly it could have been the fluttering wings of a moth. "Only you." I felt the sweetness of his tenderness, outstretched to me like a gift. My hands were under the warmth of his, resting on his chest.

"Can we just make an effort not to provoke them, then? My father feels that you poke him with a stick at times. It rankles. You are skillful enough to do what you need to do without drawing his ire. After all, you're the most articulate man I know. You're a natural diplomat, a born orator, just like your father."

William sighed. "Anything I do is meant to create change for the better," he said. "You know that by now. I hold Dr. Graeme and your mother in the highest regard. I only wrote *Tit for Tat* because William Smith publicly ridiculed our defense proposal. He would have spit on it if he could. Smith pledged loyalty to my father, then turned on him. Now the weasel panders to the Penns as if they are his best friends in the world. Remember, we published *Tit for Tat* anonymously."

It was my turn to sigh. "Yes, yes, I know. By the way, Rebecca is quite enamored with Reverend Smith now. I have never quite understood her attraction for him. He seems to need to be far more outspoken than a minister should be."

William nodded curtly, not wanting to think about Smith or Rebecca's interest in him. His gaze bore into me.

"I do promise you, Elizabeth Graeme," he said, his heart strong as a drum under my fingers. My eyes sparked with tears. "My dark-haired beauty, I promise to protect us and our life together. *Come live with me and be my love.*"

"*And we will all the pleasures prove,*" I finished the line. Christopher Marlowe must have been overwhelmed with love, too, when he wrote that.

Chapter 6

Philadelphia
January 1757

"Betsy, I'm going to England."

I stopped skating and stared at him. The river was frozen hard this year, the trees along the water a net of black lace.

"England?"

William stood looking at me sadly, his skates like leeches against the snowy crust.

"I'll be called to the bar after I finish my studies at the Inns of Court. And I'll help my father when he needs me."

"How long will you be gone?"

It was happening, then. The Pennsylvania Assembly had voted to send Mr. Franklin to London to negotiate with the Penns on their behalf. Perhaps in person, our government hoped, Franklin could get the Penns to see reason. I knew Mr. Franklin was going, but I didn't anticipate that he would take his son with him.

"I don't think it will be long. Maybe a year."

My mood deadened, I skated to the riverside, taking care to avoid the other skaters. William came and offered me a hand as I balanced on one foot at a time to take off my skates. I shoved my boots on and tied my skates together. William took off his skates too, darting glances at me under his eyebrows. Wisely, he said nothing other than holding out a hand to take my skates and carry them for me. I shook my head and slung them over my shoulder.

We walked in silence up from the river toward town, my mind racing. I took short breaths and watched the white air float from my mouth.

"You will go in the spring, I guess?" They would have to wait for the weather to turn.

"Yes." William looked at me with concern. "We're buying passage for an April crossing."

April was only three months from now. No one went abroad for less than a year. I felt sick. Having him out west for two months in the Lehigh Valley had been long enough.

My thoughts jumbled, we walked quickly until we reached Third Street, near Christ Church. Dimly, I remember I had supplies I wanted to take to drop off at the jail for the prisoners. They suffered so greatly in the cold. I was also knitting blankets for the almshouse. The world never seemed to relieve the poor.

"You can come with me," William ventured and tucked his spare hand into my elbow.

"Very funny." I stamped my feet into the snow, then I banged my mittened hands on the low posts that separated us from the road. A year here without William might as well be a year in a dank cave without benefit of the sun.

The pain of it was I *could* imagine a life with him in London. I saw myself taking tea in great drawing rooms with bright-minded people, talking of literature and science. My mother had taught me well; I would be a good companion for him in London society. I could continue my charity work there at a workhouse or the new foundling hospital. In the evenings, so many choices. Operas, plays, concerts, salons, visits. I thought of how much I could write and read while he was at court during the day or busy with his studies. Come summer, we could visit gardens and famous landmarks and tour some of the continent together, Amsterdam, Florence, or Rome. The books I could buy! Why, I would need a trunk to ship them all home.

"Very funny," I repeated bitterly. I knew it would not happen.

"You can come with me. Let's marry."

I shook my head. My parents would never allow it. My father would view it as his daughter traveling across the ocean to oppose his friends there. Besides, marriage under the age of twenty-one in Pennsylvania was illegal without the written consent of parents. I was a year too young.

"No. We'll marry when you return," I said, more confidently than I intended. "After that, no one can do or say a thing to stop us! For now, we will grant your father's wish, and mine, and wait a year." We both had strong fathers. We both found it impossible to deny them. We would have to wait, that's all there was to it.

That's what William's parents had done; they waited until Ben Franklin returned from London, that illustrious trip that my step-grandfather Keith fobbed on him all those years ago when he was so young. Deborah and Ben had had a happy marriage, notwithstanding their poor little Franky dying. Luckily they still had their little Sally at home. Mr. Franklin credited Deborah's sturdy personality as one of the reasons he was able to retire in his early forties and leave the print shop to pursue his other interests. I admired the way Ben spoke of Deborah with such respect, as if he treasured her.

I voiced my thoughts to William.

"Have you forgotten that Deborah married some useless scoundrel in his absence who left town and subjected her to a mountain of debt?" William said, his voice tight. "They could never marry properly. We still don't know if the bastard is dead or alive since he never came back. Not to mention when my father eventually returned to Philadelphia, he arrived carting me in a basket from some mystery mother. Please, Betsy, I beg you. Come with me." I did not often hear anger in William. It never occurred to me that he resented not knowing who his birth mother was. He never spoke of it.

"Your father will never allow it, William! Nor will mine. You need to focus on your studies. And your father has to be unencumbered to go into battle with the Penns. You two will be busy saving the world. Or at least Pennsylvania."

William ignored my barb.

"Marry me in secret before I leave. Then no one can say a word about it."

He was serious. Marry him in *secret?* My bark of laughter turned into a choke. "In this town? We would never get away with it. Your father *is* this town."

William's face was like a thunder cloud, ominous and shifting.

"What if you are gone longer than a year?" I burst out. "What do we do then?"

William considered this. "I think it's unlikely. Father is fond of Deborah, and he dotes on Sally. He'll be eager to get back to his experiments. Can I not persuade you to reconsider?"

Oh, William. He thought I had a choice. Tears slid down my face. The wet drops almost hurt as they hit the cold air from the warmth of my eyes.

"And I would not wish to be gone from *you* that long," he said earnestly. "I honestly couldn't be. What would my life be like without my Betsy?"

What would my life be like if I could do as I liked?

"Philadelphia is to have a concert next week," Liza said. "Did you hear? Our first *public* concert!"

"How interesting," my mother murmured over her toile.

We were gathered in our city home. It was Saturday night. Reverend Smith had supped with us and afterwards, he and Father smoked in the wingback chairs while Mother sewed and Liza and I worked on our embroidery. I suspected Mother and Father hoped I'd want Reverend Smith for myself, but I had no interest. I would leave him to Rebecca, she had enough enthusiasm for both of us. Whenever they were in the same room her eyes sparkled every time he spoke, especially about his work at the college. She thought the rays of the sun caressed his head directly.

I kept my head bent over my work, irate with the world. I was enjoying the feeling of piercing the cloth with my needle while tobacco smoke wrinkled my nose.

"Shall we go, Betsy?" Liza asked. "Boston and New York have been having public concerts for years. We are so far behind. Stuffy Philadelphia is always last, it seems."

Stab in. Stab out. Pull thread.

"Let's get tickets," she said. "You love music."

"I do," I said flatly.

"Can you imagine, *anyone* can go to this one," Liza enthused. "As long as they have a dollar for the ticket!"

Until now, concerts had all been private events, held by a particular person and attended by invitation only from the person hosting the concert. All guests were controlled and your option to attend was decided upon in advance. A public concert was a daring idea.

She lowered her voice so only I could hear her. "The concert will cheer you up."

"How do we get tickets?" I asked.

"I think I saw it in the paper." Liza laid her embroidery hoop aside and went to retrieve the broadsheet on the sideboard. "Ah yes, here it is, in the *Pennsylvania Journal and Weekly Advertiser*. Tickets at the London Coffeehouse, a dollar each. Concert under the direction of John Palma. A continental sampling."

"Open to the public, eh?" Father said around his cigar. "I don't know about that."

"Oh, Father," I said. "There won't be a sign on the door saying *Lechers and murderers, please do come in. Lots of velvet purses for your thievery in the lounge, this way.*"

"Winter is a bad time for contagions," he said.

"Sickness can hardly be prevented, Thomas, can it eh?" offered Reverend Smith. "It's everywhere, no matter whether one's in a gutter, concert hall, or church pew. Nothing anyone can do."

"I think it's a nice idea to have concerts for everyone to enjoy," Mother said. "Much different than private ones, don't you think, when the music and guests are so predictable? This opens up the world."

Father grunted.

"It's being held in the Masonic Hall in Lodge Alley," Liza read. "Very elegant for the riffraff," she teased Father. The hall, a large brick building with columns flanking the entrance, was fairly new, not yet two years old and striking in its architecture. It was the first Masonic Hall in America, I heard.

"Perhaps you should ask Rebecca Moore," I suggested to Reverend Smith. "You two seem to get along well."

He shook his head. "A pleasant idea, but one I must decline. We are finishing our first play, and I must keep focused on that. *The Masque of Alfred* has been a significant effort for the college. We hope to perform it for Lord Loudoun when he arrives in Philadelphia. It has been quite an undertaking."

"I hear you've been working hard," I said. My friends were in it: Francis Hopkinson was a talented musician and had written some of the music and Jacob Duché was playing the part of King Alfred.

"The students are performing it as part of their oratorical curriculum," Reverend Smith explained.

Smith was proud of being the provost of the College of Philadelphia, as well he should be, proud of his stringent requirements for the students. Since the school came to life five years ago, three groups shared the building: the college, made up of young men from wealthy families; the grade school students; and the charity students from poor homes. All boys, of course. Only the Quakers offered schools for girls in the city. Ben Franklin had suggested the college years ago, working with many others to gather subscribers and see it come to fruition. Mr. Franklin and Reverend Smith had been good friends at one point, until Smith switched his allegiance to the proprietors, after all Franklin had done for him. *That weasel*, I heard William Franklin say in my mind. Now Reverend Smith went so far as to publish stinging criticisms of anyone who had ideas that opposed the Penns' wishes.

"I am not familiar with the *Masque of Alfred*," Mother said around a pin held in her mouth. "What's the story line?"

Smith shifted in his chair and sat up straighter. "Something very different!" His voice rose in excitement. "Much more than just a play! It is a dramatic production, but not just acting. We do it all; singing, music, *and* acting, with the most evocative scenery and costumes! We have added more than two hundred lines to the original, and also added new characters. I even recruited the help of a young painter by the name of Benjamin West, who shows great promise for painting our sets."

Realizing he had not answered Mother's question, he said, "Ah. The story. The *Mask* is about the redemption of England from the cruelties of Danish invasion in the year 878. At first, the Vikings are victorious in battle against England. Poor King Alfred is near defeat, hiding in a hut, unaware that twelve hundred loyal Britons are nearby. Upon the good news, another great battle takes place. This time Alfred is victorious, England stands, and the play ends with 'Rule, Britannia!' sung in honor of Great Britain!"

"My goodness, how exciting," Mother said. "We shan't miss that."

"The composer, Arne, is very popular in London I heard," Father commented. "Sought after."

"He is an excellent composer," Smith preened. "I think he would find our version of the *Masque of Alfred* quite intriguing. Unprecedented!"

"And Francis is a talented musician," I said. "He plays several instruments as well as sings." My friend was a true renaissance man.

"To think," Liza said, "a public concert *and* a musical play in town all at once!"

"So much for stuffy Philadelphia," I said to Liza. "We seem to be catching up."

"We will all go see it," Mother decided, "and celebrate your work, William. I'll ask Jane and Ann and their husbands too."

My sister Jane had been delivered of a healthy baby boy in November. They named him John. Both mother and son were doing well. Jane had been blessed with another easy birth.

"It would be my honor." Reverend Smith looked pleased.

"You are doing a fine job with that school, Smith," Father said. "It's a credit to you."

"Our first graduating class will be receiving their diplomas in May," Reverend Smith boasted. "A small group, only seven, but more will come. One day our college will rival Harvard or the College of William and Mary. I'm sure of it."

"Shall we ask your William to the play?" Liza asked me. "And the concert? And I'll ask a friend too."

Father looked in our direction as he exhaled a circle of cigar smoke, his gaze as unblinking as a raven's stare.

I put my needlework down. "Why, yes. Let's. William does love a play. And he would never say no to good music."

Spring came quickly, and before I was ready, it was time for William to leave.

I went that day to see them off. We stood in the Franklins' home, a trio of women, Mrs. Franklin and young Sally and I, amongst their trunks and bags, the room sweet with lavender and wood polish. Mr. Franklin's eyes were hooded when he glanced my way and my face tightened. Was that pity? Or just relief? I should have been going with them. I was William's wife, even if it was only known between the two of us.

I looked at Deborah and saw resignation in her face. William told me his father asked her to go with them, but she would not cross the Atlantic. I found that odd, for Deborah was an Egyptian sphinx, smart, capable, stolid as limestone. She roared like a lion when required, but refused to feel the roll of the ocean beneath her feet.

Mr. Franklin came in with an extra pair of spectacles and added them to his leather satchel. He straightened and looked at his wife. "Should you change your mind—"

"I'm not coming, Ben, you know I'm not. I'll stay here with Sally. Together we'll keep things ship shape. Who else could take care of the house and affairs the way you like them? We'll be here to welcome you home."

I glanced at their daughter. Sally looked cross. At thirteen, she wanted her father. Her lower lip thrust out against her will, her arms crossed across her chest.

"Steady on, Sally," her father said easily. "What shall I send you? The finest ribbons? A fashionable new hat? What would you prefer, a bolt of fabric, a vat of perfume, or all the stray kittens in London?"

Sally giggled.

"Ooh, ribbons." Sally brightened. "And lots of sweets."

Mr. Franklin tousled her hair, which carried him a scowl as it displaced her cap.

William entered and my belly flopped. He came to me and took my hands in his, expressions flitting across his face like starlings. I loved the feel of my fingers in his, birds in a nest, his hands warm and strong and safe around my smaller cold ones. William need not fear any change on my part, my feelings would not be diminished by his absence. We were secretly engaged, betrothed in every way except a formal announcement. Married, even, by our own vows to each other. Besides, I knew that engaged or not, our bond was strong. I smiled at him.

Mr. Franklin spoke quietly with his wife and daughter, gave last-minute instructions for practical considerations in his absence, and then stood a moment and looked around the room. For myself, I had the odd feeling of being on a stage as a scene played out. I felt both uneasy and calm, upset to see William go and, at the same time, relieved that the days of trying to avoid this moment were over. Now I could look forward to his return and beginning our lives together.

Our good-bye was over too soon. I jumped a bit when Mr. Franklin finished embracing his wife and daughter and turned to me. He kissed my cheeks with genuine affection, gave my arm a squeeze, then nodded at me and walked unhurriedly outside to the waiting coach. Mr. Franklin never rushed, he was stately. His wife and daughter followed him, the servants trailing them with the luggage. When the room emptied out, William kissed me and laid his lips on my ear, "Wait for me, my darling," he said.

"There's no worry of that. Of course I will. Be safe," I said, and willed this moment to stay with me, the scent of him, his height over me, the warmth of his hands, his face when he smiled, his eyes when caught by the light from the window. "Come back to me."

"How could I not?" he said.

We joined the others outside. Luggage was stored, then the men climbed in. Before I could say another word, the driver had clucked and the horses pulled away.

Mrs. Franklin wiped her hands on her apron, watching as the coach clomped away down Chestnut Street.

"Safe travels!" Sally called after them. "Good luck! Godspeed!"

"Well," Deborah said. The word hit the ground like a hard stone.

She needn't have worried that I would embarrass her with tears. "Well," I echoed her in a flat voice. "That's that. Good-bye, then, Mrs. Franklin."

"Come and visit, my dear Miss Graeme. Any time you'd like. We'll be glad of the company, won't we, Sally?"

Sally nodded.

I removed myself without delay. I left Deborah and Sally with their emptiness, just as I had to carry mine with me. Had I known then what the future would bring, I would not have been so stoic.

Chapter 7

April 7, 1757
Eizabethtown, New Jersey

My dearest Betsy,
Our horses are baiting, which gives me a few spare moments that I will seize to let my charmer know of my welfare.

We expected to have arrived at New York yesterday, but the extreme badness of the roads prevented our getting farther than Woodbridge. Our chaise horses tired before we reached Brunswick, which obliged us to leave them, and the carriage, behind and come forward on horseback. We shall, however, God willing, reach the place of our embarkation this day. Every morning since our departure has had a lowering aspect, but before noon the clouds have dispersed, the sun has shone, and the remainder of the day has proved most delightfully agreeable. The morning of our love, my dear Betsy, has likewise been overcast, threatening a wrecking storm. May kind heaven graciously permit a cheering sun to scatter these clouds of difficulties which hang over us, and afford a noon and evening of life that is calm and serene. I trust our conduct will be such as to deserve this mark of divine goodness; may we not then reasonably hope for its accomplishment.

An invitation from Governor Belcher to dinner cuts me shorter than I intended. That every blessing may attend you is the ardent prayer of, dear Betsy, your most affectionate,
Wm. Franklin

April 11, 1757
New York

My dear Betsy,
Never did anyone set down to write in a worse humor. A thousand things have I to say to you, and scarcely a minute to say them. My father is now impatiently waiting for me to assist him in an affair that cannot be postponed.

Had I followed the dictates of my own inclinations, I should have passed the last evening in pouring out my soul to you on paper, instead of murdering my time in a large mixed company of both sexes. Although the height of good sense and politeness prevailed, they could not divert my thoughts from a certain little corner in a certain little room, with all its long train of soft attendant ideas.

However, I must stop my imagination, or I shall not have time to tell you that we did not arrive in this city until Friday morning.

The captain of our packet is so extremely ill with consumption that we shall be obliged to throw him overboard before we are a fortnight at sea. I paid him a visit at his lodgings, found him very peevish and fretful, and though he is launching into eternity, scarce a word escaped him unattended by an oath!

The reading of your dear letter, which I have done over and over, is the only pleasure I have enjoyed since my departure. Pray let me not see a post without having one from you. The many disagreeable sensations I have felt, by delaying to write to you till it was almost too late, will cure me of the crime of procrastination; and may it prove a warning to my Betsy.

Let me be remembered to your dear mother and other friends is all that I can add at present.
Your ever faithful,
Wm. Franklin

June 2, 1757
New York

My dearest Betsy,

By one accident or another, we are still in New York. But I know not how to complain of my detention, for has it not afforded me the pleasure of another letter from my Betsy. A letter for which I cannot be thankful enough.

I must answer it in short; the time of our departure has now been positively fixed to this afternoon. The name of our packet is the General Wall, Captain Lutwych, Commander. I believe few, if any, letters sent by the packet are opened. If you direct letters for me to the care of Peter Colinson, Esquire F.R.S. in London, I have no doubt of your letters coming safe.

Once more adieu. Adieu, my dearest Betsy. I need not repeat (for you must know) how much I am your most affectionate,

Wm. Franklin

July 17, 1757
Falmouth, England

My dearest Betsy,

I have the pleasure to inform my dearest Betsy that her Franklin is safely arrived in England about two hours ago, after a passage of twenty-seven days. I am so hurried in getting our things ashore, and inquiring for horses and carriages for transporting us to London, that I have not the leisure to give you any of the particulars of our voyage. I design to do it, however, by the very first opportunity.

In general, we were highly favored with winds. We were several times chased, and met with no accident, except the night before our arrival, when we narrowly escaped running ashore on the rocks, owing to our not having discovered the *light ashore until it was almost too late to avoid them! Although our passage cannot, when compared to most others, be deemed a very disagreeable one, I cannot but be of the opinion that although the pleasures of this country be ever so great, they are dearly earned by a voyage across the Atlantic. Few inducements will tempt me to pass the ocean again, if ever I am so happy as to return to my native country.*

I question if I shall have it in my power to write again by this packet, as she will sail sometime this week. No post after our arrival in London can reach her.

I must beg you to say for me my good wishes to your good family, and let my great hurry plead an excuse for you seeing so soon the name of your affectionate,

Wm. Franklin

Chapter 8

Philadelphia
September 1757

The Stedmans' table was a dancing mirage that night as the oil lamps flickered, necklaces glinted, and gilt in the porcelain dishes threw back the light in shards. My brother-in-law Charles presided at the top of his table while my sister Ann glowed beside him. My whole family was at the Stedman table, my sister Jane and her husband James, my parents, myself. We were joined by two sets of close friends, Margaret and James Abercrombie, and Daniel and Madge Roberdeau. As he so often did, our Reverend Peters rounded out our party of twelve. Liza stayed upstairs to play with Jane's small children.

"To a bountiful harvest," Charles toasted. He lowered his glass and looked down his long table at us. Ann had chosen a good man. Charles had fought at Culloden before leaving for America with his brother Alexander. Now he was a vestryman at our church and an astute businessman with a burgeoning shipping and trade business. I knew he and my sister had money, but to me he was just the kind man who brought dear Liza to us after rescuing her from orphanhood in Scotland.

"Bountiful," we echoed and drank.

"So Benjamin Franklin has gone to negotiate for us in London," Charles said. "How well do you think that will go?" Charles had recently purchased a stake in an ironworks in Lancaster. He was always fretting about what the Penns' actions would do to local trade and commerce.

"They've arrived, then?" Reverend Peters asked.

I nodded. "Yes, they're in London and have secured lodgings."

"Held up two months in New York before they sailed, though, poor buggers," James Abercrombie said, a ship captain himself. "Loudon was holding back all the boats, waiting on reports from Canada that he wanted sent back to the king as soon as possible."

"Who?" asked Reverend Peters, tapping an ear.

"Lord Loudon. Britain hoped when they sent him that he'd manage to sort out our troops and get a stronghold on the conflict. So much for that." Abercrombie howled with laughter.

Instead, the French had wrested Fort William Henry from the British last month in New York. It was an immense victory for them, opening up Lake George and giving them access to the southern waterways. It had been a bad year for the British; Loudon's failure was a painful loss.

"This war," tutted Margaret Abercrombie. Her diamonds were huge, I couldn't help but notice. I wondered if her husband's ship brought them back from lands unknown. Africa, maybe.

"I've heard Loudon is being replaced as commander-in-chief," my father said. "Britain is sending someone else to try and get it right."

"Thank Christ for that," Charles said. "Sorry, Father."

Reverend Peters smiled benignly.

"It had better turn around soon," my father said. "We are at risk."

"Peril, I'd say," Daniel Roberdeau interjected gloomily. He had been elected to the Pennsylvania Assembly last year, although it did not seem to make him very happy. He was frustrated by his role in government. Madge told me he'd been happier as a timber merchant.

"This war with the French and their Indians is going on too long," my brother-in-law James Young complained. "The western frontier is still like a ragged coat held together by pins. France hasn't stopped eyeing us like a dog about to rip meat off a bone. It doesn't reassure me that the French have had more successes than we have."

"Aye, the Indians are still going on scouting missions for the French general along Fort Allen way," Charles said as he cut his chop. "And from the other forts from Reading to Bethlehem, adding to their scalp collection along the way."

"At least we *have* forts there now," I said fiercely. Thanks to Mr. Franklin and William and the men who had labored with them last winter. I felt the table turn to me in surprise.

"You must miss him, Betsy," Margaret Abercrombie said to me gently, the only one who seemed to realize that I had a personal interest in Benjamin Franklin and his son's trip.

I nodded once. I regretted that I had said anything. I didn't want anyone to ask me anything about William.

There was a pause, then the conversation picked up again.

I focused on the odd sound Reverend Peters made when he ate. His teeth clicked together at the back of his mouth, bottom against top. I turned a piece of pork around on the tine of my fork and listened to his teeth clacking. He was not that old, around fifty, and the meat was not very tough. I found myself almost counting in time to the rhythm of his teeth.

"Tell me, Peters," my father said. "How is the church managing these days with the all the incoming frontier folk needing help and such?"

"We are bursting at the seams," Reverend Peters admitted. The clacking stopped when he stopped eating to speak. "I'm afraid Philadelphia has become a city of refugees. Loudoun didn't help us, either, when he arrived with all the troops that needed billeting. We are grateful for the addition of the hospital more than ever. And for your medical care, Thomas."

"At least the king is finally opening his purse," Father said. "We sorely need the soldiers and the funds. Loudon has been a disappointment, but still. Better days must be ahead."

"If the French win . . ." my sister Ann said thoughtfully. "Can you imagine?" That was so brazen of her, voicing what we did not speak of. We briefly considered the idea of France winning America, wresting it from England.

"They should never have taken Fort Oswego last summer to start with," Charles muttered grimly. "That was a blow."

"Things will get better," Mother said. "The king will choose his course of action. The English have been fighting the French for a thousand years."

"Not here though," Jane countered. "Not on this side of the pond."

"We have the world's largest and most powerful navy on our side," James Abercrombie said confidently. "And the biggest empire."

"Still, at the end of the day we are only a colony, perched on the edge of a great wilderness, eh." Dan Roberdeau was not convinced the world's largest navy would help the back side of Pennsylvania. We were a colony in trouble.

"If nothing else, Britain needs our money and goods," my brother-in-law James said. "Our timber, tobacco, and crops. We provide valuable income to them through taxes on trade."

I hoped Benjamin Franklin was successful with his work in England. Pennsylvania still needed much more help than what the Penns were willing to provide.

"God save the king," Charles said loudly, raising his glass.

"God save the king," we all echoed earnestly.

It sounded like a prayer.

Chapter 9

Philadelphia
1757 & 1758

I read William's letters over and over again, especially
when I wanted to be alone with him.

My dearest Betsy, my charmer.

. . . A thousand things I have to say to you

. . . Our love

. . . A certain little corner in a certain little room

. . . Your constant, most affectionate

. . . Your ever faithful

I wondered if William could sense me with him as I felt
him with me. I had sat next to him in the coach as they
lumbered along those pitted roads through New Jersey, his
thigh warm against mine in the spring sunshine, until the
horses tired and we abandoned the chaise and went forward
with the horses. I was with him in New York, fuming at the
delays with him, cursing Lord Loudon for holding back the
packets in a desperate move to bring good news to the king.
I sat next to him as he slept swaying on the waves each
night, praying over him for a journey free from misfortune.
In my dreams, I kept their ship safe, blowing them to safety
like Poseidon from above, powering them with gusty wind as
they slid across miles of black water.

Even after nine months, I thought of William each day,
even though I had not had a letter from him in months.
Mother said to be patient. She said to remember he was
abroad for the first time and was under pressure from many
sides.

"You must be content with his affection and the
assurance of his return," Mother advised me as we sat
together in the evenings.

Mixed company of both sexes, taunted my mind. *I should have passed the last evening in pouring out my soul to you on paper . . .*

"Here it is Christmas time already," Mother said. "The time is passing quickly."

Her support of him was endearing, for I knew that she could very well use the gap in letters to sour me against him. William warned me he would procrastinate, and he had proven to know himself well. *You have more than a double portion of leisure, my Betsy,* he had written. Knowing Mr. Franklin senior's endless industry, his relentless curiosity, the task set out for him by the Assembly, and the labor of William's legal studies, I could understand the demands on their time. And yet. What if the absence of letters meant that William was ill? Perhaps he was bedridden with a bloody flux, wasting away. What if he had stepped out of a tavern and been hit by a speeding carriage? Or worse, forgotten me?

Mother laughed loudly when I said this. "Or killed by a rabid dog? Or murdered in cold blood in a dark alley by a mysterious man in a voluminous cloak? Elizabeth, turn your imagination to your writing."

The weeks crawled by. I tried to write, but more often than not I sat and read and watched the first snowflakes limp down from the ashen sky. When I wanted to be alone with William, I tucked a letter in my pocket and snuck out to one of the public gardens. Of course all the plants were brown and dead, but I liked the solace and silence of the shrubbery, the songs of the birds. I held the letter and talked to him, knowing no one could hear or see me. There was comfort when I sought him when I was alone, as if we were together again by the creek at Graeme Park.

"Are you going to sit there and mope?" Liza's arms were piled high with wool when she entered the parlor the week before Christmas. "It's not like you to be pouty. When you have finished with today's bout of melancholy, I would be grateful for your help."

"What's all this?"

"Wool."

"Yes, I see that."

"We're going to knit for the almshouse. Hats and socks for the cold days ahead. The poor need us."

"I was thinking that if I had to do any more needlework, I would poke myself in the eye with a needle. I just finished embroidering a tablecloth for Mother's ladies' group. Now they want lap quilts for the elderly. And I already knit blankets for the almshouse."

"Go on, fetch your needles. Your father has promised the priest we'll be upping the woolen hat stock in no time. Besides, I promise my conversation will be worthwhile. It's me! I'll be enchanting."

With a sigh, I flopped down next to Liza and helped her unload the skeins of wool so they did not tangle.

"I wasn't moping. I was reading."

Liza nodded at my copy of *Candide* on the chair. "Hard to read without turning the page."

"You know me well."

At least the dancing assemblies would begin again next week, which was infinitely better than visiting one sitting room after another. I was looking forward to the season this year, especially after last winter's unexpected treats in music and theater. True to his word, Reverend Smith managed to get his *Masque of Alfred* seen by Lord Loudon, and, in fact, every visiting dignitary to Philadelphia, including Colonel Washington of Virginia, the war hero, who said he liked it very much. The college had given extra performances in March to make sure the most powerful patriarchs would not miss it.

"Well, at least this keeps me from feeling bored," I said and took a ball of wool. I took my needles and cast on.

"Bored? You've hardly stopped, Betsy! You were paraded around all through the summer and fall," Liza pointed out. Mother made sure I got escorted to every bee and bonfire going between Perth Amboy and Baltimore.

"Whatever happened to that gentleman from South Carolina who was following you around at the Shippens' dance?" I asked. "After we went boating."

Liza hesitated. "I declined his admiration."

"He seemed a good prospect, I thought. He had his own plantation, didn't he? Indigo, wasn't it? Or was it tobacco?"

"I could not get past his nose hairs. I could have braided them."

"Liza!" I spluttered with laughter. "Really!"

"I don't know how anyone with a looking glass would not have run for scissors. What about his manservant? Surely he would have mentioned it?"

I almost choked. "Well, he was a little older. Maybe it was his eyesight."

"I saw it as a character flaw. I'm convinced he liked it. Either that or he didn't want to be bothered. Can you imagine twenty years from now? Some poor woman waking up to that—"

"I concede your point."

We were both still chortling when Clara appeared carrying a package.

"At last!" Liza exclaimed, beaming at me.

I dropped my knitting needles and took it from her eagerly. William's elegant, spidery script looped out the letters of my name on the brown paper. I felt a thrill as I imagined his long fingers writing my name and thinking of me—me!—all these thousands of miles away.

I took my package and moved to the window. It was a bleak day, brittle, clouds the color of gunmetal. There was refuse in the road outside. Father would not be happy. He would be on at the mayor again, pressing for cleaner streets.

"Should I leave you in peace?" Liza asked after Clara left.

"Of course not, silly. I have no secrets from you. Let me open it, and then I'll tell you everything." I unwrapped the package hastily, without looking too closely at the contents—fur and fabric, they could wait—and rummaged until I found the letter inside. I ripped it open.

"Ooooh, a long one," Liza commented.

I took the letter to the window seat.

December 9, 1757
Craven Street, London

Dear Madam,

No doubt you must be surprised at so many vessels arriving from England, without so much as a single line from the man who has so often, and so warmly, professed himself your friend and admirer. The thoughts and suspicions that must naturally arise in you on this occasion, my imagination pictures in such strong colors as to give me pain.

But, believe me, my dearest Betsy, I am not wholly without excuse. For some time after my arrival at this great metropolis, the infinite variety of new objects, the continued noise and bustle in the streets, and the viewing of such curious things engrossed all my attention. Since then, frequent engagements amongst politicians, philosophers, and men of business, making acquaintances with such men as have it in their power to be of service in settling our unhappy provincial disputes, and now and then partaking of the public diversions and entertainments of this bewitching country, have found my full employment for almost every hour.

Even the present hour is stolen from sleep; the watchman's hoarse voice is calling past two o'clock. Such is now my hurry, and such is it like to be; rather increasing than diminishing. Ought not then some allowance be made for my past, nay for my future silence, when so circumstanced? Be that as it will, I shall write to you as often as possibly I can and trust to your friendship for an apology, if it not be so often as we both desire. It may seem strange, but it is no less true, that one great reason why I from time to time delayed writing was the multiplicity of things I had to tell you. I knew not which to give preference to, and my leisure would not permit me to mention all of them. How have I longed to inform you of the pleasure I enjoyed in visiting Windsor, its castle, and its shady retreats! Places you yourself recommended to me and which I have often heard you rapturously speak of, though your knowledge of them was purely ideal. The enchanting scene at Vauxhall is another theme on which I could dwell for hours together. What would I not have given for the power of instantaneously transporting you to that delightful spot!

The many agreeable walks amidst rows of beautiful trees lighted with lamps; the elegant paintings and sculpture with which the boxes, the grand hall, and orchestra are adorned; the curious artificial fall of water; the ravishing music, vocal and instrumental; and the gaiety and brilliancy of the company would have made you conceive yourself in a situation beyond even the Elysium of the ancients. Your participation of these pleasures, with sundry others of like nature, was what I earnestly wished at the time and could only have heightened my enjoyment of them.

As politics is a subject you have no great relish for, I shall only mention it in general. As yet, I see no prospect of a termination of the affairs my father has undertaken for the province. Their little knowledge of (or indeed inclination to know) American affairs renders his task very uphill and difficult. You will think me justifiable in speaking thus of the proprietors when you consider that during the time they expressed themselves strongly inclined to settle matters amicably with my father, they were repeatedly publishing scandalous and malicious falsehoods against the Assembly and people of Pennsylvania, with a view of continuing and increasing the prejudices. They trusted that as my father was obliged to a friendly negotiation with them (which they could easily contrive to continue until the sitting of Parliament) that he would not take any notice of nameless aspersions in a newspaper. In the advantages they expected from this piece of poor low cunning they have, however, been disappointed (as you will have seen before this reaches you) by a paper I published in the Citizen. For although it might not be so proper for my father to take notice, while the negotiation was going on there could be no reason why I, as an inhabitant of Pennsylvania, now on my travels in England, and in no way concerned with conducting the negotiation, should not vindicate the honor and reputation of my country when I saw it attacked. My putting my name to the paper, and the place where I was to be found, was judged necessary, as it would be the most effective means of putting a stop to further anonymous attacks, and as otherwise the public could have no reason for giving greater credit to one representation than the other. It has had all the good effects I could have wished; but I am told the proprietor is much incensed against me on that account, though he doesn't venture to complain as he is sensible that he was the aggressor. As this paper, no doubt, will be canvassed on your side of the water, I shall take it extremely kind if you would inform me of a few of the pros and cons which you hear. It is only for my own private satisfaction I ask this favor, and you may depend no other use will be made of it.

My father has had several interviews with the proprietors at Thomas Penn's house, and they have always treated him with great civility. I have not seen Richard, but Thomas Penn I have met with several times at court, though I believe he does not yet know me by sight. John Penn, I am told, has just come to town, having been sick in the country almost since his arrival from America. Governor Morris has arrived here and I suppose will join forces with the proprietors, at least I hope so, and they will entrust him with the whole conduct of the dispute on their side. His natural propensity to tell something more than the truth cannot fail to give considerable advantage to his opponents.

My eyes begin to draw straws, and my candle is almost burnt down. I must therefore hasten to tell you that I have taken the liberty to send you one of the newest fashioned muffs and tippets worn by the ladies of quality at this end of the town.

Mr. Davis, who has been so kind as to take charge of these things, is a young Irish gentleman strongly recommended to my father by an eminent Scotch physician of this city. He intends to settle in Philadelphia. He seems to be of a good-natured, obliging temper from what little I have seen of him. I expect him to call early in the morning for this letter; the vessel in which he booked passage has already gone down to Gravesend for launch. I have hardly room to acknowledge the receipt of your letter of October 1, and am enclosing another dated June 19. The reason why I did not write from Sandy Hook was because I was in daily expectation of sailing. I thought it could be no great pleasure for you to hear how disagreeably we were detained.

Farewell, God bless and preserve you, is the sincere prayer of, Dear Betsy, your truly affectionate,

Wm. Franklin

I finished the letter and stared out the window.

"Is he well?" Liza asked anxiously. "Was there bad news?"

"He is quite well," I said distractedly.

"What then? What is it?"

I sighed. He had taken the time to write me such a long letter. And yet I was unnerved. I turned to Liza.

"There is no way of knowing when Mr. Franklin will be finished his negotiations."

"Ah. They are not yet returning, then."

"No. Not anytime soon."

"And?" Liza looked questioningly at me.

"Before he left, I asked William to avoid participating in any politics that would upset my family and make it harder for us here when he comes back," I explained. "And yet he did."

I sat down next to Liza, whose knitting needles were idle in her lap now. Her face was concerned. "The letter has made you unhappy."

My thoughts were black as boat tar. "He knew it was important to me. He *promised* me, Liza. He promised me that he would avoid any obvious politics that would be seen as offensive by my father, just while he is away. We need to prevent any obstacles to our marriage next year."

"Ah. You mean William's letter," Liza said. "The one they reprinted here from the *Citizen* a few weeks ago. I thought it was quite fair? It sounds as if Parliament was being cordial to Mr. Franklin's face and then lying behind his back. Truly malicious. A future lawyer cannot be asked to look away from injustice, can he? It is not in William's blood. Pennsylvania is his home; he wouldn't stand for that."

I chewed on my lower lip.

"Besides," Liza said, "you saw the article in the paper when it came out. You already knew."

"I thought he would explain," I said. "I thought maybe someone had forced his hand. Instead, he defended his position and asked me to tell him what people here said about it. It was as if our talk had never happened at all!"

The Penns had blamed us for our defense problems. It was ridiculous. In his article, William defended the people of Pennsylvania. He pointed out that it was the Penn family who were adding to the problem by not paying taxes. William also reminded them that a number of Quakers had *voluntarily* resigned their seats in the Assembly rather than stay and obstruct defense measures by creating problems that stemmed from their stance of non-violence. He ended by saying that Pennsylvania forces already protected much of New Jersey, Delaware, and part of Maryland from Indian invasion, without receiving any contributions from those colonies for the expense, or even compensation from England.

Liza took the letter from me.

"Betsy, he must have spent *ages* writing you this. He said he misses you and that he wishes you were there. And he sent you a *gift*. I'm sorry, but I can't agree with you on this one. What was the gift?"

I held it out the tippet and muff. Was he truly being thoughtful or was the gift meant to placate me?

"Very pretty," Liza said admiringly.

I would rather have had more letters. "He has no plans to come back."

Liza looked at me, exasperated. "William is not a child. His father cannot keep him there by force. He needs no permission to return. When his studies are completed, he'll come back to you. Look at what he *wrote.* He wants you there with him."

I felt tears on my cheeks. "You think me petty."

Liza sighed. "Oh, Betsy. What would you have him do? William has his constraints, as you have yours, I suppose. As do we all."

"I miss him," I breathed, ragged as broken glass.

Liza took my hand, squeezed hard, and we sat for a moment.

"I worry. I cannot help but worry," I said, "when I think of him so far away." The words came out as a whisper.

"You mustn't think about that letter in the paper," Liza said urgently. "He had to do what was right. You wouldn't want a man who cows to a woman when justice is at stake. I know you would not. That's not who you are, Elizabeth Graeme."

"It's just that I wish—"

"Betsy, few women are interested in politics, and few men avoid them. You must learn to look the other way, that's all. All of Philadelphia knows William loves you. He said so himself. You need to believe him. He *will* come home. Together you are like fat poured on the fire. By that I mean there is a mighty power between the two of you. I've lived with you for a few years, and there are not so many men who could meet your flame."

"That letter, though. What if my father—"

"Next week you'll be twenty-one. You can do as you like after that."

Chapter 10

Horsham
May 1758

"I still can hardly believe it," Rebecca said as we cut peonies in the garden. "I am to be married this summer! I'm going to be a *wife*. As my dearest friend, and my oldest, you must be my first visitor when I have my own home. My own home, Betsy!"

Finally, Reverend William Smith had fallen like a chess piece.

"I'm so happy for you," I said. "It's what you've always wanted, isn't it." I thought she and Smith were well matched, for her lightness seemed to balance his peculiar intensity.

"Your William will come with you, of course."

"I don't know when William will be back. He's still in London."

"He has not been called to the bar yet?"

I shook my head. "And he tells me that his father's negotiations are not going well."

I snipped another peony and placed the stem in my basket. The peonies seemed bigger this year, lusher. My father kept our gardeners busy. In addition to the exquisite perennial beds, and the ambitious annuals each year, there were plans to add a maze. I cut another peony and held it to my nose. Rebecca and I used to pick flowers when we were little girls and lace them through our hair. Peonies could be my favorite flower, although I loved most flowers. How could you argue with the magnificence of a June rose? Or the happiness of wild daffodils? Or the first tiny white flowers of spring peeking out through the still brown grass like splotches of rich cream in coffee?

"He may surprise you, I think," Rebecca said. "Sail home and arrive on your doorstep."

"That would be nice."

"I do think it is preferable that your William is older," Rebecca continued conversationally. "A man, not a boy. It makes such a difference. I know that now myself. It's an embarrassment when I think of who I used to fawn over. Your William has seen enough of the world to know himself. I remember that night at Cordelia's when he told us about the charge he was part of in the New York campaign—"

"Let's focus on *your* William, shall we," I interrupted. "What do we need to do to prepare you for marriage?"

"No, Betsy, not you too. I have enough women fussing."

"I could make you a crown of flowers," I teased. "Do up your hair like a Greek goddess." I held out a fistful of peonies. Rebecca made a face.

Rebecca and William's relationship had begun when Smith found himself thrown in the city jail in January for libel. Oddly enough, Rebecca's father was in the same situation. Their outspoken criticism of the Pennsylvania government had gone too far, at least for the local magistrate's tastes. In Reverend Smith's case, he had printed pamphlets to advertise his disgust, which didn't help him any. Rebecca's father was bleating just as loudly. The Moore family home was west of Philadelphia, closer to Indian territory; Mr. Moore's carping was probably out of fear for his family's well-being and the desire to protect his property. If either man had expressed any regret at all, or simply silenced their voices, they would have avoided jail, but neither would. That was one way to get attention, I supposed, when the head of the college and one of the landed gentry go to jail, things must be dire. They had certainly made their points. Smith's jail stint did not deter his students. They happily trudged the block and a half from the college to the jail to take classes with their teacher while he was temporarily incarcerated.

Rebecca had gone with her mother to visit her father at the gaol and, to her delight, found Reverend Smith in the next cell. Finally, Rebecca had the complete attention of the man who held her heart. He became taken with her daily visits and almost immediately after both men were released, Reverend Smith sought Rebecca's hand. They were to marry at Moore Hall this July. It seemed to be a year for weddings. Many of my close friends were getting married in the coming months.

Rebecca stopped cutting and sat back in the grass, gazing up at the clouds. "A whole new life to look forward to, Betsy, for both of us. We'll raise our babies together and they will grow up as playmates, like you and I were."

Would we? The man I said yes to was three thousand miles away and apparently in no hurry to return.

I put down my garden shears, tipping my face back to the warm spring sunshine. Rebecca laid down in the grass and drew her cap over her eyes.

I looked up at the house. Graeme Park had been my home since I was two years old. The soft edges of the round stones fell toward each other, mortar edged around them like water foaming around seashells on the sand. The masonry of my house was so different than the stiff red and brown brick houses in Philadelphia. I had a fondness for the grace of the house, admired its bones. I liked the way the roof curved over the attic like a closed lid, the honey-colored shingles covering the roof in crisp lines, the two chimneys firmly placed on top like gingerbread biscuits crowning a trifle. It was a beautiful house, regal in its pretty clearing, as solid as Stonehenge. My memories with William were everywhere here. How many times had we sat in this garden, or raced each other on the horses, or tramped through the forest.

I glanced over at Rebecca.

"Let's go in, shall we? Before I lose you to all the ladies who are coming this afternoon to celebrate your betrothal, let's have our midday meal in peace. I am sure I saw

Gretchen making a rhubarb pie this morning. We'll go find Liza and see what she's up to."

Rebecca sat up and pushed her cap back in place. "Betsy, I feel badly that you'll have to listen to the ladies fuss about me and my upcoming marriage when you are bearing the burden of absence. I confess, I was nervous to tell you my news."

I smiled and tweaked her nose. She looked so serious. "Thank you, sweet old friend. Just keep me away from crusty Adelaide Peters. I heard her telling Mother after church that I am getting too old to wait for a man."

"She did not!"

"The word spinster was said. I'm sure of it."

Rebecca laughed. "I'm not sure what that makes the Carter sisters. They are at least twenty-six."

"The goodwife Peters would like it noted that I am getting long in the tooth."

Rebecca waved a hand. "She just wants you to choose one of those oily grandsons of hers. Still, your hand is taken. You mustn't forget that."

I thought uneasily of my last letter to William. I shuddered when I remembered what I wrote; I had been upset. In a moment of temper I told him he could keep his muff and tippet and his fine ladies of London. Now I winced to think of my angry words on the page.

It *would be folly—no, madness!—to think of risking my life with you, a strong party man! Can I look to you as the person that will share my pains and pleasures during our future life?*

How I regretted that letter. I had written again and apologized almost immediately. I told William how badly I wanted to be there to see all those places he had told me about so warmly. I also sent him a love poem.

Excerpt of letter Benjamin Franklin to Deborah Franklin
June 10, 1758
London

My dear child,
I have no prospect of returning until next spring, so you will not expect me. But pray remember to make me as happy as you can, by sending some Pippins for myself and friends, some of your small hams, and some cranberries.
William is of the Middle Temple, and will be called to the Bar either this term or the next.
I think I have now gone through your letters, which always give me great pleasure to receive and read, since I cannot be with you in person. Distribute my compliments, respects, and love, among my friends, and believe me, ever my dear Debby,
Your affectionate husband
B. Franklin

Chapter 11

Horsham
January 1759

"Horsey," my nephew demanded as my sister labored in childbirth on the floor below us. "Please!"

I hardly heard him. The whole house held its breath for the delivery, as if we were balanced on the sharp point of a knife. Outside the trees shook as the wind wailed and a storm raged, while inside we tried to go about our day as the frost thickened on the windows and the candles bowed low with every draft. The servants closed every interior shutter against the wicked gales. The house was dark even in mid-day.

Jane had begun her lying-in at Graeme Park the week after Christmas with this baby. She wanted the child born in the country, far away from the fevers and their deadly contagious reach across Philadelphia, where many of the houses are pressed closely together. She had lost a baby to diphtheria last year, a boy. This baby was her fourth in five years of marriage.

Her husband James came and went to his work in the city, while Mother and I and the nurse grappled with my niece and nephew. They were like a dozen piglets on the loose.

"Aunt!" John said again, frowning at me. "Horsey."

I looked at my nephew. "You have your horse." I motioned to the toy in his hand.

He shook his head. "No. Aunty horsey."

"He wants you to be his horse," Anny explained, eyeing us from her makeshift carriage. Anny was three years old now, almost four, and little monkey Johnny had just celebrated his second birthday.

"Here, John." The nursemaid, Marta, handed him another toy horse from her pocket.

Johnny shook his head, a pink baby lip poking out. I could not tell whether he was going to cry or burst into one of his rages. "No."

Marta, and I had, rather unwisely I saw now, let them make forts from the extra furniture stored on the third floor. This room was chaos compared to the spotless nursery next door. Stacked furniture was piled high, along with boxed dishes, rolled-up rugs, and accompanying mystery boxes marked cryptically as "dining". All of it was in use each summer when we were bursting with visitors but come January, it was stored. Usually this room was out-of-bounds, but today in an attempt to keep them distracted from their mother, we were playing here. The children were shiny-eyed with excitement at being let loose in the forbidden room. A Windsor chair was now Anny's carriage, a leather-backed chair her horse, a cane chair Johnny's imaginary stallion.

"Horsey," Johnny said, pointing to the floor.

When the storm broke, I would be able to take them out to play in the snow or go sledding, if I could get Johnny to sit still long enough to stay on the sled instead of trying to jump off.

"Oh alright. Come on, then." I sank to my knees on the rug. "Neigh. Neigh. I'm a horse."

Grinning, Johnny reached his little arms for my shoulders, and I hauled him onto my back. Anny squealed in delight at the sight of us and hurled herself from the chair behind her brother and half onto him so that they were both clinging to me. Marta clucked in disapproval, her face stern. "You will make them crazy like animals," she scowled. "They must learn they cannot."

Despite the cramped space, we went two turns around, my knees aching as they lurched along the floor. My petticoats and skirts provided little protection for my bony knees.

The floor creaked as someone entered. Marta made an alarmed noise.

"Your poor Aunty's back. She'll have another of her fevers for sure," Mother said, amused.

"Elizabeth thought this a good idea," Marta said dourly.

I sat back on my haunches. The children slid slowly down my back to the floor.

"Horsey!" Johnny said to his sister, attempting to climb on her back.

"No, Johnny, no. I'm too little. Get off!" Anny twisted away from him and they both tumbled.

"Neigh, neigh," John said happily.

Mother motioned her head for me to follow her out the door. "Marta, calm them down, please," Mother instructed her as we left. I ignored the pained look Marta shot me.

"Milk and puddings?" Anny suggested helpfully to Marta, whose stern face implied there would definitely not be milk and puddings coming.

"I think you should lock it," I said to Mother in the hallway. I pushed my hair back from my forehead. "They are little beasts. Keep them in there."

Mother laughed. "All little children are beastly at times."

I had never been as fond of children as many women were, although of course I loved my niece and nephew. "I do not know how you had ten, Mama," I said with feeling. The thought was overwhelming. "Or how any woman does, for that matter."

"One at a time, dear," Mother said easily without a moment's pause, "one at a time." She shot me a wry look. "Although you do find you enjoy them more as they grow older."

I had a twin when I was born, her name was Sarah. Mother said we were born on a day so cold all of Philadelphia shivered indoors watching their windows coat with ice both outside and in. Sarah and I were my mother's last babies. Sarah came out first, strong and quick, smoothing the way for my tiny self to slide out tiredly behind her. Unfortunately, Sarah died in her sleep a few weeks later, healthy and perfect. I, on the other hand, was still here, although I was often weak and sickly. I could not recall a calendar year passing without being struck to my bed for weeks at a time with malaise or some mysterious pain. Poor Sarah and all the others. My poor mama, too. Only three babies still alive, of ten.

We went downstairs and lowered our voices outside Jane's door.

"How is she doing?" I asked.

"This baby is coming more slowly than the others," Mother said. "Still, the midwife says she is making progress."

"The baby will come today?"

"Babies come when they want."

We sat with Jane until the clock chimed two in the morning and her pains began to quicken. I watched Mother and the midwife hustle around her like bees on a hive. Tea, steamed cloths, herbs in poultices, more tea. Shuffle, fuss, shuffle.

"Out," the midwife ordered me when Jane's groans intensified, and pointed a finger at the door.

I went. When I woke, there was a blinding sun high in a cloudless blue sky. I heard the cry of a newborn and ran into Jane's chamber still in my shift. She was sitting propped up against pillows, a bundle in her arms. I hurried to the bed.

"A girl." Jane shifted her for me so I could see a tiny face in a nest of cloth.

"Hello little one," I said. The baby was pretty. She had Jane's pert nose, not my long one. When Johnny was born he had a pointed head and white bumps on his cheeks; Anny had been red and misshapen, her newborn face bunched up in ugly creases. "She looks like a painting. What will you name her?"

"Charity, after James's mother."

"Is he on his way?"

"Mother had someone go to fetch him earlier, after the storm broke. And to tell Father too, who's at the hospital. Then I sent Mama to bed and told the midwife to go home for a few hours. We've only just this moment been left alone. Haven't we, my little angel?"

"Do the children know?"

"Yes, Marta brought them in when they woke up. I'm afraid they thought her very dull."

We had a good chuckle at that.

I sat on the bottom of her bed, my feet curled up under me after the cold floor of the hall, and admired them both. Jane took Charity to her breast. I watched as the impossibly tiny mouth clamped on and the wrinkled brow smoothed.

Jane looked down at her baby daughter with wonder, her mouth curved in a smile.

"Was it easier this time?"

"It's never easy," she answered slowly, "but that becomes so unimportant in the end. You will see, when it's your turn."

The baby had light hair, like her father.

"You think you will remember how it feels to hold a child of yours when they are born, but you can't," Jane mused. "It is only when you hold a baby in your arms for the very first time that you have this joy. It is difficult to describe. Each child is unique, no matter how many babies you have."

"Ann will be so happy," I said. I knew our sister would come to meet little Charity as soon as she could.

Jane glanced at me and sadness shadowed her face. "I hope that is so," she said quietly.

Ann had been married for years and she still had no children. She desperately wanted them.

"When she is finished her feed, shall I put her in the cradle so you can sleep?" I asked. "Before the midwife comes back, and your husband arrives, and the whole world is here and we all fight over her. I could sit and watch her while you sleep, if you'd like."

Jane's eyes were already closing. "Thank you, Betsy. You always know what to do."

Wheels crunched over the snow and up the lane day after day with horses, carriages, and carts loaded with food and gifts and families from nearby farms. The floors and walls creaked and swelled and for the rest of that week, the house was hot, crowded, and far too noisy, even though everyone was feigning quiet to let baby and mother sleep. Anny and Johnny were plied with sweets and got away with mayhem when eyes were focused elsewhere, even under Marta's eagle eye. Father must have invited every neighbor for miles around to celebrate the arrival of his newest grandchild. The birth of a child, any child, during the month of January was a welcome excuse to leave the house and seek warmth and company elsewhere. New father James held court in the parlor, puffed-up with pride and alcohol.

It was all too much, even for me, who loved company. I wanted to go back to Philadelphia. I thought with longing of my friends and conversations over tea, of shops and plays and concerts. I had never liked Graeme Park in the winter. I did not like seeing my summer paradise turn white, iced with dreariness and isolation. Long, cold miles stretched between us and the amusements of town, country roads lined with naked trees and shivering stretches of bare field. You could almost watch the bleakness creep in with the first snow. It was even worse when ice covered the roads and held us hostage.

Finally, at the end of the week, when the children were playing drums with cutlery on the table and the dog was trying to hide in the wood pile, I bundled up and went for a ride on my horse.

Carmenta was just as eager as I was for freedom. We crossed several acres, moving at a good pace on the main trails. My breath came out in puffs, the air gloriously fresh and free from wood smoke and the smells of tobacco and vinegar and beef tallow. The horse and I moved as one, the gray afternoon weaving a cocoon around us, wintry pale and crystalline. I drank the land in with my eyes as we rode through, to remember for later at my desk. The berries of a holly bush gleamed bright red, and beneath, the paw prints of a squirrel imprinted the snow.

In no hurry to return, I let an hour pass, and then two. When my fingers started to ache under my gloves, I reluctantly turned for home. I approached the stables through the meadow, my neck cold under my hood. Someone ahead was waving. As I got closer I could see that it was Old Joseph. He had been with our family for so long I couldn't remember a time without him. He wasn't one of our slaves, but Father would never dismiss him from service.

"You're needed at the house," he said. "Go now. I'll take the horse."

"Is something wrong?" What on earth could I be needed for? The house was bursting with people. "Surely Mother can't be worried about me. Oh, did someone new arrive?" Or had Johnny tried to escape again? He wanted to climb to the top of the snowbanks.

Old Joseph shook his head. "Company's gone."

He must be wrong. Why would everyone have left? It was early. I searched his lined face. He was like a grandfather to me. It had been Old Joseph who picked me up from the ground when I was four and had tried to climb a tree that was too big for me. I still had the scar from where a rock lodged in my forehead. Mother stitched my wound with a sewing needle when Father was out setting a broken leg a few properties over. It was Old Joseph who rescued me when my brother locked me in the larder, and Old Joseph who comforted me when our other dog ate Miss Porridge, my favorite rag doll.

"Miss Jane isn't well," he said. He gestured for me to jump down, and held out a hand to help me down. "Go on, now."

"Do you mean Ann? My sister Ann is not well?"

He shook his head. "Please, Miss Elizabeth. Hurry."

I slid off Carmenta and handed him the reins. The silence in the house made me run up the stairs without bothering to shed my cloak or boots. I hadn't heard quiet like that for weeks.

"Mother!" I called from the stairs. "Old Joseph said—"

I stopped outside Jane's open door, which stood open. Mother looked at me and shook her head.

I took it in. Jane was asleep. My father, my mother, the midwife, James, and my sister Ann were all gathered around the bed. There was no blood on the sheets, they were as white as the snow outside. The room smelled of sassafras tea and something heavier. Bitters?

"What's happening?" I asked quietly. I had left a house filled with Nesbitts and Van Horvens and Morgans, and youngsters playing in the nursery.

"What time is it?" Jane asked in a thin voice. Not asleep, then.

"Not yet four o'clock, dearest," Mother answered. "Are you feeling better?"

"Where is everyone?"

"They went home so you can rest and be better."

When babies came, we were a family of easy births, blessed with unremarkable labors and healthy infants. It was illness that carried so many of our children to an early grave.

"How is Charity?" Jane asked. "Does she have the fever too?"

"Yes," my father answered simply.

Childbed fever. My heart sank. That morning Jane and I had joked around and played cards in her bed. Childbed fever was as cruel as cholera, it could take you swift as a flash flood following a heavy rain.

I entered the room gingerly and looked over at the cradle. The baby, uncovered, was sleeping in a ray of afternoon light from the window. The sun was low, another hour or so and it would be dark.

Father stepped away from the bed. He went to his satchel, rubbing the bridge of his nose in concentration. After a moment he took something out, then leaned over little Charity.

"We'll bleed her," he said to the midwife. "Both of them."

"Jane had a fever yesterday," the midwife whispered to him. "Like I told you. But it was only for a short time, then it went. I thought she was clear."

"So it did," my father said grimly.

"It was gone," the midwife repeated. "I was sure."

Mother and Ann busied themselves with rubbing Jane's arms and stroking her hair back from her face.

"Go tell Gretchen we need ginger tea, extra strong, a garlic poultice, and the willow tincture. And lots of ice and cloths," Mama told me.

I ran out. My boots had made puddles of water on the floor.

"Betsy?" Jane said. I stopped and ran back.

"My sweetness?"

"Warm milk. My throat."

"I'll get it right now."

The rest of that day and night were one long blur, elongated and formless. We managed to ice Jane's fever down, but the baby burned for hours. James paced the room. After a while he sat in the chair between the bed and the cradle, between wife and daughter. He placed a hand on each for a time, then got up and paced again.

I sat in a chair, reading aloud from the Bible as Father and the others moved around me. I wanted to calm Jane. I read for ages, until my eyes were gritty and my tongue was clumsy in my mouth, until the lack of light made it hard to see. I stopped when I heard a sharp intake of breath. Father stood holding little Charity against his shoulder. He stood for a moment without moving, then turned and handed the baby slowly to James with a shake of his head.

James slumped as if someone had taken his body out of his clothes. He bent over his daughter, trembling.

"Give her to me," Jane said.

Mother tucked pillows behind Jane's back to raise her. James hesitated, then put Charity in her arms.

The midwife still stood at the ready, poised, but her demeanor had shifted. Her back was straighter, her face resolute, her jaw set. She was back in the role that she knew. There was action to be taken, a woman to be cared for, a family to be consoled. This was familiar work.

My sister's hand cradled the baby's impossibly small face, doll-like and perfect. She reached inside the blanket for a tiny white hand, enclosed it with her own. They stayed like that, hands embedded, as the room grew darker.

"Take her," Jane finally said. "There won't be a viewing this time." When baby Jacob died, we laid him out in a little coffin in the parlor. The lining was a bed of velvet.

Ann stepped forward and carefully lifted Charity from Jane's arms, her face composed.

By the time the sun was up, Jane's fever was gone. She had drunk a little broth, eaten a soft egg, and cuddled Anny and Johnny, who had barely had time to comprehend they had a sister before they no longer had a sister.

"God needed Charity," Marta told them in her no-nonsense way. "Children, you must pray for her, and she will look out for you from heaven. She is with her brother Jacob now, and you are not to be sad. It will not help. Come. We will go outside."

Mother and Ann and I busied ourselves and left Jane alone to talk for a long time with her husband. He would need to return to the city.

I went back to Jane's sickbed that afternoon as Mother was bringing her a meal. "Remember, it had nothing to do with you," Mother told Jane as she laid the tray on the dresser. "No one is to blame. We do not know why these things happen."

I sat on the side of the bed and took Jane in my arms. She buried into me like a puppy, letting me hold her. Her breath was warm on my neck, her skin smooth and reassuringly cool under my fingers. I stroked her back. I ached to bring her little Charity back, to turn back the clock, to even know what to say to ease Jane's pain. But I would leave that to Mother, who understood far well what Jane was going through, when I could not. She had more children dead than alive.

I retreated to my chamber. I laid on my bed and read Plato, finding peace. If I could not understand God, at least I could curl up in bed with my book and try to forget his actions for a few hours.

I wished Liza were here, I craved the comfort of her. She was in the city, graciously creating space for the expected horde of visitors. Tomorrow I would send word to her.

I was dozing when a cry ripped my sleep. I leapt up, my heart slamming into my chest, but I knew my mother's scream and knew what it meant.

Jane was gone too.

For days, I dreamed of being an old woman surrounded by dogs covered in sores. I was in a house that had a damaged roof and many empty rooms. I climbed into my bed in the derelict house, the scab-covered dogs keening on the floor. Jane floated by holding two babies, both rosy-cheeked and glowing with health. She blew kisses into their skin, unaware of the old woman watching from bed, with half of a roof over her head.

When I woke, I was as tired as if I had not slept at all.

Chapter 12

Horsham
April 1759

It had been raining for days. By the time the laundress came, every gown I owned was caked with mud at the hem several inches deep. The mud made me happy, for it meant that spring was here. In Ben Franklin's letter to Deborah, he had said they couldn't return until spring. Spring was here! I was happy Deborah had shared the letter with my mother. That meant I would see William soon. My heart knocked in my chest at the thought. I couldn't wait to see him again. My long wait would soon end; two long years, finally over.

I worked away in my *Poemata Juvenilia* book while the nurse had the children occupied. Today I was transferring a friend's poem into my book. I had sent her one of mine, an ode to nature. My *Poemata* was a collection of poems, prose pieces and copied letters that spoke to me about our extraordinary world. I liked to call forth philosophers, historians and poets, so we could all charm each other with a wild profusion of ideas. Whether they were famous people long dead or my friends down the road, it was the act of the firing up the imagination and freeing words that was so exhilarating.

I didn't hear a knock, but suddenly Mother stood next to me. "Elizabeth."

"Mama, how formal. Have a seat." I didn't look up from my pen.

"Margaret Abercrombie has received a letter from William," Mother said, her voice tight.

"Mmm." I rubbed at a smudge of ink on my hand, wondered if Hannah meant to use that word *lucid* the way she did.

"I am sorry to tell you this. William believes you have broken off with him."

I had not heard from William in a few months, which was not unusual over the course of winter. "I'm sorry, pardon me? Who received a letter from William?"

"Margaret Abercrombie. I have just returned from her house. She bid me come at once after she opened the letter from him. I was dismayed by the contents."

"What? Why would he write to Margaret?" I asked, puzzled. "And why did she not ask *me* to go to see her? Why did you go?"

"Elizabeth. Please listen."

"I don't understand. William wrote to Margaret Abercrombie about *me* to end our courtship?" I asked stupidly. "Why did he not send the letter to me?"

Margaret was a kind woman and a good friend of ours, true, yet why involve her in our private matter?

Mother sighed. "I don't know. It is unfortunate, my darling, but William has set you free. Of that there is no doubt."

"Did you bring this strange letter home?" I struggled to make sense out of what my mother was saying.

"Mrs. Abercrombie wants you to go to her. She wanted me to tell the news to you first, privately, as I'm sure she thought you would find it upsetting, as do we. William asked you to forget him. He told you to consider finding another and said he *cannot make you happy*. Well, what he said was that he agrees that he can't make you happy, as if you had suggested it first."

There was an absence of sound, as if I had fallen under a wave in the sea and my ears were full of water.

I shook my head, tried to clear it. "I don't know what you mean. Why would he think that?"

"Something about the war, the distance, his political views. All of it. It appears he thought you were ending your courtship."

My thoughts banged together like a blacksmith's chisel on iron.

"I am sorry, Elizabeth." Mother's voice was gentle. She had been anticipating this, I realized, for two years. This came as no surprise to her.

"We had a disagreement," I mumbled. I stood up from my table and walked to the window. It was still raining, harsh and relentless, sheets of water slamming to the ground and pooling. I barely saw it. "I was upset when his letter appeared in the paper after he promised me he wouldn't be political. I mean, in a way that would cause problems for us. I felt that he was not thinking of me, or our future. I wrote an angry letter to him, it was harsh I admit, but then I sent another apologizing for my rashness. I wanted him to be frightened of losing me and rush home as soon as possible."

I turned to her. She still stood by my desk, eyes wary.

"Did you see the letter?" I asked, "With your own eyes?"

Mother nodded. "He asked why you could not have been more civil. He seems to feel you let him down. He said he always warned you he was not one for writing."

He must not have received my most recent two letters. That could be the only explanation. I thought sadly of my love poem. I had poured out my heart.

"Margaret Abercrombie!" I wailed. The news had finally sunk in. William had written to Margaret Abercrombie to get rid of me!

There was great care in Mother's voice. "She was terribly distressed by this, as you can imagine, and as surprised as we are. She knew the letter would cause you pain. It was so unkind of William to involve her. Why he did such a thing is a mystery, and unconscionable. You must go to her as soon as possible."

Where was the William I knew in this? My mind heaved, sought to steady itself. *Wait for me . . .* he had pleaded.

"Was there anything else?"

"He was dismayed that you did not care for the gift he sent. He said that you had admired the story of Sophia's muff in that book, *Tom Jones.* Henry Fielding, isn't it? He had hoped his gift would raise a similar affection in you."

I tipped my face into my hands and groaned, which turned into a sob. Mother gathered me in her arms. "He believes that you ended your courtship, my darling. It seems he wrote to agree with you. If that is not the case, surely there can be recompense."

"I know he loves me," I cried into her shoulder. Two long years of waiting sat bitter as chard in my mouth. "I mean, it's *William. My* William. He loves me, Mama, I *know* he does. Something must be wrong. I was angry, that's all. Surely he knows me well enough. How could he do this?" We had been close friends for years.

Even then, I could imagine him as if he were standing in the room. I saw his smile, heard his voice, even felt his hands around mine as I smelled the lavender and polish fragrance of the Franklins' front room.

"Then you must write again," Mother said firmly. "Apologize and ask him to return. Let him know you are unhappy without him. Confirm your affections. But you must be prepared to wait, too. That is the way of these affairs of the heart."

The letter William sent was not complete. His signature was missing. His looping W, his broad, bold F was nowhere to be seen. Of course I had not expected his usual signatory of "your most affectionate William" given our misunderstanding, yet surely he would have ended a letter with his name, as was customary? It was highly irregular.

I went in search of Margaret in her kitchen.

"Is there another page?" I asked shortly. "There is no signature."

She shook her head. "It arrived just so."

"Was the seal broken? Altered in any way?"

She looked at me sadly. "No, Betsy. I'm sorry. It came that way."

I felt a pang of remorse. Damn William for this. Margaret was a good woman, and a friend, and she faced hardships of her own. James was at sea again and would be for months. She must find it difficult to be alone with the children with her husband away at the mercy of the ocean.

I excused myself and went out to the yard. I stood with my hands on my hips and stared at the chickens. I did not think William capable of the words written on the page, but it was clearly his handwriting.

After Jane's death, unable to cope, my brother-in-law left the children with Mother to raise. I know she wanted to help James, but she was also happy to have her grandbabies under her wing and to have the house alive with children again. James rushed back to Philadelphia, saying he would come when he could. Mother hired a nurse to live in, updated the nursery, hung a new swing from the oak tree in the yard, then packed up some of her best china and figurines for an indeterminate length of time to make the house suitable for her young grandchildren.

Liza and I had to get used to having small children around all the time. Of course, to Mother, it had been strange to have just Liza and I in the house as young women, since she had spent twenty years with little ones underfoot.

I did not find it an easy adjustment. Johnny was the worst sort of little boy for getting himself in trouble. He was in constant motion, and he wrecked everything. He climbed like a monkey, nothing off limits to his curious mind. Johnny scaled everything, anything, wherever he went, with no understanding of personal safety. He tried to jump off the sideboard when he thought he could get away with it. One day I stopped him from trying to jump over the banister on the third floor. He would not have survived the fall.

And little Johnny was loud. He yelled when he was happy, he yelled when he was angry, and when he was sad, he wailed. It was hard to tell which was worse, his good humor or bad, for when he was cheerful he would frequently holler with enthusiasm, "Bang, bang, you are DEAD," at his toy soldiers before one or more went flying.

"He's two years old," Mother said mildly when Liza and I complained.

"Almost three," Liza said wearily.

I looked forward to the day when we could entertain him with a book or story.

Little Anny, in contrast, was calm but talked for hours, with enough questions to exhaust us. Her tea parties could rival a queen's. She wrapped herself in Jane's lace stole and glided through the halls advising courtiers or accepting dancing invitations from suitors. Between the two of them, the days were long, and I had to write in stolen hours. I burned through many candles in late hours. Even though the responsibility for them was not mine, I couldn't leave Mother to the task alone.

Sooner than I would have thought, with the cruelty of the very young, Anny and Johnny stopped asking for their mother. They also did not seem to mind that they only saw their father once or twice a month.

"Mama's in heaven," Johnny said matter-of-factly whenever someone mentioned her.

London
August 1759

Dearest Betsy,
I hardly deserve your consideration, and yet I appeal to you for exactly that. I have done little to keep your affections for me in recent months, and yet by way of this letter, I write to you with great embarrassment and great love.
I am ever a bad correspondent, that's true. My life here is chaotic, with too much to occupy a man's hours, and too many tasks to keep me distracted. Please accept my most sincere apology. I still consider myself engaged to you, and no consideration on earth would induce me to think of marrying another. What must I do to make amends?

William thought I had ended our engagement and hoped Margaret would intervene on our behalf as our mutual friend. He was apologetic, remorseful, consumed with reaffirming my affections. He missed me.

"Yours affectionately, William," I read aloud with satisfaction. Of course I forgave him. I felt the same way. I still sensed him with me.

I tucked the letter behind a loose panel in my wardrobe. I would write immediately and tell him everything, that Jane and the baby had died, that Mother had the parlor repainted, that Reverend Peters came every Sunday for supper and wanted to stop working for the Penns and return to the church. William would have known already that the British had won the Battle of Quebec last month. We expected the French to acknowledge defeat soon, which would end the war. Wouldn't it be a relief if the French left the continent altogether?

One thing was certain, I was done talking about William Franklin with anyone. There had always been too many people between us. Other than to confirm we were still engaged, until his return, I would be silent on my heart.

Shakespeare's Lysander had said it perfectly in *A Midsummer Night's Dream:* the course of true love never did run smooth. Surely that could change. William would come back and we could enjoy our life together.

I would keep busy. I would work, I decided, more than I ever had before. I would help Christ Church with the refugees, make more blankets or clothing, cook soup if I had to. I'd be a beacon of industry.

In any spare time, my pen would fly. I would write poems, begin new translations, create copies of classics not yet in circulation in English in the colonies. There was much work to be done.

There is a certain Elevation of Soul
A noble turn of virtue that raises the hero from the
plain honest man,
To which Verse can only raise us.
E.

Chapter 13

Philadelphia
November 1762
Three years later

My sister Ann sent word to the house that she wanted to meet me at our favorite teahouse.

I decided to drag Clara with me. Father did not like me unaccompanied, even though Philadelphia during the day was perfectly safe. You saw many women walking alone from one task to another in our crowded streets. After the French fell to the British in Montreal and surrendered Canada two years ago, the fighting effectively ended in Pennsylvania. The British are trying to make peace with the Indians now.

"I must go to the market to get salt and spices," Clara protested. "Missus Graeme wants to start the mincemeat."

"We'll stop there on the way home, and you can get what you need then," I said. "I will tell Mama and Gretchen. We'll get sticky buns; would you like that?"

We set out, walking from our house to Market Street— no one bothered calling it High Street anymore, there were so many stalls and vendors all the time—and then right onto Front Street. The day was temperate for November, not overly warm but temperate enough. Philadelphia was still growing at a rapid pace and I was enjoying all the new people and businesses appearing. I wondered how the Franklin men would perceive the changes when they returned, for there were many, including the opening of our first medical school. We had a new king, too, on both sides of the pond of course. George II had died two years ago and the monarchy passed to his young grandson, who was only twenty-two when he took the crown. They said he was very progressive, for a monarch.

We approached the London Coffeehouse, which had been built eight years ago by the Bradfords after they raised money from a group of local merchants who wanted a respectable place for trade that wasn't a tavern. The coffeehouse sat close to the docks at the south end of Market Street and was a constant hive of activity all hours of the day and night. All of Philadelphia came there at one time or another. Besides the merchants, it was always bursting with businessmen, traders, travelers, politicians. There were booths reserved for the exclusive use of the governor and other government officials to conduct their business in private. Most ship captains that anchored in Philadelphia took meals, made deals, and, more discreetly than elsewhere on the docks, secured their women there.

As we got closer, I was dismayed to see it was an auction day. A shipment of slaves must have come in. Six Negro men were standing on a makeshift platform of wooden boards that were held up by two large barrels at each end. Even though it was November, they were naked. Their eyes stared down, their faces without expression, ankles shackled. One of them was more boy than man. Next to the men, on the right, was a young woman and two small children, girls. They couldn't be more than four or five years old. Their silence contrasted to the buzz of conversation in the crowd around them.

I looked away and started to walk faster.

"Jesus and Mary alive," Clara whispered with a sharp intake of breath. She stopped to watch. I halted next to her. "It isn't godly. Thank God I'll have my papers one day."

Father purchased Clara from a carpenter in Bucks County. She was an indentured servant, and after three more years of service, her contract would be fulfilled. After that, she could seek employment under her own terms. Her parents hired her out in return for passage here from Germany when they couldn't pay their way.

A group of men in fine coats and hats stood in front of the makeshift platform and appraised the slaves. One of the men, head like a barn owl, adjusted his spectacles, then looked up at the slaves. He gestured to the chest of the slave on the far left. "That one's seen some hard labor," he said to the man next to him. "He's sure to be a good worker."

"Good strength there in the torso," his companion agreed.

"Raise your arms," a rotund man commanded, the slave trader. The young Negro obeyed without looking up.

"It's wicked," Clara breathed, horrified.

"Clara, let's go." I gave her a light poke in her back. "Some things aren't for us to see."

I shoved her to make her walk on, but her head twisted over her shoulder at the slavers. I had known this was the purchase site for the slaves who were brought to Philadelphia on the slave ships but had never seen an auction.

"It isn't right," Clara said again.

"It's not for us to understand," I said uneasily. I'd grown up with slaves. We had two left, Alex and Mars. I wasn't permitted to speak with them, all I knew was that I saw them working in the fields. They had their own quarters and Old Joseph oversaw their work. When I was younger I hadn't thought about it much, they were just field hands. Father said life on plantations gave Negroes food and shelter and medical care. He said it was a way of life passed down to us and we had to work with the way the world was.

"It's not for us to understand," I repeated.

"Easy to say if you've always been free," Clara said bitterly. It sounded like she was cursing me.

When I was a child, we had many more slaves than Mars and Alex, and one of them ran away. Father put an ad in the papers, but we never saw him again, he was never caught. Secretly, I was glad, until one day Old Joseph turned glassy eyes to heaven and moved his lips and I suspected the real reason we never caught the boy who ran. They fished dark-skinned bodies out of the area rivers all the time. Old Joseph is a Negro too but he is a freedman.

Negroes had no easy time living as freedmen in the colonies, that was certain. Old Joseph chose to never leave Graeme Park, even in the winter. At some point, I knew not why, Father stopped buying new slaves.

"Turn around," the slave trader ordered the slaves. The auctioneer stood to the side of the crowd, a tall man, thin and knobby, ready to take bids. He reminded me of a grasshopper perched on rotten fruit, bug-eyed and unblinking.

Clara and I found ourselves paralyzed by the scene before us. We stood against our will and watched from where we had stopped on the other side of the street.

The Negroes shuffled in their ankle chains to face the coffeehouse, their bare buttocks to the crowd. Two of the men had backs that were a river of silt gone dry, skin set in grooves. I looked away.

"Bend over," the auctioneer commanded them. Against my will, I looked back. The fat man, the trader, walked past and poked the youngest between his legs with a stick. "Virile," he crowed. The would-be purchasers guffawed, pleased by the promise of more workers to be born from the price of one.

"Clara," I said, "We'll go now. Ann is waiting." But neither of us moved.

One of the children looked back over her shoulder, confused by the barks of laughter, and the trader smacked her hard on the bottom with his stick. She yelped and her mother elbowed her in warning. The girl was so small.

"We are selling the mother and the girls together," the trader announced proudly. "They are equally suited to city house or country plantation. I am told the woman is a good worker but refined enough for the dining room. The little girls will make fine kitchen maids. And when they are grown . . ." his words trailed off. His face gleamed with lascivious suggestion.

"Horse's ass," Clara said under her breath. I pretended not to hear. Whatever kind of life she had with her family back in Ireland, it hadn't been one of subservience. Her family had paid a high price to come to America in more than one way. Thinking of Clara's family crossing the ocean made me think of poor Margaret Abercrombie. Her husband had gone to sea two years ago, in 1760, and had never been seen again. The ship did not come back, and James Abercrombie was presumed lost at sea. Margaret was heartsick, but coping with raising the children the best she could.

I looked at the slave auction and considered whether I should buy the woman and her two girls. Mama was kinder than many. Could a woman purchase slaves? How much would they be? I didn't know how I would pay. Perhaps on credit, until I could get Father to settle the account. I bit my lip. What was I thinking? We had no need of more help. Even after Clara left one day, we would have a surplus of servants. Mama hadn't the heart to let them go after Ann and Jane moved out, and Father had done well over the past few years.

I grabbed Clara's wrist and hurried on, feeling sick. I wished we hadn't seen it.

The tea house was a little farther up Front Street. I entered with relief, trying to shake off the slave auction. My sister was waiting.

"Hello my lovely," I said to Ann. "I promised Clara tea and a bun. What would you like?"

We sat at a little table with a red gingham cloth. Clara took a table at the back of the shop, happy with her bun, and pleased to have the hour of leisure afforded her.

"What news?" I asked my sister when we settled.

"No news," Ann said. "I just fancied an outing."

I knew better. "Ann."

She sighed. "Charles sent me out." She traced the squares on the cloth while I waited. "I just want to sleep all the time and Charles doesn't like it. I know he's worried, but I've been through these spells before. I wish he'd just let me be instead of parceling me out to my sister like a child."

I had seen this before. It was the melancholy. Ann had times where she took to her bed for three or four days at a time. Nothing seemed to help her except the passage of time. My mother assumed it was the strain of being childless, the deep sadness of her longing that drove Ann into herself during dark days.

"Perhaps you should see a physick?" I suggested gently. "Or a good apothecary? Herbs may help. Have you ever tried that?" I knew my sister would soldier on in silence, although I'm sure my father had spoken to her at some point.

"Herbs? Only God can help, but he won't. Oh Betsy, all these years, and no children, not even any that died in my womb. What can herbs do if I'm barren? I've been married fourteen years. Fourteen years!"

"What if there's a reason?" I asked, my voice lowered. I reached for her hand. "What if it is something physical, an obstruction? Why don't you see Dr. Redman? Or Dr. Bond? He's been in practice forever. Let him examine you. He has an office on Spruce Street. Ask him not to tell Father. I'm sure he will keep your confidence."

"It's so embarrassing," Ann said resentfully. "It's probably too late for me at this age. With my luck, any obstruction would probably be some kind of tumor."

"For heaven's sake, Ann."

"I thought maybe one day . . ."

"Is Charles making you feel—"

"Oh no. No."

She removed her hand from mine and twisted her thin gold wedding band. "Perhaps I should see Dr. Bond," she said slowly. "Even if he cannot help me, I would be no worse off than I am now. Promise me you won't tell Charles. Or Father."

"You know I won't."

Ann wiped a stray tear from the corner of one eye. "Let's talk of happier things. What news from home this week? Mama is well? I haven't felt like visiting anyone, so I haven't heard much."

"Well, Johnny jumped off the sideboard—again—and broke his nose. It was our first week back in the city. He is five now and still trying to fly. I thought he would outgrow it."

Ann laughed. "Poor boy. Someone should tell him humans will never be birds. Sadly, we are meant only for the ground and the water on it."

"And Anny is in trouble again for playing with Mother's best china from the orient. She broke the teapot lid after being told the china was not to be touched. Mother thought she could be trusted now that she is almost seven."

"Was she punished?"

"Mother let the nurse go and hired another. I don't think she would have been as upset if the fireplace tile had not cracked when Johnny dropped a brick on it the week before when the nurse was idle."

"A *brick*?"

"He said his toy soldiers needed a barrack."

"But where did he get the brick?"

"The shed. After he picked the lock."

Ann laughed, a long, hearty laugh that pleased me and made her eyes water. "How I wish Jane could be here to see them. They get in trouble because they are so *bright*."

"I wish that as well," I said. "I miss her terribly. How has it possible that she has been gone three years already?"

We looked up when we heard our names called. Johanna and Mia Janssen approached us in a burst of calico and feathered hats.

"Why, the Graeme sisters! How are you?" Johanna sang. She ran the spring fête every year for Christ Church. Johanna wasn't a bad sort, but she had a tendency to prattle on without saying much of anything, and I was happier relieved of her company. Besides, she did not care for reading. What would we ever have in common?

"We are very well, thank you," Ann answered. "How are the Janssen sisters?"

The two of them looked at me.

"We are so indignant," Mia said.

"Truly, we are seething," Johanna added.

"What do you mean?" I asked. "Is the seamstress out of buttons?" I winked at them to show that I meant no spite.

Ann laughed at me.

Johanna paused and exchanged a look with her sister. "My goodness, don't tell me you haven't heard."

Ann and I looked at each other. Heard what?

"May we sit?" Mia asked.

Ann nodded toward the empty chairs. "Please."

"Well, we were so pleased to hear *Doctor* Benjamin Franklin returned to Philadelphia yesterday. Apparently they call him doctor now after France was so taken with his electrical experiments! He arrived on the *Sweet Mary* just yesterday."

Was William home? My pulse quickened. Our letters over the past year had been infrequent, but he sent me newspaper clippings from time to time, and accounts of the funny characters he met in London. Oh, please tell me he was finally home.

"Mrs. Franklin and Sally must be delighted," Ann said.

"Dr. Franklin surprised everyone," Mia explained. "Not only did no one know he was coming home, he left London three weeks before his son's wedding."

She threw the last sentence down like a body dropped in a grave.

Johanna took a breath. "It turns out William Franklin married a woman whose family owns a sugar plantation in Barbados. She had been living in London for the past year or two. They are returning to America soon, for William is going to be governor of New Jersey. He has accepted the post."

"I feel so badly," Mia said. "We thought you knew. My heart goes out to you, Elizabeth. How awful that he kept you waiting all this time. How long has it been? Five years? What sort of man does that?"

"I blame it on London," Johanna said. "That city rots men. Sarah Drinker was on the *Sweet Mary* too and said there is even talk that William had a son last year, and *not* with his new wife."

I was still seated in my chair but my mind had left my body. I could not have responded even if someone shoved a hot poker though my bare foot.

"A bastard baby," Mia said softly. "They say he's doing the boy right, though, and paying to have it fostered. He plans to claim the poor baby eventually, I heard. I just hope he told his new wife before she said yes to marrying him. How strange, isn't it, for him to repeat what his own father did and have his own illegitimate son?"

I wished I could jump off a sideboard and break my whole head.

Clara appeared at the table. "Don't forget the market, Mistress Elizabeth," she said with an unusual efficient briskness. "Gretchen is desperate for nutmeg and cloves. Your mother will have my head if we dawdle. The mincemeat can't wait and all that."

Ann's hand was on my elbow.

"Good day to you both," Ann said politely.

Clara smiled at the Janssen sisters sweetly. "Oh dear, you have something on your fichu, a stain," she said to the air, yet they both jumped and reached for their necks.

Somehow we made our way toward the door.

"In truth, no man returns to a woman after five years," Johanna said to her sister in a lowered voice, although her words carried clear as a ship's horn. "No matter how rich she is. I don't know why she ever thought he would."

"Love turns people into fools," Mia murmured.

God help me, it was true. William had married an Elizabeth Downes in London, at Covent Garden Church, on the fourth of September. I wondered what I had been doing that day. He was finally coming home, with a new wife at his side and an illegitimate son from another woman in someone else's care.

I stayed in bed for three days. Sometimes Liza would come and lie quietly next to me, and sometimes it would be my mother. On the fourth day, with ice in my soul, I decided to go to the Franklin home to expunge myself of the scourge of William Franklin forever.

"Darling, I'll come with you," Mother said quickly as I threw on my cloak and prepared to march up Chestnut Street to the Franklins. She ran after me, struggling to keep up with my brisk pace. "You don't need to do this, you know."

"Yes, I do," I said stiffly. I was not going to slink away from that damned family like a dog with my tail between my legs. Even nervous old Aurelius would not have done that, God rest his soul.

Mr. Franklin himself opened the door.

"My dear," Mr. Franklin said, surprised. His eyes went to my mother and he nodded respectfully. I was grateful for the lack of pleasantries. I could not have borne any *"It's been such a long time"* or *"How are you?"* platitudes. But no, Franklin was too much of a diplomat for that. Sly, always sly, then and now.

I thrust my letter at him. "Please see that your son receives this."

I turned to go.

"Come in, won't you?" Deborah said kindly from behind Mr. Franklin. Against my will I felt my mother nudge me forward into the warm house, the smell of ginger wafting toward us.

Franklin slipped my letter in his pocket without comment and swept his arm toward the sitting room. "Let me play my armonica for you," he offered amiably. "It's a brand new instrument that I designed and brought back with me. I know how much you love music, and this instrument makes the most glorious sounds."

I wanted to run, but we entered the parlor. His invention sat off to one side of the room. What had he called it? An armonica? At a glance, I could see it was beautiful, long and sleek and unusual, like no instrument I had seen before, about the size of a child's coffin. Orbs of glass lay on their sides in a long row of concentric circles, there had to be more than thirty, growing ever bigger. The row of glass circles was anchored at each end to a metal wheel, which in turn were attached to wooden sides, like book ends.

"The foot pedal makes the glasses spin," he explained, and sat on the stool in front to play. We watched him dip his fingers in water from a cup, then run them along the glass edges to produce vibrations that rang into clear, sweet notes as his foot pumped the spindle near the floor. Oh, and what notes they were! My ears perked like a cat's. The musical notes that emerged were haunting and high; they had a lightness of clear sound, an astonishing purity. This was music from an angel's realm. The only comparison I could muster was the memory of a boys' choir, young voices lifted up like bells made of crystal.

As Franklin played his armonica, I studied his profile, the line of his jaw, the softness his body, the high forehead. He had not changed much in appearance. How strange that I hadn't stood in this room for five and a half years, and yet it felt like last week. I was determined not to let Franklin or his music soften me. I would not ask him about William's marriage, or his bastard grandson. I wouldn't mention William at all.

No consideration on earth could induce me to think of marrying another.

Shut up, I told him in my head through gritted teeth.

"Tea?" Mrs. Franklin asked, when her husband finished his song. "Coffee? Or some apple cider?"

I shook my head. Mother declined as well.

"It is magnificent," Mother said to Franklin. "You said you invented it?" Her voice was full of wonder.

"I happened upon a young man at a dinner party playing wine glasses with a wet finger shortly after we arrived in England," Franklin said, lost in the memory. "I thought I could make something that would be less laborious, a wonderful new kind of instrument."

Before we could rise, Franklin began another song.

I watched his strong printer's hands as they delicately stroked the glass orbs to create that haunting music. I looked at Deborah, who gazed upon her husband with love. She was almost beaming. How could she welcome him back so easily after five years apart? Yet they seemed no different.

As I stood there listening to that eerie music, I felt as if I had aged decades. What a foolish, stupid girl I had been, waiting year after year when I must have been the only woman in all of Philadelphia who knew he would not marry me. And still he led me on, continued to tease and hold on to me until I was irrelevant as the rags lining a bird's cage.

That evening in my chamber, I wedged a hard-backed chair under the doorknob, then climbed fully dressed onto my bedstead with my cache of betrayal. One summer day two years ago I had taken the letters from their hiding place in the wardrobe and put them in a coffee tin with some expired lottery tickets on top. The lottery tickets reminded me of William, of how it was when we were first together.

I found his letter from 1759, begging my forgiveness, and ripped it soundly in half, then tore it carefully into quarter-inch pieces. *No man returns to a woman after five years, no matter how rich she is.*

I had spent five of what might be the best years of my life, five years of my *youth*, being loyal to someone who was not loyal to me in return. He was only coming back to America now to become governor of New Jersey. Where had the man I loved gone? Who had William become?

I methodically shredded half of his letters, the most recent ones, over my quilt. Our relationship was spread out over a nine-patch pattern like cotton bolls on a barn floor. I climbed off, gathered the pieces, and went to the fire. I crouched down close, the flames hot in my face, and burned each tiny fragment one piece at a time, the paper sizzling in a little pop of flame. One by one they crinkled to black and were swallowed whole. The last pieces had my name in fragments from the address. I watched William's pretty script fling by, sweeping *G*'s, big *E*'s. The flames ate my name.

Miss
Elizabeth
Graeme
in Phila.

He never wrote Philadelphia out in full. It had been charming to me once, one of his endearing quirks, a sign of his restless quick mind.

I thought burning his letters would give me satisfaction, but it did not. I decided to keep the oldest letters intact, the letters from the first two years after he left. They would help me remember when what we had was real, when what we had was love. I could not account for William's change of heart, of the malignancy that had seeped into his character.

People would talk of course. They would say he had been long gone and point three years in the past to Mrs. Abercrombie for proof of my delusion. They didn't know how it had been, how he wrote me again and pledged his soul, how we exchanged letters for another two years. Well, now they would never know. I had destroyed the evidence. Still, let them talk. What did it matter now?

I put the remaining letters back in the wardrobe under the loose board and threw out the coffee tin and the lottery tickets.

When my father first heard the news, he cried. He did not try to conceal his emotion; he let the tears slid unchecked down his face. That gave me pause, for I had only ever seen him cry when his children and grandchildren died.

"Thank God you escaped William!" he cried out. "He is a most dangerous man!"

Oh Papa. Did I escape? I wasn't sure. Did we have any control over our lives, or did our lives simply happen to us? What if I had said no to William when he asked to marry me? What if I had refused to wait more than the first year? Or what if I had insisted I go with them?

Are choices still choices if you don't recognize them as such?

Chapter 14

Philadelphia
1763

"Go abroad?" I laughed. "Ha."

My parents exchanged a knowing look, which made me cough on my tart.

"Just like that?" I scoffed. "I'm needed here. With the children."

"They are hardly orphans, Betsy," Mother said sharply. "They have me and your father, and Liza. We have the nurse. You can spare the time."

Liza nodded.

"You need a different climate," said my friend Benjamin Rush, a new addition to our Saturday dinners. He was an apprentice under Dr. Redmond and planned to go to Scotland next year to earn his medical degree. He was young and handsome and extremely bright. "A change. You were ill all winter."

I shrugged. Where? The sugar islands? I had no reason to go and no one to go with. Besides, the West Indies made me think of another Elizabeth who was probably lounging around New Jersey in her dainty Fras Poole shoes from the most popular shoemaker in London.

"I have been considering a trip home to Scotland," Reverend Peters said. "To see my family, and have the church recognize my new position." Peters had recently become rector of the twin parishes of Christ Church and St. Peter's, released from twenty years of working for the Penns in different government positions.

"Aye," my father agreed. "And it wouldn't hurt you to seek care from Fothergill while you're there. He's one of the best physicians in England. We are not as quick to embrace new treatments over here."

Reverend Peters's health had deteriorated this year. His heart, apparently.

Peters nodded. "I haven't seen my sister in thirty years. I've never even met my nieces and nephews."

At his age, it might be his last chance to travel.

"Then go," my father urged him. "Persuade Elizabeth to go with you. Someone can step in for you at church."

"Come with me, then, child," Peters encouraged me. "I need a companion, and you need a chaperone. You can see London. Let's have a true adventure."

"Yes. Why not?" Rush said.

"Are you sending me away to find a husband?" I snapped irritably. If that was the case, England be damned. Everyone laughed. I considered the invitation. Peters was more than twice my age. He'd be safe enough as a male companion.

"If that's the case," Liza said, "they would have to send me to find a husband too. They'd get rid of the both of us."

"We wouldn't dare," my father said wryly. "You two wouldn't listen anyway."

I found myself smiling. A glimmer of possibility was being offered to me: the lure of travel, the unknown, beckoning me away from here, the only place I'd ever known. A chance to see the world! As Reverend Peters said, an adventure.

"Come with us," I suggested hopefully to Liza. She shook her head, it was not in her nature. After she made the crossing from Scotland to the care of her uncle Charles as a girl she had no desire to cross the ocean ever again. It reminded her of everything she lost, her family, her country, her life there.

And just like that, there was a journey to plan. From my end, it was simple enough, letters to friends we would stay with, arrangements for travel money, what to put in my trunk. Reverend Peters had weightier matters to consider: his replacement in church; the needs of his congregations while he was away; official letters to notify authorities of his impending visit. We realized it would be next year before we could sail, for Thomas Penn wanted the transition to our new governor to go smoothly, and asked Reverend Peters to help with the transition following the resignation of the latest governor, James Hamilton. They never seemed to stay long, those ill-fated governors.

For the first time in my life, I had a purpose. How many times had I envied the merchant ladies, working busily alongside their husbands in various trades. How good they must feel after producing some of the goods actually needed in the world. I considered this for a time, and wondered if I dared start a business, but Father frowned upon the idea. Mother reminded me it was good fortune to be a woman whose hands were free from toil. To be educated was no small thing, it was a true luxury.

Indeed, but an educated woman without husband and children was a spinster, saddled with idleness, and then what value did her life have? At one point, I offered to teach at a charity school, but Father said, "You are a Graeme." That was the end of that.

Horsham
May 1764

I only doubted my journey once, the day I heard a bang and went down to the parlor and found my mother wrestling with the weaving loom. It was spring, and we were back at Graeme Park. Hyacinth, hollyhocks, daffodils, and tulips stood swaying in the bed outside each window, heads high.

"I'm fine," she said when she saw me. "I want to switch this with the spinning wheel. The light is better by this window, here."

I helped move the loom where she wanted it, and as I did so, I noticed what she was working on. "What is this, Mama? Not a funeral cloth?"

"I must be practical," she said. "I'm getting older."

"This is for yourself? Are you ill?"

"No, my darling. I wish to be prepared."

"You are in good health," I protested. "You're only in your sixties. That's young."

"My body is tired."

"Nonsense. You must rest, that's all. You do too much."

She shook her head. "I have a feeling, Betsy. I want to be prepared when God calls me home. If I sew this now, it will take the burden off others. You and Ann and your Father."

"No."

"I am not afraid to go home to the Lord."

"You are talking nonsense, Mama. We need you here. Anny and Johnny are still children. Father, me, your friends, we all need you. Besides, we've had quite enough death in this family for a while, don't you think? Prepare your shroud if you must, but you will not be requiring it anytime soon. And if you believe you do, I shall not leave."

Mother wagged her head at me, dismissing me. "You are sailing next week, my darling girl. I remember the excitement of my own crossing. I do not believe you will regret it, not a whit! What a marvelous time you'll have."

"Well, you making your funeral cloth, for one, deters me from going," I said pointedly.

She sighed. "Oh, Elizabeth."

I let it go. "I fear Reverend Peters's health is so poor that he may not make the journey, Mama. If I were to arrive and find myself alone . . ."

"I confess I've had my own doubts, watching him at suppers and during services. I discussed it with your father, however, and Thomas feels he is well enough. The sea air will do Peters good; to delay may be more unkind. Your father says reaching England quickly will help him the most. Once you arrive, Richard will be in good hands there with Dr. Fothergill. And, of course, you'll travel with servants. You won't be alone. Father has seen to that."

"What if he dies there before we return? What would I do?"

I meant with his body, but I couldn't bring myself to say it. Reverend Peters was a sixty-year-old clergyman who had twice married and left both wives before leaving for America thirty years ago, although his marriages happened innocently enough. He believed his first wife dead when she was not, and she reappeared when he unwittingly married the second. Besides all that, surely Peters would want to be buried at Christ Church? Was there such a thing as an ocean passage to return a corpse?

"Pray that he does not. And pray that you and the servants remain well."

New Castle, Delaware
June 1764

I, Elizabeth Graeme of Horshamtown, was about to cross the great ocean that separated us from our mother country. I supposed I should have been frightened, but I was not. I was standing on the deck of a merchant ship as a passenger! I could hardly believe it. Here I was, twenty-seven years old and unmarried, and about to sail to England! What a great adventure!

My temporary home for the next several weeks would be a cabin on the *Britannia* with three other women of my class from Philadelphia, and our maids. Reverend Peters was similarly ensconced in his cabin along the way with male companions and their manservants. For the next month, we would rely on God's grace and good winds to see us safely to a shore three thousand miles away. God bless the black water that had to swirl about our boat to deliver us there.

Our sleeping space was sparse but clean, with enough comforts and simple elegance to make the journey bearable, a perk of the ticket price we paid. As I expected, we were in close quarters, there was barely enough room to turn in a circle without bumping into a bunk or the small table. Storage was a narrow cupboard behind the door. At least we had lantern that swung from the cabin ceiling.

I put away my things. I had tried not to bring much. I placed my books under my bunk, Laurence Sterne's *The Life and Opinions of Tristram Shandy, Gentleman* and Edward Young's *Cynthio*. I had my pens and ink and three blank books to write travel journals to send home. I had also brought two decks of cards to while away the time and a small series of needlework canvases and several skeins of thread.

"This is my first time on a ship of this size," I told Reverend Peters above deck as we looked around at the flurry of activity around us.

"She's a beauty," he said as a lock of white hair bounced over his forehead. "This is certainly an oceangoing craft."

Seagulls circled us, hungry for food, as we stood and marveled at the sights before us. I drank it all in, tried to hold it in my mind to write about later, the crew and the complexities of the boat, the ropes and ladders and gear. Men young and old scurried about and called to each other, crew with faces the color of boiled lobsters and brown trout, skin wrinkled as raisins. I watched them load a cow onto the ship to provide butter and cream, I guessed, and several chickens and crates of apples, oranges, and pineapples. We were informed by a crew member that breakfast would be at eight each day, dinner at one, supper at nine.

My exhilaration was short-lived. For three days, we waited for the weather to oblige as we slowly lurched across New Castle harbor what seemed like an inch at a time. The anchor was dropped in short segments, whenever they could get a whiff of breeze. Finally, on the fourth day, the crew found wind that filled the sails and bore us eastward. We were under way! The boat surged through the water like some great mythical beast.

Many years ago, I'd heard Dr. Franklin tell tales of his first time sailing to England as a boy in the 1720s. He hunted dolphins from the boat and jumped from the ship to take baths in the salty sea. It all sounded so grand and so terrifically *free*. Now that it was my *own* feet on the deck of this sailboat, I could not imagine jumping in the dark water, unfathomably deep and cold, or hunting dolphins. I suddenly understood why Deborah Franklin refused to make the journey. As the *Britannia* picked up speed, I wondered if I had made a mistake. I had no diplomatic business to conduct, no business at all for that matter; no husband to reunite with, no family save for remote cousins in Scotland that I had never met. What was it William had said? That he did not want to undertake the journey a second time given his near-perilous arrival in England, when his boat was almost wrecked on rocks off the coast. God help me. But it was too late to turn back now. We were in open water.

I looked up at the brilliant blue sky and said a silent prayer. Underneath my shoes the deck was worn smooth from years of the beating of feet and salt. The sails billowed above us, vast and white, the seagulls crying as they soared and dipped.

I watched as land fell from view. Excitement, nerves, terror, exhilaration, I had every emotion at the same time. I looked at Reverend Peters, who winked at me. He had made this trip already and possessed sufficient confidence that we would arrive in one piece. He fully expected to be reunited with his family in a few weeks.

Just last Sunday I had sat in our family pew at Christ Church and listened to him say a farewell to the congregation. Peters asked the congregation for prayers and good wishes, which came in droves afterward as we were hugged and kissed with the goodwill of hundreds. I would miss Liza terribly, and Anny and Johnny, and Mama of course, but I was comforted that they would continue on in my absence until I returned and fill me in on all that I missed.

As the days passed I found myself an able sailor, free from seasickness despite the temperamental roil of the sea. I spent many hours in fine weather on the main deck with Reverend Peters and the ladies as we gazed in awe at the interplay of sea and sky and wildlife. I watched osprey fly by and sharks slide past. Schools of mackerel glimmered in the sun, and whales leaped from the water, immense and breath-taking. The sky itself was a canvas that painted itself through a range of dazzling blues to solid walls of gray. At sunset streaks of molten red and orange and pink blazed over the horizon. I especially loved when great white clouds shifted and rolled across the horizon like bags of white down. Oh, if I could paint what my eyes saw!

One afternoon I had the sensation of becoming the sea and sky and boat all at *once*, as if there were no division at all between me and the world. I was free, without form. That night I tried to describe it in my journal:

I could not help observing that whatever way the ship moved we appeared to be in the center of a circle, for the sea seems to be a perfect circle, surrounded by clouds that look as if they bent down at the edges to join it, so that our own eyes form the horizon, and like self-love, we are always placing ourselves in the middle, where all things move around us.

With my own eyes I had seen one of the finest sights there was to see, I was sure of it. I felt as if I had glimpsed God himself, sensed the immense beauty of an unspeakable glimpse of eternity.

When the weather was bad or I felt unwell with my one of my headaches, I was content to lie in my bunk. If my pains were mild, I would converse and play cards with my companions, or read. One of the ladies had a passion for backgammon, although sometimes we played chess. I did my needlework, although not often; the sway of the sea made my hands unsteady.

Poor Reverend Peters was often poorly. The pains in his chest confined him to his cabin often, although he did his best to make light of his situation. After we made landfall and spent time in Liverpool, we were going to go to the baths at Scarborough to take the healing waters there. I had high hopes for the cures of Dr. Fothergill, who had an estate that was said to have an unusual garden filled with healing plants. When Father was the port physician he had met Dr. Fothergill's brother when he visited Philadelphia. Father spoke highly of the family and their many talents with medicine and healing.

Overall I was content with my passage on the *Britannia*. The food was not too bad, the ship in good repair. The crew seemed well trained and obedient to our captain. We were blessed by mostly good weather.

After four weeks at sea, our captain announced that we would soon make landfall. England at last!

Chapter 15

England
July 1764

Liverpool teemed with life and dwarfed Philadelphia by
its size and exotic flavors.

"Aye, Liverpool's the second most important port in
Britain now," one of my fellow travelers said as we
approached, himself a Brit. "Have you heard of the Liverpool
Triangle? They export our manufactured goods from Mersey
to Africa for slaves, then sell the slaves for plantation crops
in the West Indies. Liverpool is one of England's biggest
ports now, as important as London and Bristol. You can get
anything you want here from anywhere in the world."

The onslaught of strange accents as we disembarked
was both hard on the ear and a reminder that I was far from
home. I felt like my delight would bubble over. We had made
it! I was standing on English soil!

"Over there!" Peters yelled to me. He pointed.

"Sorry?" I called back. I could not hear much.
Everywhere people were crying out greetings as crates and
trunks banged together and workers called to each other.
Then I saw that he was pointing at a woman hurrying
toward us.

I expected Peters's sister to be like him, round-faced and
soft-bellied, with that implacable air of steadfastness and
patience. She was not that.

"Lass!" she screamed as she launched herself at me, and
threw her arms around my neck. She was hardly bigger
than a knitting needle in girth. She was slender, bony,
almost, her face lined so that her cheeks looked as if they
had been divided from the rest of her face with a surgeon's
knife, so deep were the trenches on either side of her nose.

She wasn't ugly, no, she was a handsome woman, dressed well, but she had none of her brother's refinement.

"I've heard all about you!" she screeched, and held me at arm's length to look in my face. "I didn't expect you to be a beauty," she added with a frown, as if that were an unexpected problem. "Richard didn't say. Anyway, what do they call you? Lizzie? Beth? Betty?"

"Elizabeth is fine," I answered, wiggling from her close grasp. I did not want her to call me Betsy. It reminded me of the easy familiarity of my mother and sisters. Peters's sister was already too familiar and we had only just met. I knew she would order me about as easily as one of her children if I allowed it.

"Call me Abitha!" she yelled, and launched herself at her brother a second time. "Oh Ricky! Thirty years! How could you do that to us!"

Reverend Peters gathered her in his arms and hugged her close.

"That's our ma," a slight man said with a grin in my direction. He thrust out a hand. "I also am Richard. Nice to meet you, Elizabeth. Welcome to Liverpool."

"Named for your uncle." I smiled.

"I'm Lydia," a woman said quietly, Richard's sister. To my relief, Abitha's grown children were far less exuberant than their mother.

"I'll fetch your baggage," young Richard offered with a glance at our servants, "and get you home to get settled. What a long journey you've had."

"How lovely to arrive in England in the summer," Abitha said as we walked down the dock towards the waiting coaches. "We'll show you everything there is to see! Your mother is from St. Albans, isn't that so? I have never been there myself, but I have friends who have, and I'll introduce you."

The Peters lived in a modest home not far from the water. Abitha was a gracious hostess, and attentive, but it soon became apparent that her yelling was a cover for a body in decline. She tired easily, and did not each much at meals. Abitha appeared once a day to put on a show of liveliness, then the effort seemed to diminish her, and she disappeared to her room. She often asked her brother to take tea with her in her chamber. It was her children who escorted Reverend Peters and I around town and through the countryside.

I was fascinated by Liverpool. It was easily the richest town I had ever seen, although I hadn't been to London yet. The houses were built high over the streets in brick and stone, and the city was far cleaner than Philadelphia. The town hall was grand, imposing, and there was a stately financial exchange. Young Richard explained the wealth was from brisk sea trade, abundant wool production, and a burgeoning cotton industry. Shops and trade were plentiful. Even the poor seemed to fare far better than the poor in Philadelphia.

A month later, we'd had our fill of parlors and tea and seen what we could of the surrounding countryside. We appealed to Abitha let us be on our way to Yorkshire and the spa. She agreed on the condition that Reverend Peters return before we sailed.

If Liverpool dazzled me, the spa was another world entirely. It was a true spectacle. Many said they were there to take the waters for their health, but few actually seemed ill. Whatever their illnesses were, the complaints did not stop spa guests from parading about in clothes more suited to fashionable salons in London. Every day I met odd characters that tickled me to no end. I carefully wrote down my impressions in my travel book, picturing Mother and Liza and Ann in fits of laughter over my descriptions.

Our daily routine was more a holiday than a medicinal cure. Every morning at eight we climbed into a carriage of glass that was as big as a house, really, it was so large. We watched the beach draw closer as the horses padded down to the shore, pulling the glass carriage. We waded into the sea in our flannel swimming costumes, and bounced in the curative waves. The water was cold, which made it hard to enjoy, and I wondered at the reality of the professed benefits. After our swim, we made our way back into the carriage and up to the spa to change and have breakfast. After the midday meal, another coach arrived in the afternoon to take us to the horse races at Scarborough. I thought it an odd combination, for illness and excitement seldom made good healing partners. I was sure Father would find it a strange thing too. Often several unhappy participants lost money and left with empty pockets and a sour face. After the races, we went back to the gathering room for cards and dancing. We always ate a late supper.

Reverend Peters began to tire of the cold water and biting breeze each morning and refused to keep going. He preferred the comfort and warmth of the lounge and began to spend all his time there. There was no shortage of company for him. I didn't like drinking the water but I still forced it past my lips three times a day. The water stank and tasted as awful as bad eggs. I felt no different for having endured the drinking of it, either.

I myself seldom turned down an outing. Just being there, not in Philadelphia or at Graeme Park, felt healing to me. I enjoyed the sensation of being untethered, the physicality in my body that went with the feeling of being free. I never tired of my feet covered in sand, or the wind that played havoc in my hair, or the sharp cold bite of the water. When I bobbed in the waves and looked around me, it was all entirely refreshingly new. How gloriously unencumbered I felt.

I savored my freedom. How thrilling it was to be no one at all, completely anonymous. When I was in Philadelphia, even three years after the end of my engagement, people would still warn me if William Franklin and his wife were in town, or about to pass through, as if I should hide. Years later I was still being whispered about behind raised fans. Would I ever get past being the jilted woman?

Each evening at the spa almost five hundred people made their way to the gathering room for the evening's activities. I could move through any room as a femme mystérieuse. I could say what I wished, meet someone without them already knowing my father or having been to a party, or six, with my mother or sisters. Impossibly, I had been liberated from the confines of the small world of Philadelphia. How exciting to be just another woman in a pretty gown!

I could even, if I wished, yell at the racetrack, as I was doing now. I stood on the balcony with a group of new friends from the spa and surveyed the list of horses on a paper in my hand to pick my next horse. A tall man next to me turned to me.

"Who do you think will win?" he asked, his eyes on the sleek hind muscles of a horse being walked to the starting line.

"I will bet on the horse that no one thinks will win," I answered glibly.

His eyes met mine in surprise. "Whatever for? You are guaranteed to lose your money."

"Ah, but the race is never really awarded to the swift, nor the battle to the strong, is it, sir?" I replied carelessly.

His face creased in a grin, and he turned fully to me and extended his hand. When I met his gaze I saw he was handsome. He introduced himself as Laurence Sterne.

"Not the writer!" I gasped.

"Guilty as charged," he said. "But you must try to like me anyway."

"I read *Tristram Shandy* on the way over from America," I said, wanting to pinch myself. My pulse thumped wildly. "I have read your books!"

He acknowledged this with a graceful bow but did not want to speak of his work. We watched the horses race, talking of everything and nothing for ages. Laurence Sterne had an easy intelligence and wit, and a mocking attitude that suited me fine in my current mood. All too soon the races came to an end, and our group was called back to the coach.

"A shame you did not win," he said with another grin. "I daresay it might have been your strategy that caused your downfall."

"Likewise, I'm sure," I said smartly, for he had fared no better and had enjoyed no winnings.

"I wish we could speak longer," he said with feeling. "Sadly, I am returning home tomorrow."

"A shame," I agreed. "We are leaving for London soon as well."

"I believe you said you are staying in the spa lodgings? Will you be at the dance tonight?"

"I will." My heart was in my throat.

"Then I shall visit you, if you allow me the honor. I find myself quite enchanted by you, Miss Graeme. Permit me to call on you."

"I would be happy to continue our acquaintance," I said, with real pleasure. "But I warn you, Mr. Sterne, hundreds attend the dance. You may find me hard to find in the crowd."

"I shall look for you tirelessly," his eyes crinkled. "Surely Apollo will lend me his torch so I may find you."

I tore myself away from him against my will as I returned to our waiting coach to return to the spa.

I could not wait to get back and find Reverend Peters and let him know that I had met Laurence Sterne and that I would see him again tonight! *The* Laurence Sterne who wrote *Tristram Shandy* and so much more. I still could not believe my luck. Laurence Sterne had called me wise and amusing and so many beguiling things. I floated down the hall feeling like the girl I had been ten years before, replaying our conversations from the day over and over in my mind.

Later that night I talked Reverend Peters into going to the assembly room with me and held him hostage until the early hours of the morning. I chose my brightest dress and wore my hair in the way my mother liked, piled high in the front so the light could catch it, a single braid tied with a ribbon curling over the front of my shoulder. My eyes kept going to the door. At midnight, I asked the front desk if Laurence Sterne had arrived.

No, they said, he had not.

I never saw him again.

We spent several more weeks at the spa, though Peters stopped drinking the waters altogether, claiming intestinal distress. He was weary of the spa's clientele; their foppery annoyed him and made him yearn for the earnestness of a church congregation.

"You are better suited to this crowd than I, Elizabeth," he remarked. "You are like a songbird, flitting among them, singing to those who are blessed to hear your song. There is no one who isn't better for your company."

"Sometimes I prefer a more serious audience, too," I remarked.

We left the spa at the beginning of September. Peters was keen to reach London and see his friends, Thomas and Juliana Penn, and conduct his church business. The Penns had two homes, their summer home at Stokes Poges in Buckinghamshire, and their London house near Charing Cross, called Spring Gardens. Reverend Peters would stay with them at Spring Gardens while I stayed in rented rooms on Craven Street. I would have stayed there too but they only had one unoccupied bed left.

I gaped like a fish as our carriage rolled through London. The city was ancient and overwhelming and impossibly large. Some streets stank with despair, reeking of sewage and offal, but others glittered with wealth and sweeping architecture. Everything I'd known in Philadelphia was magnified to the power of ten or more. There were people everywhere, both rich and poor, in a startling expanse of humanity.

Peters laughed at my wonder. "Close your mouth, child," he said good-naturedly.

Pigs and dogs ran freely in the street, skirting around the horses and carts and heavy pedestrian traffic. The Thames was clogged with more boats and wharves than I could count. The dome of St. Paul's Cathedral towered over the skyline, more beautiful than any building I had seen in my life. We drove past beggars sleeping on church steps and scruffy small children pushing carts of wares to sell, and men of high station striding along with their shoe buckles glinting in the sun.

By the time we arrived at the Penns, I was bursting with what I'd seen and eager to write my thoughts in my travel journal.

The Penns had the wealth of Midas, judging by Spring Gardens, yet Lady Juliana seemed unaffected by her earthly riches. I found her humble, without affectation, and I liked her immensely. She was very beautiful, her body had the fluidity and grace of a bolt of unraveled silk, even though she was halfway through a pregnancy. Her husband, Thomas, I noted, had to be thirty years her senior.

"You just wait, Elizabeth," Lady Penn said, "until we show you London! You may not ever go home!"

"I'll send you to your rooms with my manservant, Edmund," Peters said decisively. "He'll look after you."

My Craven Street accommodations suited me perfectly. I had rooms within walking distance to Trafalgar Square and St. James's Park. My sitting room was large, tastefully decorated, and fine enough for entertaining. I had my chamber, a water closet, and everything that I could possibly wish for in terms of food and drink and comforts. I liked my landlady, Mrs. Bloop, who was a pleasant widow who mostly kept to herself.

I was pleased when Juliana Penn's eighteen-year old niece, Hannah, came to visit and we spent two weeks walking the city, the servants in tow, seeing the sights, dining out, and accepting dinner invitations from friends of friends who had been in Philadelphia, or knew Reverend Peters, or my father, or the Franklins. We even called on Liza's distant relatives, the London Stedmans. We walked through the newly opened British Museum, saw *Macbeth*, listened to a symphony at a music hall, and shopped for new gloves and trinkets on Oxford Street. I sent my nephew Johnny a writing desk, and chose a new gown and stomacher for Anny. For Mother, I chose perfume; for Father, a new pipe made of walnut. For my sister Ann, I selected fabric in a deep emerald color that would make her pale skin look as clear and fine as alabaster.

November came before I knew it, and with it came heavy skies and long evenings devoid of sunlight. Reverend Peters went back to Liverpool to spend time with his ailing sister. I was surprised to find myself alone in London with a bad head. I tried to treat my headaches, but they only got worse, and eventually I asked Dr. Fothergill to call on me.

Fothergill was in his fifties and unmarried. I knew he lived with a sister who was also unmarried. He was a Quaker, gentle spirited, easy to be with. There was no lack in our conversation, for he had a lively interest in the world around him, all aspects, and as well would entertain me with medical stories from his work at St. Thomas's Hospital. In turn I tried to tell him what life was like in Pennsylvania. He was particularly interested in the trials we faced with the Indians, although it had been relatively peaceful since 1760, and quite uneventful since the Treaty of Paris was signed.

"How long have you suffered?" he asked me over tea in my sitting room.

"How long have I suffered from headaches? All my life," I answered. "For as long as I can remember. They come and go. There doesn't seem to be any rhyme or reason to them."

"I meant now, this time."

"Almost two weeks. I thought perhaps it was the air, the coal fires are insufferable. They suffocate me to no end." It was an element I despaired of in London. On cold days, the sky turned dark, hanging low and thick as black wool.

"You're not used to it, I'm afraid."

"We burn wood at home. A wood burning fire smells so fragrant."

"Unfortunately, we destroyed most of our forests in the middle ages. England is a relatively small island. No danger of running out of coal, mind you. Most people, especially the poor, have no choice but to put up with coal smoke if it means being warm in the winter."

"Understandable. And how fortunate that our colonies can provide the timber to build your English ships," I said, thinking of the carts straining under their piles of logs, headed to the docks back home. There were twelve shipbuilders in Philadelphia when I left, and I expected new ones to be there when I returned home, to meet the soaring demand.

Fothergill nodded. "Indeed."

"I'll be fine though," I added. "My headaches are a part of me."

"What about your humors? Have you been missing home?"

"Yes. Well, no. I mean, of course I miss home, but Philadelphia will be there when I return. My family and friends, they'll all be waiting for me. I don't know when I will be able return to London again, so I am soaking up my time here. The sights are so wonderful to someone from Pennsylvania. I just sent another travel journal home yesterday. They will scarcely be able to believe what I've said."

"And tell me, what impresses you most?"

I thought a moment. "I think the experience of being here, of being able to walk around and see the sights of a thousand years. The size and history of London is unimaginable until you are here. When I walked through Westminster Abbey, I thought I would burst."

He laughed, a rich, robust laugh that reached his eyes and made them crinkle at the edges. He felt like a dear friend and we'd barely known each other a month or two.

"I felt that Shakespeare and Milton were right next to me in the abbey," I explained. "Like invisible companions. I couldn't help myself, I recited some of their work aloud, wanting to impress them."

"It's enchanting to me to see London through your eyes, when it's all I know. I'm so used to it I can no longer see the forest for the trees. You must come see my garden at Upton," Fothergill said. "We'll bring Reverend Peters as well. I planted a botanic garden filled with herbs for healing. I don't believe there's another garden like it. I'm a rather keen botanist."

"I would like that very much."

"For your headaches, take this tincture." He reached for his medical bag and took out a brown glass bottle and something wrapped in paper. "The herbs are to be steeped and drank three times a day. Valerian and comfrey. If you're really in a bad way, send for me. Otherwise I'll check in next week."

When he left, Mrs. Bloop took the herbs to steep them. "He'll never bleed you, you know," she said. "He doesn't believe in that. He says bleeding should go the way of the torture rack in the Tower. Medieval practices."

I nodded. Somehow, that sounded like Fothergill and what I knew of him so far. I wondered what Ben Rush would think of that, up and coming doctor that he was. And I wished my father could meet Dr. Fothergill. He would find him inspiring.

Reverend Peters did not return to London in December as planned, for his sister continued to struggle with her health. For the first time in my life, I was truly alone. This made me miss everyone at home, but especially my mother, who was always my comfort through the years. I looked forward to her letters, and hung on every word. Her most recent post said that Clara, my maid, had finally earned her freedom and was gone, and that our cook Gretchen had taken ill and they were in the process of hiring another. I resolved to send a note to both of them to wish them well.

Silence pervaded my hours. I found myself missing the sounds of Graeme Park, the constant whirl of people, the noise of Anny and Johnny, the squeak of carriage wheels and good-natured banter of guests. There was no flurry of people going about their business, no dog barking, no sound of women talking and the fields being worked outside. I missed Liza's jokes and my sister Ann's chattering away about fabric and paint and whether she should change the curtains or update the cushions. I even missed the sound of my father flipping the pages of a medical journal by the fire in the evenings.

After the cold weather set in I stopped going out as much. I tried to sleep off one headache after another. Christmas was fast approaching, and it appeared for the first time in my life I would spend it alone.

"You should appreciate this time of solitude as it will bring you closer to God and the true meaning of Christmas," Reverend Peters wrote from Liverpool in his usual paternalistic style. Dear Reverend Peters, so well intentioned and so discouraging without meaning to be.

I knew his sister needed him, and it would be his first Christmas with his family in many years. Luckily, Reverend

Peters' health was also improving under Fothergill's care and he had more wind in his sails.

After the church service I sat in my empty rooms by myself that Christmas. The servants had the day off. I considered my life. I felt a hundred years old, although I was still not yet twenty-eight. I listened to the steady tick of the clock on the mantel, which made me think of our tall clock at Graeme Park. I looked around me at the porcelain and tapestries, the potted plants, the harp in the corner, the big brocade armchair, and calculated what my course of action should be. In the spring, Reverend Peters and I were going to Scotland, the last leg of our trip. If these were my last few months in London, I might as well enjoy them.

For the first time, I had the gift of solitude, which at first was daunting, but then became appealing and jolted me with power. All my years I had been surrounded by others, being told what to do and say and how to act. It occurred to me that without the watchful eyes of Reverend Peters on me, dear as he was to me, I could do as I liked. I almost jumped from my chair. I could do as I liked! Although I possessed no carriage and horses of my own, and no footmen or the means to rent them, there was nothing to stop me from inviting people here. I brightened at the thought. I would be queen of my own estate, unanswerable to *no one*, for the first time in my life!

I went to the door. "Mrs. Bloop," I called, my plan forming in my mind, "how are we for tea and cakes? Shall we go to the market?"

My time as a London socialite was intoxicating. In no time at all, I received six calls for each one I made. They came in a steady stream of damp overcoats and shoes wet from the London winter drizzle, bearing presents and bottles of wine and the pleasure of their company. I never said no to anyone who asked to call. The Penns; the St. Clairs; the Barrows; the Browns; the London Stedmans; and people I met at the theater and opera and music halls, or simply by walking in St. James's park. Dr. Fothergill became a close friend and came three times a week, not to treat me, but to visit and talk about any number of things. He really was the most agreeable man, and possessed such a fine character. Dr. Fothergill's goodness was palpable to me. I had on occasion wondered why he had not married, but caught myself when I realized the same could be said of myself with regard to taking a husband. I never once felt Fothergill's visits had an ulterior motive, he was not a man in want of a wife.

I also formed a close friendship with Juliette Ritchie, Jules, who had separated from her husband and was living in London after returning from Philadelphia last year. For her birthday, I gave her a fan and wrote a poem for her on the back of it.

All in all, I was having a wonderful time.

This evening Colonel Gram and his wife were here, friends of my parents. I visited them at their home a few weeks ago, and they were returning the social call.

"Has Mrs. Penn had her child?" Mrs. Gram asked, a thick finger with a large ruby ring tapping her armrest.

I nodded. "She has, a little girl. They have called Sophia. Hannah is thrilled to be able to be there to help care for a newborn."

"Ah, how wonderful." Mrs. Gram nodded in approval. "Juliana's well? The birth was not too taxing on her?"

"It all went very soundly, from what I hear."

"Splendid," Colonel Gram said. "We'll send a gift."

"I do wish Mrs. Penn had had the chance to introduce you at court before her confinement," Mrs. Gram said to me. "For then I could have taken you as my guest at the party to celebrate the king's birthright next week. Frank, can you have Elizabeth introduced at court before the party next week?"

I shook my head quickly. "Oh no, really, that is not necessary." I had no desire to meet the king. That was for other people, not for girls from Pennsylvania.

Frank chewed a piece of fudge and considered it. "Yes, perhaps I could."

"My dear, you are in London," Mrs. Gram admonished me. "Why shouldn't we use Colonel Gram's station to introduce you to His Highness? This is England!"

I demurred again, but to my astonishment, many weeks later, at the insistence of Colonel Gram and his wife, I found myself standing in front of King George III at a reception. I realized with some surprise we were less than a year apart in age. The king was pleasant, and I found him sensible and calm, even pious, and said so in a letter home. The public did not seem to dote on him in the way I expected. The people of England claimed their king was too fond of domestic life at home. It seemed King George III was committed to his wife and young sons and did not wish to take a mistress, making him a far cry from other salacious kings. His subjects saw this as a sign of weakness, as if his personal contentment would lead to a complacency in his empire's political power.

One afternoon not long after I met King George, I reluctantly received one man I would have rather not seen: Dr. Benjamin Franklin.

"You look well, dear," Franklin said, sitting down on the sofa, rubbing at his stiff leg.

Mrs. Bloop was there to defend my honor, and sat crocheting in her chair in the corner, in her good dress, I noticed. I had explained Franklin was an old family friend and she need not be there. "Still," she'd said, fixing her cap and eyeing the oil painting on the wall, her mouth set.

Really, the companion I required was Reverend Peters, so I could see more of London than was available to me as a single woman, even with his manservant Edmund in tow, and my maid. I needed the asylum and protection of a man with status. But there was still no word from him.

"I *am* well," I said to Franklin. "Very well, thank you. London is a wonder, is it not? I have even met the king; can you believe it! He was very gracious. And are you well, Dr. Franklin?"

He had aged in the past couple of years. He must be about sixty now, his hairline receding more steeply, showing more of his forehead. His hair was long at the back, straight and gray, to his shoulders, and he wore no wig. He still had those keen eyes, belying the genial expression on his face.

"I have just passed my fifty-ninth birthday, so any accommodations I must make for this aging body are to be tolerated," he said. "It seems an age since I was swimming and leaping off cliffs in my youth. Still, age is an honor not bestowed on all, so one must be grateful for it."

I poured a glass of port for him at the sideboard and another for myself.

"We all admire your industry, sir. A day in your life is never wasted," I said, thinking of his civic work, his diplomatic missions, his electrical experiments, his business interests, his stove, his armonica. The last thought I pushed away, remembering that sad day in his parlor when the armonica played a mournful elegy to my lost dreams. "What brings you back to London? I did not know you were coming."

"After I lost my seat in the Assembly, I was sent to persuade the king to take Pennsylvania away from the Penns. I am pleased to hear you think him gracious."

"And make it a royal colony?" Like New Jersey, where his son still sat as governor.

"Ah my dear, I have missed your sharp mind. You don't miss a thing. Colonies run by a family in power make it unnecessarily complicated to govern well. The interests of the people get lost. A royal colony, however, directly governed by the king, will—"

"Take out the middleman, so to speak," I finished for him.

"Just so," he agreed.

"A weighty problem," I murmured. "You have your work cut out for you."

I did not wish to discuss orders of government. I thought of my friends the Penns, and how what Franklin was proposing would impact them.

I took a sip of my port, then another one. "I have only been in London a few months, and you were here for years. Tell me, what sights must I see?"

"First, I promised your mother I would inform her of your well-being in London. Tell me, what shall I relay? I will compose a letter to Deborah tonight."

"Tell her I'm happy and that I have recovered my health here. Tell her I do not want for visitors and friends. And that I look forward to being in her company again."

I glanced toward the corner and caught Mrs. Bloop staring at Dr. Franklin, her crochet hook still. How curious, that he should garner such admiration everywhere he went. He had only been here a short time, minutes in fact, and Mrs. Bloop was gazing at him with open curiosity. And admiration? Normally she did not raise her eyes, lost in whatever work was on her lap. She saw me looking and dropped her head and returned to her crochet.

"Consider it done," he said. "I will write of your good health and high spirits. As for sights, have you been to St. Paul's Cathedral? You'll visit Parliament, of course, if you haven't already. And if you can, you must see the art at Windsor Castle."

"Oh I did, I went to Windsor! I saw the paintings by Rubens and Van Dyck. I marveled at St. George and the Dragon, that spectacular horse and cloak. And how glorious is Saint Martin and the Beggar! They have similar subject matter, yet they are worlds apart! Van Dyck makes you doubt what you are seeing on the canvas, for it's almost too real to be a painting. The way he achieved the nuance in the musculature defies belief. I couldn't believe the way the pictures are just hanging there on the wall, as common as a simple wooden cross, as if one could simply reach out a hand and take a painting as they walked past."

"I am sure they are well guarded, despite appearances."

"One would hope."

"You've been to the plays here, I assume?"

"No armonica concerts, though. Sadly."

He grinned, then chuckled.

"Did you know the shell collection at the British Museum is not as beautiful as Dr. Fothergill's?" I asked. Dr. Fothergill and Dr. Franklin were friends. Come to think of it, Dr. Franklin seemed to be friends with every soul he met, except for the Penns.

Franklin smiled and shook his head, then took off his spectacles to wipe them with a handkerchief.

"You have such a faculty with words, Miss Graeme, as usual. I admire you. I can see why half of London cannot stay away."

To whom had he been speaking? How would he have known that?

"So what news of Philadelphia?" I asked. "How is my family? Is Father faring well at the Philosophical Society meetings?"

"All are fine and missing you," he said simply. "I have heard nothing to the contrary. Your father beams with pride and talks at length of your letters and journals. From what I hear your travel journals have caused a sensation in our city of brotherly love."

"And what other news?"

His general news matched what I knew from the papers. Since the end of the French and Indian War and the worst of the Indian uprisings, the colonies were enjoying a time of peace. France lost Canada and gave Louisiana to Spain, which eliminated France's claims in North America and effectively removed France as England's rival in the colonies. Now America was stronger than ever, firmly under Britain's command. King George III gave the Indians the protection of the Ohio Valley and ordered his American subjects to honor the boundary line. Franklin said that Pennsylvania still needed access to the king's ear, representation in Parliament, and a say in how we would be taxed and governed. The colonies were still disgruntled and apprehensive at their child-like status under Britain.

We talked easily, and an hour later Franklin stood to go.

"Thank you for letting me call on you," Franklin said sincerely. A stray thought of William swept through my mind like the fall of an autumn leaf.

"England has been kind to me," I said. "No one need worry about me here."

He bowed his head in acknowledgment and said farewell.

Mrs. Bloop stood too, her eyes on him, gleaming, as he left. What was it about Dr. Franklin that he managed to gather women everywhere he went, especially at his age?

Chapter 16

London and Bristol
Spring 1765

"We're going to visit Bristol for three weeks," I told
Fothergill. "Then we're off to Scotland after that."

I would finally get to meet the Balgowan Graemes, then
we would head home.

"I hope I won't regret leaving your medical care!"
Fothergill had seen me through the worst of my wintertime
maladies, including a gallbladder attack and a bout with
kidney pain.

Fothergill was unconcerned. "Bristol is not so far. Drink
the waters there and bathe in the hot springs and you'll be
fine. I am more worried, Betsy, that yesterday you were
made a slave of."

He must have heard about the suitor Mrs. Gram
introduced me to, a minor lord from Kent. The man was far
too bland for my liking.

"Sir, I am slave to no man, I assure you," I retorted. "My
heart and my hand are entirely free." Why were men always
so quick to put a woman in bondage? We must ruffle their
sensibilities and make them nervous if we are uncaged.

"No, not a man, my dear, the Stamp Act," Fothergill
said, deeply amused. "England has levied its first direct tax
on the colonies to raise revenue. Fiery Massachusetts will go
mad. The Act becomes law in September."

Massachusetts was well known for its rebellious
thinkers who pushed back against the long arm of England.
Some of the men there formed a secret group they call the
Sons of Liberty, which advocated for colonists' rights and
fought unfair taxation. It couldn't be much of a secret, I
thought, if I knew about the group's rebellious agenda.

Fothergill explained the Stamp Act would place a tax on all paper documents, including newspapers, playing cards, and all legal items, including licenses. The colonies were used to taxation as a part of trade, but the Stamp Act was something entirely new. We would be taxed without receiving any benefit. The tax dollars raised would all go directly back to England, and not stay on our soil to benefit the colonies.

"I wonder how that will go," I mused. "If you consider that for a hundred and fifty years we've loosely done whatever we wanted."

"It was an expensive war," Fothergill said drily. "And even if it wasn't, the king wants to fill his purse. There will be rioting in your American streets, you can count on it."

I did not care for drinking the waters of Bristol any more than I liked drinking the waters of Scarborough. If they possessed healing powers, the elixir fell flat on me. I thought more highly of Dr. Fothergill's healing herbs and tonics.

Reverend Peters joined me in Bristol for three weeks before receiving word that his sister's health had declined again. He rushed to Liverpool, and I returned to London.

What a different place London was in the spring! The brick buildings of Craven Street were covered in climbing ivy, wisteria, honeysuckle and clematis. Gardens were bursting with May roses of all shades and varieties. Everywhere I looked there was light and color and growth.

I might have begun to miss my friend and companion, Reverend Peters, but instead fate brought me a breath of fresh air.

"I am Nathaniel Evans," he said at a dance at the Bowery, and bowed low over my hand. "Pleased to make your acquaintance."

"Nathaniel Evans the poet," Jules Ritchie said. "I've heard of you! I used to live in Philadelphia. I'm Juliette Ritchie. Please call me Jules."

This Nathaniel Evans was slim, almost slight, and dark-haired. I noticed his fingers, slender and white, like fluttering paper birds. These were not the hands of a tradesman or farmer.

"My friend is a poet too," Jules said. "You have much in common, for she is visiting from Philadelphia as well."

He raised an eyebrow. "Elizabeth Graeme, I presume?"

We spluttered at the recognition.

"I'm flattered that you know me," I laughed. "You do presume correctly."

"I was sent by Reverend William Smith to be ordained here," Nathaniel explained. "His wife is a close friend of yours, I believe? She told me about you with great enthusiasm."

"Rebecca!" I exclaimed. "She certainly is a close friend, my very dear friend. What a small world it can be."

We spent the evening getting to know the young poet. Nathaniel Evans was earnest, he felt the cares of the world deeply, and yet there was something almost childlike about him. He did not possess the wit of Laurence Sterne or the shrewdness of William Franklin, but had a thoughtful quiet intelligence. His eyes took in the smallest detail in someone, the slightest flicker of emotion. Although in some ways, he reminded me of William, for Nathaniel also wanted social justice and spoke at length of helping the poor. You could cut yourself on William's intellect; Nathaniel's mind had fewer sharp angles. His expressive mind was smoother, more serene. He took longer to make his point, and did it more gently, but he was no less intelligent or insightful.

"What is your background?" Jules asked him with interest over a glass of sherry.

"I graduated from the College of Philadelphia," he replied. "I thought I would be a merchant, putting out saffron and silk to sell."

"And instead you'll be putting out sin with salvation," I quipped.

Nathaniel laughed. "Reverend Smith told me all about you, you know. You are missed. He said the city is very dull without you."

"Don't be fooled, I think he was warning you about me," I said.

"Do I need protecting?"

I was being flirtatious with someone I had only just met. I could banter with him as I did with Liza or my sisters, no, make that *sister*. I would never get used to losing Jane.

"Probably," Jules said. "She is dangerous. Very."

"He said I should be wary of your many talents," Nathaniel teased.

"It's true. I make a very smooth cup of chocolate, very velvety. I don't know if I can boil an egg, they won't let me near the kitchen house." Why did my voice sound husky?

Jules cleared her throat.

Nathaniel took a step back and fingered the embroidery on his silk waistcoat absently, then changed the subject.

"I may be guilty of the sin of pride," he said with a glint in his eye. "Reverend Smith said my poems are awful compared to yours."

"Probably true," I said quickly for effect, which made us both laugh.

I thought I saw Jules make a face.

The three of us, Jules a happy third, trotted around London doing as we liked, which mostly involved talking for hours as we strolled through gardens and streets alive with spring. Reverend Peters, satisfied with my companions, took his manservant Edmund back with him to Liverpool.

Nathaniel was a tonic for my soul. It had been almost eight years since I could speak as closely with a man as I had with William. Nathaniel was a good conversationalist with a keen ear for listening carefully, and for a minister, he had a surprising sense of humor, laced with irony and enough of a bite for me to feel entertained. He retained his piety for when it mattered.

When we were together, hours disappeared without being marked as time spent. We discussed literature, tossed around Greek mythology, argued over Roman history and philosophy, deconstructed scripture, and laughed like children at small things. Jules was a contented companion, leaving us to prattle away but joining in when the mood struck her.

I learned Nathaniel was five years younger than me, only twenty-three, although his wisdom stretched far beyond his earth years. He was gifted with words, spoken and written, and they tumbled between us, meeting up with mine, like two creeks that met at a fork and surged into a river.

June arrived. I had been away from home for a year.

I was happy.

Philadelphia
June 1, 1765

Dearest Betsy,
It is my deepest regret to have to tell you that your mother has died. On the 29 of May, our Lord took her home. She begged us not to tell you she was ill.

The letter came in mid-July as I was about to leave with Jules and four of our friends to drift along the Thames on a barge toward Chiswick for the day. At the same time, I had also been packing that morning to go to Dr. Fothergill's summer home, Lea Hall. I had added my cloak to my bag and placed a battered copy of *A Midsummer Night's Dream* on top of it when I heard the post come.

The letter was one of many gathered together and tied with a string. They were dated from the middle of April to the middle of June. One of the letters was in my mother's handwriting.

I fear this illness will be my last.

That line, in her familiar hand, almost broke my heart. My mother was gone. My mother, my constant source of love, my earliest memory of this world and my last memory of home in Philadelphia. She was the thread that stitched us all together, and now we would be forever void of her company. The thought of my absence in her time of need made me cry out in pain. I had not been there for her, had not even known she was ill. After all she had done for me my whole life, I had not been there to comfort her during her last days.

Jules Ritchie spent the day with me as I mourned. Every now and then she quietly gave me a cup and made me drink. First water, then tea, and after night fell, gin.

My poor mother was dead and I was stuck in England. I ached to rush home but could not. Reverend Peters was still in Liverpool with his sister and would be tied up for at least another two months with family matters. We had not yet booked passage home. It would be months before I could set my feet back in Pennsylvania.

Nathaniel brought flowers, Mrs. Bloop hovered with food, and Jules came to hold my hand, but I wanted no company. I sat and cried sometimes and read my Bible and cried again.

"My life will never be the same," I said to the potted plant, not knowing just how true that would be.

"You should still go to Scotland, Betsy," Jules said encouragingly two weeks later. "And to Fothergill's country estate. Your mother would want you to. Besides, what good will rushing home do for your mother now? She's gone. You may as well go. There's nothing anyone can do."

I made the journey with Dr. Fothergill to Lea Hall. Reverend Peters met me there, and together we prayed for the souls of my mother and his sister, who had also passed.

Dr. Fothergill's gardens were as extensive as he had promised. I admired his rare plants in hothouses that were over two hundred and fifty feet long. He said he had three thousand species, which included a tea plant that towered above my head.

"Let me show you my Hortus Siccus," Fothergill said. It was a book from the mid-sixteen hundreds, filled with flower specimens. Each was labelled in Latin with its botanical name, in alphabetical order. "It's similar to a compendium of plants at the University of Padua from the seventeenth century," Fothergill said, almost reverently. "I collect as many as I can."

A garden of its size didn't grow by itself, and Fothergill employed an astounding fifteen permanent gardeners. "And artists," he added when I commented. "To record the new species I grow."

My admiration for him was significant. When I got home, I would tell Benjamin Rush about Fothergill's great healing garden. Perhaps a smaller version of a medical garden could be started at the Pennsylvania Hospital.

"I won't be coming to Scotland with you," Peters announced over toad-in-the-hole one evening, his teeth clicking as he chewed. "I'll send Edmund with you. I need to go back to London to finalize the paperwork from the archdiocese. I also need to spend time at Spring Gardens with the Penns before we sail. There will be no other opportunity. My sister took more of my time than I planned for."

Traveling to meet my relatives at the Graeme ancestral seat was one of the reasons I came on this trip, and the only achievement of any importance I'd hoped to take home with me. How was it fair to simply toss away our plans?

"You made a commitment to me," I said, annoyed. "We said we would go together. Our plans were agreed upon long ago."

"I wish I had the leisure you do," he answered. "You'll tell me all about it, my dear. You'll go without me. Edmund will look after you."

I fumed for days.

"His sister just died," Nathaniel answered soothingly when I wrote to him. "He has lost someone too. He is more aware of time now. The clock waits for no man."

I thought of going back to London, but Nathaniel was still there and I did not want him to think I was returning solely for him. I wasn't sure whether the affection between us was simply friendship from finding comfort with each other in a place away from our normal lives, or a greater connection. In any case, there was no hurry, we both had to return to Philadelphia. We could wait until we got home to renew and explore our acquaintance there. Besides, I really did want to see Scotland. I couldn't be this close and leave for Pennsylvania without making the effort to go.

We sent word to the Scottish Graemes of our impending arrival, hired a coach, and headed north.

Scotland! Scotland was so beautiful words to describe the landscape eluded me. It was late August, and we were gifted with good weather. Every description I thought of failed to convey the sheer majesty of the land before me. I felt as if the mountains and valleys and lochs possessed an ancient magic. When the sun was out, there wasn't one view, there was many, as the light shifted and slid over a land bursting with inexplicable beauty. Rocky peaks dropped dramatically down to glens dappled in purple heather and shrouded in ethereal mist. I thought sadly of the massacre at Culloden, where my brother-in-law Charles had fought twenty years ago. England did its best to end the clan system after that, and suppressed the Gaelic people.

"Still, we go on," my cousin, another Thomas Graeme, said cheerfully when we finally arrived at Balgowan. "Scots are strong, lass."

Thomas welcomed us warmly and proved an excellent host, along with his family. Edmund and my maid joined the servants in their quarters. I was embraced into the family fold, and grateful that I had come. There were many long meals and even longer nights by the fire, getting to know each other.

In my free time I wrote in my journal, took long walks in the gorgeous countryside, and explored my ancestral homeland. Sometimes while I walked, I felt my mother beside me. I could hear her soft voice quietly telling me not to worry. I had re-read all of the letters from the past year before I left London, combing through them for clues. Was her penmanship shaky or weak in places? Had her writing changed? Was she trying to tell me she was unwell without coming out and saying it? No, all the letters looked the same, read the same. I thought of her working on her funeral cloth that day at Graeme Park. If she had known or even just suspected, she had deliberately pushed me toward England anyway.

"I must return to London," I said to my cousin as we rode horses at the end of another beautiful day. "I have so enjoyed these past three weeks, Thomas, I can't begin to tell you how much this means to me. But I must go home."

"You've been just what we needed, lass," Thomas answered. "A fresh slice of the world. I doubt we'll ever make it to America, not at our age. Which reminds me, I want to send something home with you. Come to the library when we get back."

My interest piqued, I duly found the library a short time later. Thomas handed me an armload of books containing his bookplate.

"A gift," he said, showing me the inside cover of the book on the top of the pile. "Something to remember us by. We Graemes have to stick together."

"Thank you," I said, touched and intrigued. I ran my finger over the crest. "The Graeme family coat of arms. How beautiful."

The bookplate was timeless. It made me think of great families over many generations, of wars fought and lost, of royal standards flying high, of the ongoing rhythm of life, of what we leave behind. Maybe it was time for me to stop waiting and step up to my life. I resolved to find an engraver in London. I would design my own coat of arms to create a bookplate for my library at home. Just for me, one woman. Only a woman, but a woman with her own bookplate! I felt a frisson down my spine.

We planned to sail in October.

I was busy. I decided on the design for my coat of arms and paid to have the engraving done. I particularly liked the bird in the center, which reminded me of Graeme Park.

When I got home, I would embroider a silk sampler of my crest.

I said my good-byes. I thought I would be pleased to be heading home to my father and sister, to Anny and Johnny and my real world, but melancholy gripped me in the final days. I could hardly separate pain from pleasure, hardly knew whether I was happy to be sailing or filled with sadness at losing those I cared deeply for here. Even the sight of plain Mrs. Bloop bent over her needlework filled my eyes with tears.

I had no way of knowing if I would ever return to this dazzling city. In London, if you had your health, you could seek and find knowledge and pleasure in so many pursuits, in every mode of life. There was such a variety of arts and sciences and hobbies to explore. There was goodness and virtue here. On the other hand, overindulging in every desire this city offered could cause great weakness in morality over time. I'm sure many lost their way here; London could definitely be a doorway to spiritual decline. I could not help but wonder if that's what happened to William Franklin.

I was delighted by a thousand things in England, had come to love this bewitching country. I had been treated with humanity, respect, and politeness, and received real friendship from so many people, many of them my superiors in life. My dear Mama was born here, so it would always have a piece of my heart. And England had given birth to so many great men whose writings had helped to form our education in America.

One good-bye I did not need to make was to my young poet, for Nathaniel Evans was coming with us. We booked passage on the *Zephyr* and were scheduled to leave from Gravesend on October 7.

England would soon be behind me. What was ahead?

Chapter 17

Philadelphia
December 1765

Land! Home at last! I left the *Zephyr* without a backward glance, free after three interminably long months, much of it battling shrieking gales in the Atlantic. I practically ran off the boat, or tried to, my legs jelly underneath me as I struggled to find equilibrium without water heaving under my feet.

"I'll come see you," Nathaniel called after us. I waved and blew him a kiss.

We missed Christmas by a day. The captain steered us into Philadelphia on December 26. I searched for the city's church spires from the river, feeling as if I were in a strange city on an unknown continent. I had been gone only eighteen months, yet everything was different. I might as well have been gone twenty-five years.

"Thank goodness you're home," Liza threw herself at me in our city home. "It felt like you were away forever."

I embraced her back tightly. "I missed you too. So very much."

I tried not to look for Mother, but she was everywhere. Her unfinished knitting lay balanced on the chair arm, no one had moved it. I counted backward; it had been lying there for six months. Her book was on the table, an embroidered linen strip marking her place. Her green shawl was over the back of her chair, her slippers peaked out from under the footstool. We had embroidered the top of that footstool together, in crewelwork.

My shrinking family gathered in our front room. I looked around. Liza looked healthy. My father seemed thinner. The children had grown taller while I was away, as children do. Anny was nine now and becoming willowy, like her mother.

She was more serious, I thought, more cautious. At seven, Johnny was still a young child, loud and exuberant. My sister Ann and her husband Charles looked well.

I handed out my gifts. Anny and Johnny disappeared upstairs shortly afterward with their arms filled with sweets and toys.

"She didn't want you to know," Liza said when she saw me looking at Mother's empty chair. No one sat in it. "She forbade us to tell you."

"Was she very ill, at the end?" I asked, looking at Jemimah on the mantel, Mother's porcelain doll from childhood. She loved that doll.

"She was," my father said simply. He looked tired, crumpled as a discarded cotton shift. "It was her bowels. Ailments of the intestines are impossible to treat. Mercifully, it was a rapid decline but it's never fast enough when you have to endure pain like that."

"I was with her at the end, Betsy," Ann said. "She was relieved to be going, looked forward to being happy in Christ's love. It was what she prayed for, what she wanted." Her face twisted with emotion. "She told us not to mourn for her."

Charles held his tricorn hat in his lap. "She left us with a message for you. She asked you to forgive her. You know, for not bringing you home."

We all sat so stiffly, as if relaxing may shoot us through with arrows.

"She said we must be sure and tell you that it was her desire that you stay in England until you came back of your own volition," Liza added.

"She could not bear for you to see her suffering," my father said.

"How proud she was reading your travel books," Ann chimed in. "She adored them! We all did, Betsy. You made us feel as if we were there."

"Those journals of yours passed through an untold number of hands," Liza said. "There was always a rush to be next! At one point people were in line. Mother had to promise them she would write down the order."

"You created quite a fuss, you did," my father said proudly.

I looked at my hands folded in my lap. My journals seemed so small and insignificant at this point, all the prattling I did about the clientele at the spa, on meeting Laurence Sterne and the king. I once spent a whole page talking about the height of wigs and hats. None of it seemed to matter now.

"How was the journey home?" asked Charles. "We expected you back in November."

"Horrid. We got caught off the Isle of Wight for three weeks waiting for wind. It took us almost an entire *month* to clear British waters, and then we were tossed about on the sea for another two months after that. It was nothing like the smooth sailing on the way over. I was sure we would never get here."

Ann groaned. "What a tortuous time." She turned to her husband. "See, Charles? That's why I won't go. All that time in a boat and you could drown at a minute's notice!"

"Was it worth it, Betsy?" Liza asked earnestly.

I paused. I thought of the great balls, Westminster Abbey, Windsor, the striking beauty of Scotland's highlands, and all my new friends, dozens of them.

"It was," I answered softly. If it wasn't for Mother, I would have no regrets at all. Nathaniel's steady company saw me through the worst days of mourning in London, and then again as a steadying presence during the hellish trip home. How grateful I was for his friendship. We talked for ages on that boat, and played cards until our eyes swam. Reverend Peters considered him a close friend now as well. I would tell my family about Nathaniel, but not when I had just gotten home, not before discussing Mama.

I looked around again. What would I do without my Mama? I could not begin to fathom the emptiness of this house, of our lives.

"We're beginning to find out just how much Mama took care of," Ann said. "Graeme Park is in a bit of a mess. Summer without her was so . . . difficult."

"I tried my best," Liza said, the words trailing off. "The servants can be so wicked."

"It is wonderful to have you home," my father said with obvious relief. "We'll bring you up to date."

Of course. There it was, dropped in my lap like a heating stone: I was to run Father's household. I was expected to take up where Mother left off. My future was being handed to me, as the last unmarried child, the responsibility was mine. Ann had her husband to look after, and they were busy building a beautiful new house on Third Street. Father needed a hostess. Not to mention he had no other unmarried daughters to help him raise Anny and Johnny until they were old enough for their father to reclaim them. I was the only one left. I would need to become my mother.

For one terrible moment, I thought longingly of my freedom in London and hot tears filled my eyes. I felt ashamed of myself. Of course I would help my aging widowed father.

I looked up and caught Liza's eye. She gazed at me sympathetically. I could hear her thoughts: *We'll do it together.*

I found Philadelphia much changed. True to Dr. Fothergill's predictions, my hometown had become an angry place. Protest meetings were being held over the Stamp Act, and everywhere heads were lowered, voices whispering urgently. Tax collectors were openly harassed in the streets and frequently attacked. The increase in violence and discontent was noticeable. Palpable, even.

"We are boycotting British goods," Liza explained. "Until Parliament repeals the Stamp Act. We're all going to wear what we have for the next while, or make our own manufactures."

In New Jersey, someone hung an effigy of a tax collector by the neck from a tree. The papers made an engraving of it and reprinted it at length across the colonies. The tree was named *Liberty*. They left that effigy hanging for days, its fabric limbs twirling grotesquely in the wind as a warning.

"If the king can levy the Stamp Act on us," my friend John Dickinson argued, "what else will he do? There is no end to his power over us. We all feel the rough twist of rope against our neck. This is not just about money! Our very way of life is threatened."

Even my father was unhappy. "Such a tax," he muttered. "Brought down on our heads without so much as a whisper."

"It's only a tax," I said, hoping to relieve the tension.

"A tax brought down like a club, from across a vast ocean. We had no say in it. Sets an example, aye? And where will that money go? Not here."

People were up in arms everywhere, in the market, in taverns and coffeehouses, in private homes, on the street, in churches and meetinghouses and in the shops. The consensus was roughly the same—after a hundred and fifty years of relatively autonomous control in our local governments, none of the colonies appreciated the slap.

I thought of what Fothergill had said to me. "Parliament has the power to do many things which they have no *right* to do. Taxes should be levied only by the same people *who are going to pay them*."

There was no denying the general foul mood of the city. This only increased when Commander Coville ordered the seizure of every vessel that attempted to dock without with the required stamp on their papers. Philadelphia simmered with rage.

"People think Dr. Franklin had a hand in the Stamp Act from London," Liza explained to me. "While you were gone a mob stormed his house here in September, and Deborah held them off with a pistol. They tried to burn down their house. She is lucky she escaped with her life. A pack of local men came to her aid."

I struggled to understand. Franklin had helped create so much of Philadelphia: our college, hospital, fire insurance company, first free public library, and more. If a mob had stormed the house of one of our most respected citizens, the face of Philadelphia, when his wife was home alone, we were entering calamitous times. Who else would they attack?

The notion that Benjamin Franklin had a hand in the Stamp Act was ridiculous. I knew it couldn't be true. He reached adulthood with nothing, not even noble birth. He was a tradesman, a man who had built his fortune with his bare hands. As a printer, and the eleventh son of a candlemaker from humble means, Franklin of all people understood the real cost of taxes on a worker and his family. He would not have been in favor of it.

"It's not true," I told Liza. "It can't be."

Acclimatizing to my position as lady of the house was not easy. Why had I not paid more attention? I had no idea how a house was run. Liza and I were frequently frustrated, and I hadn't even gone to Graeme Park yet. Surely running the estate in Horsham would be even more challenging, based on the sheer size of the property alone.

My mother left two letters for me. In the first letter, she asked me to look after my father, and Anny and Johnny, and gave me tips on managing the household. I still hated housekeeping so much that if I did not have to attend to it, I never would. I wished I had paid more attention when Mother was alive. How had she managed it all?

Despite my aggravation over the house and our affairs, it was the second letter that brought me up short.

Dearest Elizabeth,

We women have it only in our power to deny, I cannot call it a choice. I hope you will never bestow yourself on any other than one who is generally reputed a good and sensible man; with such a one, a woman cannot be unhappy. When you meet him, take him with all his faults and frailties (for none are without), and when you have him, expect not too much from him. Like all things, the higher your ideas are, the greater will be your disappointment.

I frowned. Mama meant to advise me on choosing a husband, but what if I used my "power to deny" and told my father I wouldn't be his housekeeper, what then? Where would I go? What would I do? In truth, I had nowhere else. According to my mother, we women had no choices, only refusals. And no one was offering me an alternative.

I felt the world pressing in on me from all sides. I said as much to my sister as we took a walk along Water Street a month after I came home. There were more warehouses and foundries than when I left. You could see the leap in industry, even in so short a time.

"I feel ill prepared for the task that has been given me," I complained. "Housekeeping is a great trial to my temper and I despise it. Surely I will fail."

"You haven't been home very long," Ann said cheerfully, sliding her arm through mine. "It is an adjustment after your adventures. You should write something, that always makes you feel better, doesn't it? Or why not invite your new friend over, the poet you met?"

"Nathaniel? I already see him in town quite often."

"Has he asked Father to court you?" my sister pressed.

"He's struggling with his health. The time on the ship weakened him. The weather was awful, everything was so damp all the time. Father says he'll invite Nathaniel to Graeme Park in the spring to take the country air."

"Well, that's good. You can get to know each other better without feeling pressured."

"I must focus on the children," I said sharply. "And our father, a man who just lost his wife of more than forty years. Haven't you seen how he wanders like a ghost?"

"All that will sort itself out with time," Ann soothed. "You'll see."

"The servants don't listen," I said wearily. "I'm supposed to understand what supplies we have, and magically know when we need more, and where to get them at the best price, and do the ledgers, and solve disputes, and handle it all like a fairy godmother. Father doesn't seem to know a thing about running the house, and doesn't want to. If it's not about medicine or husbandry or agriculture he sticks his head in the ground."

Ann pushed back the hood of her cloak. "Betsy, you must learn to be in charge. The servants need to see you as a taskmaster. If the staff are bickering or uncooperative, you must replace them. Be stern. Let them know you'll go to Father, and that he has placed power in you for their dismissal."

I heaved a sigh of disgust. I wanted to write and read in peace. Either that or attend dances, not order servants about. I was twenty-eight years old, not fifty.

"As your sister, I'll speak plainly," Ann said. "Mother made it look easy. I myself find it quite challenging, and I don't have children in the house, let alone have to manage a plantation the size of Graeme Park. You're going to have to get tougher, my sister, that's all there is to it."

We walked along in companionable silence, elbows linked. Ann had turned forty while I was overseas. We both knew there would be no children for her and Charles now. Perhaps I should have acknowledged it sooner, after all, they had been married eighteen years, but I couldn't bear to see her hopes dashed. Although after Jane died, taking tiny Charity with her, I was less eager for Ann to be with child than I'd been before.

"Your new house is so large and lovely," I said warmly. "I cannot wait to see it finished. Your very own palace. It's so grand."

Ann smiled, pleased. "It will be handsome indeed. Can you come by later? I want to show you some of the plaster options. I'm having trouble choosing fruit or leaf motifs. You must help me throw a ball next year. I hope it will be our first of many."

Philadelphia
Winter 1766

January churned on, February trudging in after it on frosty heels. I wanted to curl up in a little ball in front of the fire, yet I put one foot in front of the other. The education of Anny and Johnny was pressing, and they had lost months of lesson time. Father needed a well-appointed home to entertain in, too, and there was work to be done in that regard as we wrestled with creating a home that didn't include my talented mother.

As I put together lessons, I realized my niece and nephew were growing up. Their skills were more advanced, which made their lessons more interesting for me. In a couple more years, when they were a little older, Father would be able to bring specialized tutors in for languages and philosophy. He would send Johnny to the Philadelphia Academy and have Anny focus on music performance.

We returned to learning in the makeshift schoolroom in the study.

"Don't go away again, Aunt Betsy," Anny said again. She kept saying it over and over.

"Oh, my darling girl. I'm here now. You are like a daughter to me. And a son," I added when Johnny looked over.

"We're glad you're back," Johnny said. "You're our best teacher."

I dropped a kiss on both heads.

"Tell us about London," Anny begged.

"Again? I don't think I have any stories left that you haven't already heard."

"Tell us about meeting the king!" Johnny enthused.

I shook my head. "Again? No. Time for lessons."

They both had an affinity for language. Johnny liked to read and discuss what he'd read, while Anny wanted to write verse and have me tell her how to improve what she'd written.

"What are you working on, Aunty?" Anny asked me. "Are you writing?"

I wrote a poem about returning from England but found no joy in it. Joy was not what I felt these days. I was not comfortable in my skin, not comfortable in our house, not comfortable in moody Philadelphia where the streets rattled with anger. I especially dreaded the thought of returning to Graeme Park in the spring, which meant memories of my life with Mother next to me by the day and week and year. She had been beloved friend, tutor, parent.

"Never mind me. Let's talk about you two. What have you been working on?" I asked them. "I must catch up. You've both grown so accomplished."

"After Nana died, they didn't make us do work during the summer," Anny explained.

"Then in September, Cousin Liza helped us," Johnny added. "Well, she tried."

"She's not as good at teaching us as you are," Anny explained. "But she means well."

"Let's start by reading some of the psalms in Latin," I said. "Open your Bibles to Psalm 67 and read it to yourself." It was what Mama used to do with me when I was young.

We would linger over each word of a psalm, say it aloud so the musical sounds would roll off our tongues, and to practice my penmanship, Mother would ask me to then copy the psalm into my book.

The children settled in at the table.

I watched them for a moment and then opened my own Bible. I read Psalm 23, mentally translating to English from the Latin: *The Lord is my shepherd; I shall not want. He maketh me to lie down in green pastures; he leadeth me beside the still waters.*

I reached for a pen. On a whim, as the children read, I used Shakespeare's classic iambic tetrameter to rephrase the first line of Latin into English, this time choosing my own words. I kept going, ending with:

Or by meaning water's sides;
Where murmuring fountains smoothly glides.

I liked taking the sacred words and rephrasing the verses that had soothed me when I was a child. I transcribed another psalm the next day while the children worked, and then another the next. I liked finding rhythm, deciding how well I could make each line slide to the next as I went along. I chose the words carefully, the lines dancing along with a life of their own. It was a pleasing distraction. It did not matter if my translations were clumsy or awkward or even plain awful, I only did it to suit myself. My efforts kept my mind busy.

At the end of February, Ann sent for me. When I got there, my sister lay on the sofa, covered in a quilt, her face pale.

"I feel so ill, Betsy," she said.

"Perhaps you should go to bed."

"I have been in bed! I cannot stand another moment there!"

"What can I do?"

"Just stay with me. The servants look at me like I'm a miasma of infection. Charles must work, and I don't want to be alone. When I am, I think of Mother, and the sadness weighs too heavily on me. Can you open a window?"

She said her stomach hurt.

I stayed with her. I gave her the medicine that her doctor had left, and dandelion tea, and pressed cool cloths to her face. To amuse her, I told her stories about the ribald plays in London, and the prostitutes lining the alleyways of Covent Garden.

I was not worried. She had been sicker at other times, we all had. This would pass in a few days' time.

"You'll feel better soon," I reassured her. I really thought she would get better, but she turned a corner for the worse. Days later, the neighbors in each direction on Third Street could hear her shrieks of pain.

My sister surprised us by dying the next week.

"No, oh no," were her last words.

Ann can't be dead, I though in bewilderment. Her house isn't finished.

Horsham
April 1766

There is something about children that insists one must continue on, for one look at them and you know you are needed. The presence of young Anny and Johnny was the only comfort for Liza and I in those days.

When would our losses end? I shuddered to think of what would happen to my world if I lost Liza. She was all I had left, for although I loved my father, only women can lift and bolster other women.

Spring came, and we returned to Graeme Park, grateful for every gift of emerging life, for the flowers that bloomed, the new baby deer, every tiny shoot and spark of green. We clung to the smell of the earth unfolding, and the fuggy smell of growth in the mud.

In April, my father arranged to bring Nathaniel Evans to Graeme Park to stay for a few weeks. "For his health," he said to me nonchalantly, although I thought I saw him stealing a look in my direction.

Poor father, he looked so old. First Jane and the baby went, then Mother and now Ann too soon after. He and my sister Ann shared a deep inexplicable bond. They'd always been very close. We all knew Ann had been his favorite child and none of us ever minded, for they seemed to go together so perfectly. He loved all of us with his huge generous spirit, but Ann was his special daughter.

Father needed time to recover, I told myself. I would make sure he wasn't working too hard.

"I have a friend I would like you to meet," I told my niece when I knew Nathaniel was coming.

"I don't want anyone to come," Anny said, angrily, her face sullen. She had lost her mother, her grandmother, and now her aunt. She wanted me to herself.

"Somehow," I said gently, "we have to find a way to go on after people we love die. We need to do normal things and try and be happy, if we can. Life is a gift."

"No."

"You don't have to stay with us," I said patiently. "You can say hello to my friend and go elsewhere. He's coming this afternoon and I expect you to receive him cordially. I've told him so much about you and your brother, he'll be so pleased to meet you. He knows how much I treasure you."

A muscle in her cheek quivered. Her arms remained crossed in defiance. "No. I'm too sad. It's not good for me.

Aunty Ann probably died of a broken heart from being too sad after Nana died."

"Oh, I don't know about that. My sister was looking forward to lots of things, like more time with her husband and her new house being finished—"

"That's right, you *don't* know."

I left it. You could not argue with the anguish of a nine-year-old girl who had seen too many of the women in her life die. I wondered why her father didn't step up and spend more time with her. Surely James' business wasn't so pressing that it was more important than his children. I'd heard from him more frequently by letter when I was in England than I'd seen him in person since I'd been back.

Nathaniel arrived as the clock in the landing struck three. I had missed hearing that clock while I was away, it was an anchor to my childhood, to my life. We gathered in the hall, Father too.

"My, he's so handsome, Betsy!" Liza whispered when she peered out the door at his trim well-dressed figure. "I think he looks like a Bernini sculpture. Are you courting?"

"No," I answered tartly, my mother's advice needle-like in my mind. I wondered briefly if Liza would consider Nathaniel for herself, but she had never seemed interested in men. Mainly she was content caring for those around her.

Nathaniel entered with the grace of a visiting dignitary, elegant and refined.

"How do you do, Mr. Evans?" my niece asked him formally, conscious of my warning to her. Anny's voice was an eerie echo of my mother's. Her eyes ran over him in a way that was too old for her, assessing him shrewdly. Anny would be a quick-witted woman one day, she missed nothing. She also had a robust liking for critical thinking, and Lord knows she was stubborn.

He smiled at her, and nodded his head very seriously in return. "How do you do, Miss. . ."

"Young," she replied with affectation. "My father is Mr. James Young of Philadelphia. But you may call me Anny. Everyone does."

"A pleasure," Nathaniel said, his lips curved in amusement. "I am acquainted with your father, Miss Anny."

"How?" Johnny asked shortly, suspicious. He demanded an explanation from Nathaniel impatiently.

"John," my father said warningly. "Don't be familiar."

"I met him in church," Nathaniel answered easily with a nod at my father. "He speaks of his children with pride."

"What is your occupation, sir?" Johnny asked. "Are you a ship's captain?" His eyes lit up at the thought.

Nathaniel smiled at the boy. "I am a new minister, son, and something of a poet. Alas, I am not a ship's captain, however I did recently get to sail all the way to England, where I was fortunate enough to meet your wonderful aunt." He gave me a warm look.

My father watched us thoughtfully.

Johnny considered this. "Did you see any pirates?"

Nathaniel laughed. "Only if you count the king's tax collectors on the docks as worthy of such a title."

My father made a weird sound, half laugh, half strangled cough. Johnny looked confused and turned his attention back to his toy.

"Come in," I said. "No need to stand in the landing."

"What kind of poet are you?" Anny asked, leading Nathaniel to the parlor. "I myself like writing poems about nature."

"I do too," Nathaniel told her. They looked endearing, young girl next to grown man, talking so earnestly. "Maybe we can share our poems with each other?"

And just like that, Nathaniel had young Anny wrapped around his finger.

Nathaniel grew robust in the fresh air and under Father's medical care. We fed him fatty spring lamb, eaten with peas and mint from our gardens, and the best beef. We made him eat desserts, sweet puddings and cakes washed down with creamy milk fresh from the cow. I tutored the children each morning and we all went exploring or riding with Nathaniel in the afternoon. In the evenings, Father plied him with spirits and we played games in the parlor while Father read another medical journal or some new book on farming.

"I suspect Nathaniel could live to be a very old man," Liza remarked to me one day as we watched him mount a horse. "He has none of the recklessness that William did. I don't worry about him breaking his neck while he's out riding."

"That was a long time ago," I said. It was true, though, Nathaniel was a softer version of masculinity. He didn't look for wars to fight or mountains to climb.

"I don't like the sound of his cough. What does Papa Graeme say about it?" Liza asked.

"To me very little, he respects Nathaniel's privacy."

Liza nodded. "Betsy, Nathaniel seems fond of you. Very fond."

"Oh Liza. What are you saying?"

"Some people aren't meant for games of the heart. He's not like that."

"I'm not playing games!" I was offended. "I am not doing anything. I'm hosting a friend."

"You're not discouraging him either."

"I've been preoccupied. After Ann died—"

"He has been here for weeks, Betsy."

I considered this. I was fond of Nathaniel, but was it enough to deepen into something more? Could I be the wife of a minister? Did he even think of me that way? Our friendship had been very platonic thus far, which made me feel warmly toward him, for our affection did not threaten me. I still wasn't sure I wanted to be a wife.

The days were long and warm, and getting hotter by the week as summer approached.

I showed Nathaniel the special places from my childhood. I took him to the nook where the bluebells grew;

showed him my favorite sycamore tree, the old trunk twisted and thick; charmed him with the spot in the meadow where wild rabbits hopped each year. We climbed over forest floors thick with green, collected twigs, splashed in the stream where frogs croaked and the children hunted for tadpoles.

"I wrote a poem about Graeme Park," he announced one night when we made a bonfire outside and sat around it on tree stumps. Nathaniel fished it out of his pocket. "I'd like to read it, if I may."

Anny clapped her hands. "You love it here!" she exclaimed. "We got to you! Can you stay here with us for always?"

"Will you permit me to read you my poem, Lady Young?" he asked formally, standing and bowing.

"I will!" Anny beamed.

"They call my aunt Lady Graeme now because she met the king," Johnny interrupted.

"It's true," Liza agreed.

"Your aunt is a noblewoman indeed," Nathaniel murmured, "in every way."

"Go on, then," my father said. "Don't keep us in suspense."

Nathaniel positioned himself theatrically and cleared in his throat in a manner befitting a Shakespearean actor. With a sweeping gesture of his arm, he deepened his voice and began.

> *"How breathes the morn her incense round,*
> *And sweetens ev'ry sylvan scene?*
> *Wild warbling thro' the groves resound,*
> *And op'ning flow'rs bedeck the green."*

He stopped. "That is the first stanza."

"Oh, do continue," Anny breathed, eyes glowing.

His poem took me back to our dawn walks, my arm linked with his, the sky sweeping lilac to blue, the robins warbling their timeless song.

Nathaniel smiled at Anny and continued.

> *"Thus musing o'er the charming plains,*
> *(Where Graeme the just and good retires*
> *Where Laura breathes her tender strains*
> *Whom every graceful muse inspires)—"*

"Aunty Betsy you are Laura," Anny explained. "Am I in it too?"

"Or me?" Johnny asked.

"I could have a special pen name too," Anny said. "I'll be Evangeline."

"Let him finish," my father intoned around his cigar.

Nathaniel winked and read on until the close of his ode.

> *In heav'n thy name shall be enroll'd, and others*
> *learn like thee to live.*

"Aw, you forgot me and Anny," Johnny said, disappointed. "You just mentioned Grandfather and Aunt Betsy."

"And me," Liza teased. "He forgot me too."

"I most certainly did not," Nathaniel deferred. "I simply couldn't find words that were special enough. You three shall be the subject of my next poem."

We all agreed it was the most wonderful poem ever, and Anny took Nathaniel's place on the imaginary stage to read one of her own. My heart tugged. She looked so small and so grown up all at the same time. Mama would have loved this, I thought. Would the ache ever lessen?

The evening grew late, and we retired inside away from the bugs. The children were sent to bed, then Liza pleaded a headache and retired. My father stayed firmly planted in his chair.

"What will you do when you are finished with the psalms?" Nathaniel asked me. I was still working my way through them, transcribing as I went.

"Betsy is writing her mother's epitaph," Father said, "for her gravestone at Christ Church. And Ann's as well."

In truth, I had been putting it off. I didn't want to think about them both being gone.

"And after that?" Nathaniel asked me.

"I have been thinking about translating one of the classics from Greek or Latin," I admitted. "I'd like to tackle a new challenge. I'm still deciding." Although I still wrote poetry regularly.

It was pitch black outside; no moon glowed. My father drank his whisky, and it loosened his tongue. He began to speak brightly about a new irrigation system he wanted to try, talking at length about rainwater and soil levels. I half listened, drowsy with warmth and wine.

"Would you give me a hand with it?" he asked Nathaniel. "I thought I could break soil once we—"

"I would like to, Dr. Graeme, but I will be in New Jersey by then," Nathaniel said.

We both looked at him, surprised.

"I accepted a missionary post in Gloucester County," he said quietly. "I leave Sunday."

He had been here for six weeks. He had become part of our family.

"Where exactly?" I asked, trying not to sound irritable.

"The vicarage at Haddonsfield. Across from Philadelphia, on the other side of the river. Not far from here really, about fifty miles all told. Maybe thirty miles from Philadelphia. Certainly not far compared to how far we traveled from London."

"Well," my Father said and rubbed his chin. "A man of God is always in need. That will suit you fine, son. Just fine."

"You didn't say anything," I said, feeling hurt.

"The letter of acceptance came in yesterday's post," Nathaniel said apologetically. "I didn't want to say anything in front of the children until I knew for sure. I applied when we got back, months ago, and had almost given up hearing."

"Oh," I said. What had I expected? A man needed a vocation. He wasn't going to float around Graeme Park all the time writing poetry. That's what women did.

"Perhaps you could visit me, Betsy," he offered.

"Or you can come here," my Father told him without missing a beat. "Or to our house in the city. My daughter is—"

"Yes, yes, of course," Nathaniel agreed, too quickly

His daughter was what? Was I too respectable? Sickly? Or perhaps too attractive to go visiting a younger man? Ha. That one stuck in my throat as laughter.

"Congratulations, Nathaniel," I said. "We are happy for you."

He was going far away, relatively speaking, from us.

Two days later Nathaniel headed to New Jersey. The household came out to watch him climb into the coach, including Old Joseph, our new maid, Sally, and the cook and the kitchen maids. The air was thin, no one wanted to see him leave. The presence of a young man here breathed life back into these walls.

He kissed my hand. "I'll write to you, my dear friend."

I nodded. Another man had made me such a promise once.

"Me too!" Anny said. "Write to me!"

Nathaniel laughed. "How about if I write one letter and it can be for all of you? I may not have much time once I'm working for my parishioners."

"I hope you meet a pirate," Johnny said hopefully.

"Probably not in church," Nathaniel answered with a straight face.

"Best of luck, Nathaniel," Liza said. Father inclined his head in agreement.

"Thank you, Thomas." Nathaniel pumped my father's hand. "Thank you for everything. Thank you for feeding me back to life!"

His carriage disappeared down the drive as we waved and waved.

I was getting used to patching holes made when people left us. As soon as he was gone I put Anny and Johnny to work on the violin and flute and turned to my own task of writing Mama and Ann's epitaphs. It was hard to choose words worthy of eternity.

I worked for days, crafting and discarding and writing more, and crying in spurts. My poor dear Mama, my poor sister, how I longed to see them.

Finally, toward the end of July, I had a verse that felt right. It was done.

> *Forgive, great God, this one last filial tear!*
> *Indulge my sorrow on a theme so near:*
> *This earth born strain indulge, that mourns the blest,*
> *And doubly mourns, because they were the best,*
> *Tho' truth remonstrates, self-love will prevail,*
> *And sink the beam in nature's feeble scale,*
> *A God incarnate once wept o'er Lazurus dead;*
> *The power divine recall'd his soul when fled*
> *A poor frail being weeps a mother gone;*
> *The tomb scarce closed before a sister's flown.*
> *Each was a guide, a pattern and a friend;*
> *She prays to join when fleeting life shall end.*

The epitaph was agreed on, and chiseled in stone.

I didn't know what to make of Nathaniel. I thought perhaps I had imagined his feelings for me, then a letter and poem arrived when Liza and I were playing chess together one rainy July afternoon.

> *Yet, if the happiness, fair maid,*
> *That soothes me in the silent shade,*
> *Should in your eye, appear too great,*
> *Come, take it all and share my fate!*

"I told you," Liza said, a touch smugly.

"You think it's an invitation?"

She snorted. "A man asks you to *share his fate* and you have to wonder if he's interested?"

"Well, I teased him about what an easy life he'll have as a country parson. I said he'll become fat through indolence and leisure time! He wasted no time sending this rebuttal, bold as a rooster."

Liza laughed. "I cannot imagine Nathaniel gone to fat. Did he give you any hint of his affections before he left?"

"No, although he may be afraid of Father."

"He does tend to growl at the single men, doesn't he? Well, more importantly, what are your thoughts?"

"I'm not sure." I thought longingly of the excitement of London. Even if I didn't go back, there was Philadelphia, which was growing fast as a bed of weeds. Besides, I had Anny and Johnny to raise. If I went to New Jersey, who would take the children? I couldn't leave Liza to fend alone. I couldn't leave Father. And for sure I wouldn't send the children back to their father.

I also didn't know if I could be a country parson's wife. If I couldn't have London, at least I had Philadelphia.

Philadelphia
1767

I made my decision. I decided to translate *Telemachus*!
There was no copy in English available anywhere in the
colonies, that I knew of.

"You must be mad!" Liza exclaimed. "It's hundreds of
pages long!"

The idea had been dancing in my mind for a while,
Telemachus had long been a family favorite. It was originally
published in France in 1699 as *Les Aventures de Télémaque*
by Francois Fénelon, who imagined Odysseus's journey
continuing after Homer finished with his telling of it in *The
Odyssey*. I knew copies were available in America in French,
but there were none in English, and the French copies had
been specifically imported by certain individuals.

"It will take me years," I agreed. I was almost thirty now,
but I had time, with no husband and children to dictate my
hours. "Besides, I finished with translating the psalms."

My friends were delighted that I had translated the
psalms. Three years earlier we had celebrated when Francis
Hopkinson published *A Collection of Psalm Tunes, with a
few Anthems and Hymns* himself for Christ Church
parishioners to sing. Francis was my biggest champion,
remembering the days we had tossed ideas around for his
book.

"I only did this this for my own amusement," I cautioned
Francis when he called one day. I took down the two leather
volumes and showed him my work: one hundred and fifty
psalms adapted from Latin in seven months.

Frank took the books from me. "Two volumes! And you
had them bound."

"My handwriting is terrible," I said. "Everyone says so.
The one part of me that Mother despaired of."

He opened one to the inscription. "*For Reverend Peters*,"
he read. "Kind of you."

I nodded. "He is very special to me, and a great inspiration. He helped guide my faith, for years. I'm going to surprise him with these, as a gift."

"These are impressive translations. You are a woman of great talent, Betsy. The world should know who you are."

"Bah, you haven't looked closely enough. Some are them are awful, but I don't mind. They were a pleasant enough distraction, they served their purpose in taking my mind off my mother and Ann. I'm moving on to my next project, did I tell you? I'm translating *Telemachus*."

I wanted to make my translation as literal as the different languages permitted, which, when added to the complexities of verse, would be sure to make it long, but I was up for the challenge.

With the new year, my grief stopped its frantic scrabbling inside me. I began to feel more peaceful. *Telemachus* was my road forward.

I was pleased, too, when my brother-in-law Charles Stedman announced he was re-marrying, a year after my sister Ann's death. He asked Margaret Abercrombie to be his wife.

I pushed Nathaniel away after his letters became suggestive.

My saucy friend, I admonished him, *if you choose a spouse, I will call her friend too!*

We saw each other occasionally at events in town and in Christ Church, but he was reluctant to leave his post for any length of time during his first year as pastor. His parishioners were just getting to know and trust him.

I believed our fondness for one another might develop into a union in the future, when Anny and Johnny were grown in a few short years, and I looked forward to that.

What I needed now was the opportunity to be in one place long enough to feel the world stop moving. I needed my feet under me again after the huge shift in my life that was Mama and Ann's deaths.

Ah, but what did I know about the future? Clearly nothing.

The pernicious white plague stole my beautiful dark-eyed poet. Consumption took my Nathaniel. His obituary gave no indication of how brightly he shone in life. I wished I had been asked to write it for him.

> *Obituary for Nathaniel Evans*
> *Died October 29, 1767*
> *On Thursday last, departed this life, in the 25th year of his age, the Reverend Nathaniel Evans M.A., missionary from the Society of Churches of Gloucester and Cole's Town, in New Jersey. His remains were interred in Christ Church.*

Chapter 18

Horsham
October 1771
Four years later

There was a screech, a bang, and the sound of feet pounding along the third floor. Anny came racing down the stairs, with Johnny in hot pursuit.

"Give it back!" he yelled.

"Not until you give me back my hair combs! And the pen from my writing box!"

"I don't have them!"

"Yes you do, I know you do!"

Anny yelled as he grabbed the back of her skirt on the landing between the first and second floor to stop her from getting away from him.

"Pig!" She whirled on him, brandishing a toy lead cannon above her head, poised like a knife. Johnny leaped on it like lightning, yanking it out of her hand as Anny gave a yelp of fury and lunged for him.

Liza and I appeared from the parlor to see what was going on. They ignored us, but they both froze when my father opened his office door. Liza and I raised our eyebrows at each other in anticipation. Let the show begin.

Father stood looked calmly at both of them, rocking slightly back on his heels like a general assessing his troops. At eighty-two, he still cut an impressive figure, especially if he pulled himself up to be tall and authoritative. He was hard of hearing now, and had a mild cough that never left him, yet he still had the vigor to manage Graeme Park and walk five miles each day at dawn. Even if he didn't hear the yelling, he would have felt the pounding on the floor above him.

Anny and Johnny looked at him, not daring to retreat from the landing.

"Grandfather," Anny said, and stepped slowly down the last flight of stairs to stand before him. "Did we disturb you? I apologize. I did not—"

My father cut her off with a shake of his head.

They both waited.

Anny looked worried but Johnny looked defiant. He had a small cannon clutched in one hand, the other fist was clenched by his side. At thirteen, he was small, still a child, his body not much bigger than when he was eleven. Manhood was slow in coming to him.

"John," my father said in his justice of the peace voice, "give your sister back her things."

Anny was pink-cheeked after the exertion of running from her brother, her cheeks flushed. Wisps of hair escaped around her face. At fifteen, she stood at least four inches taller than her brother in a woman's body. She looked as if she were ten years older than Johnny.

Johnny looked at the pine planks under his feet.

"Don't take them again," my father said. "And don't enter your sister's chamber without permission."

"She—"

"No matter how fierce the battle, son," Father added, his voice softening with amusement, "a good general knows to prepare without relying on reinforcements that may not come to his aid in time."

Johnny brightened at this until Anny smirked at him.

"Ann, you are far too old to react to him in such an unruly manner, even though he maddens you," my father said with the cool imperiousness of a colonel. Anny looked at her grandfather, her eyes still sparking with the heat of combat and injustice.

"Your brother is still a boy," Father said to her. Johnny's face pinched in annoyance. "You, however, my dear, must find equanimity in all things. That is what your sex must do."

With that, my father turned on his heel and returned to his office. He closed the door behind him.

I stepped forward before they could start up again and gave Johnny a hard look. "You heard. Replace the things you took."

He turned to climb the stairs, defeated. "I needed the quill to load the cannon," he muttered under his breath.

"And my hair combs?" Anny demanded as he disappeared around the stairwell. "Why did you thieve *those,* you useless knave?"

"Stop," I said. "You heard your grandfather. It's time you stopped reacting to your brother. You are no longer a child."

"I'm not a child either!" Johnny called down.

"Let's go whittle twigs, Johnny," Liza called to him. "That will do the trick. We'll get those cannons loaded in no time."

"That is all he cares about," Anny seethed. "His stupid pretend battles! He's too old! I should throw his wretched army in the necessary and watch them sink into the—"

"Go." I gave her a push. "He is a boy, but you can act like the young woman you are. And start packing your things. We are returning to Philadelphia soon."

I watched Anny run up the stairs, her slippered feet light compared to her brother's hard stomp. I turned to Liza. "What on earth would he need her hair combs for? I'm afraid to ask."

"To secure a line of bayonets," Liza said confidently. "I'm willing to bet he needed a base to keep them upright and get the right formation to lance the enemy. War is a real and present danger in Johnny's mind."

We both laughed. Of course, back then we could. It was only 1771.

Philadelphia
November 1771

Our coach drew up before our house in Philadelphia as
the daylight waned, charcoal shadows laced against the late
afternoon like the reach of a gloved hand. I looked up at the
house, pleased to be back for the winter. How I loved this
town! As much as I loved the countryside, I would hate to
live in the country year-round and miss all the joys of city
life, which were always so exciting to me.

"Can we go to the confectioner's?" Johnny asked.
"There's a new one on Walnut Street. Or maybe it was Water
Street."

"We've only just got here," Anny told him. "You shouldn't
be asking, little boy."

"Anny," I chided her.

"One day soon, John," Liza answered.

"They put an ad in the *Gazette*," Johnny said,
undeterred. "They're selling liberty drops, barley sugar, and
plum cake. And biscuits!"

"Hungry again?" I asked him wryly as we alighted from
the coach and made our way through the gate.

"Always."

"Can we hold a dance?" Anny asked. "I'm old enough."

Liza and I looked at her. In my heart, she was still the
little girl I helped raise when Jane died, but in truth she was
now the age I was when I began meeting up with William
Franklin. The thought made me swallow hard. Time was a
slippery eel.

"I expect we will," I answered easily.

"And when can I come to your Attic Evenings?" Anny
demanded. "I know you'll hold them every Saturday night
like you did last winter. I want to come."

"And you talk about *me*," Johnny said, flicking a dried
leaf at her. "Let Aunty get in the front door, will you, *little
girl*. Maybe one day you'll get to go to the ball."

Liz couldn't help herself, she laughed.

My Attic Evenings in Philadelphia were modeled after salons I went to in London, which were most likely copied from those in Paris. All matter of topics had been discussed when I attended, from the ridiculous to the sublime. It was so thrilling to meet with bright like-minded people and not just talk of trivial things! We could discuss anything from Socrates to James Macpherson, or the latest popular novel taking Europe by storm, or a new scientific or medical discovery. Both men and women were welcome.

Mama had kept regular Saturday evening calling hours in the city for years, and it seemed a fitting extension to expand her tradition of hospitality into a structured literary gathering. Over the past five years my Attic Evenings became my lifeblood. I'm not sure how I would survive winter without these sparkling nights, warmed by fire and wine and exciting conversation between friends with sharp minds. My father chose not to attend, he said he would let the young people sharpen their wits without the old dullard, which of course he could never be. Father was so pleased and proud to open up his home for the Attic Evenings that there was never any limit on spending. Not when the best of Philadelphia arrived at our door.

"I'm going to have an Attic Evening the first Saturday in December," I told Liza. "I ran it by Father and he has no objections."

"Already," Liza answered. "Don't we usually wait until January?"

"We had quite a crowd last year when we broke for the season," I said. "I'm keen to keep the momentum going and catch up with everyone."

My friends John Dickinson, Jacob Duché, and Francis Hopkinson were regulars. Francis had a new wife, Ann, who introduced us to her brother, Elias Boudinot, who became a fast friend. Benjamin Rush always came, back from studying medicine in Scotland. He was Dr. Rush now, a bright young force in medicine. Julia and Richard Stockton came regularly from Princeton, and the Morgans and Redmans and Roberdeaus. The list went on.

Liza and I decided on Homer as the evening's topic. I had completed my translation of Fénelon's *Télémaque* two years ago, in 1769, after three years of consistent hard work. I painstakingly wrote out twenty-four books and tens of thousands of lines. Finally, my *Telemachus* was finished. Now that I was not working on it anymore, it didn't feel as self-serving to discuss Homer's *Odyssey*.

December 7 arrived clear and cold. I couldn't wait to see everyone, and to be able to gather in one room again instead of around town in a piecemeal fashion.

I lit candles and oil lamps in the parlor and hummed under my breath.

"Can I stay?" Anny interrupted my thoughts.

She watched from the loveseat, feet tucked under her, nose peeking above a book. She had my love of literature. In another year or two, there would be no difference between her efforts at writing and my own.

"You're going out with your father," I answered. "Aren't you?"

She sighed. "Why yes but why can't I tell him—"

"Next year, after your birthday," I said. I would not be able to put her off much longer. I had always planned to keep her at her schooling until she was at least sixteen. After that, I could not hold her back from adulthood.

"Just promise me you're not talking about Nathaniel's poetry tonight."

"I promise you we are not. In any case, it's not finished; we're still finalizing subscriptions and negotiating with printers. It will be a few more months before the book is printed and ready."

After Nathaniel died, Reverend Smith and I began working on compiling a book of Nathaniel's poetry. We wrote letters across all the colonies and beyond to get subscribers who would contribute the money to finance its publication. It took us five years to secure the money, edit his work, and be in a position to finally publish. To my utter astonishment, more than four hundred and fifty people signed up to buy the book! I expected the orders from Philadelphia and London, but we also received requests from people in England, Scotland, Canada, France, Barbados and other places in the West Indies. The subscription list included governors, lawyers, doctors, teachers, merchants, ministers, college professors, craftspeople and more. Altogether, Nathaniel's friends and admirers ordered almost nine hundred copies. We've called the book *Poems on Several Occasions*. I liked to think if he were here, Nathaniel would have approved. I couldn't let him die in obscurity. At least this way, his work would live on.

Anny stared at me, petulant.

"Oh Anny. I promise I will let you stay for that one, at least for the first half of the evening. You were Nathaniel's friend too. Remember that summer night when we read poetry outside by the bonfire? We won't forget him. Now, go get ready. And remind your brother to wash before he sees his father." Boys. Personal cleanliness was never a priority.

She left, satisfied for the moment. My thoughts returned to Nathaniel.

Some of the poems we chose to include in *Poems on Several Occasions* were from correspondence that Nathaniel and I exchanged. I did not want my private poems or letters to be included, but Reverend Smith argued that Nathaniel's poems about Graeme Park—and me—had no meaning without the poems and lines from my return letters. For Nathaniel's sake, for the memory of his friendship, I reluctantly agreed.

I could not believe he had been gone five years. On the day I finally finished *Telemachus*, I went to his grave at Christ Church and told him. He was the first person I told. Sometimes, when I'm alone and having tea, I pour a cup for him too, when no one can see. If he were here, I'm sure he would be more pleased for me over *Telemachus* than for the publication of his own poems. That's the way he was, big-hearted.

"I wish your harpsichord was here," Liza said, walking in with our new dog, Fidele, in her arms. She was wearing her favorite embroidered yellow silk gown I had sent from Bath. "I love when we sing at the end of the evening."

I nodded. "When everyone's had enough to drink."

I recently added "The Lass of Peaty's Mill" and "Tweed Side" to my repertoire.

"I'm not sure I made the right decision to leave the harpsichord at Graeme Park year-round," I added. "I thought I would be easier to have it there rather than carting it back and forth."

"Perhaps Francis will bring his violin," Liza mused. She looked around the room. "The winter greenery looks lovely."

"I like the oranges studded with cloves," I said, sniffing the bowl. "The cloves seemed an extravagance, but the scent is so delicious. And the nutmeg reminds me of Christmas cookies."

I looked up at the clock on the mantel. "I'll go and change. Could you ask Sally to put out another bottle of Scotch?"

I glanced at the table. Figs, salted nuts, and various types of crackers and cheeses and sweetmeats. There were also candies and gingerbread and cakes. Two dozen crystal glasses and white cloth napkins lay surrounded by an arc of glass bottles and a bowl of punch.

"It's fine," Liza said, seeing me eye the food. "We always have too much. Don't fuss."

When I came downstairs, carriages were in front of the house.

"William and Rebecca Smith," Liza announced, still carrying Fidele.

"And Jacob and Elizabeth Duché," I added.

"I see Reverend Peters walking up," Liza said. "John Dickinson is with him. Oh, and John and Mary Redman. And Hannah and Cornelia and their husbands." I loved to see my old friends from our dancing assembly days. Most of them were long married. Only Liza and I were still single, adding our names to the roster of spinsters in town.

In no time our parlor filled with people.

"Annis!" I exclaimed when the Stocktons arrived. "What a surprise! I didn't know you were in town."

Annis and I had known each other as small children in Philadelphia but lost touch. When I returned from England, she wrote a charming letter saying she had heard of my travels and my fondness for poetry and would very much like to be friends. I count her counsel as among my most valued. I often spend time at Morven with her, in Princeton. What a grand estate the Stocktons had.

"Richard had business here in town," she said with an affectionate look at her husband, a lawyer, "I accompanied him as an excuse to get away from our children for a few days! And of course, to see you, Betsy dear."

We all laughed.

The servants filled glasses as we settled into chairs and loveseats, a couple of the men sitting on footstools by their wives.

"Betsy, will you publish *Telemachus*?" Jacob Duché asked. "It's an impressive work. We all admire you for taking it on. There must be a printer who wants to get his hands on it."

I had my handwritten pages bound in two thick volumes of red leather, the title tooled in gold on each spine. Then I added the page numbers by hand. There were more than four hundred pages in each book. Sometimes I secretly marveled that it was my own work.

"Publish? Women don't benefit by being published," I answered modestly.

"That's true," Annis said, an accomplished writer herself. "Much better for us to be cloaked in mystery so we may lay our cards as we choose, unobserved and unchallenged."

"Although it would be nice to have it printed," I conceded. "My handwriting is terrible. And a few times the ink was thick and blobbed on the page. Or too thin." How luxurious it would be to have access to a compositor, trays of type, and a printing press.

Telemachus was the largest piece of work I'd under undertaken. Sometimes I went and added notes to certain pages for the benefit of future readers. The final touch was a poem I wrote and added to the beginning. I was proud of my *Telemachus*, it had been an epic effort, one that I had often struggled to complete. I had underestimated what a grueling process it would be over three years.

"It's good to have British ale again," Richard said, holding up a bottle of Dorsett beer from Thomas Dale, the London brewer. "After the restrictions."

For a while after the Stamp Act was passed, the colonies continued to punish Britain by refusing to buy or use imported goods. Since we had no representation, we voted with our money. Less than a year later, British merchants squawked to Parliament that they were being crushed, and the Stamp Act was repealed. Our relief did not last long, for the Townshend duties were passed two years later and were only repealed last year. It seemed Britain was determined to crush us with taxes of some sort, determined to make money off us.

I thought we should have continued with the import restrictions. The colonies shouldn't fund tyranny. We must learn to produce more here, or go without.

John Dickinson objected to Richard Stockton's praise of the ale. "Just because we're swimming in British luxuries again doesn't mean we face any less of a threat. We haven't come that far. One must only look to Boston to see the magnitude of our challenges. We should continue to resist without violence."

Dickinson, an accomplished orator, had been chosen to represent Pennsylvania at the Stamp Act Congress in 1765. He drafted an eloquent resolution against the act that colonists took to heart. It was hard to know whether Britain would have repealed the Stamp Act anyway, but Dickinson was known for his successful part in its demise. After the Townshend Acts, Dickinson published *Letters from a Farmer in Pennsylvania* in a series in a local paper, under a pseudonym.

I wrote a long poem in response to Dickinson's *Letters from a Farmer*, which I called *The Dream*. My poem urged colonists to do their patriotic duty and forgo the goods of England, told in an imaginary dream state to illustrate our evolution from William Penn, and transition us back to the simple rural life where farmers are their own masters. I think I may have gotten a little carried away from my fervent pace of *Telemachus*, for *The Dream* was over six hundred lines long.

"The redcoats are entrenched around Boston Bay now," Duché said. "I'm sure the Sons of Liberty are beside themselves with indignation."

"It's the women who suffer," Elizabeth Duché argued. "The Quartering Act forces the goodwives to have soldiers in their homes, even when children are in the house! Who knows what manner of barbarity ensues."

"That's what happens when Parliament asserts the authority of the British legislature over the wellbeing of its colonies," Dickinson agreed.

"It makes no sense," Richard Stockton said. "You would think after the past five years, Britain would yank its head from its arse. Parliament can't seem to get it right."

"Or the king alone would get some sense," agreed Reverend Smith.

"You've become quite a celebrity in France, John," Duché said. "Voltaire has compared you to Cicero in ancient Rome. Your pen packs a punch."

Dickinson shrugged. "We do what we can. We must speak out against wrongs."

Dickinson was being modest. His pen had fueled resistance far and wide, up and down the colonies, from New Hampshire to Georgia. Ironically, the Townshend Acts had been repealed the same day the bloodshed in Boston took place last winter. The redcoats said they fired in self-defense against hecklers in the common that night. Two men died, and more were injured. Not much of a massacre, but the Sons of Liberty found it a convenient way to condemn the British and start a smear campaign against them.

Rebecca Smith sighed. "Can we lighten this mood? Let us talk of something besides politics!" My dear friend hadn't changed much over the years, although now she was the mother of four children.

"Hear, hear," agreed Elizabeth Duché.

"Betsy, start us off," Annis cried, raising her glass. "Please."

I stood up. "Tonight, ladies and gentlemen, we ponder the writings of Homer. Did Homer actually exist as a man? Or were his writings a collection of oral stories that had been gathered together and assigned to an imaginary author?"

There was a smattering of applause and the clinking of glasses. Then more clinking of glasses.

"Shall I read a passage?" On Attic Evenings, we read a portion of the original text, and a lively debate ensued. I dutifully read the passage from Homer.

We dove in with enthusiasm, laughing and drinking and shouting out our opinions. Time flew by.

"I still say Homer did *not* exist," Duché yelled when we were interrupted by movement in the hall.

"Excuse me." My maid, Sally, was in the doorway, and behind her, two men in overcoats and tricorn hats. "Dr. Rush, ma'am, and a guest."

All eyes were on the stranger next to Rush.

"Hugh Henry Fergusson," the man said, bowing. He had a thick Scottish accent. "Henry."

"Are we too late to join you?" Ben asked me.

"No, no, of course not." I moved toward them. "Do come in."

"I received a letter of introduction for Mr. Fergusson from a doctor in Virginia," Ben explained, taking my hand. "He is newly arrived in Philadelphia and I thought perhaps we might welcome him."

I turned to the man. "Yes, of course. Welcome, Mr. Fergusson. Do come in." There were murmurs of greeting from the room behind me.

"I've heard a great deal about you, Miss Graeme," he said in his Scottish accent, his voice like music in my ears. "They say you are as silver-tongued as a mystic."

"I don't know about that. How long have you been in America, sir?" I asked.

"Two years ago, I arrived in the colonies to help my brother Robert with his plantation in Virginia. I am from Perthshire in Scotland. My father, newly retired, was thirty years in the British army."

"This is your first time in Philadelphia?"

"It is." He had a voice like warm honey blended with aged Scotch. I shivered.

"Let me introduce you," I said. We circled the room to make his acquaintance.

"I thought Henry would be a good match for your evening soirees," Dr. Rush said, his eyes flashing with warmth. "He speaks several languages and, like yourself, is

in possession of a classical education. When I told
Fergusson there was a lady in town of refinement who held
salon evenings, and that this lady was a dear friend of mine,
he beseeched me to bring him to you."

"We like to think of ourselves as the Athens of North
America," Annis said with a wink at Mr. Fergusson.
"Philadelphia's intellectual elite. Ha ha."

"The salons of Paris have nothing on us," Liza agreed
light-heartedly.

"Don't let them fool you," Rebecca objected. "We just
have a lot of fun."

"And wine," Reverend Peters added drily.

"Thank you, then, for your hospitality," Mr. Fergusson
said with a little bow to me. I shivered again. He grinned.
"C'est mon honneur d'être ici."

"Piacere di conoscerti," I answered in Italian. I switched
into Latin. *"Hinc tibi grata sint." Pleased to meet you. You
are welcome here.*

He mimicked me in kind, switching from Italian to Latin
and then Spanish. I smiled at him, amused.

Mr. Fergusson returned my smile, his eyes traveling
down me from head to foot. Later I would try and remember
that night, that moment. Simply standing next to him was a
physical sensation.

"Have a seat," I murmured. He would have to make do
with a hard-backed chair brought in from the office.

"What brings you to Pennsylvania, Henry?" Duché
asked.

Fergusson shrugged, a light easy movement. He seemed
to be made of air and light. "In truth, I do not know.
Perhaps I fancied an adventure of sorts. I came to see
America's biggest and bustling city. I may look for work
here, or I may return to Scotland. I was a soldier before I
went to help my brother."

He was young, I realized, my eyes scanning him. His
face was worthy of Gainsborough's brush, he had strong
features, large expressive eyes, a masculine sweep of jaw.

Outside, a December wind rattled the windows. Our discussion on Homer was lost. Fidele wandered in to give everyone a sniff before sauntering out again to find a less noisy place to sleep.

"I've heard you're a writer, Miss Graeme," Mr. Fergusson said. I could listen to the lilt in his voice all day.

"There are many writers in this room," I answered. "Mrs. Stockton and Mr. Hopkinson, and of course you know John Dickinson's pivotal work."

"Speaking of writers, what is the latest news on Evans' book?" Francis Hopkinson asked.

"Betsy and I are producing a book," Reverend Smith explained for Fergusson's benefit, "containing the poetry of our late friend Nathaniel Evans, who died some years back. We have managed to collect several hundred subscriptions."

Smith turned to Hopkinson. "We're getting prices from printers, so we are getting closer. It should be soon."

"My condolences on the loss of your friend, and I look forward to purchasing a copy of Mr. Evans's book," Mr. Fergusson said smoothly. I felt his eyes on me. Were they blue or grey or green? It was impossible to tell by candlelight. Who was this man who made me feel so transparent and unsteady?

"Are you a writer yourself?" Rebecca asked him.

"No, despite the fact that every Scot seems to think every drunken thing they utter is worthy of infamy."

The room roared with laughter. Our newcomer was uplifting, and the room was fascinated with him. Mr. Fergusson was clearly at ease in social situations. He laughed and talked without self-consciousness, and in turn people were drawn to him.

"What does your brother farm?" Liza asked. "Tobacco?"

"Yes, and has made an excursion into indigo," Fergusson answered.

"Two years in Virginia and no wife yet, Mr. Fergusson?" Reverend Peters enquired.

"I am twenty-four," he said with a smile. "Still time to find a suitable match. I find I'm quite particular."

"Hear, hear," Dickinson agreed heartily. He was still a bachelor at forty.

Was it my imagination, or did Henry Fergusson look at me too often? I cursed the responding flutter in my chest. I wasn't one to fall for charm. I'd had enough men through my parlor over the years to know the weaknesses of their sex. They were a dangerous species. But more truthfully, I was of an age where fewer men were interested in the time it would take to break through my objections. At age thirty-four, why would I marry now? I was set in my ways, and not upset that I did not have children of my own. I had Anny and Johnny, they were my children.

"Are you a farmer yourself, then, Mr. Fergusson?" asked Annis. "Do you harbor hopes of farming your own land?"

"I wouldn't mind," he answered. "I'm no stranger to hard work, whether it's farming, business, or soldiering."

I liked the sensual way his finger and thumb rested around the curve of his glass, the manner in which his body held the poise of an agile cat. There was a quality about him, a sleek restlessness.

He navigated his evening among strangers well, I felt, this Henry Fergusson of Perthshire, during his first night in our company. He took his teasing gracefully and delivered a few barbs of his own. Beneath his friendly banter was something a little more serious, even mysterious, the type of man who had dark crevices in his surface. I was intrigued despite myself. He was too young, I told myself, ignoring the heat spreading through my body like warm mead.

We drank and talk and laughed and even with the discussion on Homer abandoned, it was an engaging evening. The candles were low when most of our friends left after midnight. Dr. Rush and Mr. Fergusson were the last to leave as the clock struck two.

"I've got patients in the morning," Ben groaned as he slipped on his coat. "Can I send them to your father?" he joked.

"Alas, Dr. Graeme doesn't practice medicine anymore. My dear father is almost deaf and well over eighty now. He deserves a rest."

"We can't keep him still on the farm, though," Liza chimed in. She linked her arm though mine and rested her head on my shoulder. "Papa Graeme still works like a boy in that regard. He enjoys it."

"Ah well, back to work then," Ben said, rubbing his eyes and yawning. I knew it was all talk; he loved being a physician and had new ideas on containing contagions.

Fergusson's eyes were on mine as he thanked us for our hospitality. He left with a tip of his hat. Liza and I watched the two men walk out into the clear December night, the moon high and bright.

"I saw you," Liza accused me after the door closed behind them. "You like him! The two of you might as well have been alone in the room."

"I admit I like him, why wouldn't I? He'll be a friend to me as Ben is. Nothing more."

"If Mr. Fergusson was the flame, you were like a moth banging on a lantern."

"Liza! That's unflattering. Maybe even unkind."

"A bear to honey? A bird on summer suet?" She was enjoying herself, laughing at me.

"I am not interested in romance," I scoffed. "I'm past the marrying age. I am content."

It was true.

"Uh huh."

"Besides, it is not as if I have lacked for offers." That was also true. I could have taken a husband many times over the years.

"Did any of those offers come from a handsome young Scot who seemed to have a mysterious and striking connection with you the first night you met? I bet he can even quote Fénelon."

"Good night, my dear schemer." I turned to climb the stairs.

"At least you didn't say I embarrassed myself," I added over my shoulder.

"I give you more credit than that," Liza answered. "You are more self-possessed now than when we were younger. Both of us are. Besides, Mr. Fergusson wasn't frivolous either. He looked at you in . . . a certain way. I think our new Henry likes you, too."

"I am *content*," I repeated firmly to the stairs in front of me. "As I am."

"Shall I bet you a shilling?" Liza said. "What's the date today? December 7? Let's record it for posterity."

Chapter 19

Philadelphia
March 1772

"He's not the man for you, Betsy," my father said, implacable.

I stood in front of his desk like a child.

"I want your blessing," I said stubbornly.

"He's not the man for you," he repeated.

"How would you know," I cried. I turned on my heel and paced back and forth in his office.

"You've known him how long? Three months?" My father stared at me as if confronted with madness. "There are good men you've known for *years* and you would still be cautious. It's not like you to be so intemperate." *At your age,* he could have added. I credited him with not saying it.

"There is nothing wrong with me! I'm not intemperate or immoderate or impractical or *anything*! Would you have me be alone forever?" I spat the words. "Drying on the shelf like a brick of old bread! Why not marry if I choose? I'm thirty-five years old!"

"Christ! By all means, marry! Just not Henry. Or at least not so soon."

He paused, struck by a thought. "Dear God, you're not ... with child?"

I stared at him, incredulous. "The mere suggestion proves you do not know him!"

"I know he is eleven years younger than you are."

"And no young man could find me attractive at this age?"

"Damnation!" My father banged his hand down on his desk. The ink pot and the letter opener jumped. "What do we know about him? What do *you* know about him?"

We glared at each other. I would not list Henry's attributes like a heifer at the fair.

"I thought you would be pleased," I said finally. "He is kind, and hardworking. Everyone likes him, including people *you* trust. What issue do you have with him?"

My father raised his voice. "Can he support you? What possessions does he bring to a bride? Does he have the means to ask you for marriage at the age of twenty-four?"

Enough. I was tired of talk. I had let them steer me from William Franklin fifteen years ago, and I had talked myself out of my feelings for Nathaniel in the aftermath of the shock of my mother's death.

"Four months ago we had never heard of him," my father added. I crossed my arms across my chest and set my jaw.

I found Father's argument about Henry supporting me disingenuous. We had Graeme Park! I was the only remaining heir. Although still youthful in body and mind, Father was aging. Why would he not welcome a fit son-in-law and train Henry to work his land, at least for my sake? It was not as if I had anyone else after Father passed. It occurred to me suddenly that this was a subject Father and I had never discussed. What would I do when he died?

"I want you to be happy." My father softened. "I have wished you to marry for many years, my darling. All I want is your happiness. I adore you. I simply fail to understand your choice. Why do you insist upon—"

"Why do you not care for him?" I demanded. "What is it really?"

"He is a stranger," he said. "Henry's character is unknown to us. He's from another country."

"Your country, in fact. Scotland! Not some strange threatening faraway land." I refused to be swayed. I wasn't a little girl. I no longer believed in any future than the one immediately in front of me. "I see no stain upon his character. Unless you consider his affection for me to be a blemish."

My father gave a heaving sigh, leaned back in his chair, and crossed his arms over his chest. We were mirror images of each other. The sigh made him cough, a rusty shudder deep down.

"One year," he said finally. "Betsy, please. Court each other openly in Philadelphia this year. And then next spring, if you still love each other, I will bless this union. I will shout it from the rooftops, no, from the belfry of Christ Church! Darling girl, if he is as right as you say he is, he'll wait to spend his life with you. What's a year, measured against decades?"

I groaned. Not this trick again. This was the same scheme he'd pulled with William and I all those years ago, and it worked. William Franklin came home married to someone else, and that woman was now the wife of the New Jersey governor, enjoying a fine house in Perth Amboy.

"Henry doubts my affections," I said under my breath. I wasn't a girl any longer. Why did I need to wait?

"What?" he said, leaning forward and motioning to his ear.

"Not a year," I said. "A year is too long. Henry and I want to be married. We love each other."

"Six months, then."

I laughed without mirth. Was I a deal to be negotiated?

I was about to open my mouth to argue again when I looked at my father and saw him as other people must see him. In that moment he looked old, wheezy and frail through his shoulders. No longer a physician or person of status, just an elderly man holding on to his last daughter. His wife was dead, nine other children and two grandchildren also long gone and buried.

My anger seeped out of me. I sank into the chair in front of his desk and pleated my skirt into folds. I smoothed the fabric and then made folds again.

"Would Mother like Henry, do you think, Father?"

"She always respected a learned man," he answered slowly. "Any man who reads books knows how to use his own mind. She would want you to have a husband who was devoted to you and your happiness, whatever you believe that to be."

I looked at the vase of hyacinths from our garden on Father's desk. Our head gardener was one of the most accomplished around and had been with us for years. I could smell the flowers from where I sat, so sweet after a long winter. Their dainty petals radiated a jewel-like lavender blue color.

"Fine," I muttered. I looked at my dear father and lied to his face.

"Six months," I said.

A month later, I arrived as a bride at Olde Swedes' at nine o'clock at night. They sky was dark, almost completely black, the April moon hiding under a thick layer of cloud.

We moved silently from the road to the churchyard. Every sound under foot, each crinkle of leaf and crunch of pebble, sounded like thunder.

I'm sorry, I said in my mind to my father as I tiptoed down the very long path to the toward the shadow of the church. He would be at home, possibly with a friend, one of the Penns, perhaps, or a Nesbitt, nursing a drink, unaware that his daughter was secretly getting married without him. Betraying him. Soon, in just a few months, I would tell Father, and he would accept it, I'm sure. Henry needed to go to Scotland on family business for a couple of months in the summer and neither of us wanted him to go until we were married.

I looked over at Liza. We were pale as moonstone in the inky shadows.

She smiled at me. "It will be fine," she mouthed.

Behind us were John and Mary Redmond, and dear Benjamin Rush. It was Ben who supported Henry and I most of all. Perhaps he felt responsible, having dropped Henry in my lap, or at least in my parlor. I had asked John Dickinson to come, but he declined.

Conspicuously missing was my family. If Father wasn't there I also couldn't invite Anny and Johnny, or Reverend Peters, or anyone from the congregation of my own church, which I had attended all my life. Their absence hurt more than the lie.

"I'm getting married," I whispered to Liza in disbelief. Liza squeezed my hand.

We arrived at the church and stood by the side under a maple tree.

"Should I go get the rector?" John Redmond asked in a low voice. "He doesn't know we're here."

"Not yet," I whispered back. "Wait until Henry gets here."

Henry was upset when I told him what my father had said that day. He wanted the legendary Thomas Graeme to welcome him with open arms.

"Why would he oppose me when you're old enough to know your mind?"

"I don't know. I'm between Scylla and Charybdis," I told Henry miserably, and it was true. Choosing either man's wish would wreck me, and still leave me to face the other.

"Marry me," Henry had urged. "I am not looking for just any woman. I cannot be without you, Elizabeth Graeme. You have stolen a part of me. I've never met a woman like you. I've never felt this way."

"It's not that easy," I objected. "I love my father. I feel badly. I'm all he has left."

"You have it in your power to ruin me," Henry said fiercely. "Only your love matters. If you want to wait, we'll wait. I won't force your hand."

Oh, but I didn't wait. For the first time in my life, I chose love. Unconditionally, inconveniently, rashly. I chose love.

When I was young I never imagined my wedding day, which was just as well, for I would not have been able to see myself standing secretly in a churchyard in darkness, surrounded by a cemetery. The gravestones formed a shadowy line of sentry around us, miniature soldiers of slate that stood at attention. If I squinted hard I could see the glint of light of the river behind us. I wished Rebecca could have been there, but she was confined to bed, recovering from the difficult birth of another daughter this week.

Liza squeezed my hand again. "You are so beautiful," she whispered. "Timeless as Aphrodite."

The darkness quivered as a figure slid down the path toward us and stood next to me. Henry. I felt giddy.

"You can go fetch him now," I said to Redmond. John disappeared in the church and returned with Reverend Swenson.

Dr. Rush lit a tin lantern and held it up, its yellow light seeping across our whispering party. Henry's hand reached for mine. I shifted my bouquet of wildflowers to my other hand. The warmth of his skin made me think of babies, and the squirming warmth of Rebecca's newborn that afternoon. Earlier today I had visited and held her daughter, a tiny silken creature, named Elizabeth, after me.

Would I have children of my own? For the first time, it was possible. I was old for child bearing, but Mother was thirty-seven when she had me and my twin. Maybe one day Graeme Park would be noisy with my *own* grandchildren, the boys tall like Henry, the girls slight and dark-haired. I would tell them how their great-grandfather Thomas Graeme purchased our home from his father-in-law, a lieutenant governor of Pennsylvania. I'd point out the deer farm and tell them how my father had ingeniously built the fence with raised beds around the exterior so the deer could hop in but not out, and how we organized the cleared land into crops. I would show them the trees in the orchard, cherry and peach and apple. I would point out the knot in the parlor paneling where I got my finger stuck when I was six. I would tell them about the sumptuous parties we hosted and how long people talked about them afterward. And I would tell them about their luminous great-grandmother Ann Diggs Graeme, and how she taught me to tell stories that would make an audience gasp and clutch their chests.

"Let's begin," Reverend Swenson said softly, hold up a bible. "Who gives this woman?"

"I do," Dr. Rush said.

At our request, the ceremony was brief. Henry and I couldn't stop beaming at each other. We barely heard the vows, until Pastor Swenson pronounced us man and wife in a thick Swedish accent. Henry leaned down to kiss me to murmured approval from our small gathering. I was Mrs. Henry Fergusson, a wife!

"God be with you," the pastor said. "Don't take each other for granted."

We accepted the embraces and good wishes of our friends and turned to make our way into the church to sign the registry. I stepped toward the path and stumbled.

Seconds later I was sprawled on the dirt, momentarily stunned. A strangled cry left my lips. My pretty new cloak was tangled under me.

"Betsy!" Mary exclaimed. "Are you hurt?"

"I don't think so. I tripped over something."

Ben rushed toward me with the lantern held high so they could see me. Liza retrieved my bouquet.

I reached down to push myself to my feet and felt something hard and cold. I had tripped over a gravestone embedded in the earth. I tried to read the inscription on the stone, see a name, but Henry's hands were on my waist. He pulled me up and led me inside, away from the dark and into the light.

Very early the next morning I slipped into our house on
Second Street as the first swirls of color painted the
morning to life. I did not remember opening the door or
tiptoeing up the stairs, for my mind was on my husband.
We spent our wedding night at an inn, in the nicest room
they had.

I was not shy.

As we planned, Henry and I lived separately after our
wedding night. I assured him it would only be for a few
months.

"Tell him," Henry urged me daily when we met in town.
"Tell your father today. Waiting will only make it worse."

"He only just agreed to the idea of you," I protested.
"When he learned you're going to Scotland, he suggested the
marriage take place when you get back. His acceptance is
an improvement, my love. I'll tell him after you leave, I
promise. It will afford you, us, the safety of distance. When
you return, all will be well."

Henry shook his head, frowning.

"I promise," I said. "I'll tell him before you get back in
the fall. You know I hate this deception." I didn't know if I'd
ever lied about anything before in my life. Kept secrets, yes.
Lied deliberately, no.

In June Henry boarded his ship for Scotland. I didn't
know how our secret remained a secret, but it did. It
certainly helped that the season in Philadelphia was over
and everyone had scattered to their summer homes and
pursuits like billiard balls. I was wracked with guilt sitting

in our family pew each week listening to Peters's sermon. I'm not sure how my guilt wasn't written on my face. I felt terrible keeping my secret from my dear friend Reverend Peters, but keeping it from Anny hurt me the most. It was like lying to my own daughter, made worse by the fact that Liza was in on the secret, which turned Anny into an outsider. My heart felt wretched.

"You can't undo what you did," Liza said to me one night at cards in August. "Tormenting yourself won't help. Perhaps you should just get it over with and tell Papa Graeme. What are you waiting for, anyway?"

I didn't know. I certainly didn't regret marrying Henry. I was afraid of hurting my father, but I had already done that, hadn't I.

Ben Rush was no help. "You should have chosen someone respectable when your father sent you to London to find a husband," he joked. Even though there is ten years between us, Rush had become one of my closest friends over the past five years. He liked to talk as much as I did. His mind was like fireworks.

I smacked him. "Fine words from a bachelor such as yourself."

The summer passed. Every day, I tried to find my voice, and every day I failed.

Instead, I wrote a fifty-seven stanza poem called "Farewell to the muses written by a young woman soon after marriage." One of my better pieces, I thought.

Horsham
September 1772

How could it be September already? I did not have time to delay any longer.

I took a deep breath, and went in search of my father one afternoon.

"Where is Mr. Graeme?" I asked Sally, who was folding napkins.

"He went toward the barn." She nodded toward the east.

I found him looking at the north fields, surveying the hay. The farm was alive around us. Farmhands were stacking bales of hay and sorghum, the Indian corn growing high over my head in the field.

I linked my arm through my father's. "There you are Father."

"Isn't she a beauty," he said, gesturing to the land. He patted my arm. "Forty years, and I never tire of it."

"You have done well," I said. "I remember how it was here when I was small. This is a different place now. You've worked hard."

We stood and watched the land, the sun shimmering on the golden crops. A hawk flew high, its wings spread wide, and made a large sweeping arc over our heads.

"I wish your brothers were still alive. They were to carry on Graeme Park. A man needs his sons. The land demands it." He turned to me. "When I'm gone, this will be yours, Betsy. You know that, I hope?"

I nodded.

I have been married for five months, Father.

"I have something I would like to discuss with you," I said. "Will you take a walk with me?"

He lifted his hat, wiped his sweat on his sleeve. "A problem at the house?"

"No, nothing like that."

He nodded, and we moved forward.

We had reached the path by the distillery when Old Joseph rushed up on horseback. "Mr. Graeme, you're needed, sir. A fight broke out between field hands. Blood has been shed."

My father left to deal with the disturbance, and I returned to the house, my stomach clenched with tension. Nothing was ever easy.

The next morning I woke and paused at the window to admire the sky, a dazzling blue, when I saw my father coming up the avenue toward the house, hat set low on his brow. For an old man, he moved quickly, sure-footed. I watched the speck of him grow bigger, coming closer, until at last he reached the outer edges of the garden. I glanced over at my wardrobe. I would dress quickly and go to him.

When I looked back, I saw my father pitch forward. In an instant, he was on the ground, an arm trapped under him, hat thrown off.

I ran downstairs in my shift and bare feet, calling for help.

We ran out to him, but it was too late. My father was lying on the ground dead.

Selfishly, I was feverishly glad I had not told my father of my marriage before he fell. I would have thought myself responsible for killing him.

I loved my father deeply, but his death did not bring the anguish to me that my mother's had, or my sisters'.

I found myself tasked with writing yet another epitaph:

The soul that lived within this Crumbling dust
In every Act was Eminently just.
Peaceful through Life, as peaceful, too, in death,
Without one Pang, he rendered back his breath.

As expected, Father left me Graeme Park. His will spelled it out in detail: my inheritance included the house, the land, and everything growing on the land. I also was the beneficiary of the household furniture and plate, and the obligation of our rented house in Philadelphia.

"Can we buy a ship?" asked Johnny. He was a boy who dreamed of going to sea.

"Not likely," I answered.

The eight hundred and thirty-seven acres of Graeme Park left to me included crops, livestock, tools, twenty acres of orchard, our two slaves, Mars and Alex, and seven servants. In his will, Father ordered that we were no longer to consider Old Joseph a servant; we were to care for him for the rest of his life. I decided I would release Alex and Mars one day, but for the time being I needed them so I could keep the farm operational.

The will also stated I had to pay James Young, my late sister Jane's husband, a thousand pounds, at a time of my choosing. James and his children, my Anny and Johnny, were also left two pieces of land in Northampton County, one a thousand acres and the other five hundred acres. Those properties were of little value. Liza was not listed in the will, because Father knew that I would always provide and care for her, just as I would Old Joseph.

At first glance, it seemed a handsome legacy. At closer inspection, it did not take long for me to realize that we were completely broke.

Unknown to me, there were many outstanding debts against Graeme Park. My father's will did not address any of these. More than fourteen hundred pounds would have to be paid back—a small fortune—without any information on which assets would cover the debts. Unfairly, I was required to find a way to pay all the debt that was now under my name, yet James Young's inheritance of a thousand pounds would be untouched. How could that be?

I went over and over it with Liza, but the numbers remained the same. We were in financial trouble. I needed Henry, and he was thousands of miles away. A letter would take weeks to reach him. I was dizzy with worry. Even when he came home, he had no experience running a farm on his own, let alone a plantation of this size.

There were more immediate problems. The world did not know I was not a single woman. From a legal perspective, the consequences were staggering. Even though the inheritance was mine and I had lived at Graeme Park from the time I was a baby, any action now required Henry's approval since we were married. John Dickinson volunteered his legal services to me and counseled me to publicly announce our marriage in order to keep creditors at bay.

"You have no choice, Betsy," he said. "Everything belongs to Henry now. While he's away, you need his approval to sell what's his. I'm sorry, but it would help if people knew." I wondered if Dickinson had a feeling that this would happen, if that was why he hadn't wanted to come to my wedding, such as it was. Richard Stockton also counselled me, but none of it helped.

I had been married for five months, and known my husband less than a year. Of our five married months, Henry had been overseas for three of those. The first two months we had spent living apart, meeting in secret. Yet by the marriage and couverture laws, he now owned outright everything that was mine, even down to my undergarments and the shoes on my feet.

"If that's true, when Henry dies, why does everything return to *me* and not go to *his* estate?" I asked my legal counsel.

"The laws are changing, but not quickly." Dickinson was sympathetic, but the law was clear, Henry owned Graeme Park, and by extension, me.

I had no choice. Reluctantly, in Henry's absence, I informed Philadelphia that I had married. Most people were stunned into disbelief.

"Jesus Mary and Joseph!" Mrs. O'Rourke said in her fabric shop as her mouth gaped in surprise, revealing her black teeth and the gummy peppermint within. "I didn't think it could be true, Miss Graeme! Not you! Begging your pardon. Er, Missus Fergusson."

Reverend Peters simply looked wounded, and pressed his lips tightly together without saying much. Some reacted with humor: Rebecca cheekily reminded me that *I* was the one who had boasted the whole world would get matrimony in their heads before I would. Luckily, Anny and Johnny took it in stride without hard feelings.

"It's like a novel," Anny breathed. "How romantic."

"Why did you want to do that?" Johnny said, perplexed.

No matter which way I turned the figures over, I couldn't find a way to ease the numbers. Was there someone I could ask for money? I thought briefly of my former brother-in-law, but Charles Stedman was in financial difficulty after his business investments fell through. The embargo of British goods following the Stamp Act and the Townshend Acts had hit him hard. He even sold the beautiful house that he had been building with my sister before she died. Charles actually added to our debt problem, for my father had co-signed for an eight hundred-pound loan for him that was now up to me to repay.

"What do we do?" I asked Liza.

"The obvious step is to get rid of the house in town."

The decision was a painful one. I loved Graeme Park in the summer, but the thought of living there year-round through the winter left me limp with despair. I had no wish to live so remotely, so far from civilization. Still, it had to be done. Even without the city house, I didn't see how we could make Graeme Park profitable. Even if Henry did his best with the farm, we were so far under water it would be hard to get ahead.

I realized belatedly Father had never provided for his family on the income from Graeme Park. His money had come from his work as a physician, and through the generous public appointments that had been granted to him over the years by the Penns.

Barely a week after my father died, two men came to the house to rifle through our belongings. The four of us, Liza and Anny and Johnny and I, watched the men manhandle the contents of our home.

"Why do we have to let them do this?" Johnny asked.

"They need to calculate our worth so we can settle our financial reverses," I answered.

"They're assessing the value of the estate," Liza added.

"It's worth it if it helps us in the long run," Anny said.

Snuff-stained hands turned over possessions both prized and mundane. Nothing went untouched, including Father's shaving kit, the locket containing a braid of Jane's hair, Liza's gold bracelet, even the dog's basket.

Johnny's face was rigid with anger. He was half-man, half-boy. Anny simply wove her fingers through mine and huddled close to me.

How could Father have left me this mess? Did he know? He must have. I wished he had made arrangements, or at least discussed his financial situation with me.

"Will they take our things?" Johnny asked.

"I don't know," I answered truthfully. The world was upside down.

Maybe we could keep the house and a hundred acres, I thought, and sell the rest. I would look for what I could hawk for money. Perhaps my filigree brooch, the best of my fine dresses, some of the silverplate. Not my writing desk. Definitely not that.

I was still a newlywed. This was not the way I imagined my first year of marriage would go. I wished Henry would return, but I advised him not to travel in winter. If he couldn't get here by Christmas, I told him, he should wait until spring. Storms on the Atlantic were far too treacherous in January and February. My passage had been enough of a nightmare in November and December.

It was almost laughable. James Young and I were co-executors of the will. Of course Father had named him as an executor: James was the father of his grandchildren, even though I'd barely seen him over the years while I was raising his son and daughter.

Despite James having the same access to the numbers as I did, he insisted on asking for his inheritance. The problems did not concern him, he said, he wanted his thousand pounds. He refused to listen to reason.

After being absent for years, he began to come to the house several times a week to press for his inheritance. We quarreled, each time worse than the last. I could not connect the man I had known for years, and even sometimes called friend, with the man before me now. He was ugly and ill-tempered, and beyond impatient.

"James, I don't understand how you could think the debts don't affect you," I said, perched on Father's desk as the assessors rattled through Mother's china in the cabinet on the other side of the wall. I cringed as I heard the clank of two pieces banged roughly together. That china was over a hundred years old. Mother would shrivel to see this. "You've seen the ledgers yourself. How can I pay you money I don't have? "

He shrugged. "Sell land."

I spoke strongly. "The will explicitly states that the timing is to be *of my choice*. I would not hold back your thousand pounds if I could easily give it to you!"

"You got it all, Betsy, the house and over eight hundred bloody acres. You got it all! All Thomas left me was a scant thousand pounds and some land nobody wants! I'm the father of his grandchildren! If Jane was alive—"

"I raised your children." My voice was icy cold.

"Just sell. Give me my thousand pounds."

"Will you *listen*? Even that takes time. A buyer must be found. Otherwise, I can't pay the fourteen hundred in debt against the estate and still pay you."

"What of Henry's money?"

"Henry's still in Scotland." I didn't think Henry actually had any assets, in any case he'd never said he did. Still, I hoped he would return from his family in Scotland with good news, surprising me with a windfall.

My brother-in-law was unmoved. "Get Henry to give you power of attorney. Write to him. Have the lawyers draw it up."

In the coming weeks, I learned James was even refusing to repay his own personal bills from purchases in the neighborhood that he had charged to Graeme Park, including for his stockings, chewing tobacco, and even his own boots. He was siphoning everything he could from me when his children were still in my home. He was a cad.

In moments alone, I prayed and asked Jane if she had really known this man, for if she had, how could she have ever loved him? James's behavior was confounding; he was *family*. Nothing we said shifted his opinion or persuaded him to be less aggressive. He had no interest in working with me as co-executor in any useful way.

Our creditors were knocking hard at the door. The irony was rich: I could not claim a single coin from debts owed to my father, yet every coin we owed was being called in, by litigation too, if it pleased them. I went back and forth from Graeme Park to the Philadelphia house during the months after Father's death to sort our affairs, leaving Liza at home with Anny and Johnny.

In February, finally a small victory. I was able to sell a small plot of land Father owned south of Philadelphia.

I returned to Graeme Park after two weeks away relieved and bone weary.

How I hated Graeme Park in the winter, I repeated to myself as I looked through the carriage window. Snow, snow, and more snow, topped by a steel-gray sky and a house framed by dreary brown trees. I guessed I should be grateful it still wasn't as bad as England's black coal skies.

We had so much work to do. Reports came in with alarming regularity about broken fencing, leaking water pumps, crumbling mortar. While I was happily writing books and holding literary evenings, Father had let things go.

"Did you see James in town?" Liza asked as I pulled off my lambskin gloves and dropped my packages on the table. I bought the bare minimum: Sugar, flour, a headache tonic.

"No." I was glad I hadn't seen him. I handed my cloak to Sally. I harbored no illusions about ever having a civil relationship with my brother-in-law.

"Our Philadelphia house has new renters," I told Liza. I sat down on the chair in the hall and tugged off a boot. "I sold most of the contents, that was a relief. What's left will arrive by cart next week. And I managed to sell the Moyamensing lot, although it only fetched two hundred and thirty-three pounds. I had hoped for three hundred at least. Still, it's in the right direction."

I looked up. The house was too quiet. I expected to see Anny bounding toward me with outstretched arms, as she usually did. And Johnny was never this quiet.

"Is everything—"

Liza shook her head. "They're gone, Betsy." Liza's face was pinched, skin the color of wig powder.

"What do you mean, gone?"

"James came for them," she said sadly. "Just yesterday. I didn't see this coming."

James had laid his hand, and took the children away. My punishment had been delivered. He may as well have put a knife in me. I instinctively knew they would not be coming back to us.

"Collateral for his thousand pounds," I muttered.

"Anny didn't want to go," Liza said, disturbed. "She put up a fuss. She was very distraught."

Anny, my sweet girl. And Johnny, my feisty boy. He had already been like a bow pulled tight after his grandfather died, upset and irritable all the time.

"James is ruining us!" I blurted out. This was worse than having financial troubles. "Surely he's won't expect young Anny to live with men—"

"He arranged for her to live with Charles and Margaret Stedman." I still thought of her as Margaret Abercrombie.

My legs would not hold me. I sank heavily to the floor, my skirt wet with snow and mud. "And Johnny?"

"James apprenticed him out. He said he's old enough."

Chapter 20

Horsham
1773

"I'll always be your loving Liza," Liza said, blowing a kiss as she left us. "I won't, however, come between a man and his wife. I shall stay in the city."

Henry and I moved into the large east chamber that had been my parents' for so many years. I wished Liza hadn't left. I was lonely, and even thought I felt bad for thinking it, I craved female company. Henry worked out on the land all day while I stayed in the house or garden. We had few servants left. At first we kept our coachman and gardener, which we deemed indispensable at the time, as well as the cook, and one housemaid, Sally. A short time later we let the gardener go, and then the coachman.

I knew Henry was doing everything he could to save us, so I didn't complain, but I hated the solitude of my day, with not enough money to go visiting. No help came home with Henry. I wanted to invite friends over, but I could no longer afford to entertain. Close friends like Mary Campbell came from Burlington, and Rebecca and her children, for they were like family, but other friends had to wait for better times. I played my harpsichord for hours at a time some days just to fill the gaping wounded silence.

Henry enthusiastically dove into being "laird of Graeme Park," as he liked to jest. I wished I could be as fond of farming as my husband, but I wasn't. Farming and housework both seemed like drudgery to me. Working the land was certainly hard on Henry; when he returned at the end of the day he was worn out, tired and too spent to wish to talk. Fortunately, in our marriage bed there was joy between us, so we had that.

Sometimes I walked the nineteen miles to Philadelphia to stay with the Stedmans and got a ride back. I could visit Anny as often as I liked as she was living at Charles and Margaret's, but Johnny was staying with the dry goods merchant that he was apprenticed to, and I had less opportunity to see him. Charles was irate with James for his behavior over the will, and the two previous brother-in-laws had parted ways in anger, which meant that Johnny was no longer allowed to enter the Stedman home, where Anny was living. It made no sense. Another one of James Young's strange punishments.

"I am sorry, Betsy, that you find pastoral life so challenging," Margaret said to me while she boiled the kettle. I went to the Stedmans' home to take Anny her birthday gift, a sampler I had stitched for her.

It was difficult for me, still, to think that Margaret was married to my sister's husband and that Ann was long dead. It was even stranger that it was the same Margaret that William Franklin had written to all those years ago, before poor James Abercrombie was lost at sea. An eternity ago. So many changes had happened since my carefree youthful days. To think that one day I had thought all our problems would be solved if we could only get the Indians to stop murdering people; and get the French out of America. It was laughable.

"I do hope you do not feel too isolated," Margaret added sympathetically.

"I keep busy," I said. Occupations that had been happy pursuits for me now felt tedious. I was fed up with reading and walking and needlework, for I did all of them alone. I thought marriage would end seclusion, not create it. "Henry and I are happy."

"Would you like tea?" she asked me. "It's Dutch tea."

Margaret wouldn't dare serve British tea after parliament passed the Tea Act, which allowed the East India Tea Company to bring tea shipments to the colonies without stopping in England first. It was meant to drop the price of tea to below the cost of the smuggled Dutch tea, but the move ignited the disgust of colonists. Another game was being played. England was still moving us like game pieces.

"They can't trick us," local merchants cried bitterly. "'Tis not for our benefit, it saves the East India Company from bankruptcy and milks us! Why can't we choose whose tea we drink?!"

"No British tea must land," Ben Rush commanded. He had added his voice to the general outcry over the past three years. Ben was deeply involved in the resistance movement now, and an active member of the Sons of Liberty chapter here in Philadelphia. The rebellious sentiments that began in Boston had swept through the colonies like ignited gunpowder.

"To think," Margaret sighed, "all this fuss over tea. Tea! You would think the last war would speak for itself when we rid the continent of France and placated the Indians. Honestly, where would we be without the protection of England? Sometimes I am not sure what the rebels are thinking. They must be mad. These are times of trial."

Charles and Margaret were loyal to the crown. And yet she still served Dutch tea, not British, for if they openly supported Britain, the rebellious colonists would paint them as traitors. "British tea contains the seeds of slavery," the rebels thundered. Even John Dickinson, my quiet friend and newly installed volunteer legal counsel, had abandoned his voice of reason. "If anyone assists in unloading, landing, or storing the tea, he shall ever after be deemed an enemy to his country!" John Dickinson pronounced. In a very rapid period of time, my friends and family had separated into one acrimonious camp or the other: for the crown or against it.

"Ah well, let's talk of other things," Margaret sighed. "How is it with Henry home now?"

"He's out in the fields most of the time," I said. "Sometimes he doesn't even come in for his midday meal. Yet as I said, we are happy."

"Are you lonely?" she asked sagely.

"I miss the pleasures of living in Philadelphia half the year," I confessed. "And I miss Liza very much." I did not mention pining for Anny or Johnny, since Margaret had kindly taken Anny in.

"I miss your Attic Evenings."

The thought caused a pain in my chest. "Our fortunes may change again," I said. "Henry is a good man. I feel fortunate that he brings me a happiness that had previously been unknown to me. A great deal of happiness." I did not want her to think I had regrets.

"I heard hesitation in your voice. Are you sure you are in a pleasing position?"

"I am," I said. I paused. "Well, every newly married couple must get to know each other, both the light and dark, mustn't they? I'm sure it was like that for you and Charles when you married?" She had been happy with her first husband before she lost James to the depths of the sea.

"Dark?" Margaret looked at me with concern.

I wished I hadn't said anything.

I laughed, a little too forcefully. "I just meant that Henry has moods. Don't we all? Sometimes he's silent and I feel he doesn't want to speak to me. He can be almost unapproachable, in one moment, and then talkative and attentive the next. I haven't lived with anyone like that before."

"Could it be the stress of learning to run Graeme Park? He must be tired."

"Yes, of course. Of course. I'm being silly. I suspect I am puzzling to him as well! Too needy, perhaps, at the wrong times. Please believe that we are very happy."

"You both have gone through many challenges over the past year, haven't you?" Margaret paused. "It will pass. You will just have to visit me more and stay as long as you like!"

My niece came in then, eating a pear. Her face lit up when she saw me.

"Aunty!"

"My darling girl, how I've missed you."

Anny often told me her years with me at Graeme Park were her happiest. *". . . And now that I am of an age to know and return your tenderness, I have left you,"* she had written to me with love, and a touch sadly.

This trip to town for her seventeenth birthday was a convenient excuse to embrace her again, and spend much needed time together.

In October, Henry and I tried to sell seven hundred acres of our land. No one wanted to buy them.

In November, groups of bitter men in Philadelphia met to plot how to get away from the long insidious reach of Britain.

In the middle of December, the Sons of Liberty, dressed as Indians, dumped more than three hundred crates of tea, from three different ships, into Boston Harbor, under the cover of darkness. The tea was worth a small fortune.

The following week when a shipload of tea headed toward Philadelphia, it was emphatically turned away while piloting up the Delaware River. The captain came ashore to plead his case, but eight thousand people showed up at a town meeting to angrily tell the ship's captain what he could do with his tea. The captain, his ship, and the cargo of tea slunk back to England at the end of the month.

"That captain is lucky we didn't tar and feather him like we do the tax collectors," Anny said fiercely to me over the rejected Philadelphia tea. "Or slit his throat."

I looked at her, surprised. "You have strong feelings," I commented mildly.

"I do," she agreed. "We should not be governed by an island three thousand miles away where we have no say. After they turned that ship away, the captain had no business arriving in town to try to bully us into accepting his cargo."

My little girl, now a woman, had become a patriot. Her brother, when I saw him, talked incessantly of joining the British army. Brother and sister, each taking an uncompromising stance. These troubles with England were severing families, and my family was no exception.

"You must know that Margaret and Charles support the crown," I said to her in a low voice. "I trust you're tempering your opinions here in their home."

"Of course I am," Anny said a touch scornfully. "Tell me you're not a loyalist too?"

I was taken aback. It was a bold question. Anger against any citizen who supported England festered like an infected boil across Philadelphia and beyond. Even church leaders maintained careful neutrality. They could not side with the resistance, for if they did they would lose half their congregations and be seen as treasonous. They also could not side with the loyalists, for their churches would be vandalized and their names dragged into hostility. They would face violence or have their homes burned to the ground; their families would suffer. No one was safe, not anymore, on either side.

"My sympathies are with the colonies," I finally answered, which was true. Of all people, I wanted to be honest with her. I felt danger creep toward us as certain as the tide, although Henry had done nothing but scoff at the uprisings as piffle.

"I feel that the colonies will work with Britain toward resolution of these matters," I added. "Listen, Anny, please don't—"

"I know," she said flatly. "This is between us. I'm not a fool, Aunty."

I was grateful to see the end of 1773, even though it would mean another long winter imprisoned in my white wasteland while my husband wondered why I wasn't with child.

I was hopeful for 1774. Surely we were due for a good year.

Horsham
May 1774

"They are finally getting Massachusetts under control,"
Henry said approvingly after Parliament passed the
Intolerable Acts in the spring. "Fair enough, since Boston
refuses to pay for the tea they destroyed. They have no
remorse. Imagine if it was Spain or France. We'd rip them
apart."

"I can't see how taking drastic measures is going to
make Boston feel more conciliatory or repentant," I argued.
"That never works. Boston is being held hostage as
punishment. The British have closed the port and taken
away their right to govern themselves and hold meetings. All
this over tea?" I thought of the women raising their families
there, and what the impact would be on their ability to get
food and everyday supplies for their families.

"The king needs to get to the leaders of the Sons of
Liberty and shut them down," Henry said. "All those men
sneaking around, plotting to undermine honest rule.
Treason is treason. They'll even recruit a wharf rat if he is
interested in making trouble for the fun of it. Better for the
king to come down with a heavy hand than let them breed
more rebel rats. He needs to capture Adams and Hancock
and the other ringleaders to solve the problem."

I was caught between two worlds, and sadly, there were
people I loved dearly in each.

After almost two decades of writing, sometimes around
the clock, especially with *Telemachus*, my pen fell silent.
Despite my rural captivity and the long days, it felt
unappealing to write or translate literature from another
language when the world around me was writhing with

conflict. Even Graeme Park was in a bad way. The Intolerable Acts may have been in effect in Massachusetts, but we felt them from as far away as little Horsham in Philadelphia County. There was talk of a formal committee forming to address the British problem. The wind held whispers of words we hadn't heard before. *Liberty. Freedom*.

Last year Virginia created a Committee of Correspondence to keep informed of issues as they arose, then every colony added representatives to the committee. Ben Rush liked to say that it was the first time each colony thought about another. Now all thirteen were linked for a common cause: keeping an eye on Massachusetts and Britain's heavy hand there. We were in a fight against oppression. Pennsylvania's delegate to the committee was Robert Smith, the man who designed Carpenters' Hall.

One by one, my friends and family chose a side. The loyalists, convinced they were right: my husband, my nephew John, the Stedmans, the Morgans, Rebecca and William Smith, the Redmonds, and so many others. The patriots, equally as convinced they were right: My niece Anny, my dear Liza, Dr. Rush, Annis and Richard Stockton, James Young, the Redmans, the Hopkinsons, the Duchés, the Boudinots, Joseph Galloway, and so many others.

It was like a line drawn down the middle of my parlor.

John Dickinson opposed the tax and trade laws but didn't want to openly rebel against Britain or agitate violence. Many others were on the fence, too, conflicted, or kept changing sides. A great canyon was cracking open between us. Each week more people pounded their stake in their respective ground, or somewhere in the middle, confused.

It was bad enough to experience the split between my friends, but to see my own *husband* on the other side? I hardly knew what to think.

Horsham
September 3, 1774

"Liza and I are going into town today," I reminded Henry as he kissed my collarbone. Liza had been here for a week, and I decided to accompany her back to Philadelphia. We would walk, it was a beautiful day, more summer than fall.

"Is there anything you need?" I asked as I watched him slide out of bed.

Henry shook his head and reached for his shirt. "Just what's on the list."

He paused, looking down at me. "You are beautiful."

I stretched languorously for his benefit.

"I'm staying with Margaret and Charles for a few days," I said. "I'll probably be back on Tuesday or Wednesday. I'll ask Charles to bring me and if he can't I'll ask Ben. He usually goes to see patients this way."

"Be safe, love," he said. "Stay on the main roads."

Liza and I set off two hours later as the sun crested the top of the trees. I was pensive as we walked to the end of the property. I looked around me dejectedly. A few short years ago Graeme Park buzzed like a hive with people coming and going, work in every direction the eye could see. These days we survived on willpower and a minimum of hands, the remaining workers scattered like spiders. Our world got smaller daily. Even the baker who benefited for years from our bread order stopped letting us purchase on credit. Thank God for the farmers who leased some of our land to farm.

"It will get better," Liza said, reading my thoughts. She was one of the few people left who had been here during the days when we glimmered with abundance. "You'll see. A few good harvests, a few acres sold."

I nodded, although I did not see. We were not making any significant improvements, and every day a new problem arose. The simple, endless days slid together with only endless toil to link them. I had spun all the flax I cared to spin, carded wool until my wrists ached, wove blankets and shawls until I wanted to cut my hands off. If we could only find a buyer for some of the land. Or perhaps we could rent out the house and land and live in Philadelphia. Either way, we need a buyer or a renter with money.

I walked faster, and Liza adjusted her stride to match mine.

"Perhaps if you have a baby, you'll feel happier," she suggested tentatively.

"Henry has been home a year," I said. "He doesn't suffer from lack of rigor in our marriage bed. Any obstacles on that front are with God."

Liza nodded. "A year isn't long with all the worries you've had," she said kindly.

"My sister Ann was married for years and years without a child. Not even a stillbirth. Maybe I'm barren too."

We walked on in silence a while, breathing in the morning.

"Look, black walnut seeds," Liza said, pointing to the ground. She scooped up two in her hand, then added a third and attempted to juggle. "Remember how you used to collect them for ink? You were convinced you needed all the ink you could get. You were afraid you would run out."

I smiled. "I needed barrels and barrels. I think I asked Father to plant more walnut trees."

"Are you writing?"

I had only written two poems since Henry returned. Last year I wrote odes to the seasons, and sent them to Annis Stockton in Princeton. I liked my ode to spring the best.

"I should start again," I said.

"You should," Liza agreed. "It makes you happy, and few women in the world can write like you do. You don't seem like yourself."

We walked east along County Line Road to the Horsham Friends Meeting House where we stopped to speak to our Quaker friends leaving Meeting, then continued down to Old York Road and on to Bethlehem Pike toward Germantown.

It was a fine day, a comfortable temperature. Our boots barely kicked up dust in the road.

By noon, we had been walking for a few hours and we were hungry. We had bread and dried meat with us and a flask of cordial, but we planned to stop at the Rising Sun tavern for a rest and a hot meal.

"Let's keep going until we get there," I suggested.

"I fancy a lovely steak and kidney pie," Liza sighed. "Dripping with gravy."

"Smoked ham," I said. "With fresh peas."

"Roast potatoes with onion strips!"

"Malt ale."

"I'd rather have cider," Liza countered.

"Fresh cherries," I offered. "With a plate of cheese and grapes."

"No. Sweet apple cake with clotted cream."

We were interrupted from our food reveries by the sound of a group coming toward us. We could not see them; the road curved and was hedged on both sides by elderberry bushes. I heard horses and a cart, and male voices.

Out of habit, my hand moved to the knife in my pocket. We didn't usually have problems on this road; it was well traveled and relatively safe. Mostly we passed houses and farms and said hello to cows and sheep and children along the way.

We moved to the side of the road and hugged the bushes. When the party emerged around the corner, we could see they were no threat, mostly teenaged boys on horseback. Two horses pulled a cart loaded with crates of vegetables and sacks of what appeared to be grain, being driven by an older man, who looked to be the father of one of the boys, judging by the matching yellow hair.

They dipped their hats to us.

"Good day, ladies," the man called. "Everything alright?"

"We are very well, sir," Liza answered. "Good day to you."

The man nodded. "If you're on the way to town, you'll find it a busy place."

"Why's that?" I asked.

"On account of the meeting."

"What meeting?" Liza enquired.

"The continental congress that's gathering at the Carpenters' Hall. Over the troubles."

That was this week then.

"We are headed to Boston," a boy explained. He looked to be Johnny's age, about fifteen.

"Just like you to chat up the ladies, Andrew," one of the boys jeered.

I stopped walking. "You're going to Boston with food? Is the situation that bad already?" I directed my questions to the man.

He nodded. "It will be soon enough. My wife's family is there. The port has been closed for four months. Boston is choking. Any supplies will be sorely welcome come winter. Seems a good idea to make the trip while the roads are good."

After all these months, Boston was still being strangled until the king was satisfied order had been restored. In addition to the port being closed and thousands of British soldiers flooding Boston, the local government remained shut down. The courts had been overtaken. Even holding a benign town meeting was illegal. Bostonians were being held powerless as continued punishment. Ships rocked idly at the piers, sailors walked the town aimlessly, shops sat empty.

"Good luck to you," Liza said sincerely.

"What can we do?" I asked.

The man shrugged. "If you have a farm, send food."

"People there used to be able to leave, but now they can't," the man's son said. "British troops have Boston circled. My aunt Chrissy says the soldiers fire their guns on the town green all the time for no reason except to scare people, the bastards."

"Abe."

"They're not even allowed to fish without a special pass," another boy said.

"And you can imagine how much the regulars are charging Boston folk for a fishing pass," the driver said sadly.

With the port closed, food and money were drying up too. All the citizens were trapped, surrounded by General Gage and his four thousand redcoats.

The driver sighed. "Never thought I'd see the day." He tipped his hat and clicked his tongue. "Move on," he said to the horses. "Good day, ladies. Fare thee well."

Liza and I rested at the Rising Sun for an hour. When we set off again, we were in high spirits, our meal warm in our bellies. We saw blue jays, a woodpecker, a cardinal, and armies of squawking geese overhead. We called greetings to passersby, one carriage at a time, and stopped often to talk with the women along the way, or the children enjoying the last beautiful weather before the chill of fall moved in.

We reached the edge of town around late afternoon and heard beasts and carriages coming up hard and fast behind us. This group was clearly different from normal traffic, they moved with urgency. There was a stiff-looking man on a horse leading in front, dressed in formal livery. The travelers were well guarded by men in uniform flanked around the carriages on horseback, muskets at the ready.

"They're on the way to the Continental Congress," Liza said in awe. "They must be."

"Did you see who it was?" I asked.

"I thought I saw John Jay," Liza said, "of New York. They were at the Christmastide ball that the Shippens gave last year, do you recall?"

I felt a small thrill. The Continental Congress was actually going to happen, and in our own hometown! Joseph Galloway told me he was going to represent Pennsylvania. I heard Thomas Mifflin was attending, and several others that were not personal friends. Most colonies were sending more than one representative.

"If they're caught, they'll hang," Liza breathed. Joseph Galloway had already received death threats.

"The Intolerable Acts have pushed men to the point where they will risk their lives," I said, my voice full of wonder. Impossibly, it was true.

I knew the Congress was being held to discuss the problem of the king stripping away freedoms. After the uproar in Boston for the past three or four years, and the taxation acts, we couldn't assume that England would give America representation or even a fair hand.

"Our liberty is at stake," Ben Rush had said over and over. "They're taking away a way of life we've had for a hundred and fifty years. All of a sudden."

"I wish I could participate," I said, watching the coach go by.

"We're still British subjects," Liza said, frowning. "I don't understand this."

"I don't think they're trying to overthrow Britain," I told Liza lightly. "No one wants a civil war. The colonies are asking for the same rights that men in England have. Aren't we *all* the king's subjects, both in England and America and in the other British colonies around the world? I know Henry wants the Congress to ask King George to address the grievances in an orderly manner. It's business."

"I thought Massachusetts isn't allowed to be at meetings or have anything to do with government?" Liza said. "And yet they're here? I can't believe this is actually happening! Madness to think all thirteen colonies sent men."

"Twelve," I corrected. "Galloway told me Georgia isn't sending anyone."

"Georgia must have some sense," muttered Liza. "Tell me, Betsy, if it's not hostile, why are there war ships in Boston Harbor with cannons aimed at the town? And why was that group armed?"

Philadelphia
September 3, 1774

"Here you are! You made it!" Margaret Stedman welcomed us with open arms. Despite my efforts to the contrary, I still thought of her as young Margaret Abercrombie, although none of us were young now.

"We got lost in a field of sunflowers," Liza said. "The sun was hitting them in the most perfect way, and they were almost as tall as us. We could not resist their loveliness."

The maid stepped forward to take our traveling clothes. She was pretty, I noted absently, hair the color of ripened wheat, and a tiny waist. She was small, with dainty features. I had seen her before and not really looked at her. I smiled at her when I caught her staring at me.

"Prepare some small beer, Jenny," Margaret told her. "It's a hot day and we're in need of refreshment." The girl nodded and slipped away.

"Liza. Betsy." Charles came into the hall and reached out to embrace us one at a time. "All my favorite girls are here now. Let's call Anny too."

"Come," Margaret said. "Your feet must be wailing." She pointed us toward the parlor. "How good of you to walk here."

"We saw some of the men on their way to the Congress," Liza said. "They flew by us in fine carriages, looking very determined and serious."

Charles grunted. "Philadelphia is spewing like molten metal."

We seated ourselves in comfortable chairs.

"I think you should consider leaving for a time," I told Charles fiercely. "Philadelphia is a rebel city now. I'm worried for your safety, you and Margaret. At the very least, come to Graeme Park." I must have said it a dozen times since the spring.

Charles dismissed me with a wave of his hand. "Tempest in a teapot. It will pass. The king will subdue the rebels and the rebels will back down."

"Aunty Betsy!" Anny ran down the stairs. "Liza! We expected you earlier."

I laughed. "Permit these two ladies a slower walking time, my sweet. We are a little older than you are. Although I am grateful for your enthusiasm."

"I think we played as much as we walked," Liza said.

"I had to stop her from dancing in a cornfield," I said. "Even after the sunflowers."

"Ah, there's a reason for the lass's eagerness," Charles said, with a fond look at Anny. "Go on now, tell them."

"I am quite taken with a certain gentleman!" Anny hugged herself, looking delighted. "I have been dying to tell you both in person!"

"Oh?" I asked.

The object of her desire was a Dr. Billy Smith, a graduate of the medical school with a stellar reputation for being proficient with healing herbs and medicines. No relation to Rebecca's husband, another William Smith. Anny gurgled for ages with news of her doctor, her face alight. I watched her, thinking of three-year old Anny marching around draped in her mother's lace stole.

"She should wait at least a year," I said to Liza when we were alone. "Take her time. She is young and it's too soon."

Liza scoffed.

"This is different," I said meaningfully. "I was a woman of *thirty-five* when I married. Anny is a *girl*. And far too open with her feelings for such a short courtship, it's not comely. I will speak to her."

Liza laughed in my face. "I wouldn't bother. She seems to have made up her mind."

"I don't want Anny married to a man who may not be who she thinks he is," I said.

Liza stared at me. I felt my face flush.

"Maybe he is who she thinks he is," she said mildly.

Philadelphia
September 5, 1774

Liza and I were headed to the shops on Monday morning when we saw from the steady stream of traffic headed toward the Carpenters' Hall that the Congress was about to begin.

"Ooooh, let's go watch." Liza steered me over to Chestnut Street.

One man after another arrived at the hall. Some walked, some came on horseback, others were delivered by chaise.

We watched dozens of men young and old climb the stairs to the main door. They were well groomed and fresh, in wigs and without, wearing new silk stockings and freshly polished shoes. Our friend Joseph Galloway nodded to us and we waved at him enthusiastically.

"Why meet here and not at the statehouse, I wonder?" Liza asked, shifting her empty basket from one arm to the other.

"Less obvious of a revolt?" I guessed.

"I wish I could be a fly on the wall in there," Liza said. "I wonder what they'll say. Especially the men from Massachusetts." I thought of John Adams, the loud barrister, and his cousin, Samuel Adams. Those two were voluble all on their own, without dozens of others trying to contribute to the conversation.

"I am more interested in what John Hancock has to say," I said. "It's well-known that Mr. Hancock and his Sons of Liberty aren't known for patience. Or meekness."

"There'll certainly be no shortage of talk. All those politicians will be shouting over each other."

"I wonder what South Carolina thinks of all this," I mused. "Boston must seem as far away to them as Antarctica. Perhaps that's why Georgia didn't send a delegate."

"South Carolina has probably had enough of being told what to do with their tobacco and indigo."

"When you put it like that, you begin to realize Boston's only a small piece of this," I mused.

"Look at this man coming along," Liza commented. He was very tall and smartly dressed, and cut an impressive figure framed against the imposing red bricks of the hall.

"That is Mr. Washington from Virginia," I said. "Mr. Franklin introduced him to me. They worked together in the back country. Believe it or not, I even entertained him once."

"Washington, the French and Indian War hero," Liza said admiringly. "I heard his horse was shot out from under him at Fort Duquesne. He must look mighty fine on a horse. He's so big and imperious looking."

"No doubt his wife is appreciative," I said drily.

"Who is that with him?"

"Patrick Henry, I believe," I said. "Also from Virginia. He's been one of the most outspoken. I don't know who the third man is, probably another Virginia delegate."

"Do you know how long they'll meet for?" asked a woman next to me, juggling a baby in her arms.

I had no idea, but surely these men would need to get back home to their families and their work. I guessed a week or two at most.

"British soldiers will shut this down by day's end," someone said.

The fifty-six men of the Continental Congress labored away inside that hot, close room for seven long weeks, until the end of October. Some of them came and went, and a few came late, but the meeting churned on and on. At the end of their time together, they sent a written request to the king. His expected response ignited a hotbed of speculation across the colonies.

I read the paper to Henry as we sat in the garden having an evening meal on an unseasonably warm fall night. "It says that if the Intolerable Acts aren't repealed, the colonies will stop sending exports to Britain. And they'll hold another congress next year."

"It says *what?*" Henry asked.

I read aloud from the resolutions. "After the first day of December next, we will not import into British America, from Great Britain or Ireland, any goods, wares or merchandise whatsoever—"

"The merchants won't survive."

I continued reading. "No more molasses and coffee from the West Indies, or wine from Madeira, or foreign indigo. No tea, especially from the East India Company."

"God's blood," Henry muttered.

"And no dealings with any man *anywhere in America* that does not agree to the above," I finished.

The rules were clear. Anyone in America violating the new import-export rules would be punished. Their names would appear in the newspapers as an enemy of the country, and their business would be boycotted by other citizens.

In other words, this was a new America. Tories would not be tolerated. The die had been cast. Britain needed to negotiate with us, not issue orders.

"They've gone too far."

"I don't know. Look what is still happening in Boston," I said. "The soldiers even torment people on Sundays leaving church. Nothing seems to be beyond civility."

"Elizabeth," Henry said, "I think you forget yourself."

I put down my pudding. It did not seem to matter what I ate, my waist remained small and my hips slim. I wished they would widen and give Henry the child he wants.

Henry stared at me, an odd look on his face. "We can't support traitors. Rebels have killed British soldiers tasked with peacekeeping."

"By accident. In a fracas. General Gage ordered that all molasses be turned over to make rum for his soldiers. Does that seem right to you? There's no grain left for children of the poor, and they're making rum for the troops."

Henry shrugged. "Gage is responsible for following orders and subduing the revolutionaries."

"Henry, the British aren't just going to walk away from Boston. They've had their pound of flesh and it still isn't enough. It has gone beyond that."

"America can't exist without Britain, Betsy." Henry clanged down his cup. "We are part of the world's largest empire. In contrast, the colonies are a few people bundled up on the coast. Most of this land is still wilderness heaving with Indians."

And just like that, my opinion was thrown away.

"I think you should spend less time with Anny," he said. "She's proving herself to be inflammatory. You married a Scot, you father was a Scot, your mother was English; why are you so willing to throw away our heritage?"

I bit my tongue. Henry had been more and more outspoken in recent months regarding his Tory sympathies.

I feared for him on his visits to town. One day the patriots would beat him senseless. Where was the man who had appeared at my house three years ago, erudite and elegant?

Henry had an almost childlike way of deciding he was right and then ignoring anything that contradicted his opinions. I had seen him like that many times at social gatherings. He made inappropriate comments without thinking of the recipient, and then didn't notice the ensuing awkwardness. Embarrassed, I would bring it up later with him, but he never seemed that concerned.

"I'm not throwing away our heritage," I said. "Sometimes the old ways stop working. Look at ancient Rome."

Chapter 21

Horsham
April 1775

"Bang!"

"Dead! You're dead!"

"Nah, I got you first."

Young boys, children of the workers, were in a musket war behind the barn.

I appeared around the corner to see a black-haired boy throw a stocky boy to the ground. Four other boys had their imaginary guns at the ready.

"You're dead. My bayonet pierced your heart."

"That's not my heart, you idiot. My heart's on the other side."

"Don't call me an idiot, you loyalist scum. I'll burn your house."

"If I'm dead, I can't live in it anyhow, idiot. Long live King George the Third."

When they saw me, they leaped to their feet.

"Missus Fergusson," they muttered, dropping their heads.

"Stacking hay, boys?"

Silence.

I smiled. "That looked like a fierce fight. Who won?"

They looked up at me cautiously.

"The rebels," said the black-haired boy.

"Mr. Fergusson says the rebels will hang," said the thick boy. His cheeks were pitted with pox scars. "When they're caught. All of them."

I looked down at the tense faces. "You best tend to the hay now."

"There's been a real battle," the black-haired boy boasted. "In Massachusetts. Way more redcoats died than our minutemen."

"Who told you that?"

"Old Joseph heard it. He told Isaiah's father when they were unloading the timber."

"I'm Isaiah," the stocky boy said proudly.

"Back to work now boys," I said abruptly.

I hurried in search of Old Joseph and whatever papers I could find. The boys spoke the truth. It took five days for news of the fighting at Lexington and Concord to reach Philadelphia. Blood had been shed, although no one knew which side fired the first shot. The day after the news reached town, thousands of men gathered at the Pennsylvania statehouse to volunteer to bear arms for the cause.

I knew one thing for certain, if I was a man I would have gone to the green and added my gun and voice to the cause. I only hoped I could win over my husband. People switched sides every day.

"Are we at war?" Johnny asked me with eager eyes when I went to see him. He was seventeen now, a man, and prime fighting age. His toy soldiers were long gone, but he still dreamed of battle. I wished I could hold onto him and keep him safe.

"I don't know," I said. "Farmers with no fighting experience are forming militia companies and arming themselves against the British. They're being told to be ready at a minute's notice."

The news out of Lexington and Concord was confusing. It seemed that British intelligence had gotten word of an arsenal being hoarded by the rebels and marched troops east from Boston to Lexington to take it. Members of the resistance saw them and rode ahead to warn the locals and minutemen. As the British approached the town of Concord, on the way to Lexington, fighting broke out. No one seemed to know who fired first. If you believed the rumors, by sunset on April 19, two hundred British soldiers were dead.

We were at war with our own country.

Horsham
May 1775

Summer came early, and with it, soaring temperatures and rotting sewage that made Philadelphia fetid. Anny came to stay with us at Graeme Park to escape the heat and stench. Her father had loosened his hold on his daughter's exile from me in my home, for she was a grown woman now, and soon to be married. I didn't speak to him myself, James Young and I still avoided each other.

I asked, almost begged, my husband and niece to try not to provoke each other while we were all under the same roof, but my pleas went unheeded.

"Give me liberty or give me death," Anny taunted Henry one night, quoting Patrick Henry. They had published his speech across all thirteen colonies after he brought down the house with it at the Second Virginia Convention in March.

"Britain will crush this pitiable rebellion," Henry said, amused.

"What gentleman would choose *oppression*?" Anny said disdainfully.

"Why expose us to the horror of war?" Henry countered. "Our cities will be destroyed, our fields will go uncultivated, and everywhere will be strewn with death and ruin. To what end? Only suffering, that is all. Against the most powerful military in the world, the rebels cannot win. Then we really *will* be enslaved."

"You're a fool," Anny spat.

"Anny," Liza reprimanded her.

"Women need not concern themselves with matters of state," Henry said. "You cannot be held responsible for your uneducated misconceptions."

"Men need not be stupid, and you *can* be held responsible for that," she shot back. For a woman she was dangerously outspoken, and I only hoped it was because she felt she was within the protective circle of family.

The Intolerable Acts had not been repealed. A second Congress was going to take place in May, at the State House this time. Benjamin Franklin was going to attend, back in Philadelphia following his long diplomatic mission to London. He was fed up with Parliament, and now fully engaged in the fight for an independent America.

An independent America! They were words we had avoided until now, dared not even think them. After the petition to the king yielded no results, everything changed. The colonies claimed they were being backed into slavery.

"I heard Franklin has broken ways with his son," Henry said. "William Franklin is a Tory through and through, and Franklin's taking up the cause. They don't speak anymore. My money's on the son."

I peeled back the years to remember the Franklin men. They were inseparable companions and good friends, as affectionate as any father and son could be. Surely their discord would not last.

Margaret and Charles steadfastly refused to leave their home, even though Philadelphia had become the official seat of an insurgent government. Tories in town were getting harder to come by. They were leaving in droves.

I received a letter from Margaret that John Hancock had arrived in Philadelphia to open the second Congress. She said that hundreds, maybe even thousands, went out to meet him. "Charles and I could scarce believe it," Margaret wrote. "Two men rode before him with drawn swords. The whole city flocked to see him, as if he had descended from the heavens and was different from other mortals."

Through all of this, my husband refused to hold his tongue. He wrote letter after letter urging reconciliation with Britain, asking leaders to consider the strengths of the union. There was no one he considered beyond the reach of his quill. He wrote to men of influence: Ben Franklin, Dr. Benjamin Rush, Jacob Duché, Frances Hopkinson, Patrick Henry. How long before his loud opinions saw him tarred and feathered when he went to town? They set people's houses on fire for less.

I found myself at a loss. I couldn't have my own voice, no woman could, and yet I didn't agree with my husband's opinions. There was no action I could take.

My only option to fill the uncertainty in my life was by throwing open our doors to anyone who would come, money be damned. I could no longer be alone with my thoughts. Sometimes I would take the coach myself and drive two ladies home and then pick up three more on the way back. I no longer cared. It brought Henry into the house to entertain in the evenings. Music was back in our parlor. We sang. We played games late into the night. If we kept busy enough, we could almost ignore the sound of the world cleaving open around us.

In June, George Washington was elected commander of the Continental Army, less than a year after Liza and I watched his lithe form stride into the Carpenters' Hall.

"General George Washington!" Anny said, triumphant. "The perfect man for the job!" I heard he had no official training, had never commanded a standard unit. His involvement in the French and Indian war had been a scrabble.

The old Pennsylvania government was still officially in place but no longer met, the governor gone mute. A rogue government sat gathering power and taking its instructions from the new Congress.

The message was clear: Resist England. Obstruct. Take up arms. Remove women and children immediately to safe places.

Henry entered our chamber that night as I was stepping out of the bath.

"I'm wet," I protested when he drew me to him. He looped his fingers through my hair, caressing the wet strands. My insides instantly leaped to life. A lazy finger followed a drop of water sliding down my neck, a tender motion, slow and unhurried. We always had this.

"Where's Sally?" he asked.

"I asked to be left alone."

"Lucky me."

He leaned forward to place his lips at the hollow of my neck. His right hand snaked out to my breast.

"You're wearing too much," I whispered as he laid me on the rug.

"Then you'll have to help me," he said. "What should I take off?"

Afterwards we stayed on the rug, watching the fire die. His fingers stroked my back tenderly.

"I received a letter from my brother," he said. "He asks that I go to Scotland. His health is poor. There are matters to be settled."

Relief flooded me. He should go right away. It would be good for Henry to be absent while the trouble played itself out.

"Then you must go to him," I said softly. "Give me power of attorney while you are gone. I may be able to sell some of our land and give us ease."

He nodded. "I'll ask Richard Stockton to oversee any sale and transfer the proceeds to you."

"When will you leave?"

"As soon as I can book passage."

I nodded. "By the way, does Richard know his daughter is falling in love with Benjamin Rush? Ben made me promise not to tell Annis until he had spoken to Richard to ask for Julia's hand."

Henry laughed. "Seems a good match. They're well suited."

"Ben is beside himself with nerves. If she does not say yes, it will ruin him."

Henry drew me closer. "We haven't had it easy," he said, "but if you hadn't said yes to me, beautiful Betsy, it would have ruined *me*. Know that I love you."

"And I you. So very much."

We fell asleep in each other's arms, with not a stitch on. When it became cold I pulled the blankets from the bed to the floor and covered us. Sally didn't come back for the tub.

Henry made the crossing in September in the company of Richard Stockton's brother Samuel. Not wanting to linger, they left right after a hurricane sent trees flying and threw ships onto the shore along the coasts of New York and New Jersey. He wrote that they were settled on a merchant ship and hoped for a smooth crossing.

I was glad he was gone. A crowd of patriots had dragged our friend John Kearsley from his home in the city and carted him through town. "An enemy to the people," they cried as they hoisted him and hit him. His crime was meeting peaceably with other loyalists. Kearsley was betrayed by one of his servants who overheard him toast the king. He was still in jail. Jails were disease-ridden, odious places, better suited for dying than living. The Kearsley family, part of our church congregation, was wild with grief. There was nothing we could do since Philadelphia had become a vigilante city, with extralegal justice being dispensed. Weeks later John Kearsley died in that jail.

In Henry's absence, Liza moved back in to keep me company. We prepared for Anny's wedding to Billy, which took place at Graeme Park on a soft November day in a soft grey and white landscape of watered-down ink.

It was a tender marriage ceremony, with Anny and her groom beaming at each other. Jane would have been happy to see her daughter marry at the family home, the house she had grown up in. I hoped all their spirits were there, Mama and Father and Jane and Ann and all my other brothers and sisters, to see a luminous Anny and her doting groom be married by a very old and shaky, but proud, Reverend Peters. He had been so ill this past year that he resigned his rectorship, but he insisted on marrying my niece. It was a nod of honor to my father, and to me.

James Young did not approve of his daughter's marriage, but he attended reluctantly, thin-lipped and frowning. Johnny could not leave his apprenticeship to attend his sister's marriage, even for a day. My dear friend Benjamin Rush attended the wedding as a groomsman. Ironically enough, in Henry's absence, it was a gathering of patriots.

August 23, 1775
Proclamation for Suppressing Rebellion and Sedition
We do accordingly strictly charge and command all our officers . . . to use their utmost endeavors to withstand and suppress rebellion, and to disclose and make known all treasons and traitorous conspiracies . . .
King George III

Chapter 22

Horsham
January 1776

"I hope I'm with child soon," Anny said, a hand on her belly, her face radiant. "It's too early to know."

I embraced her, my own innards as empty as an underground grotto.

"That would be wonderful news," I murmured into her hair, genuinely hopeful. "Our family needs to grow again."

"Although, this isn't the best time to have a child," she said, her brow creased. Anny was exiled with us at Graeme Park until her husband felt Philadelphia was safe enough for her to return.

"There is no good timing," I said. "If my mother were here, she would tell you that. Your grandmother. She had ten children, in many different situations across the years, probably none ideal. A baby is a gift, a blessing, no matter when they come."

"But the conflict," she said. "Philadelphia in turmoil, the British occupying New York City . . ."

It was better she focused on the troubles than the fact that her own mother died from childbirth.

"Hand me that, would you?" I motioned to the brass cleaner. The candlesticks needed cleaning.

I pulled the heavy woolen shawl that had been my mother's tighter around me. It was cold everywhere in this house, no matter how high we built the fires. Every bit of icy wind seemed to seep through the windows as if the glass had holes in it. Would January never end?

"Betsy!" Liza burst in, panting. "We've had news! Johnny has joined the British army!"

"You must be joking," Anny said.

Liza shoved a paper in my hand. "He has already gone! He went to New York and boarded a British warship. The note says the general accepted his service and is transporting him to Boston to join the army."

"Who brought this?" I asked.

"A messenger. No one we know."

"He can't have," Anny said, disbelieving. "Johnny knows we're working for the resistance. Father is a known Whig."

My mind worked. Johnny knew we would have stopped him from going, so he ran.

"He's gone," I said. "He sent this from New York on purpose." So we would not stop him.

"We must bring him back," Liza said. "Let's go to James at once! Johnny is too young to know what he's doing. His father will get him."

Johnny knew full well what he was doing. He had often stated his loyalty to Britain. In recent months, Johnny had commented in detail about the movement of British troops. Naively, it had not occurred to me that he was making plans to join them. I thought it was a carryover from his fascination with war as a boy. Perhaps I hadn't wanted to know more than that.

"The British army will not turn John away, or release him," I said flatly. "They'll sign him as a volunteer without pay and be glad of him."

"How can you be so calm?" Liza cried. "Johnny is just a boy. Our boy! He'll get himself killed. What does he know of fighting? He doesn't know anything."

"And if he doesn't die, my father will kill him," Anny said. "It's bad enough to have Englishmen stomping on us, but to have my own brother turn?"

I shook my head. "He made a choice, Anny. One that is his to make, even if we don't like it. And Liza, you're wrong. He's not a boy anymore. He chose a side, just like we did, as a man. He walked in with his eyes open."

"How could he do this to us?" Liza said. "We should have sent him to Scotland with Henry! Now we have to worry about him."

Johnny had abandoned his apprenticeship, burned his bridges. I thought of the way James had excoriated me over the will, and that hadn't involved his son pledging allegiance to the British. I shuddered to think of his reaction when he found out. I sincerely hoped I wasn't there.

Ben Rush came to visit with Joseph Galloway, and to deliver a publication they considered important. Ben handed me a pamphlet called *Common Sense*, written by someone called Thomas Paine. We sat in the dining room, it had a bigger fireplace from the days when it had been the kitchen, before Father had the kitchen house built outside. Liza was out with Anny, visiting Mrs. Wechter, who had a broken arm after she lost her footing on the ice.

"Read it, Betsy," Ben urged me, excitement in his face. "I think you will find it remarkable. Paine manages to express our predicament perfectly! His suggestion is startling, but plainly *obvious* all at the same time."

I glanced at Joseph. He looked pained.

"This will start a war," Joseph said. It was clear that Joseph did not agree with whatever this *Common Sense* said. "A war for independence."

"Independence," I breathed. It was still a startling word. Astonishing.

"We argued all the way here," Ben said cheerfully, grinning at his friend.

"There will be blood," Joseph warned. I could feel Joseph's discomfort. Joseph had been a delegate at the first Continental Congress, but he argued that we needed to find a way forward and work things out with Britain. By the time the second Congress was held seven months later, he wanted nothing to do with it and refused to participate. In comparison, Ben had been an enthusiastic supporter of the resistance movement from the earliest days. I suspected Joseph was getting cold feet and backing away from the cause.

"There's already been blood. We can't reconcile with a king who ordered his troops to shoot *his own citizens*," Ben returned.

Joseph frowned. "Even the rebels didn't expect this, not at first. It was supposed to be about seeking representation, asking for change. This *Common Sense* is putting flint to gunpowder."

I looked back and forth from one to the other of my friends.

"I'll read it later," I said, "but first I want to enjoy time with two dear friends who I hardly get to see these days."

"How is Henry?" Joseph asked, accepting my redirection. "We miss having you in the city."

"He is well. His brother passed peacefully, he had a cancer. After that Henry went with Sam Stockton to London with a letter of introduction from Ben Franklin. Henry says they've been attending Mrs. Stevenson's Wednesday calling hours. They send their regards."

"Any news on potential buyers?" Joseph asked. Our friends knew of our financial struggles, I'm sure everyone did. The assessments of our belongings after my father died was well known. People talked.

I shook my head. "That would be nice, but no, not yet."

"It's harder now," Ben commented. "In times like these, purchasing property takes a brave stomach and a fortune teller's divining rod."

Philadelphia
April 1776

Liza and I did our part: we went out to canvass for the cause.

"Stay together in pairs," Mrs. Robinson called. "You each have your assigned streets. Approach everyone you meet. Everyone, you hear me? If they have no money, accept silverplate or jewelry. Take anything that has potential value. Bullets too."

Liza and I looked around us. We were standing outside Mrs. Reed's house. Two dozen women were paired up to hit the streets of Philadelphia and thrust out baskets for donations. At the center of this effort was the passionate and larger-than-life figure of Mrs. Esther Reed. Mrs. Reed, a Brit, had only been in America for a few years and had in no time formed the Ladies Association of Philadelphia. She was almost single-handedly recruiting the women of town to rise up and raise money for the American army. She called us the Daughters of Liberty.

"We will not rest, ladies," yelled Mrs. Reed from the stoop. "We will *not* stay in our kitchens and parlors when there is work to be done! We will *not* be idle! Our support of the cause is every bit as important as our husbands' soldiery!"

A roar went up in response.

"Do not take no for an answer," Mrs. Reed called. "Follow people that walk away without acknowledging your plea. Hound them! We must think of the men to whom we owe our future peace. For liberty!"

Another cheer. "For liberty! Huzzah!"

"Go on, then, ladies," Mrs. Robinson said. "Spread out. We'll meet back here this afternoon."

"All monies raised will be sent to Mrs. Washington," Mrs. Reed called in parting. "To be dispensed to her husband, General Washington."

Esther Reed was the wife of Joseph Reed, a lawyer who left his law practice to join George Washington's army and was now Washington's personal aide and military secretary.

Liza narrowed her eyes at me as we headed to Fourth Street. "Are you not worried about what Henry will do when he finds out you're volunteering with the Daughters of Liberty?"

"I can't think of that right now."

Liza shook her head. "Betsy, be sensible. Henry is a loyalist if ever there was one. When he finds out his own wife has joined the rebels—I mean, you're taking *action*. It's not just words anymore . . ."

"I've never been a bystander," I said quietly. "It has been almost ten years since John Dickinson wrote his *Letters from a Farmer* and I responded then by—"

"John Dickinson is loyal to the crown now. He's not a Whig. He couldn't bring himself to fight for separation. But back to the point, Henry wouldn't like what we're doing."

Neither would my childhood friend Rebecca Smith, or the Stedmans, or Joseph Galloway who, as I suspected, had turned loyalist, or so many other of our dear friends. Or even my own nephew. Yet still, I felt strongly that this was the right thing to do.

"The patriots are gaining strength. Henry may have changed camps, if he were here," I said.

"What do you mean?"

"Well, he left before the rebels stole the cannons at Ticonderoga and dragged them to Massachusetts to point them at the British, which forced their evacuation from Boston. It's different now. He may feel differently."

"Or he may feel the same way. And you're his wife."

I was annoyed. "Enough about me. What about you, Liza? Will you stand firm when we are made to face the consequences of our actions?" Anger hardened my jaw.

Liza stopped walking. "Betsy! You of all people know my heart. My time and actions and resources are with the

Americans. All those visits we made to the jails and the workhouse, how could you say such a thing?"

"I just feel so . . ." I mulled over my feelings. Fed up? Would I have married Henry if I had met him four years later?

"So what?"

"I love him, Liza," I blurted out. "The truth is I really do. Sometimes I wish I didn't, but I love him."

"I know," she said softly. "Let's not speak of it anymore. I'm sorry I brought it up."

I pushed down my feelings of despair. I could take them out later when I was alone. I linked arms with her and took an exaggerated step. "For the cause!"

She laughed, and heads back, we marched up the street.

"Let's head to Grogan's Inn," I said. "Maybe we'll find some travelers who are new to town and have money in their pockets."

"Let's hit all the inns and pubs on our route," she agreed. People always had coin for a drink.

We swindled money out of men in the Indian Queen pub, begged a goblet from a silversmith, and were just approaching a family walking along when someone grabbed my arm.

I turned and found myself looking into the intense eyes of my brother-in-law.

"We need to speak," James Young said urgently. "Please Elizabeth," he added when he saw me set my shoulders.

I motioned to a small park up ahead. "Whatever it is, Liza can hear it."

He nodded, and we ducked in and stood under a weeping willow.

"Johnny was shipwrecked," James said urgently. "He never made it to Boston. The Americans took him prisoner."

"Oh God. Is he hurt?"

"I have seen him. Mercifully, he is unhurt."

I waited.

"I know we haven't had an easy time of it lately, Betsy, but for the sake of our family—"

"What is it, James? What do you want?"

"I believe I can convince Congress to be lenient with Johnny if I can tell them that he's confined at Graeme Park."

I heard Liza's sharp intake of breath and the sound of the snow falling off the trees behind us.

"Safely in the custody of his aunt," he finished. "You."

My mind spun. Any bitterness I held against James faded against the need to protect the boy who was like a son to me. I had a sudden image of two-year old Johnny trying to jump off the sideboard, his face earnest, his little arms spread like wings.

I nodded once. Anything to keep my nephew out of prison and alive. Kearsley's death in the filth of the Carlisle jail was all too recent. "Do you think they'll agree?"

"I'll use every shred of influence that I have," James said fiercely. "Hancock knows what I do for the cause."

"Then bring our boy back," Liza said firmly.

"Yes, you must," I said. "Soon as you can."

Horsham
May 1776

A letter came from Henry that spring.

I would be more happy with you, from my soul I would, in a cottage in the Appalachian mountains of America, than rolling in the luxury of London without you. Yet since I am here, please come to me.

"It must be a good letter," Liza said. "You look pleased."

"Henry wants me to go to England." I frowned.

"And?"

"I'm needed here with Johnny now," I said. "And let's not forget Graeme Park does not run itself."

"Henry should come back."

"No. No, it's better that he isn't here. It's safer."

I had no intention of leaving Anny to have a baby without me, and I wouldn't abandon Liza with a struggling farm and not enough money. Our situation remained grim. We relied on each other now, the three of us women. I had scrimped to hire an overseer to help manage the daily work of the farm, but it still wasn't enough to make a difference.

"I won't go to him," I said firmly. "I'll let him know why."

"Be prepared," Francis Hopkinson told us at dinner one night. "The British will want to invade Philadelphia and take out the rebel government."

"I know families who are preparing to flee," his wife Ann added. "So many are hoarding cash and personal necessities to take when they run."

"Where is Howe's army now?" Liza asked. "Does anyone know?"

General William Howe had been sent to assume command of the British forces last year. He first brought reinforcements to Gage in Boston, but had withdrawn his army after they faced the rebel cannons in Boston.

"Halifax," Francis answered. "But he'll swing back south soon enough, you can bet on it. There are dark days ahead. Prepare yourself. Stock up on what you can."

Any illusion of avoiding a full-out war was long gone. I prayed Henry listened to me and stayed away.

"We'll prepare," I agreed, although I didn't know how. Liza and I exchanged worried looks.

"Enough of all this talk of war," Ann said decisively. "I'm going to change the subject. I want to talk of something more agreeable, like our dear Betsy's recent achievement. Congratulations, Betsy, on the publication of your poem!"

I waved her off, embarrassed. "Thank you," I murmured. "It's nothing, really."

"It's not nothing, it's tremendous!" Francis chimed in. "Our very own Betsy has a poem printed in the *Pennsylvania Magazine*!"

"It's almost a shame, dear," Ann Hopkinson said to me, "that you were born a woman. If you were a man you'd be like Milton or Dryden or some such well known writer. Such talent you have. It's unfortunate that you toil away in obscurity without reward."

"Not anymore!" Liza said. "She's a published writer now!"

"Well old friend, we wish you many more published poems to come," Francis said encouragingly, "in several fine publications. Maybe you'll even have a book of poems published one day."

"I don't think I'd want that," I said. "It wouldn't be right."

Each month that passed, with painstaking slowness, took us closer to the edge of a precipice that we could only dread. Which way would the pendulum swing? Was it possible to even think we could win a war against Great Britain? How could we beat the greatest navy in the world, the biggest empire, the king of England?

At the end of June, Congress made a declaration. Anyone waging war against Pennsylvania by helping or siding with the king was guilty of treason. Treason. Pennsylvania would immediately take the guilty party's land and all their possessions. Loyalists would lose everything.

The risk couldn't be more obvious to me: my husband, a firm loyalist and the legal owner of Graeme park, was faithful to the crown. Graeme Park, my lifelong home, my refuge, was under attack.

I was going to lose Graeme Park.

"Don't worry," Liza said urgently. "Henry's not even in the country. He's not here."

I wrote Henry right away and told him it was more important than ever that he stay away. I was grateful when he wrote back to tell me he was going to Paris. His French skills were needed for some sort of government negotiation. I breathed a sigh of relief.

Johnny was not pleased to be back.

"I would rather be in jail," he snarled the day James brought him to Graeme Park.

"You might get your wish yet," his father retorted, cuffing him on the side of the head.

When I received word they were coming, I sent Anny to the free library in Hatborough to donate some books. I would spare Johnny her wrath, at least on arrival.

Liza stepped forward. "You must be hungry, John. I feel like we shouldn't call you Johnny anymore, you're a man now, aren't you? Would you like a meal? Or ale?"

"I'm leaving." James stroke to the door. "Stay here, son, or I may have you hanged. It's what you deserve."

He banged the door on Johnny's expletive.

"We missed you," I said to my nephew. "Despite your unfortunate circumstances, welcome home. You are very much wanted here. Liza and I want you to know our affections for you remain unchanged."

John stood in the hallway, mute. His face was unreadable. Would he run again?

"Also," I continued, "I was hoping I could call upon your sense of charity and put you to work on the farm. I know it's not what you'd like to be doing, but we are in a bad way. A very bad way. We need your help. Please consider this for my sake." I wasn't afraid to pull any emotional strings I had with him. This was the only home he'd known, and if I had to remind him that Mother and I raised him, I would. The British army couldn't have him.

Johnny softened. "I am hungry, actually."

I exhaled. A minor victory. He had not said no.

"Then let's feed you, and hear all about your bravery," Liza drew him to the dining room.

James voice rang in my ears. *I may have you hanged.* What kind of father says that to his son, no matter the circumstances?

July 1776

God in heaven. The colonies have declared independence from Great Britain. Independence! The declaration was written down, signed by fifty-six men, and sent to King George. They've gone and done it.

May the Lord have mercy on us all.

Henry's voice floated back to me. *Our cities destroyed, our fields uncultivated, and everywhere will be strewn with death and ruin. To what end?*

Oh, Henry. What will we do?

There were no answers anywhere. What I would have given to have my father and mother back again, if only for a day, an hour, a moment. I craved the comfort of their presence and their counsel.

That summer, there was no cause for celebration. The papers trumpeted the news, but the lurch toward independence felt like a wave of darkness descending over us. Any remaining loyalist holdouts fled Philadelphia.

Houses were left empty, gates gaped open, livestock abandoned, pets deserted in the streets to fend for themselves. All pretense of civility was gone. It was hard to find liberty in the mewling maw of a half-deserted and disintegrating city.

As if he was part of the exodus, our dear Reverend Peters died a week after the declaration was inked. His passing and burial were swift; he was interred before I could get to Christ Church. My poor old kind friend, he had been like a dear and well-loved uncle to me. I chose to remember him on the boat to England as he stood on the deck with me, wispy hair blown about his gentle face, the screech of seagulls overhead. He had such enduring love in his heart, he walked this earth with such faith.

Jacob Duché succeeded him as rector at Christ Church.

Chapter 23

Horsham
August 1777

We did what everyone in dark times must do: we kept going. We had no other choice.

Liza and I heard the fife and drums before we could see the men that held them. We went outside to watch as the Pennsylvania Sixth Division lumbered into Graeme Park, a long train of carts and horses and soldiers on foot. They drooped in the August heat, faces wet with sweat, bodies lumbering. There were hundreds of them.

A short time later Brigadier General Anthony Wayne stood in our parlor. He bowed deeply to Liza and I, his eyes searching the room behind me.

"We are grateful for your support of the American army, Mrs. Fergusson," Wayne said formally. He nodded at Liza. We must have struck him as odd, two middle-aged ladies in a house that had seen better days.

"We welcome you," Liza said. "We are patriots. We embrace the cause wholeheartedly."

Mad Anthony, they called him. *Crazy as a beast*. He was clear-eyed and long-nosed, shrewd looking.

"What can we do to help while you're here?" I asked. "Of course you and your officers will stay in the house."

We had no idea why they had landed in our fields or how long they would stay. Ben Rush believed Wayne was on his way to corner the British, who were moving south. Howe and his army had left New York City and been spotted in Delaware.

"My men require water, food, rest. August is a damnable month for soldiering. This heat."

"The creek has running water," I said. "We are fortunate to have many deep, cold springs. You are welcome to whatever food and supplies we have. The past few years since my father's death have been challenging, yet I suspect we'll find enough. We'll do our best to meet your needs."

"We'll convert this room to a guardroom," he said. He was a man used to giving orders. I didn't know much about him, but I heard Francis Hopkinson say Wayne had provided the rear at the Battle of Trois-Rivières during Benedict Arnold's invasion of Canada. "And he led the forces at Fort Ticonderoga," Hopkinson praised him. "He is single-minded in bringing down the enemy. That's why they call him Mad Anthony. He's fearless on the battle field, and bombastic in his support of the war."

"Will you be staying long?" I asked, mentally calculating how long it would be before our supplies were depleted.

"General Washington is in hot pursuit of the enemy, madam," General Wayne replied drily. "We camp here until we receive orders to move. How long that will be, I have no idea."

"Of course," I agreed.

"We'll dig the latrines in a line at the rear of the camp, near the woods, away from the water. The men will fix booths before their tents to shelter them from the heat of the sun."

"We could be put to work," Liza suggested.

"Ladies have no place in a military camp, notwithstanding the inevitable camp followers or ladies of ill repute. They cling to the men like nits. There is not much we can do about that."

"Miss Stedman and I will move to the third floor," I decided. "You and your officers may take the rooms on the second floor. You can move the contents of this room into storage if need be." I had no idea what a guardroom entailed. "We'll keep busy spinning flax to make cotton for bandages and shirts for the troops. The men will be in want of extra this winter."

General Wayne looked us up and down. "Who else lives here?"

"My husband is abroad," I said. "Last I heard, he was in Paris using his proficiency with the French language for the cause. My niece, Anny, is with child and was here but recently returned to the city to be with her husband when the baby arrives. My nephew John helps with the farm while Henry is away. The rest are servants, slaves, or seasonal workers. There are few of us left, as you can see."

Anny had finally fallen pregnant after Christmas, and we were all eagerly awaiting the child's arrival.

"Have someone show us the grounds," Wayne said curtly. I did not feel he was rude, he was very focused on the task at hand. "We'll need to see the creek. We need hay for the horses; meat for the troops. How much beef and pork can you spare? We'll ensure our slaughter pens are far from your water. And give us whatever you have in the way of vegetables, herbs, and fruit."

"How many of you are there?" I asked.

"Four hundred. This is not my whole division."

"Where is General Washington, if I may ask?" Liza asked.

"Nearby, ma'am, in Crooked Billet. I would not offer this information if it were not already well known. You cannot hide the thousands of men camped with him."

I knew Crooked Billet and the surrounding area. Washington must have been at John Moland's house. John had passed away many years ago, but his family was well.

"Tell General Washington he is welcome here," I said. If he came, I wouldn't tell Henry.

"We drill late each afternoon after the heat of the sun fades," Wayne warned. "Do not be alarmed. Beginning at the hour of five o'clock, you may hear training shots. We parade daily."

Liza and I nodded.

"Take what you need, General Wayne," I repeated. "Old Joseph will show you the property."

General Wayne saluted and turned to go. Liza and I followed him outside.

Men were calling to each other, noise and movement in every direction. Tents were popping up like clover in a wet spring field. There was the sound of hammering over top of more hammering. Horses were being led this way and that, carts unloaded. Another cart went by carrying what looked like crates of spirits, rum or bourbon maybe. Our curving sweep of green land was disappearing under a sea of white tents and the gray and blue of the Continental Army.

"Unload the bread ovens," yelled one man. "Set them up over there."

Liza and I stood for a long while watching. Once, long ago, we had had a spring fête on this lawn, with twinkling lanterns and pretty white flag banners and posies of daisies for the tables. My sisters had argued over what color ribbons to put in our hair. Now I had an army on the lawn, filled with men joining up to wrest America from the clutches of England. I normally cursed my sex, but now I felt grateful not to have to face my end on a battlefield looking into the barrel of a gun or seeing a bayonet thrust toward my heart.

The next week, with Wayne's men still outside firing daily into the late afternoon sun, we received word that Anny had been delivered of a healthy daughter. She labored for thirty hours, calling it the "severest pain that any human could suffer." They called the baby Elizabeth after me, which made me weep.

I saved a copy of the Declaration of Independence from last summer for tiny Elizabeth and the newspapers from August. One day I would tell her, "This is what happened the summer you were born. We hosted an army in our back yard."

Ten days later, Wayne and his men were gone as abruptly as they had come. Our property was worse for wear. We walked the empty fields, Liza and I, staring down at the crushed grass, the pitted earth where tent pegs had been. The ground was littered with the debris of four hundred men: animal bones, pieces of ripped cloth, nails, crushed glass, wood buttons. They'd also stolen two oxen, a wagon, and both of Father's slaves. I still couldn't bring myself to think of them as my slaves. I would not have minded the desertion of Alex and Mars if it meant they could be free. The loss of the oxen and wagon, however, was a blow when we had so little as it was.

"This is . . . unfortunate," Liza said, staring at the singed ground where a circle of black land stared up at us like an open eye. A fire pit. There were many of them.

"We're alive," I answered. "We'll go on."

Despite the destruction to my property that Wayne and his men had brought, I had no qualms about them being here other, of course, than what we had left to eat and sell afterwards. I found General Wayne to be an amiable man. He revealed that he had a wife and two small children at home, and was interested in securing an American future for his son and daughter. Liza and I spent several pleasant evenings entertaining him and his officers, enjoying the company of the newcomers. Friendship bloomed between us. My nephew hid on the farm, although he managed to be polite in the officers' company.

"Why don't you set a reward for the return of Alex and Mars?" Liza suggested. "They can't be far away yet. Folks around here know them. I'm sure they can find two runaway Negroes."

I shook my head. "Let them go. It's wartime. Let them serve with the American forces. I'll petition Congress for compensation of the theft of the oxen and cart."

"And damages to Graeme Park," Liza added. "They ate a great deal."

We walked the breadth of the field to the tree line. The latrines were gone, the holes filled in. A little farther away there were also several mounds where new earth had been turned over. Wayne said that Washington was particular and ordered the offal from the slaughtered animals buried every day. He also made the men wash once a week.

"I saw officers using oil from the offal to lubricate their guns," Liza commented. "Rotten smell."

We surveyed what remained. Our grain stores and vegetable stores were low. Our fruit trees had been picked. Even our wine cellar was reduced.

"Winter," I said. "We are going to need a plan."

"Winter," Liza agreed. "We'll sell something."

John had run again, this time to join Howe's forces at Germantown, thirteen miles away. Brigadier General Wayne's presence at Graeme Park reminded him of how much he wanted to join the British to fight the Americans. His heart was with the crown. This time we said nothing. We had to let him go, there was no way we could hold an able-bodied young man hostage, not one who was intent on being elsewhere.

I wondered where General Wayne and his regiment had gone, but I didn't need to wait long. Two weeks later, word came.

September 14, 1777
Dear Madam,
I shall always remember the kind reception I met with under your hospitable roof and the easy politeness of you and Miss Stedman. I hope one day to have it in my power to repay some of those favors.

I am happy to inform you I am not wounded—but I have lost some officers whose friendship I esteemed—and whose death is rather to be envied than regretted.

The right wing of our army met with a misfortune, but our left in return gave a timely check to the right wing of General Howe. This has obliged him to remain on the spot ever since, taking care of his wounded and burying his dead.

The villain who stole your cattle is at Carlisle. I shall take care to take hold of him as soon as he returns.

Present my best compliments to Miss Stedman and Mr. Young and believe me yours most sincerely,

Anthony Wayne

September 16, 1777
Sir,

I am much obliged to you for saying that the time you spent at my house was not disagreeable to you. Rest assured, sir, that if in the hurry of your first coming, anything that might have occurred that you wished to be otherwise was not intended. I wish the general cause of America most sincerely well.

Since I have been favored with your acquaintance, I am particularly interested in your safety. I hope if opportunity affords you will pop in on Graeme Park, which will be the most convincing proof you can give me that you liked your quarters here. I will admit I would prefer seeing you without quite as large a retinue as composed your train when you were last here!

E. Fergusson

"Betsy we're leaving," Rebecca Smith said when I ran out to greet her one-person horse cart. She quickly stepped down. "We are going to our island, taking our children to safety. I can't stay. I only came to say good-bye, Betsy. I begged William to let me come."

Rebecca and William, longtime defenders of old Philadelphia while the city had long been a firebrand for change, were finally, at long last, being driven out. Rebecca's husband had had the foresight to purchase an island in the Schuylkill River last year as a refuge, anticipating that the situation would only get worse.

I clasped her hands. "We must pray for a speedy end to the war."

"The British are attacking Washington at Chads's Ford near Brandywine Creek," Rebecca said. "You can hear it for miles; every traveler on the road talks of nothing else. The ground is shaking but that's nothing compared to the screams of the men. They say the British have a force of thousands, maybe more than the Americans. Make plans for your own escape! I'll pray for you."

"Thank you, dear heart," I said. My eyes searched hers in good-bye. We embraced each other.

Chads's Ford was not much farther from Philadelphia than the distance from Graeme Park to the middle of town. Maybe another ten miles more. That meant that a great battle was taking place only thirty miles south of here. I had faith in General Washington. I prayed the Americans would not fall.

"Oh, Betsy," Rebecca said, rather sadly into my shoulder. "Betsy." She pushed me away to look at me. "Do you remember when William Franklin left for England all those years ago? How upset we were, and how foolish. Did you ever think we'd be here?" She laughed, half crying. "Our troubles were nothing compared to what we face now. We were so young. What children we were."

"Twenty years ago," I agreed. How much have we lost since then?

"Promise me you'll come to us if you need anything, Betsy," Rebecca said urgently, "Or if the war comes to your doorstep. You are all welcome, you, Liza, Anny, the baby, Anny's husband, and Johnny, of course. We put friends first, no matter the side, but I beg you, be loyal to the king. Do what's right. Think of Henry. Be a good wife to him, in the end that's all there is. Nothing else matters."

"Thank you. I know I can count on you," my voice was husky. "Look after all your sweet babies. Go safely."

She jumped back up to her seat and took the reins, urging the horse to race up the driveway.

Rebecca had not been gone long when a letter arrived from Margaret Stedman.

Dearest Betsy,

How I tremble as I write this! I had wished to write to you earlier today but was forced to stop until my hands stopped shaking. We can hear such terrible noise! The fighting—it feels as if the very earth is shaking—began around seven o'clock this morning and has not stopped. The cannons fire on and on. The sound is from hell. Around three o'clock this afternoon a man came to ring a bell and order all the houses be shut up! He commanded every man who could carry a gun to appear on the common to join the fighting. Everyone is wild with terror and overwhelmed with distress. So many wounded are being brought here— hundreds. Men outside are chanting, "Die or be free, die or be free." This is what Philadelphia has become. Let me know your welfare.

Margaret Stedman

A week later, I fell to my knees in shock.

The bang brought Liza running. I was sprawled in front of the empty fireplace, throwing figurines at my father's paneling. Eventually I stopped and stared sightlessly at the Delft tiles.

"What is it? What?" She stepped around the contents of the table strewn on the floor. "Betsy, have you had some sort of fit?"

"Henry is back. He landed in New York weeks ago." I picked up a book and hurled it at the window, where it hit with a thud but didn't break the glass.

"He's coming home?"

"No, he's bloody fighting with the *British*, Liza! He's in Germantown behind British lines, asking me to go to him." My voice was shrilled, panicked.

"Is he with Johnny?"

"I don't know! He didn't say!"

"I don't understand," Liza said, puzzled. "Why is Henry in Germantown with the British? Why can't he just come home?"

"He says he landed at New York when Howe's forces were there. Somehow he came back with them. He said they sailed south and then came up the Chesapeake and overland. Of all the places to arrive! New York, the loyalist stronghold! He was at the battle at Brandywine, near Chads's Ford. He fought with Howe *against the patriots.*"

"Oh God," Liza choked. "He's a redcoat."

I picked up a vase and threw it at the wall. It didn't break, the vase was pewter.

"They won't let him cross the war line," Liza said, understanding. "That's why he can't come. Why you have to go to him."

I flopped onto my stomach and laid my cheek against a floorboard. "I told him, Liza. I begged him. He knew what was at stake. He could have stayed in London, or Paris, or anywhere. I begged him to wait!"

"Perhaps you shouldn't go to him," Liza warned. "If you don't cross the line, they can't question your loyalties. Thousands of families are divided this way. You wouldn't be the first."

I stayed with my face pressed into the floor. I pounded my fists against the wood.

"He is my husband. I have to go to him. I want to go to him."

"You'll need to request a pass," Liza said.

"He has wrecked us!"

"Perhaps you should speak with Henry before assuming to know his motives," Liza suggested. "He may have taken the only opportunity there was to get back to you."

"Really? Why do so?" I asked. "Why not come home discreetly from another direction and take stock of the situation first? He could have sailed south to Virginia, or north, and slipped through the back country on horseback. Even if he did plan to join Howe, he could have come to see me first. He's been gone two years, Liza! And now this!"

"Go see him," Liza said, tugging at the back of my apron. "And sit up. Betsy. Please."

Hundreds of patriots and redcoats died that day in the battle at Brandywine, when Henry was there. They fought all day, the acrid smoke wafting for miles as the earth shook. Only the fall of darkness stopped the fighting. Days later military generals asked townspeople to volunteer to bury the dead, who were starting to rot and putrefy where they had fallen.

It was a hard loss and retreat for Washington, especially after his artillery horses fell and the British took the American cannons.

Two weeks later, the British marched on Philadelphia and took the city.

I did not know what to do, so I wrote to General Washington.

September 29, 1777
Graeme Park

Sir,
I take the liberty of addressing you on behalf of my
husband, Mr. Fergusson, who has returned after an
absence of two years in Britain.
In brief, his situation is as follows: He went to Britain in
September 1775 on some business of a domestic nature.
From there he sailed to Jamaica last February, and after
passing a month there, embarked for New York where he
arrived the evening before Lord Howe sailed. My husband,
in order to get home, sailed with Howe and is now in
Germantown. He is extremely desirous, after so long an
absence from home, to return to it. The intention of this
application to Your Excellency is to know if you will give Mr.
Fergusson a probation for a month, to stay in his own
house. He will give his parole that he will not give any
information to the enemy. He will be confined to such limits
of space as thought proper by Your Excellency.
As I am very anxious to know Your Excellency's
determination. I have applied as early as possible. Knowing
how critical this important time is, I make many apologies
for troubling Your Excellency about a single individual.
One thing I must emphasize on the subject is that my
dear Mr. Fergusson never took a decisive part on either side.
I will not detain your time, which is very precious, but
sincerely wish Your Excellency health and happiness. I
remain, Your Excellency's most obedient humble servant,
Elizabeth Fergusson

The days waiting for Washington's response seemed an
eternity. I paced and fretted and read the news, which was
dire: The British were burning the homes and properties of
known patriots to the ground. Congress had fled to
Lancaster. All church bells were also carted to Lancaster

and hidden so they would not be melted into ammunition by the British. Carpenters' Hall became a makeshift hospital.

When Congress had learned in July that Howe was headed for Philadelphia, it began arresting any prior officers of the Crown. Those who would not sign allegiance to the patriot cause were dispatched by force to the back country and held against their will.

Congress also published a list of forty men that were enemies of the state. Many of the names on the list were our friends, including William Smith, Rebecca's husband. I couldn't wrap my head around it. She had just stood in my driveway embracing me, and now her husband was a wanted man.

Three days later my reply came from Washington.

Head Quarters
Skippack, PA
October 1, 1777

Madam,
I wish I could grant the request contained in your letter of 29 September: a permission for Mr. Fergusson to come out and remain at Graeme Park for thirty days implies his intent to return at the expiration of that time into the quarters of the enemy.
I confess it appears to me very odd that a gentleman who has been so long absent from his family should wish to remain so short a time with them. Whatever might be my private inclination to indulge you, my duty obliges me on this occasion to refuse a compliance with your wishes on the terms proposed.
George Washington

Washington did, however, issue me a pass to go and see my husband. I decided I would go to Germantown to see Henry but no farther. I couldn't bear to see my hometown under British occupation.

I stared out the window at Germantown. Redcoats were everywhere, the town in chaos. Many families who refused to quarter British troops had left for elsewhere. I saw no children, heard nothing of the sounds of normal life. Germantown had become a military barracks.

Henry was lodged at the Taunces Inn. When I arrived, an elderly man waved me to the second floor. "Third room on the right," he grunted over his giant drinker's nose, red as a poppy.

I knocked, feeling like I couldn't draw a breath. I had not seen my husband in two years.

The door opened and there stood Henry. He looked the same, his face bronzed by sun and wind. Stubble shadowed his jaw.

I stood stiff and uncertain, my insides shaking. He reached for me gently and drew me into the room.

"It's you," he said tenderly. "My wife." He looked hopeful, and wary.

My lips curved into a smile. His handsome face, those piercing eyes. *Henry. He's here.*

He bowed to kiss me, and my teeth knocked his lip. I laughed self-consciously, awkward. He kissed me again, more slowly this time.

It's Henry.

Henry kicked the door shut. I pulled away and glanced around, taking in the sparse furnishings and his canvas travel bag. My heart fluttered in my chest like a caged bird trying to find its perch. Strangely, it was like no time had passed at all.

"I have missed you," he said simply, and moved to sit on the narrow bed, patiently letting me find my way in my heart. He watched me quietly, love shadowing his face.

My eyes took in his sandy hair, a little too long, the breadth of his shoulders, the new freckles from long days in the sun. I looked into his eyes. *He is the same. It's just my Henry. He's back.*

I walked over and sat next to him on the bed. We breathed in silence for a few moments, until I laid my head on his shoulder. He turned and dropped an emotional kiss on my forehead.

"Let's not do that again," Henry said huskily, and stroked my hair. "I couldn't bear another two years without you."

"I love you," I blurted out. Where were the words I planned to say? I had been crafting them in the dark for days as I lay staring at the ceiling, a diatribe of errors and faults stocked like arrows in my quiver, ready for the white rage of my aim when I saw him in person. *What were you thinking, not telling me you were coming back? Why didn't you sail somewhere else and bring a horse up? What are you doing to us, fighting with Howe? How could you? What's the matter with you? What does this mean for us?*

Time slid away from me, as intangible as air, taking with it all the offenses and hurts, the feelings of betrayal. Within minutes, it was as if he never left. We fit together the way we always did.

My heart found a steady beat. The next time we kissed we did not speak again for a very long while.

I told Henry that Pennsylvania had changed a great deal while he was away, and now nothing less than independence would be accepted. Henry said the victory at Brandywine was a sign of what was to come. "We'll be rewarded for my service," he assured me. "Our future will be secure."

Henry and I were not allowed to be together at Graeme Park, and I couldn't stay in Germantown with Howe's army. I returned home after five days to news that Johnny was serving with the Pennsylvania Loyalists, a cavalry troop. *That will make him happy*, I thought. *My fighting boy.*

"How are things with Henry? Are you still getting along?" Liza asked, worried. "He doesn't have bad feelings for you, or you for him?"

"Strangely, we do get along," I answered uneasily. It was difficult to describe the dance Henry and I did around each other, difficult to describe how we could even get along and be in the same room, let alone be lovers. We didn't talk of the war very often.

The next month, in October, Henry sent word that I should meet him at the Rising Sun tavern. I requested another pass to cross the line and made my way there.

"I need you to deliver a letter," he said to me over a bowl of fish soup. "Will you do that?"

"A letter to whom?"

Henry paused, his hand sliding out to cover mine. "General Washington."

"Why? Who's it from?"

His eyes were serious. "Reverend Duché."

Jacob Duché, our close friend and Reverend Peters' replacement at Christ Church. Why would Henry, a Tory, be asking me to deliver a letter to Washington from Duché, two patriots? Last summer Jacob met with the church vestry and passed a resolution that King George III and the entire royal family were no longer to be part of church services. Duché removed the king from his Book of Common Prayer and refused to say his name out loud. It was courageous, bold, and an act of treason, for as an English clergyman, Duché had taken an oath of loyalty to the king when he took his vows. The following week, Congress elected Duché as first official chaplain of the Continental forces. What business between those two would concern Henry?

"What does the letter say?" I asked.

"Betsy, I don't know what it says. Honestly, I don't. It just needs to be delivered."

"Why can't someone else take it? Why not someone from the church?"

Henry paused to eat his soup. "I was asked to help. Since I obviously can't go into Washington's camp myself, I thought we could ask you. Duché is a close friend of ours, I thought you wouldn't mind."

I considered the request. The continental forces had lost another battle at Germantown four days ago. Perhaps Jacob was offering encouragement to Washington. Or maybe he was relaying an important message to Congress, which was still hiding in Lancaster while the British sat in Philadelphia.

Or maybe, I thought hopefully, Duché was trying to turn Henry and being devious about it. The thought was comforting.

"Didn't Jacob resign his chaplaincy with Congress?" I asked.

"Yes, but he's is still a reverend and a friend," Henry said. "The Anglican Church may have put pressure on him to step away from the rebels."

"I'm not comfortable delivering a letter without knowing its contents. Have him send someone."

"Surely we can do this one favor for a friend, my sweet," Henry pressed. "In wartime, it's much safer to deliver a letter by hand, using someone trustworthy. Besides, Duché assures me you and I aren't even mentioned. It has nothing to do with us."

If that was the case, I would deliver the letter. I'd be a messenger just this once if I wasn't part of it. I knew Jacob well.

Washington was camped fifteen miles from Graeme Park at Kulpsville, recovering from the losses at Brandywine and then Germantown.

I arrived at camp and was announced by Washington's manservant, Billy, a dignified Negro man. "This way, Mrs. Fergusson." He motioned me into Washington's private tent, a vast structure, as large as a cottage. Washington's other servants were milling about outside, his washerwoman, housekeeper, and cook. Between Washington and his officers, there must have been a dozen servants at least on hand to meet their needs.

"Mrs. Fergusson." General Washington bowed from his great height, his voice the soft drawl of a gentleman from Virginia. He and I had met a few times before, at parties. I noticed he never wore a wig. He tied his hair back and powdered it white. Once he and Martha even came to one of my Attic Evenings in 1770 when he was in town to see Franklin. He was charming and deeply intelligent, his wife warm and earthy. I held great esteem for the both of them. I liked Washington immensely.

"Sir. You must miss Mount Vernon," I said with sympathy. "And Mrs. Washington, of course. Thank you for your service."

"It is true that I miss my home," he drawled, his voice a lilt of sound. "Yet I believe wholeheartedly in the cause of America and the necessity of our liberty. Fortunately, Mrs. Washington will join me at our winter camp in just a few months."

Mindful of his time, I set forth to my task.

"Thank you for receiving me, Your Excellency," I said humbly. "I bring a letter from Reverend Jacob Duché, who, through a friend, has assured me it must reach you directly."

He took it from me and sat at his desk to read it. I was unsure of what to do; should I leave? Or was I expected to wait and take his reply? I hesitated, and Billy waved me to a chair. I sat, my fingers pleating and un-pleating the fabric of my skirt.

It was an interminable wait. Once unsealed, the letter was very long. Of course, I had no idea what it said. Washington's face was inscrutable as he read, although a muscle tightened in his jaw and his eyes narrowed.

He finally finished reading, and stood up and began to pace back and forth. He seemed agitated. The minutes stretched on. Finally, almost an hour after I arrived, he finally turned to me, his face like stone.

The dread that had been growing in my stomach grew to the size of a canyon.

"Madam, I have always esteemed your character and endowments," he began.

I sat frozen. His words unfurled above me like the hissing of a boiled kettle.

"I am entrusted by the *people of America* with sovereign authority. Were I to desert their cause and consign them to the British, what would be the consequence?"

Dear God. What had Duché written? Had the letter asked Washington to surrender?

"Your Excellency—" I interrupted, feeling sick, but he paid me no heed. "I didn't—"

"It will be the *object of my life* and ambition to establish the independence of America in the first place; and in the second, to arrange such a community of interests between the two nations as shall indemnify them for the calamities which they now suffer, and form a new era in the history of nations."

I swallowed hard. "Sir, I had no—"

Washington went on. I dropped my eyes, feeling them burn. I would not cry in front of George Washington.

"Madam," he went on, "you are aware that I have many enemies. Congress must hear of your visit, and of this letter. I would be suspect if I were to conceal it from them."

He stared at me sternly, his face a tight mask. His voice belied his anger.

I felt my face drain of color. "I'm sorry I—"

I stopped. His face was like a granite cliff as he towered over me. What would my protests achieve other than to prove my very great stupidity? He knew Henry had arrived back with Howe's army and was intent on serving the British. I was Henry's wife, guilty by association. He thought I had chosen to deliver a Loyalist manifest. Why would he believe me that I didn't know? I bowed my head and watched the earth spin and break around my feet.

Henry, what have you done?

"You are free to depart," he said finally in a voice of that would freeze a lake. "But this letter will be transmitted without delay to Congress. *Without delay.*" It might as well have been a shout, but he was far too powerful for that.

I am a patriot, I screamed silently to the space over his left shoulder. I barely saw the flap of the tent to exit; my eyes swam with tears and the gritty despair of betrayal.

Sir, I want an independent America too.

Chapter 24

December 1777

"Humanity itself calls upon you to desist," I read aloud to Liza and Anny, my voice thick with disgust. Jacob Duché's letter to Washington was long and awful. "That's what he said. It is *revolting.*"

Duché's letter to General Washington was read in Congress on October 20, then widely circulated, and published in the *Royal Gazette* in November. Although I was not named, everyone knew the "married lady of character, having connections with the British army" was me. It was all anyone could talk about. I had become a traitor. Me, who canvassed with the Daughters of Liberty, sewed shirts for Wayne's army until my fingers numbed, and repeatedly took money and food to the patriots in jail even when we didn't have enough ourselves.

Duché was trying to destroy the cause. Piece by piece, his argument tore down the Continentals. Of the army he said, "The whole world knows that its only existence depends upon you; that your death or captivity disperses it in a moment, and that there is not a man in America capable of succeeding you."

Army, navy, Congress, citizens, French influence—all ineffective, Duché declared. The message was clear: Washington was delusional. The Americans would lose. Liberty was a pipe dream. We were guilty of collective madness, and we would all die for our troubles.

"I still can't believe it," I said again.

"I heard that Howe and his men got hold of him when they swept into Philadelphia," Liza said. "Torture tends to loosen the tongues of men."

"Although in the letter he claims it's how he really feels."

"Maybe they had a pistol to his head."

We were shivering in front of the fire on a biting December afternoon, Baby Elizabeth napping in her cot. Anny was knitting a cap; Liza a sweater. I was sewing another soldier's shirt until my disgust rose again and I grabbed the newspaper for the hundredth time.

"*How fruitless the expense of blood*," I read.

"Don't talk of it anymore, Betsy," Liza said. "We all know what happened, and it certainly was not your fault."

"Washington doesn't know that."

"I still find it odd." Anny frowned. "Why would Jacob do it? A change of heart I understand, but to send a damning letter like that, going on about how you only supported the cause at the beginning because men around you were keen and you felt pressured by them? That makes no sense."

"The British got to him," Liza repeated. "You can be sure of that."

"Duché paid a high price for it," I said flatly. "Congress seized his house and assets, and he was forced to flee to England. Congress only left his wife and children enough money to get to him in London."

"Yet still," Anny persisted. "Jacob's *best friend* was one of the signers of the Declaration of Independence! Francis Hopkinson risked his life to put his name on that document. Would you knowingly sabotage your best friend when it could mean his death? That's exactly what Duché did when he approached Washington. I would wager even the English think Duché a fool."

"Worse, Jacob is married to Francis's sister," I added. "He damned his own *brother-in-law*. What must Mary think?"

"Look at our own family," Liza said. "Young Johnny couldn't get to the British fast enough while his father and his sister are laboring for the cause." She motioned to the baby asleep in her cot. "War rips families apart."

"And then there's you and Henry," Anny said bitterly. "But we won't speak of that."

"Probably wise," I agreed.

Our circumstances were unimaginable. Henry was in Philadelphia and was now, ironically, commissary of American prisoners. When American soldiers were captured, Henry had them in his charge.

"The British treatment of Americans has been deplorable," Henry said to me when he accepted the post. "I can change that, Betsy. I'll treat the prisoners well."

On the flip side, and somewhat ridiculously, my close friend Elias Boudinot, Annis Stockton's brother, was commissary of British prisoners. The world as we knew it was gone. How could we make sense of this?

"Why won't you leave him, Aunty Betsy?" Anny asked me. "How can you stand—"

"Anny, he is my husband."

"Henry sent you to General Washington like a sacrifice," Anny scowled. "Wouldn't a man be killed for that? They hang traitors on the public green with a crowd to watch. And applaud."

Henry still claimed that he didn't know the contents of Duché's letter or his intentions. Perhaps that was true. How would I ever know? When Henry and I were together, he was a kind and caring husband. There has always been a true connection between us. We still dreamed of a future on the other side of madness. Despite everything, I couldn't abandon him.

"He's my husband," I repeated. "I believe him."

Anny opened her mouth to argue and then closed it again.

"My heart goes out to the soldiers," Liza said. "They must be suffering terribly at Valley Forge. This cold cuts like a scythe! On a devil of a day like today, without adequate shelter and food, how do they bear it?"

Anny looked at her baby daughter with a mother's fierce protection. She was thinking of the mothers of those boys in uniform, the young continental soldiers. "That's why we make these garments," she said. "Any relief we can, we must provide."

"I heard some of soldiers bleed on the snow for want of shoes," Liza said.

"That's the least of their problems," Anny scowled. "They're dying of dysentery and typhoid fever in droves."

Dr. Rush had visited the camp and told us of their misfortune. He was busy writing out medical practices for the army. After the battle of Princeton, where he served alongside Washington as army physician, he felt that there were military protocols that would save lives if they were followed.

"Next month the calendar turns to 1778," I said thoughtfully. It had been two and a half years since the shots rang out at Concord and Lexington. "The war has to be over soon."

"Henry's still in Philadelphia?" Liza asked.

"Yes," I answered. "For now."

"Keeping our soldiers as prisoners." Anny's voice was piercing as a whip, a cat-o'-nine tails whipping past bare flesh.

"Anny." I spoke slowly, punctuating each word with a pause. "I am not my husband. I do not make his choices. Just as you are not your brother. I wish I could control both men, yet I can't. Can you?"

A raw silence.

"Henry will alleviate their circumstances if he is able," I said. "I know he doesn't wish for them to suffer. His preference was to return home to us, but that option was denied to him."

"Denied by his *own* hand!" Anny flared. "By his own actions! If *I* had been gone for two years from my spouse, I'd do anything, everything, to rush back to my husband's side. I wouldn't join the British army and lord over American prisoners! Or worry about the risks of crossing some war line to get home to my wife!"

The cat-o'-nine tails landed, parted flesh. I imagined my back red with blood, skin buckled like pork fat.

"Oh Anny!" Liza exclaimed.

My hands stilled. The needle dangle from the thread. Tears slid down my nose and dropped in small circles on the fabric in my lap.

Anny was at my feet, kneeling before me. She put her head in my lap. "I'm sorry, I'm sorry, I'm so sorry."

My fingers reached for her hair, stroked the chestnut strands. Thick hair, like mine and Mama's. Anny's hands covered mine.

"I spoke thoughtlessly, forgive me—"

"Shh."

Anny lifted her head and searched my eyes, her face full of alarm. I shook my head.

"I didn't choose this," I finally said.

I chose love. That was all. Would I be punished forever?

Anny laid her head back in my lap, and we stayed there until the baby fussed.

Anny's husband took her and their daughter away to the safety of Allentown for the winter.

If Liza and I expected to be alone at Graeme Park for Christmas, we were wrong. Instead, an army rolled in and we were joined by a thousand men, led by Major General James Armstrong. On New Year's Eve, Brigadier General James Potter joined them with his brigade. There were almost two thousand men camped in my fields! It may as well have been ten thousand. Compared to General Wayne's camp of four hundred, this was a wave larger than we could withstand. We strained at the seams in every regard.

"Mrs. Fergusson, I thank you again," General Potter said, hat in hand, as he stood on my doorstep. "I know it isn't easy for you to carry the burden of the army being camped on your land."

"Come in, General." I swept a hand into the hallway. He stood, shoulders sprinkled with snow, cheeks red as plums from the crisp air. "Will you take coffee with us? Or a spirit to warm you?"

He shook his head. "I came to see if we might offer you assistance in some regard. I have been made aware of your reduced circumstances."

"We are pleased to serve the American cause," I said firmly. "We are surviving well enough, when so many others are not."

"There must be something my men can put to right. Household repairs, perhaps?"

"If you are willing, chopped firewood would be welcome. Our servants are low in number, and winter is here."

He nodded, satisfied to be able to offer me a small token of service, and took his leave.

The next day a young boy appeared outside the barn, chopping logs on a stump. I peered outside the window at him on and off, watched him swing his axe.

Curiosity roused me. I gathered my cloak and went outside.

"Thank you, sir," I said. "We are in need of that wood."

He stopped swinging the axe. "I'm first shift. There'll be others, missus. We'll see to it." He was so young. Younger than Johnny.

I handed him the steaming cup I'd carted out. "Chocolate for you. I insist."

A smile flashed across his features. He took a sip and closed his eyes, his expression one of rapture.

"I imagine you do not get many comforts very often in the army," I said. "What is your name?"

"William Hutchinson, ma'am."

"How long have you been in service?"

"I signed up in October of '76 with a volunteer infantry company in Chester County."

"You saw combat?"

"Not at first. Our first detail was to patrol Philadelphia at night. After Howe took it, we moved out. I fought at Trenton and Brandywine and Germantown, with various units."

I considered this. Duché claimed everyone would be a loyalist again if Congress dissolved and Washington gave up. He spoke of a silent majority that was against separation. "Tell me, young man, do you believe in the success of the war? For America?"

"With all my heart, missus. That's why I keep signing up for more active duty when my contracts are up. My ma says I'm in love with the cause instead of a girl."

"Are the British as cruel and barbarous as the papers would have us believe?"

He hesitated.

"Speak freely. I ask out of genuine interest. I will not repeat your words."

"After the Paoli Massacre, a Quaker man came to our quarters. He had a man with him that he'd found in the woods. This man was so badly injured his clothes were stiff with gore. So much so that his coat would have stood up on its own if we had taken if off him."

He paused and looked at my face uncertainly before he continued.

"The injured man was from Virginia. He'd survived the massacre and, as such, was an easy target, if you know what I mean. He said a dozen British soldiers with bayonets formed a circle around him. One man at a time stabbed him in a different part of his body. They took turns for the fun of it. I don't know how, but he managed to get away, but not before a bayonet gashed open his head. When the Quaker man found him, he'd been lying in the woods bleeding all night. His legs and arms were covered with mud and sand and blood, all stuck in his wounds. His feet too, he had no shoes by then. Our captain sent for a doctor, and the man's still alive. The redcoats did it for sport, after the battle was over. They counted forty-six bayonet wounds in him."

If he feared he would shock me, I was not shocked. I wondered why the British hadn't just killed the poor man and be done with it, after they'd had their sport.

"Your faith in the cause gives me hope," I said warmly, to reassure him I was not offended. "May God protect you, son. Thank you for your service in the continental army. And thank you for my firewood."

"You'll be warm now, ma'am," he said.

I wanted to ask him so much more, but I could see concern across his young brow. He was afraid he'd said too much.

"Missus," he called to me as I walked to the house. "American soldiers, sometimes they're no better. I don't want you to think that we are. It's war."

"Yes," I said. "I understand. I understand war."

Liza and I watched as hundreds of soldiers left in segments over the first two weeks of January. Some were headed elsewhere; others were going home, their contracts about to expire. In mid-January, Armstrong and Potter were replaced by Brigadier General John Lacey Junior. He had none of the cheerfulness of Armstrong or the warmth of Potter, who had arranged the firewood for us. Lacey walked the camp and pronounced the conditionals deplorable. "Equipment strewn everywhere," he yelled. "A mess! No order, no efficiency." He proclaimed the remaining six hundred men as new recruits who were confused, demoralized, and leaderless.

By January 24, the last of the troops were moving out. Liza and I sighed with relief until six thousand cartridges stored in a tent blew up unexpectedly one day. We thought hell had arrived. The smoke rolled like fog for ages, the stench and debris stretched across the land like the apocalypse in Revelation. Six men had died in the explosion. After that I knew what a battlefield looked and smelled like: fire and smoke and melted skin, pierced by shouts and screams.

Finally they were gone and we had peace. If we had been depleted after Wayne's regiment tore through Graeme Park, we were almost destitute after John Lacey Junior took his leave and left us scraped bare. I estimated, in roughly a month, the army had eaten over two thousand pounds of our beef.

Henry was still twenty miles away, living at the Stedmans and guarding American prisoners.

I was more miserable that winter than I'd ever been in my life. The world was tragic. I could not see the future or even imagine it. I was wretched indeed.

Henry begged me constantly to come to him. Each time I went, I needed to cross the war line and enter British-occupied Philadelphia. I learned that there were three ways to secure a pass: from Congress, from the War Board, and from General Washington himself. I obtained passes to visit Henry when I could, which was not often, as I was frequently denied. In all, we spent two weeks together all winter.

Our visits were like maple syrup on bitter bark. I asked him to surrender. Henry pleaded honor and conscience; he could not bring himself to believe in an independent America. It was too much to ask of him, for Henry, it was anarchy, a refusal of the natural order of things. As his wife, it was my duty to obey him, and yet his obstinacy was mirrored in me: I could no more have crossed to the British than I could have grown a third arm.

"I cannot even consider it," I told Liza.

"Perhaps you can," Liza replied evenly. "We've lost New York and Philadelphia, and so many of the battles of the past year. Perhaps your place is with Henry now. We are losing."

"We won Saratoga!" I objected. "And what about my home and family? I raised Anny, she's like my daughter. I couldn't leave Baby Elizabeth, or you. My dear Liza, I won't leave you." The farm, the mansion house, my lifelong friends. Dear Old Joseph, our remaining servants, and the ghosts of my parents, my brothers and sisters, even Governor Keith. How could I leave? I had to stay; my soul was bound with Graeme Park.

I used the trips to see Henry in Philadelphia to take more food and clothing to the prisoners of war on both sides. They were a miserable lot, dying from hunger and cold far too frequently. Elias Boudinot wrote me a letter of thanks for these small efforts, but what I brought was so meager I felt it deserved no thanks. I took what I could, but it wasn't much. None of us had much by then. Cash was hard to come by, inflation was climbing, and the British controlled any goods coming into the city, from all directions.

Surely Thomas Paine was right: we cannot be governed by men three thousand miles away. These were indeed the times that tried men's souls. It galled me, however, that Paine could write eloquent essays that caused men to walk away from their homes and families and take up arms, but not fight himself.

In April, Elias Boudinot reached out to me to complain that any efforts made by Henry to improve conditions for the American prisoners were rejected or ignored by his British superiors. Two prisoners had been beaten with an iron jail key by the provost and later died. Elias begged me to appeal to Henry. I felt I was slowly falling off a cliff, with no way of seeing what was beneath me to stop my fall.

"Stay," Henry begged me when I went to him at the Stedmans. "Leave Graeme Park and stay here in Philadelphia with me. Commit to the British, and we'll be rewarded after the war ends. Positions, land, money. Far more than your father's land. You know he would have wanted you to look after yourself."

I shook my head, and reached for my shift where it lay over the back of the chair. "You know I can't, Henry. I won't."

Henry sank to his knees in front of me and buried his face in my waist. "The patriots can't win. Why can't you see that?" he groaned.

"What if you're wrong?" I said to the top of his head. I still believed in an independent America. "They'll kill you, Henry! Seek a pardon before it's too late, before the end is decided. Leave the British now, while you still can."

Henry let me go and stood. He went to the window. Below, redcoats were patrolling in the street. "For God's sake, I'm not wrong! Look around you, Betsy! Who do you see? The Regulars, not the Continentals. We're winning."

I went to the door and stood with my hand on the doorknob. "If you won't leave the British army, then at least invent a reason to return to Scotland. Come up with another family emergency."

Henry swore. He was wearing only his shirt, his long legs bare. I looked at his feet, white and naked, incongruous on the warm honey color of the wood planks.

"For me, Henry. Please. I don't want to have to watch my husband hang."

"I plan on staying alive, with my wife. Betsy, only Congress is pushing the war along. Howe was almost unobstructed when he landed and strode overland to Philadelphia. The capital of the new America, the so-called rebel city, fell like a house of cards. England will try and separate the colonies next, create a rift between north and south and divide the people. The war won't last much longer. The Continentals can't win."

"According to you."

We both stood and faced each other in frustration.

I stepped forward to kiss him. *"A light gleams forth to lead her back, where peace and safety tread,"* I said against his lips. It was from a poem I wrote him when I turned down his first offer to move to town and be with him. It was a play on the words of Aesop's city mouse-country mouse fable.

"My country mouse," he said and pulled me to him. "My very stubborn, very lovely country mouse."

"My heart," I answered, my fingers sliding over his chest to where I could feel the beat within.

"I do miss you," he said. "The life we had there. I miss the farm, I miss nights with you. Graeme Park is an opium of sorts."

He clearly was thinking of Graeme Park before several armies rolled through.

Graeme Park was in danger.

Congress was actively seizing the property of anyone who helped or served the British in any way. Thanks to Henry, and to my unwitting action as a courier for the enemy, Graeme Park was in the lineup of houses to be confiscated. If we lost Graeme Park, we had no way to survive. Where would we go?

The winter of 1778 continued along its hellish path. Liza and I spent every minute of our time writing to friends and acquaintances who might be able to influence the authorities. We begged them to advocate on our behalf. In person, we asked everyone and anyone to intervene and speak well of us. Then we spent days documenting the efforts we had made over the past few years to support the American cause.

During those months, Henry was safe with the British, and I was grateful he was unharmed. The few times I could visit him, I poured out my fears about the confiscation rule. He repeated his confidence that Britain would win. "After the war, we'll have Graeme Park and so much more," he assured me.

I didn't tell him that we had entertained George Washington's officers recently. They had lodged overnight when they had to attend to business close by and were away from their quarters at Valley Forge for a short time. I also didn't tell Henry that I still believed Washington existed in the highest sphere of men. I was entranced by him, by his intelligence, the mountain that was his moral character. I hated myself for delivering that letter. I always would.

I hoped for relief of some sort, but none came. Darkness rolled into more darkness.

I prayed that spring would see a turn in our fortune, but in May, Henry was accused of treason. He had until June 25 to report to the Supreme Executive Council, the new governing body for Pennsylvania, and turn himself in. If he did not, Graeme Park would be confiscated, and Henry would be executed.

Three days later Johnny's name was added to the list. My husband and my only nephew both faced death.

Chapter 25

Philadelphia
June 1778

For days, I was haunted by the imagined eerie cries of my parents, wailing from deep in their graves in Philadelphia at Christ Church, while redcoats paraded by their feet, muskets in hand. *Fight Elizabeth*, they cried. *Fight.*

Sometimes I dreamed of Governor Keith shaking his fist at me. *I may have been terrible with money, but you! Look what you did. You gave it away, everything I worked for. Gone!* Keith's face would fade and become Henry's, dead and slack-jawed, twirling from the hangman's noose.

I desperately had to see Henry. I would beg him to do anything he could—anything!—to avoid being caught and executed. Maybe he could get the British to send him to fight in Minorca or somewhere else. I requested another pass to cross the war line.

I decided that after I saw my husband, I would to go to Lancaster to petition Congress to remove his name from the list of men accused of treason. As a Scot, Henry had never been a citizen of Pennsylvania, therefore he couldn't be guilty. He hadn't even been in America when independence was declared. If I explained this in front of the rebel government, surely they would see reason.

When I received my pass to enter the city, I sent word to Margaret and Charles Stedman to let them know I was coming, and bringing Old Joseph with me. It was safer for me to stay with them and meet Henry in secret than to risk moving Henry about in daylight and alerting potential spies.

Margaret sent me a note back saying that they had a visitor, but there was a bed available for me. The visitor was a governor, some English commissioner who had been dispatched by Parliament to settle the differences between Great Britain and America. Ha! Settle our differences! It was about ten years too late. How ridiculous. I would do my best to avoid him. I was sure he was a pompous fool.

We arrived in Philadelphia to find it barely recognizable after eight months of British occupation. This wasn't the town I grew up in. Destruction was rampant, the streets unkempt. There were holes like pulled teeth where wooden buildings and fences had once stood, ripped down to burn as firewood against the cold. Stores had been plundered, emptied of goods; most cattle and horses taken or eaten. Most merchants had little left on the shelves or were closed entirely. The streets were quiet and ugly. Basements and alleys had been used as latrines, the stench was overpowering.

An old Quaker lady selling corn brooms told us Howe had ordered citizens to clean in front of their property, and after the snow cleared, he insisted residents spend one week a month in general street cleanup. It seemed to me that his orders had not been obeyed. I would need to watch my step carefully.

Philadelphia's population was cut in half again when the British swept in, leaving a motley assortment of loyalists, Quakers, and the poor and elderly. I wondered what Howe's men had done all winter in this half-empty place.

"Cockfighting," the Quaker lady told me, her mouth turned down disapprovingly. "Horse racing, dining, weekly balls! And acting out plays in the Southwark Theater. I'm not jesting. They passed the time alright, don't kid yourself about that."

I felt so sad. The British played while the continental soldiers shivered and hungered and died of disease at Valley Forge. How would we ever win this war? Doubt niggled at me like the ragged fingers of Beelzebub.

"Well, only the officers played like that," the Quaker woman continued. "The regular soldiers were sent into the countryside to forage for food. Most of them stole whatever they could find, women included. So watch yourself, girl." I nodded but pointed at Old Joseph. I wouldn't come alone now, not anymore.

The Stedman house stood strong, although it looked a little worse for wear. No flowers on the step in cheerful pots, chipped paint on the door. Old Joseph went to tend to our horse and carriage. Margaret and Charles welcomed me gravely.

"We know about Henry and Johnny," Margaret murmured sympathetically. She drew me into an embrace. Charles nodded compassionately, pensive. He had aged.

How strange, I thought, that I was sheltered in a loyalist house. Dear friends, but loyalists still. I wondered how my sister Ann's sympathies would have played out had she lived. Would she have turned her husband Charles to the patriot side? Somehow I did not think so; she was my father's daughter through and through, loyal to the English and the old ways.

"General Howe announced his retirement in April," Margaret whispered, as if we were on the street and not in her front hall. "They were pushing him out anyway. We think Henry is moving out with the army. I know you came to see him but he was called away; he only just left. We think they'll go soon."

My heart sank. Henry wasn't here? What else must I endure?

Charles nodded, and said in a lowered voice, "The British don't seem that interested in holding Philadelphia any longer. Something's afoot. There are signs of an evacuation. The troops can smell it, they're restless."

"The brass put on a party for General Howe to send him off. You should have seen the fuss!" Margaret said, still in a whisper. "It was a show: decorated boats on the river, officers dressed as knights. They were jousting, setting off fireworks, dancing, feasting. It wasn't right. The Quakers were appalled. Can you imagine: all that gross excess in a time like this. Frippery!"

A shadow fell on the wall behind Margaret.

"Governor!" she said with forced cheer. Her voice returned to full volume. "Let me introduce you to our dear friend, Elizabeth Fergusson. Mrs. Fergusson is the sister of Charles's first wife, before he was so sadly widowed. You will recall, I believe I told you, Elizabeth's husband is commissary of British prisoners, very much esteemed by General Howe. They reside at their country estate in Horshamtown, Graeme Park."

I turned to meet Governor Johnstone, my mind on Henry. How could I find him? He must still be in the city if he had only just left. If the British were going to evacuate Philadelphia it had to be to get to Washington and shut down the continental army.

Wherever Henry was, he was not within my reach. Thwarted, I planned my trip to Lancaster to petition Congress. Henry would have to escape or turn himself in, one way or the other. He couldn't be executed.

Although I wanted to, I could not avoid Governor Johnstone; we were staying in the same house. Against my will, I found him a reasonable and pleasant man, and we formed a cautious ease of sorts, aided by sultry June evenings sitting in the Stedmans' garden.

"This heat," Johnstone panted one night over treacle tart, swatting at the swarming insects. "Ghastly," he said, wiping sweat from his forehead. The mosquitoes were out in full force while sheets of lightning chased the darkening summer sky.

"Philadelphia is a mercurial place," I answered. "We suffer in the cold for months until the summer charges in with her searing sun and reminds us why we must be grateful for the freezing lash of winter. I'm sure you find it uncomfortable, for there isn't heat like this in England, is there?"

"Let's go inside," Margaret said. "The bugs have gotten the best of the evening." She motioned to the maid to tidy up the garden table. What was her name? Jenny. The blond girl. She looked Norwegian. When I glanced back, she was staring at me again.

"Scotch?" Charles asked Johnstone, rising.

Margaret's hand on my arm drew me back. "He knows," she whispered. "We didn't tell him, but he knows about Henry's attainder. And he knows that you aren't a Tory. Someone told him. It wasn't us, I swear. Be careful."

Mercifully, the parlor was bug-free apart from a few spiders. Even the mugginess didn't deter our relief from escaping the mosquitoes.

"I must let you know, Mrs. Fergusson, now that we are more acquainted, how sympathetic I am to the American cause," Johnstone said from his easy chair. "You mustn't think me your enemy. No, that wouldn't do. I can understand the American people's struggles, their dream of liberty, such as it were."

I didn't like the way he said *dream,* the slight mocking emphasis. I knew that he had been dispatched with two other peace commissioners to craft some sort of reconciliation with the colonies. Burgoyne's defeat at Saratoga had shocked the British. They had counted on an easy victory.

"It is well known to me that the American people will accept no other outcome," I said easily. "I am confident of victory."

"Mrs. Fergusson," he drawled, a cigar in one hand and a Scotch in the other, his shirtsleeves rolled up. "I see that you are an intelligent woman. Permit me a personal observation, if I may, for I find myself fascinated that you hold strong patriot views, even in the face of your personal, er, alliances."

"You will not find my situation uncommon here, Mr. Johnstone, in a city that was the head of our new Congress but is now under British occupation. Many families are divided. My husband and I understand each other and will make do with whatever is handed us."

"You must call me George, please."

"Mr. Johnstone, you have been sent by the British government," I said. "I am aware of your task and the work you plan to do here. It would be unwise for us to form a friendship."

He waved his cigar, leaving a wispy plume of white smoke. "I am here as part of a peace commission, yes. And I am here on behalf of the crown, it's true, but I have no evangelical streak in me. I am not here, Mrs. Fergusson, to convert you. I cannot browbeat every strong-headed woman I meet." He paused, then smiled at me. "I would be exhausted."

In spite of myself, I smiled back.

"America has been at war for three years," I said. "You will forgive me if I find your mission unreasonable. There were years when it would have been welcome. Where were you and your peace party then?"

"We believe the people here would abandon the idea of independence in an instant if your Congress stands down and George Washington resigns his position. The people who don't want separation are the silent majority, and they're imprisoned by their circumstances. Joseph Galloway has assured us as much."

I laughed bitterly. "Then England does not understand America." Dear God. What was Joseph doing? I knew he had turned loyalist, but to tell authorities such a thing? My unwitting foolish friend.

George Johnstone had arrived far too late to be holding an olive branch of any kind. Margaret told me he was shocked to find the British army about to evacuate Philadelphia and head back to New York City. One of his superiors, or maybe several, had gotten it wrong. England shouldn't have sent the commissioners in the first place.

"Liberty is an entirely reasonable virtue to want," Johnstone said conversationally, taking a sip of Scotch. "But does liberty have to mean separation? Bloodshed? No. Perhaps the king's shortsightedness, his mistake if you will, was being too slow to recognize other possibilities. While I regret that you do not share your husband's sentiments, I am interested in learning of your own, Mrs. Fergusson. If you will take the time to educate me, perhaps I will be better prepared for my task of helping the people of the colonies understand what we can offer them. What if every British subject could live equally empowered, if you will, whether in America or elsewhere?"

"You are too late, sir," I said. "We have the support of France now. The winds have changed. Any information from me will not help you."

Dr. Franklin had gone to France to negotiate a pair of treaties that were signed in February. The French fleet was on its way. Even French nobles like the Marquis de Lafayette had joined the continental effort—Lafayette had fought at Brandywine and wintered at Valley Forge with Washington.

Johnstone twirled his glass thoughtfully. He picked at the skin around the base of his nails, I noticed, where the skin was red and rough. A nervous man?

I excused myself to retire to bed. I was displeased by Johnstone's hapless optimism that he could change the tide of war, as if Americans hadn't already died fighting. This was 1778, not 1773. The time for talking was long gone.

The next morning I was dismayed to find Johnstone in the Stedmans' breakfast room. I had entered, it was too late for me to retreat. I sat down at the table reluctantly.

"Mrs. Fergusson, you are an admirable woman," Governor Johnstone told me over his bread and butter. "If you ever come to England, you must come visit my wife and I. She would be very taken with you."

Margaret and Charles busied themselves with their coffee.

"You're returning home?" I asked. The blond maid—Jenny—poured my coffee. I added fresh cream. I felt her eyes on me. When I looked up, she looked away.

"Yes, I hope to sail by the end of the month. I was waiting to hear back from Joseph Reed." Reed had signed the Articles of Confederation and was a rising star in Pennsylvania's new governing judicial system. Johnstone had written to Congress, then. I could not imagine Joseph Reed wanting to have anything to do with Johnstone or the flurry of letters he was frantically sending Congress to request an audience. His wife, Esther Reed, was still tirelessly rounding up and spurring on the patriotic ladies of Philadelphia with fundraisers and rallies.

"Governor Johnstone, I repeat, I am certain nothing short of independence will be accepted," I said, thinking of the American prisoners rotting in the recently built Walnut Street prison. *The lucky ones die on the field*, Elias had said.

"We each have an opinion," he acknowledged amiably and reached for the cream.

"We do," I agreed.

"Fresh raspberry preserves?" Margaret asked.

"The end of the war is not in sight, Mrs. Fergusson," Johnstone said somberly. "After Brandywine, Germantown, and Paoli, the outcome is clearly favored toward the British. This bloodshed will continue if we *do nothing to stop it*. So many more men will die. If we can take measures to end the war, shouldn't we do that?"

Charles made a croaking sound behind his newspaper.

"You need not lecture me on the perils of war, Mr. Johnstone," I said stiffly. "The army has been in my garden and my house. My farm has been destroyed. I have been in the prisons and witnessed the terrible suffering, and sometimes death, of lifelong friends. I am no stranger to the pain of the wounded. More dead have been at my feet than I ever want to see again."

"Yes, yes, it's all too much! And no place for a woman alone. I counsel you to obey your husband and return to him," Johnstone urged. "Go to him at once. Or at least wait for him in England until the conflict ends."

Anger flashed through me.

"Sir, you needn't counsel me," I snapped. "Your advice is unwelcome."

Silence fell. The maid came in with a plate of bacon and dropped her eyes when I thanked her. Perhaps the servants were staring because I was speaking too harshly.

I stared at Johnstone mulishly.

"I confess I suspected that would be your reaction," Johnstone sighed. "Which brings me to another matter. Could I kindly ask you to pass along a document to Mr. Morris and Mr. Reed at Congress, on behalf of myself and the peace commission?"

Grim memories of my ill-fated delivery to Washington leaped to mind.

"No, Mr. Johnstone. Absolutely not. The passes to see my husband are difficult enough to obtain. I believe you said you have already written to Mr. Reed. Perhaps you should write again."

"I must rely on a direct method of delivery."

"I cannot help you."

"Governor Johnstone, Elizabeth's husband is wanted by the rebels," Charles said. "You can understand her difficult situation."

"I must fulfill my duty," he said. "Americans might consider repealing the Declaration of Independence if we can reach them. The peace commission—"

This was too much. I turned sharply to Charles. "Do you know someone who can deliver Mr. Johnstone's papers?"

"No one comes to mind." Charles looked at his wife.

Margaret shook her head. "Whigs don't come into Philadelphia during the occupation. A chicken would not stick its head into a fox's den by choice." Alarmed, remembering me, she looked at me apologetically. "It's different, of course, for you, Betsy."

"That's why she could help," Johnstone said earnestly.

"Governor Johnstone, I'm sorry, but I will not," I repeated in a louder voice. "Your request makes a mockery of how much has been sacrificed. America will have independence. That's what you must report back. Liberty or death. That was the call to arms, and nothing has changed. That remains the call to arms. Liberty or death!"

"For your husband's sake, Mrs. Fergusson, I hope for a different outcome," he hissed, his voice thick with venom.

Margaret and Charles dropped their eyes.

"Pork rashers?" Jenny asked into the tension, holding the dish. "More bacon?"

Somehow word reached Henry that I was in town and looking for him. He sent a message asking me to meet him in the alley next to the jail the following day.

To my intense irritation, Governor Johnstone entered the Stedmans' tea room the next morning as I was about to vacate it. I thought if I ate earlier I could avoid him.

"Good morning." I nodded curtly, my cup of coffee cradled in both hands. I inched for the door. There was no sign of Margaret or Charles.

He returned the greeting but stood blocking the door.

"Here, this is yours," I said. I handed him back his book that he'd insisted I borrow, a slim volume on why the colonies should reunite with England. I didn't read it.

"I wrote to Mr. Reed again," he said in a pleasant voice. "Just this morning."

"Safe travels to you, Mr. Johnstone. I wish you good fortune with your crossing."

Johnstone took a step toward me. "If you do see Mr. Reed upon your arrival in Lancaster, please give him a message from me, Mrs. Fergusson. Just a spoken message, no paper. Surely you can do that."

I shook my head and opened my mouth to object but before I could he added quickly, "If Mr. Reed can settle this situation in our favor, he will receive ten thousand guineas and the best post in our government. Tell him that."

Johnstone dropped his gaze, his one hand picking at the cuticles of the other.

"Mr. Johnstone."

He looked at me, eyebrows raised, a slight color in his cheeks.

"Do you not think Mr. Reed will look upon your offer as a bribe?" I asked coldly.

"It's not intended to be, Mrs. Fergusson. Men, in general, frequently appeal to a man's interests when we are asking him to step forward for a cause. It is within the custom of any negotiation. *Men* understand this."

I wanted to strike him.

"Surely if Mr. Reed wanted a reunion with British interests, he would do so without reward," I said. "And if he does not, no reward would alter his mind."

Johnstone bowed and turned on his heel to leave.

How could I have thought him agreeable? He was a snake.

"Where?" I asked Henry when he told me he was heading out with the army. "When?"

He shook his head "I can't tell you." He took me in his arms. "Unless you come with me."

"Henry."

"Come with me, come with me, come with me," he said, his face pressed into my neck. "Betsy please."

"I can't," I whispered.

"You can."

I changed tactics. "Richard Stockton says you can't be guilty. You're not a citizen, and you weren't even here when the war began. It was bad timing, that's all, you arriving so close to Howe and getting mixed up in that. You didn't know."

"Betsy, stop."

"Henry, please! Richard's a good solicitor and the most trusted of friends. Surrender, then we'll fight the charges."

"I love you. Remember that."

"Don't say good-bye! Why won't you press your case? For me! You still have a week. I know they would listen to you. You could return home, and we'll sell land and make Graeme Park grand again. We'll be together, like we want."

"Come with me," he repeated.

A day later, my husband left Philadelphia with the British army, still wanted for treason by the Americans. It was June 18. The date stuck in my head.

I did not need to make the trip to Lancaster, for Congress was returning to the city after the British left. When I learned only days later that Reed was in Philadelphia, I wrote and requested an audience with him. Joseph Reed was an important player in the new Pennsylvania government. He had Washington's ear, and I desperately needed the support of our commander. Surely Reed's wife would vouch for my loyalties. Mrs. Reed would tell him how much I did for the cause, how much we gave to the troops.

Reed agreed to meet me at Christ Church in the late morning. We sat in an empty pew, no one around us. The church was empty. I asked him for his advice on what to do about my property. It was all I had left in the world.

"Graeme Park is everything to me," I said urgently. I reminded him that I was the step-granddaughter of one of

Pennsylvania's governors. My father had served the city for
decades as a physician, justice of the peace, and naval
officer. I was an upstanding citizen.

Reed listened thoughtfully but said little and offered no
advice. I realized that Reed knew that I had transmitted
Duché's letter, knew about my humiliation at Washington's
hands. I could feel Reed's suspicion, the growing weight of
his judgment. In his eyes, I was a spy, married to the
enemy.

I changed tactics. I had to show him how much I
supported the cause. I would be truthful.

"I was with the Stedmans earlier this month," I began.
"Charles used to be married to my sister Ann, before she
died. They were hosting Governor Johnstone. He claimed he
wrote to you and received no reply. I confess I found him
quite distressing, sir, and his conversation most improper."

"Oh?"

"He mistakenly believes that Americans want to repeal
the Declaration of Independence. I told him of his error, I
assure you, in no uncertain terms. I made sure he knew
that liberty is our choice and independence our future."

Reed grunted and reached in his pocket for his snuffbox.

"I did receive his letter while I was at Valley Forge," he
confessed, chewing. "I did not desire to meet with the man."
He said *the man* as if he were spitting out gristle.

"He asked me to tell you he regrets not being able to be
obtain an audience with you. He said he wished to discuss
business with you." I told Reed what Johnstone had offered
him, knowing it would disgust Reed as much as it did me.

Reed's face went white, then red. "I will not be
purchased," Reed roared. "Not even the king of England is
rich enough to buy me."

"Yes, of course," I agreed. "That's exactly what I told
him. Johnstone is a scurrilous man."

Satisfied that Reed understood, I ended our meeting. I
had passed along Johnstone's message, so my conscience
was clear on both ends.

"Mrs. Fergusson, I must ask you," Reed said as I was leaving the pew, "why have you not renounced your husband? It puts you in a very precarious position. You must see that."

"The matter has resolved itself, sir. My husband has left me."

Joseph Reed could report that back to Congress. Let them think our marriage was over, and they could leave Graeme Park alone.

"You can see where my loyalties lie," I pressed. "I have stayed and not fled. I've sewn for the soldiers, worked with your wife in the Daughters of Liberty, assisted American prisoners. I've hosted the armies of Wayne and Potter and Armstrong, sacrificing crops and meat and most of my income. I did not know the contents of Duché's letter, I swear it. I believe in the future of a new and free Pennsylvania. *This* is my home."

I'm sorry, I said to Henry in my mind. *But you're gone now. After the war, you'll come back, people will forget, we'll go on.* For now, I did what was needed.

I had to survive.

I presented my petition on June 26, the day after Henry's deadline to turn himself in for treason.

I looked around the room. Congress's vice president, George Bryan, was a friend, and I acknowledged him with a nod and a half smile, not wishing to appear too familiar. The others, I did not know. I gazed at the men in attendance, hoping for leniency, but I couldn't guess their thoughts. Would it be different if I had an audience of women?

"Graeme Park was willed to me by my father, Thomas Graeme," I began. "As his last living child at the time of his death, I received it unconditionally. At the time of my own death, it will go to my living heirs, not to my husband. Those heirs are Anny Smith and John Young, the children of my deceased sister Jane and her living husband, James Young."

I was suddenly aware of my skirt; it was loose around my waist. I had lost weight.

I continued on, explaining the timing of Henry's trip to Scotland in 1775 and the series of unfortunate events that followed when he returned.

"My husband accepted the position of commissary of prisoners as a way to try and relieve the suffering of our soldiers. The cruelty of Mr. Cunningham at the Walnut Street Jail is well-known. He is far too adept at beating men with the jail key."

I recounted my efforts to serve the cause over the years.

"I would be grateful," I finished, "if the Council could prevent my estate from being forfeited. If not, I will consider it my duty to bear this for America. We are bound in this, our plight, and together we must share in the horrors."

In July, Pennsylvania ordered agents to seize Graeme Park without delay. All of the estates of the enemy were to be sold as soon as possible to fund the war effort.

It was over. I had lost my home. I had lost my husband.

I struggled with knowing it was Henry's actions that had sealed my fate. My own hard work, loyalty, intelligence, even my charitable work, none of that mattered. I thought back six years to when Henry showed up at my Attic Evening that winter night shining like a rare jewel. Had it been worth it?

I was no longer recognized as a person. Only a wife.

320 • Wendy Long Stanley

Chapter 26

Philadelphia
Fall 1778

Thousands of Tories fled Philadelphia with the British, frightened for their safety, and many patriots returned home.

Elias Boudinot and my other friend Daniel Roberdeau, now a brigadier general of Pennsylvania troops, spoke to authorities on my behalf, but there was little they could do when so many of the resistance leaders were intent on punishing anyone suspected of helping the British. Thanks to my husband, I was a marked woman.

"We can't just sit here, Betsy!" Liza cried. "There must be something we can do. Are they going to turn out two women on the street? Will we have to join the workhouse so we don't have to go begging for a crust of bread? Or shall we spread our legs and bed ten men a night down by the wharves?"

I didn't blame her for being upset. "We have to try and be calm," I said. "Perhaps we could stay with Anny and William and the baby." None of my petitions and in-person appeals to governing bodies and the authorities had merited any favorable responses.

Anny and her husband were in the city again. As soon as I suggested staying with them, I knew it wouldn't work. Anny had a young child and another baby on the way. She was building a family of her own; she didn't have the room for two women to live with her for the long term. We could not impose on her for an extended and unknown length of time.

If we rented rooms, we'd need furniture. I applied to the Supreme Court for an allowance of furniture and minor supplies. I asked for the minimum to fill a living room, bedroom, and kitchen. We also needed to eat, so I added to the request the remaining grain and flax stored at Graeme Park, of which there was little. And, of course, my books. The war effort didn't need those, and I wouldn't sacrifice them as kindling. I made sure I applied to keep my papers and bound work, *Telemachus* and my journals that held years of my poetry and other writings. The court granted me these requests, but not a single item more.

They said we could stay at Graeme Park until they arranged for its sale, but we had to pay rent, and the number they named was far too high. I was going to have to pay money to stay in my own house.

The worst winter of my life was followed by the most horrendous time imaginable. I was shocked to hear that for unknown reasons, Joseph Reed published our conversation about Johnstone's message as if it had been *me* offering Reed a bribe from the British! It was ludicrous. Why would I attempt to sway Reed? I only met with Reed to ask for his help keeping my property! I was only a woman. I had no clout! I certainly didn't work for the British.

It didn't matter how much I protested or denied it, attempted bribery was treason. If Congress believed I attempted to bribe Reed, I could be executed.

I was shaken to the core. Without exaggeration, I didn't know whether I would live or die.

I found refuge in a visit from the Stocktons. Just the sight of our old friends lifted my spirits, although Richard was a shadow of his former self.

In the fall of 1776, after he signed the Declaration of Independence, the British got to him. Richard was taken and tortured, starved and exposed intentionally to freezing cold. While they had him in jail, the British stayed at the Stockton home and all but destroyed it. Washington finally got Richard back in a prisoner exchange, but his health had been badly damaged. He was released by the British on the condition that he stop working for the cause.

"We'll get through this," Annis comforted me. "All of us."

"If they wanted to charge you with treason, they would have done it by now," Richard told me matter of factly. He looked so thin and beaten, even more than a year after his release.

"That's good, I would prefer to live," I said. I had intended to be humorous, but the words fell flat.

"Did you know Joseph Reed was Richard's law clerk?" Annis asked. "Years ago, when he was barely more than a boy. Reed had his own law practice when Washington asked him to leave it and become his aide-de-camp. I'll write to him and remind him of our esteem for you."

"He has no interest in my character," I said. "He's accusing me of being mentally unstable." I didn't need Joseph Reed to like me, I just wanted him to stop trying to destroy me. He could despise me all he liked. Clearly there were snakes on both sides.

"He will try and take your property," Richard said. "You can count on that. You and others, to make an example of you. Congress has demonstrated a fairly tolerant stance on loyalists, but Reed's intentions border on a thirst for vengeance. But you need not fear for your life."

"Well, there's that, anyway," I said, reaching for humor again.

"Why does he hate Betsy so much?" Liza asked.

"Reed finds quarrel with anyone even mildly smelling of loyalist sympathies," Richard explained, "partially because he was suspected of it himself after the letters he shared with General Lee questioning Washington's leadership back in '76. Washington never had the same trust in him after that. Reed's ruthlessness is the element he wields to propel him from soldier to politician and prove he's serious about independence. He already has egg on his face, you see."

"But I've done nothing!" I cried. I had made a powerful enemy simply by speaking the truth. I cursed Johnstone. Will men always ruin the lives of women?

"Don't make an enemy of Reed," Richard warned me. "He is basically the new governor of Pennsylvania. His authority is absolute, and his power grows."

"Too late for that. I fear I already have."

"Don't correct him, either. He is not known for softness. He will make you pay."

September 17, 1778, dawned sharp as a meat hook in my side.

There was a rap on the door shortly after eight o'clock. Liza and I exchanged looks, then I slowly went to open it. Two men stood there.

"Mrs. Fergusson," Dr. Archibald Mclean said courteously. Colonel Robert Loller nodded but avoided meeting my eyes, his spiky white eyebrows in a sharp line above his nose.

"You are here for the inventory," I said. I motioned them inside.

Colonel Loller reached a hand out as if to place it on my forearm to comfort me, then thought better of it. Both of these men had known me all my life. "We are required to inform you we are under oath to form an accurate account," he said apologetically.

I said nothing.

"We'll start upstairs, then?" Dr. Mclean asked. I shrugged.

They headed to the stairs with ledgers, their boots thudding on the wide planks.

I found Sally and the cook and sent them to the kitchen house. "Return when you see them leave," I advised.

Liza and I sat stiffly in the parlor and listened.

The men were in my chamber. I heard my wardrobe door opened, a slow squeak. I had been meaning to oil it for weeks. They were handling my dresses, my stomachers, my petticoats, my stays, my shoes. I heard footsteps go around the bedstead and then the sticky slide of the drawer on my Bible table. I had a lace fan from England and a vial of perfume on top. Within lay my mother's Bible she brought from England in 1731.

A knot formed in my throat. Memories from that room tumbled through me like marbles. My parents had slept there for years. Jane gave birth there, then died there. I had loved Henry in that chamber.

I heard the second wardrobe open, the sound of Henry's things being moved.

Liza and I sat on the loveseat, frozen. She reached for my hand.

"Congress is afraid," I said. "They think if they let me keep Graeme Park, I will sell land and send the money to Henry and the British will benefit."

Liza sighed.

An hour later the men came downstairs and went through Father's office, the dining room, the parlor. The busts of the poets were lifted, turned over, jostled for weight. The men looked at the samplers on the wall, the portrait of me as a baby, my brother's sketch of a squirrel that my mother thought showed such talent. They handled my instruments, went through my books. I resisted the urge to provide a tour guide's commentary of our possessions: *"Did you know I asked Francis Hopkinson to buy me that harpsichord in London and ship it to me?"* I stayed quiet.

So many books. We had already donated a large number to the Hatborough Library. I watched the men work. Surely they were not going to record each title? Loller wrote down *History of the Stuarts* and the four volumes of Edward Young's work, added a few more, but gave up after the nine volumes of *Spectator.*

He looked up. "Are there—"

"Four hundred," I answered. "There are four hundred books."

Later, when I received a copy of the inventory, I noticed they left my clothing off the list, and my jewelry and silverplate. The kindness of neighbors.

Small mercies.

Henry was in New York asking to see me, but Council refused to grant me a pass. He remained camped on Long Island, waiting for deployment to England, with me at Graeme Park, while agents made plans to sell my ancestral family home.

The contents of Graeme Park were to be auctioned off on October 15, and at a later date, the house itself be would auctioned, and all our land. The agents wanted to get the most they could from my possessions first, and so the contents sale was widely advertised in the Philadelphia papers. The proceeds of the auction were going to the war effort, so they intended to draw a large crowd.

"You don't need to put yourself through that, my dear," Daniel Roberdeau said kindly. "Spare yourself. Let me be there on your behalf."

"I have to be here. For my parents. I owe them that. Liza can go to the Campbells."

"You aren't to blame, my dear."

"Am I not?" I said rigidly. I married Henry against my father's wishes. What if I had never gone to that churchyard that night under cover of darkness?

Roberdeau looked troubled. "Then allow me to sit next to you as your friend."

"Thank you," I whispered, trying not to cry. I was crying anyway.

In the end, Liza and I both stayed.

October 15 dawned warm and sunny, the trees shimmering red and gold, heavy with leaves, too beautiful for an execution of sorts. Carts and carriages clattered up the lane as if we were having a party, but all those people had come to steal my things. Most of the men and their wives in attendance were not from Horsham, not my friends or Quaker neighbors. More small mercies.

The auction began without a thought for me. I was just another face in the crowd, not the mistress of the estate.

I purchased a few items that had been my family's for as long as I could remember: an easy chair, four rush-bottomed chairs, four beds, a tablecloth, and four pigs. These were in addition to what the court had granted me in the summer. I spent all the money I had, just over fifty-three pounds. I was broke long before the auction ended. Liza and I ignored the hostile looks we got from strangers from beneath their hats and bonnets. *Don't feel sorry for her, she tried to bribe Reed for the British! Her husband imprisons our men! They should get rid of her, exile her with the other treacherous wives! Send her to the prison ships anchored at New York. With any lucky she'd die there. Traitor!*

Oh, how wrong they were about me. I wondered what they would do if I screamed aloud.

One by one, my possessions were sold out from under me. I sat there, straight-backed and rigid, as time dragged by and the gavel slowly skewered me with every item sold.

Finally, finally, it was over. Carts were loaded, horses roused, and a hundred people strode out again without a backward glance, many merry over their good bargains, carrying out pieces of my life.

Liza and I sat on the floor of the parlor on our purchased tablecloth. The room was mostly bare, the rugs sold too. My beautiful harpsichord, gone. My mother's silver tea set, gone. My father's gold timepiece, gone. All sold with the quick bang of a gavel after a lifetime of use. The inside of my home resembled the streets of Philadelphia after the British army had stripped them bare and ugly.

"Now what?" Liza asked.

I began to laugh until the laughs came in one mad rush, tears streaming down my face.

Liza did not laugh with me. I rolled on the floor, howling and crying in fits until I could not breathe.

When I stopped, I flopped on my back, staring at empty walls punctured by nails. At least we still had the furniture I had been granted, and the chairs and beds I purchased today. What if I had listened to my father? *Wait a year. What's a year, measured against decades?* None of this would have happened. But then, I might not have had love, either. I couldn't bring myself to hate Henry.

"We can stay here if we pay the rent," I said. "Until it's sold." Unbidden memories leaped to mind of all the dazzling parties and balls this floor I was lying on had seen through the years, when my biggest concern was having a new dress made.

"We can't afford the rent. They're making us pay the taxes too. It's too much."

"Liza, we'll have to make do. The tenants will keep farming the land. I don't know what else to tell you."

If I had wanted to run, I would have gone to my husband. He kept sending letters asking me to go to New York. I started laughing again, tears sliding down into my ears, tendrils of hair sticking wet to my forehead. Until the final axe fell, this was still my home.

The thought made me giggle and cry harder. Staying to fight had been my patriotic stance, my invisible musket, and here I was, crying on a tablecloth on the floor of an empty parlor in a house no longer mine.

Henry wrote to me through October and November, hoping I would be given a pass. Then in December he announced he couldn't wait any longer. The year 1779 was upon us. In January, he would be sent to England.

Who could have imagined the war would last this long? My husband was on the executioner's list, I was accused of being a traitor, my nephew was off fighting with the redcoats, and my house was being taken out from under me. I had lived in this town, in this house, for almost forty years.

Chapter 27

Elizabethtown, New Jersey
January 1779

In the end, it was General Washington who inexplicably sent me a final pass to see Henry in January. I had begged the Council and the War Board for months with no success.

Henry had arranged for us to meet in Elizabethtown, New Jersey. I traveled to meet him, accompanied by Old Joseph, on a gray January day, the sky the color of sour milk. Elizabethtown was cold and bleak. We slowly jolted up to a large brick house on a hill, the home of a local widow who Henry said would be grateful for the few shillings he could pay her. Her husband had been killed at the battle of Princeton.

We were shown into a well-appointed house. I imagined a widow down on her luck, not a house of finery. A Negro man with a white mustache took my winter cloak as a small girl waved me toward a room where music played.

"I'm Grace," the girl announced. "I'm older than I look. Who are you?"

"I'm Mrs. Fergusson," I told her, curtsying. "Pleased to meet you."

"How old do you think I am?" she demanded.

I looked her up and down. "Eight?"

The girl put her arms over her chest, frowning. "How did you know? Everyone thinks I'm six!"

"You gave it away. You shouldn't give hints."

"I can play the harpsichord," Grace said brightly. "But my brother hogs it."

"I can as well," I confided to her.

"We could play together. Shall we?"

"Grace!" A woman bustled toward us. "I do apologize, Mrs. Fergusson. My daughter is far too outspoken for a child. Since my husband died, she has become unruly."

I looked at Grace with a smile. "See if you can find a duet for us."

"I'll find one that's not too hard," she said helpfully.

"I'm Faith Becker," the woman said. "We are pleased to have you, Mrs. Fergusson. I hope you'll feel welcome here." She was pretty, her skin unblemished, her slender form showing collarbones as dainty as a robin's legs.

There were three other children in the room. Grace's older brother was seated at the harpsichord playing a lively jig, and two girls nearing womanhood sat on a sofa playing cards. An elderly woman dozed in an armchair. The room was filled with wealth, expensive stuffed chairs and sofas in the finest fabrics, shining wood tables with intricate details. There was art everywhere and several bookshelves double-stacked with leather volumes.

"Is Mr. Fergusson here?" I asked. I wanted to see him so badly.

Mrs. Becker shook her head. "He went to fetch something, for you I believe. He said he'll be back soon."

I swallowed my disappointment. I had not seen him in eight months.

"He speaks of you with great affection," Mrs. Becker said warmly.

"We are very close," I said. I wondered how much Henry had told her.

"Girls!" Mrs. Becker raised her voice above the music. "Thaddeus, stop playing. Let me introduce Mrs. Fergusson from Horshamtown, Mr. Fergusson's wife. She is our guest."

The girls rose and curtsied, then stood respectfully with their hands clasped in front of their skirts. Thaddeus stood up and bowed, a little jauntily, before he sat and played again. These children were happy and secure; they had been raised in a loving home. I noted that the elderly woman napping had not stirred despite the noise. A slight rattling snore underscored her breath.

"That is my husband's mother," Mrs. Becker said wryly. "She will wake soon enough. You're sure to be thirsty, Mrs. Fergusson. What can I get you? Lemon cordial? No, something hot, I think, on a day like today. Tea?"

"Tea, thank you. Is there someone to see to my manservant?"

Mrs. Becker nodded at the Negro man, who inclined his head and left. A maid slipped out behind him.

I sank happily into a soft armchair. It felt decadent after hours on the hard seat of the coach, banging against frozen earth.

"Call me Faith," Mrs. Becker said. "I know you have been without your husband for many months; the children and I will make ourselves scarce."

"Oh, please don't do that. That is kind, but this your home. Do not put yourselves out. And please call me Betsy. All my friends do."

Little Grace abandoned her search of music books in order to dance to her brother's jig. She twirled on the Turkey carpet with her arms outstretched. She reminded me of Anny at that age.

Faith watched her, a faint smile dimpling her cheeks. "I know I shouldn't allow it. But with Zachariah gone . . . Well, I hate the quiet. There you have it, but I do."

"You cheated!" the girl with dark hair chided her lighter-haired sister. "I know you took two cards and not one!"

I smiled. This house was like the one I had grown up in, before . . . before.

Grace appeared in front of us. "Cake, Mama?"

"Let Mrs. Fergusson get in the door," Faith rebuked her gently.

"That child is a miscreant." The voice from the armchair was low and gruff, humorless.

The harpsichord stopped abruptly. Thaddeus got up and made a beeline for the door. "I must attend my French," he muttered on his hasty exit. "Monsieur LeBlanc will have my head."

"His tutor," Faith explained.

The girls fell quiet at their cards, and Grace sank back to the carpet with her pile of music books.

"Mother, this is our visitor, Mrs. Elizabeth Fergusson, Mr. Fergusson's wife."

"Stoke the fire," Mother Becker ordered in a deep, raspy voice as the maid came back with tea. "I'm cold."

Mother Becker was a large woman, wide and stout as a woodpile, with three chins rolling down to rest at the top a dark brown dress like a dollop of cream on a chocolate custard.

"Mother, this is—"

"I heard you, I'm not deaf." The old woman eyed me. "You look too thin."

I lifted my tired limbs from my chair and went over to the family matron. I took her hand in both of mine. "A pleasure to meet you, Mother Becker."

Her eyes were a startling blue as they sized me up, the bright blue of a young girl. Wrinkles ran in deep fissures down her face. Her cheeks were a map of lines, cutting in various directions like meandering roads.

"You look to me like you have more sense than your husband," she huffed.

I returned to my seat. "Most men are lacking in sense, I find."

She laughed, a throaty guffaw that ended in a gasp. "Cake," she barked to the maid when she rose from the fire. The girl left to do her bidding. Grace's eyes lit up at the thought of a sweet treat.

"How long are you staying?" Mother Becker intoned in her deep voice, not taking her eyes from me.

"Mother, really," Faith protested. "Don't make Mrs. Fergusson feel unwelcome."

"I'm afraid I don't know," I said. "I've been separated from my husband for a time because of the war, and now he is scheduled to leave for England. A few weeks perhaps?"

She continued with her lizard's gaze, nothing on her body moving apart from her eyes. Her limbs had barely moved after she went from being asleep to awake. Her arms were folded around her large middle like a Buddha's.

"My husband and I came here sixty-five years ago from France so we could practice our faith without persecution. They were burning Huguenots like pinecones."

I waited.

"We started in Canada, but my husband wanted warmer weather for his gout. I told Elijah way back then, these colonies would be better without some old codger sniffing at us from over in his palace."

Faith's face grew stern. *"Mother."*

Grace and the two other girls stared at their grandmother.

Mother Becker sat like a sixteen-pounder, chin wobbling with each word. She waved a chubby finger and continued. "We raised our son to think like us, but he picked the wrong side anyway and paid for it, God rest his soul. And what about you, girl? Have you any sense?"

The arrival of cake spared me and we used it to change the topic of conversation. It had been many months since I had tasted such a sweet indulgence. Faith and I discussed the difficulties of securing fine flour and sugar.

My fork clanged down when Henry strode in. I put down my plate and rose to meet him. Before I had time to feel awkward, he picked me up and swung me around. Grace laughed and clapped her hands.

"You smell like mincemeat and wintergreen," I said. Under the chill of his skin was the warmth of him, large and alive and *here*.

"You came," he answered.

As always, Henry's presence made me feel giddy. I smiled at him, feeling like a young girl.

He turned to the room, his arm around my shoulders. "This is my wife!"

"You state the obvious." Mother Becker surveyed him dourly.

Faith stood. "Girls." She held out an arm to dispel them from the room.

"Please don't leave. We wouldn't want to drive you from your own parlor," I protested.

"We have work to do," Faith said firmly. "We have been too long weighed down by sadness and escaping our melancholy with frivolity. Your presence here reminds me that we must return to our studies. The girls are behind in their Latin."

The children obediently filed out. Faith turned to her mother-in-law, eyebrows raised, hands on hips.

"I think I'll stay here," Mother Becker said lazily, a smile on her lips.

Faith turned to Henry and I. "Come, let's show your wife your rooms. She must be tired from her journey. I'll have some warm water brought up so you can bathe."

"What did you tell them about me?" I asked Henry as we lay in bed.

Only a single candle flickered in the darkness.

"That you're running our farm while I do my duty."

"Loyalists both."

"Mrs. Becker lost her husband to rebel grapeshot. I didn't want to put you in the same camp as his killers. I had to see you."

Our chamber was large, bigger even than the one we had at home. The four-poster bed was draped in chintz curtains, the walls papered in expensive wallpaper. Fine damask curtains covered the windows.

"I wasn't sure if you would come," he said after a pause.

"It took many attempts to secure a pass."

"Voglio passare il resto della mia vita con te," Henry said.

I want to spend the rest of my life with you too. I traced his chest hair with my finger.

"Was it very bad?" he asked. "The auction. I'm sorry, my darling. I prayed it wouldn't come to pass."

"It was, but let's not talk of that. When will you return?" I had to ask, even though I knew he couldn't tell me.

"When I can."

I nodded. "When it's safe."

Henry's hand slid around to my ear, stroking the skin where it met my cheek. "Tiny fairy ears."

"Pointy and sticking out?"

"Small and perfect, for an enchanting woman."

"Je t'adore." I switched from language to language, telling him in every way I could think of.

Henry pressed his nose to mine. "If you come with me, you can choose where we live. You were happy there once. London, Bath, Edinburgh, anywhere. It doesn't matter to me. We'll hold your evening salons and go the opera and eat sweets and get fat. I will find work. You'll write books. Lady Juliana will take us in until we get settled."

"Henry."

He sighed. "I thought, this one time, after all this, after losing Graeme Park, you might choose me."

The words were like glass in my breast.

"I haven't lost Graeme Park yet." I pulled his face toward me. "Henry, please. Listen."

His eyes met mine.

"They auctioned off the contents but the auction date for the house hasn't been set yet. I need to be here to do everything and anything possible until then to stop the sale. If our house and land is sold, then I have no reason to stay. I'll come to you."

Henry looked down.

"My darling, my whole life is in that house and on that land. You knew that when you married me, and you admired me for it, and you wanted me, maybe even because of it. You even spent two years working that land, and it was our dream for it to go on. Graeme Park is home. *Our home.* Ours. I am asking you to let me see it through. I can't leave until I know for sure that it's gone. And if for some reason it doesn't get taken from us, then when the war ends we can be together there. We'll find a way."

"I knew that first night I sat in your house watching you glow that you were extraordinary."

I laughed. "It's only been seven years since that night, but it feels like fifty."

"And look at us," Henry said softly. "Here we are."

"In this great big mess," I said, my voice catching.

"I should have known," Henry mused.

"Known what?"

"That a woman who could steal the words from mortals and hold a room captive until the light shimmered around her would be no ordinary wife."

"We should detest each other," I said huskily.

"Do you hate me?" Henry asked.

"I cannot."

"I had no idea I was marrying a patriot," Henry said mournfully.

"Oh please. It wasn't like that! No one knew what would happen. You made a choice to be in America, as I recall. You couldn't stay away."

"I chose you before a civil war broke out."

I looked at him uncertainly. "Do you regret it? Please tell me."

"I will always admire the way you stand by your convictions, Betsy," he said seriously. "The way you embrace your truth wholeheartedly. I marvel at the sheer strength in you. So, no, I do not have regrets. There will never be anyone like you, not for me."

"You're saying good-bye?" I asked, alarmed.

He shook his head, eyes glistening. We both were choked by emotion.

"Come here," I said, playfully grabbing a fistful of his chest hair.

He ripped my shift from neck to hem.

On the way home, I stopped in at Morven in Princeton. The Stocktons were rebuilding after the tremendous damage their property sustained at the hands of the British.

Richard's health was even worse. He had a cancer removed from his lip but persistent pain in his throat plagued him. I promised Annis I'd look for a recipe for an effective saltwater solution.

By the time I reached Graeme Park in early February, I was rested and happy and ready to fight again, until I saw the state of the house and grounds, which had fallen further into disrepair. Liza's pale face matched the sad state of the exterior.

"Why don't we go into town this Saturday if the weather's fine," I suggested, looking at her drawn face. I felt guilty for being gone so long. "We can visit friends, maybe go to the markct."

She brightened. "Oh yes! Let's!"

My good mood cheered her. We sang as Old Joseph drove us to town a few days later. We'd stay with the Stedmans first, then Ben and Julia Rush, and Liza wanted to see her friend Clementine Gerhart.

I didn't send word that we were coming. We surprised the Stedmans with our arrival.

"Betsy!" Margaret said, a line creasing between her brows. "We didn't know you were coming." She looked taken aback.

"I apologize for not sending word. I just returned from a month in New Jersey with Henry. Poor Liza was feeling lowly after being alone at Graeme Park, and we thought we'd surprise you. Is this a bad time? You're not ill?"

"No, no." Margaret's lips pinched together. "It's good to see you both. You remember my son?"

We turned to see Margaret's grown son, Jeb, from her first marriage, who was now a reverend. I'd always had a fondness for Jeb, with whom I had enjoyed many long discussions about the responsibilities of Christianity.

He greeted us, then murmured something and excused himself. "I had hoped to spend time with him," I told Margaret, who shrugged.

Later Margaret invited us to have a game of cards with Charles.

"How is Henry faring?" Charles asked as we settled in the library.

"He's well," I answered. "We are both looking forward to the end of the war." *However that will play out*, I added to myself.

Margaret seemed distracted and distant. Charles drummed his fingers on the table between turns. I couldn't shake the feeling that something was off, or we were interrupting somehow. Margaret and Charles were not themselves.

At bedtime I asked for a bedwarmer. A new maid was called and given the task.

"Margaret, where's Jenny?"

"She is not with us any longer," Margaret said, avoiding my eyes.

"What a shame, she was quite good," Liza commented. "And she was here for so long. Ten or eleven years, wasn't it? Did she leave for other employment?"

Margaret hesitated.

"She did," Charles said. "Good night," he added, and pulled Margaret with him up the stairs.

Liza looked at me. "How odd," she said.

I shrugged.

We headed to the market early the next day. I had a small amount of money from Henry to purchase food staples and wanted to be early for the best selection. I was making my way through the fish stalls when I spotted an old friend.

"Dr. Bond!" I called enthusiastically. "Hello! How have you been?"

Thomas Bond had been a friend of my father's. He was a co-founder of the hospital, and then they worked together there after it opened twenty years ago. Bond was one of the first doctors to recommend inoculation for smallpox, which led to many hearty and heated discussions at our supper table. He was in his sixties now, yet he had still offered to organize medical care for the continental army. He and his wife were admirable, hard-working people.

Dr. Bond frowned when he saw me, then smiled.

Liza said hello to him then left us to talk while she perused the stalls.

We spoke of old friends and the price of oysters and how far away the old times seemed. Bond seemed troubled, as if he was weighed down by his thoughts. Eventually our conversation stalled and he looked pained. I expected him to offer an explanation, but he simply touched his fingers to his tricorn hat and bowed to me. "Very nice to see you, Elizabeth. I think so often of your father. He was a fine man."

He hesitated, then thought better of whatever he had been going to say. "I must go."

"Good-bye then," I said with genuine affection. "So good to see you."

I found Liza at a stall selling pins and thread.

"Everyone seems unsettled somehow," I said.

"These are unusual days. People are under such strain."

"What did you make of Margaret and Charles? They don't seem like themselves," I commented. "Maybe something is wrong. Let's leave tomorrow. I'll send word to the Willing sisters. I'll ask if we can call for a day or two before we go to Ben Rush's family."

That afternoon I took a long walk with a friend from the Daughters of Liberty. When I returned to the Stedman house, I noticed a horse and carriage outside and a man waiting atop.

"Dr. Bond," I said, surprised.

"I came to see you," he said.

"Would you like to come inside?"

He shook his head. "I told Charles I would wait for you here."

I raised my eyebrows.

Dr. Bond patted the seat. "Sit, Elizabeth. Please."

I climbed into the seat next to him.

He struggled with words, his old face rueful. "When I ran into you at the market, I was convinced I should hold my tongue, telling myself it wouldn't be right to burden you. But my wife tells me this delicate matter does not belong to me, and by attempting to protect you, I may be doing further damage."

"I'm sorry, I don't—"

"I went home and thought, what would Thomas Graeme do, if the shoe was on the other foot? If it was my daughter? I have been so torn, you see."

"Sir, I'm not sure what—"

His face was troubled. "Elizabeth, I have known you since you were a babe in your father's arms. I tell you this only out of the greatest respect for you and your character and the protection of your good name."

This time I was silent.

He sighed. "Last June, Jenny, the Stedmans' maid, came to me. This was after Henry had moved out and a few days after you yourself had gone home. I believe you were staying there at the same time as the British commissioner? Jenny asked me for medicine for feminine complaints. More specifically, to rid herself of a child."

A roar rose in my ears. Bond looked at me sadly.

"I refused to give her the forcing medicine to end a pregnancy. I assumed she had lain with a young man on a carnal impulse. She corrected me. She said Mr. Fergusson was the offending party. She claimed he forced himself upon her during his stay there at some time over the winter."

The blood drained from my face. My mind spun. This couldn't be true.

He looked pained. "I wish I did not have to be the one to bring you this terrible news. I admit at the time, I told her you must never find out. She said she didn't care who knew what Henry had done to her."

"This isn't true! Henry wouldn't do that." Even as I said the words I felt the shadow of a lie weigh down my words.

Jenny had stared at me so closely in June, and so often. Henry wasn't there when I arrived. I thought it was because the British had shipped him out. Was it because he wanted to avoid me? My gut twisted with pain. I grappled for reason, my thoughts spinning like a frenzied top.

Charles and Margaret knew! That was why they were acting so strangely.

Henry had lain with a maid in Margaret's house while I was alone in the country waiting for him to come home, worrying about the charges against him. My mind rushed for an excuse. Men made grave mistakes when they were far gone with drink. Maybe he was beside himself, sick with guilt and remorse, afraid to tell me he had made a mistake one night. Or perhaps Jenny had lured him deliberately, fed up with her mundane life. Maybe it was a rash blunder for both of them, an episode they immediately regretted and wanted to forget.

"Do you know what happened?" I said, my voice breaking. "Do you know if it was only once?"

"Jenny says Henry chased her for weeks. Unfortunately, Jeb Abercrombie, Margaret's son, heard Henry at Jenny's door one night, imploring her to let him in, months before the pregnancy. Jeb claims he was very keen. Unyielding. Oh, my dear, I am so very sorry."

"Where is Jenny now?" I couldn't hear, I couldn't breathe, the sky and the earth had squeezed tight and were choking me with their closeness.

"She went home to Chester County. The baby was born, a girl."

So Henry could have children after all. He had a daughter.

I gripped the seat. "Does Henry know?" I could barely stand the sound of my voice. "About the baby?"

"Thomas Coombe was headed to New York, so Jenny gave him a letter to take to Henry. He would have received it in August. Coombe was beyond distraught for you, but I told him not to tell you. I know now that was wrong, please forgive me, my dear. For Jenny's sake, Mrs. Stedman also arranged for someone to go to New York and inform Henry in person. When the man confronted him, Henry denied it. He won't acknowledge the baby, despite Abercrombie seeing him at her door. Since then, other household staff have confirmed Jenny's story."

My husband had seduced Margaret's maid. All of them kept it from me for months, during which time I was being dragged through the mud by Joseph Reed and accused of being a traitor. Then they announced the confiscation of my home, and I had to watch the items of my life being taken from me. Betrayal upon betrayal piled up like heavy bricks on my chest, crushing me.

Oh God! Our joyful time together in Elizabethtown, after Henry had been with another woman and fathered a baby! His words rang in my ears: *I will always admire the way you stand by your convictions. There will never be anyone like you, not for me.* Then his eyes, glistening with tears. I thought those tears were for us, over losing each other, for how we suffered. No. Those were tears of guilt.

I reached a hand out to steady myself, but the world went black.

Chapter 28

Horsham
November 1781

"Congratulations, Mrs. Fergusson," the barrister said, handing over a sheaf of papers. "I couldn't be more pleased to be the one who restores Graeme Park to you."

"Thank you," I said.

After an exhausting three-year legal battle, Graeme Park was mine again. Finally. I had outlasted Reed's reach in power. In the triumph was a hollow, aching place where my husband should have been.

"Will you be going into town for the victory celebrations?" he asked me. His bald head was patchy with dry white flakes. "The fireworks and bonfires will shake the city."

"Yes, I believe I will," I answered slowly. After six long years, success at last. A month ago, Washington's forces had surrounded British General Charles Cornwallis at Yorktown in Virginia, in concert with commander Rochambeau and his French force that had come south from Rhode Island with the patriots. Cornwallis's forces had been routed in a three-week-long siege, and Cornwallis had been forced to surrender the British position just last month.

"Thank God for the French," the barrister said gleefully. "You have to hand it to the French navy, blocking them from the sea. Wish I could have been there, to see Cornwallis pinned like that, and Rochambeau and Washington coming at them from all sides!"

"Do you think it's truly over?" Was it even possible? I was bone weary.

The papers trumpeted the British surrender and the end of fighting on the continent, but after all these years, could we trust there was an end? Or would the king order another attack? Was it possible that what began as a lofty and distant idea had finally become an acknowledged truth? *Liberty is here. We are enslaved to no crown. No monarch shall rule us ever again.*

"The Prime Minister has acknowledged defeat," he crowed. "It's only a matter of time until a peace treaty is penned. In the meantime, we've got seven thousand British prisoners in Virginia to toss back."

I had written Henry that I knew about his daughter, but he claimed innocence, just as Dr. Bond warned me he would. He denied it in every letter for two years, and through every acquaintance that returned from England.

My friends were supportive but silent. Even Dr. Rush, usually so effusive and alive with ideas, was mute on the matter, but offered me his enduring support.

I was haunted by thoughts of Jenny and her baby girl. I wanted to believe my husband, but too many people sided with the maid, including Margaret and Charles. I couldn't be a wife to Henry if he had fathered a child with another woman.

"What will you do?" Liza asked me when Henry issued me an ultimatum to go to him. "You are bound by marriage vows, for better or worse. You belong to him. You'll have to go."

"I'm going to go see Jenny," I answered.

I found her in service to the Wall family in Yellow Springs. Jenny wasn't as pretty as I remembered. Pasty-skinned and big-eyed, her face was a sullen mask. Her yellow hair was darker. All in all she didn't look as young and golden. This was the girl Henry had taken to his bed? The maid who had so enraptured him that he stood outside her door on cold winter nights and begged her for entrance while I waited for him at home?

Jenny agreed to receive me. I sat at the kitchen table on a hard chair, Mrs. Wall between us. The table was bare, wood worn smooth, a clock ticking on the wall. I had never heard a clock that loud, strident as a crow. It was mocking me. Go. Away. Go. Away.

"You think I wanted it?" Jenny said harshly into the silence. "Is that why you've come?"

"I needed . . . I needed to know," I said huskily, my courage gone. "I had to come."

Why did I think this girl would speak the truth? What business did I have being here, adding to her burdens?

I took a deep breath. "My husband denies—"

"I was a virtuous girl," Jenny spat, sharp as chicken wire on an outstretched palm. "Your *husband* forced himself on me. Do you need it plainer?"

"Were you carrying that week in June, when you saw me?"

"What does it matter?"

"You could have told me. I would have tried to—" What? Help her? Not likely. Although I didn't know. What would I have done?

She laughed, a bitter and harsh cackle. "Ha. You would have believed me? The help?"

"Is it true?"

Jenny's eyes shot venom at me.

"I want you to see something," Mrs. Wall said delicately. She took a Bible from behind her back. "This is Jenny's Bible."

She placed the Bible on the table in front of me and opened it to the family history. There was an entry for the birth of a child. Margaret Fergusson, November 1778.

Margaret. After Jenny's long-standing mistress, married to my dead sister's husband?

Margaret Fergusson.

Fergusson.

She had written it in her personal Bible, one of her few possessions. *Her Bible.*

"I'm sorry," I said. My hands trembled. "I'll go."

I never asked to see the child.

Chapter 29

Horsham, Pennsylvania
February 20, 1801

Who is here? I can hear whispering.

"She's near her time," a man is saying quietly in the hallway, his voice rough.

A woman's stifled sob echoes.

"You'll keep her comfortable?" Another man, louder. A voice like gravel.

I turn my head. The door is open a crack and three figures are standing outside. I see my dear Liza and my old friend Dr. Benjamin Rush. The other man is Mr. Lukens, who owns this house. I'm his tenant.

Me, a tenant! Whatever I imagined my life to be, my imagination has failed me repeatedly.

I open my mouth to call, "Come in," but no sound emerges. My heart flutters. *I'm still here.* I'm shivering; my chamber is so cold. My fingers stray to the soft cotton of a well-laundered quilt and a thick duvet. At the smell of wood burning and the sound of crackling, I turn my eyes to find a high hickory fire.

"How will we go on without her?" Liza cries. "How will I?"

"I'll notify Christ Church," Dr. Rush says quietly, ignoring Liza. "They will need to prepare to receive her."

"That's a fine resting place for a lady of her quality," comments Lukens. "She'll have a handsome stone next to her parents at the entrance, I hope."

"This is awful, for her to go like this!" Liza bursts out. She has been my friend of forty-five years, my constant companion. I don't know what I would have done without her. "And here! When I think of the way it was, back then. It shouldn't be this way." Her voice cracks. She is remembering all the losses, stacking them up like piles of potatoes at the market. *Don't do that*, I tell her.

"There, now," Lukens says softly.

"She is remarkable," Liza whispers.

"Ah yes, that she is." Lukens agrees, nostalgia in his voice. At one point, my funeral would have been striking. We had been a grand family—we once rivaled the mighty Shippens.

"It won't be long now," Ben says. My sweet Dr. Rush.

Who will remember me? So many are gone, and soon I will be too. Where's Anny? She should be here. Oh no, that's right, she died. Is Johnny gone too? Or is he still in England?

My mind sweeps the years. I don't want to remember any of it.

Against my will, my mind pulls up the summer of 1762, the day I was told William Franklin had broken our engagement. I was a woman of twenty-five. When I look at that girl, she is as hazy as morning fog. I can see the line of shoulders, collarbones under milky skin veined with blue, a slender waist in tight embroidered silk. We should reconcile each other to the life we have lived before I breathe my last, but that girl stays silent.

I see Nathaniel Evans walk by me. Is that Henry standing in the corner? "It's a shame," Henry says, "that you couldn't have what you wanted."

There's no malice in his face.

I glance toward the door. No one is there. I wonder where they went.

"Liza," I call, but my voice makes no sound. "Ben?"

When I squint back at Henry, he's holding two red books. Oh! My books, *Telemachus*. He holds out the heavy volumes to me, a grin on his young face. He looks the way he did when he arrived at my Attic Evening that winter night. "I could quote Fénelon to you," he says, smiling warmly.

Nathaniel steps forward. "You always wrote such beautiful poetry," he says, winking at me. "I'll keep it for you. Yours and mine."

They both fade, and all I can hear is the ticking of our tall clock at Graeme Park. As my eyes close, I realize what Henry meant. America could claim her independence, but I could not claim mine. I wasn't given a way to fight.

I hope Liza takes care of my books, my writing. I worked so hard. I'd like my poetry to be kept.

I want to be remembered. So few women are, you know.

THE END

Personal Note from the Author

As a first-time writer, I'd love to hear from you! Send me your thoughts, what you liked or didn't, or suggest what you'd like to see me write about next. Thanks so much!

www.WendyStanley.com

I spent eight years writing and researching *The Power to Deny,* my first novel. One of my biggest thrills during this process was spending a day at the Historical Society of Pennsylvania holding Elizabeth's original journals in my own two hands, seeing her handwriting slope across the page, and being filled with wonder at the thoughtful notes she added to the margins later. A pressed flower fell out of one; I carefully put it back. The flower had stained the page; is it possible that flower has been in there for almost 250 years? One page in her *Poemata Juvenilia* had ripped and she had sewn the page back together, using thin white thread in a tiny careful cross stitch. I could feel Elizabeth, could sense the hours and years she spent writing and thinking, and could well imagine her life and pain at the doorstep of the American Revolution. It became very important to me to tell her story. I only hope she approves.

Author's Note on the Text

In October 1781, British General Charles Cornwallis surrendered to American and French forces at Yorktown, Virginia, bringing an end to the last major battle of the revolution. The Americans won. When the Treaty of Paris was signed two years later in 1783, the United States formally became a free and independent nation after eight years of war.

So what happened to Elizabeth and Henry? Henry Fergusson never chose to return to the United States, although many loyalists did. They were often pardoned and peacefully lived out their lives in America, but Henry stayed in England for the rest of his life. He continued to deny fathering a baby with the Stedmans' servant girl, although many people there at the time swore it was true. For more than eight years, Henry repeatedly asked Elizabeth to join him in England. Their correspondence finally stopped around 1788. Elizabeth had no intention of going to a man who had betrayed her many times. Few details of Henry's life remain. At one point, he petitioned Parliament to be reimbursed for the loss of Graeme Park (even though his wife still owned it and was living there, and it had been her family home for more than forty years), arguing that he had been loyal to Britain during the Revolutionary War and should be compensated for his efforts. Historian Anne Ousterhout writes that he was eventually granted a modest payout. Records indicate he collected an army pension until 1801, when all mention of him ends.

Elizabeth Graeme Fergusson is largely unknown to most people today, yet in the 1760s, as England was passing tax laws that unwittingly fired up a revolution in her colonies, Elizabeth was one of Philadelphia's most accomplished, well-known, and beautiful women. Her intelligence was admired by many, so much so that she attracted the attention of the intellectual elite in Philadelphia and many famous visitors coming from Great Britain and the continent. In the Age of Sail, Philadelphia was a magnet for the educated and the ambitious. By the 1770s, Philadelphia was the largest city in the colonies, and had the busiest and most lucrative seaport. Elizabeth's weekly Saturday night Attic Evenings are believed to be the first of their kind in North America. She hosted and entertained several key players in the revolutionary war, many of whom commented on her fiery intellect. Elizabeth's close male friends included Dr. Benjamin Rush, Richard Stockton, Francis Hopkinson, Robert Morris, and, arguably, Benjamin Franklin, for he never spoke of her without respect. These men all signed the Declaration of Independence. They knew and loved Elizabeth and tried to protect her, particularly after she married a loyalist and lost her family home.

Over time, Elizabeth became part of the cabal of female poets and thinkers that emerged in colonial America. Included among her friends were the poets Hannah Griffitts, Annis Stockton, Milcah Martha Moore, and others. After the revolution, about thirty of Elizabeth's poems were published in Philadelphia magazines and newspapers and were widely circulated.

Elizabeth's two volumes of *Telemachus* remain in the care of the Historical Society of Pennsylvania. Her *Telemachus* translation was an epic achievement that begs the question of why a young woman of thirty would decide to take on such a mammoth project in the first place. Until you hold these two immense, heavy red leather volumes in your hand, it is difficult to understand what an astounding triumph these works are. She was writing long hand, with a quill pen and a pot of ink, for three years, often by candlelight. At that time, from 1766 to 1769, an English translation of the French was unavailable in America. Later in life, in the 1790s, Elizabeth attempted to find a publisher for *Telemachus* but was unsuccessful. In addition to her translations and poetry (her 1768 poem "The Dream," a response to Dickinson's *Letters from a Farmer in Pennsylvania*, is a breathtaking 657 lines long), Elizabeth wrote countless letters, journal entries, and articles. Sadly, her travel journals from her time in England and Scotland are lost. Several of Elizabeth's commonplace journals remain, however, in multiple locations.

Throughout her life, Elizabeth continued to cultivate, explore, and champion the life of the mind. She wrote and read constantly. In addition to her decades-long literary pursuits, she was a keen observer of scientific and medical developments around the world and often wrote poetry on global discoveries, such as the planet Uranus. She believed tirelessly in the quest and benefit of further knowledge and was an active and enthusiastic participant in the conversation that formed the Enlightenment and Age of Reason.

Facing money troubles and advancing age, Elizabeth finally sold Graeme Park to her niece Anny's widow, Dr. William Smith, in 1791. Dr. Smith was in no hurry to inhabit the property and, out of respect, he let Elizabeth and Liza live on there until an outbreak of yellow fever in Philadelphia in 1793 left Smith and his second family in need of an escape from the disease-ridden city. Although he offered to let the two women stay in the house, out of courtesy, Elizabeth and Liza moved out and founded rented rooms nearby. Elizabeth took the Graeme family tall clock with her when she left. It chimed the time for her for fifty years of her life.

Elizabeth's house at Graeme Park is almost three hundred years old and still stands. It is largely unchanged since the time she lived there. I found the rooms retain a haunting elegance. Although it now stands empty, she would instantly recognize it as home, for the ownership of Graeme Park changed hands only three times after Elizabeth sold it, which helped protect its original structure and avoid major renovations or demolition. The house itself has not been used as a residence since 1801. In 1958, Welsh and Margaret Strawbridge gave Graeme Park to the state of Pennsylvania for long-term preservation and protection. Graeme Park is now owned by the Pennsylvania Historical and Museum Commission. Thomas Graeme's elegant wooden paneling still decorates the parlor, the Delft tiles still grace the fireplace in the room that was once Elizabeth's bedroom, and the original windows through which the family gazed are still in place, almost three centuries later.

And what of Elizabeth herself? Writing and philanthropy remained the focus of her last years. Between 1793 and her death in 1801, Elizabeth lived first at the house of a Mrs. Todd, and then when Mrs. Todd died, she moved to a room at the house of Seneca Lukens, a farmer and clock maker. Both residences were within walking distance of Graeme Park. Until she died, she continued to pine for Henry and fret about his infidelity and illegitimate child. Maybe without the scandal of the child, she may have gone to him in England, but I doubt it. Elizabeth had already made the voyage once and was not afraid of the trans-Atlantic crossing, and it was well known that she loved London. I think the truth is that she was always a patriot who would never have moved away from her new country and her lifelong home. Her friends had fought and suffered and died for the American cause. Henry's actions simply gave her an out. In an age where wives were expected to be obedient and were punished if they were not, his adultery provided her with just cause for not having to do his bidding.

Liza (Eliza) Stedman continued to support her friend until Elizabeth's death at the age of sixty-four. They had lived together as companions for twenty-five years, and were close friends for almost fifty. What happened to Liza Stedman after Elizabeth's death is unknown.

It is worth noting that her other lifelong friend and fellow poet, Annis Stockton, died during the same month as Elizabeth, in February 1801.

Anny Young Smith, Elizabeth's niece who she raised and who had been like a daughter to her, died in April 1780 in Philadelphia while in her early twenties from complications from the birth of her third child. Anny's brother and Elizabeth's nephew, John Young, remained a loyalist. They corresponded for years until he died in England from an illness in 1794. Elizabeth had him buried in St. Martin's-in-the-Fields.

Well known during her lifetime, Elizabeth Graeme Fergusson's extraordinary life has disappeared into the recesses of time. It is my hope in imagining and recreating her story that I can help her find her small place in history. Fans and readers of American history already know the accomplishments of several of her intimate male friends, which include many of the Founding Fathers. It's less likely that they know the details that formed her life: that John Dickinson (*Letters from a Farmer in Pennsylvania*) volunteered to be her lawyer to help her get Graeme Park back after its confiscation, that Dr. Rush (who had been at the Battle of Princeton by Washington's side, tending to the wounded; and later one of the fathers of psychiatry) was one of her closest friends for decades, that General Anthony Wayne (who was sent by Washington to harass Howe's troops after the Battle of Brandywine) maintained an admiring friendship with her, and so on. Many men and women in colonial Philadelphia valued her wisdom and kindness and were in awe of her intellect.

Elizabeth is buried next to her parents outside Christ Church in Philadelphia. You will walk past her grave and will almost brush her feet if you visit her lifelong church, for she lies next to the path leading to the main door. Her gravestone reads:

Elizabeth Graeme Fergusson
The true sympathizer with the afflicted
Daughter of Thomas and Ann Graeme
Wife of Hugh Henry Fergusson
Died 1801 aged 64
Eliza[beth] caused this stone to be laid
Waits with resignation and humble hope

For reunion with her friend
In a more perfect state of existence

"Her friend" is clearly her husband. Despite everything, despite his transgressions, Elizabeth loved Henry Fergusson. She had the misfortune to fall in love right before the messiness and uncertainty of a long civil war. Altogether, they only lived together as husband and wife for about two years, but she longed for him for the next twenty-five, and intended to look for him after they both died. She hoped to find him in the afterlife.

Elizabeth Graeme Fergusson died as an accomplished female poet and proud new American.

Further Reading

Non-Fiction

Andrlik, Todd. *Reporting the Revolutionary War: Before it was History, it was News.*

Blecki, Catherine La Courreye and Wulf, Karin A., eds. *Milcah Martha Moore's Book: A Commonplace Book from Revolutionary America.*

Butterfield, L.H., ed. *Letters of Benjamin Rush Volume I, 1761-1792.*

Chernow, Ron. *Washington: A Life.*

Epstein, Daniel Mark. *The Loyal Son: The War in Ben Franklin's House.*

Fried, Stephen. *Rush: Revolution, Madness & the Visionary Doctor Who Became a Founding Father.*

Harris, Michael C. *Brandywine: A Military History of the Battle that Lost Philadelphia but Saved America, September 11, 1777.*

Isaacson, Water. *Benjamin Franklin: An American Life*

McCullough, David. *1776.*

Ousterhout, Ann. *The Most Learned Woman in America: A life of Elizabeth Graeme Fergusson.*

Skemp, Sheila L. *William Franklin: Son of a Patriot, Servant of a King.*

Stabile, Susan M. *Memory's Daughters: The Material Culture of Remembrance in Eighteenth-Century America.*

Fiction

Shaara, Jeff. *Rise to Rebellion: A Novel of the American Revolution.*

Shaara, Jeff. *The Glorious Cause: A Novel of the American Revolution.*